BROAD REACH

A SIM GREENE MYSTERY

ROB AVERY

Jack Tar Publishing
Provo, Utah

Published by
Jack Tar Publishing LLC
1979 North 1120 West
Provo, Utah 84604, U.S.A.

Broad Reach / Rob Avery – 1st ed.
www.robavery.com
ISBN 978-1-945809-06-4
Library of Congress Control Number: 2017910751

Author's Note: This is a work of fiction. Names, characters, places, and incidents are a product of the author's imagination. Some locales, businesses, organizations, and public places or names are used for atmospheric purposes. Any resemblance to actual people, living or dead, or to businesses, companies, events, institutions, or locales is completely coincidental.

I have been to the British Virgin Islands many times and consider it to be one of the safest and most beautiful places I have taken my family and friends for vacation. Much of the writing of this book occurred aboard boats anchored in clear waters near white sand beaches surrounded by coconut palms and steep hills filled with greenery. In one day, however, hurricane Irma swept across this island nation destroying homes, harbors, and vegetation. One friend tells of wind gusts reaching 245 miles per hour. Coconut palms—famous for the ability to survive tempests by bending with the wind—snapped their trunks like wooden matchsticks. Paraquita Bay, one of the usual hurricane holes, became a maritime wasteland with hundreds of boats strewn atop each other like children's toys tossed in a box. Satellite images of the islands, once green and verdant, now depict a brown emptiness devoid of vegetation. Many of the resorts, restaurants, and harbor facilities have disappeared.

There is good news, however. One month, to the day, after Irma struck, I had the opportunity to speak with some of my BVI friends at the United States Sailboat Show in Annapolis. The Bitter End Yacht Club—one of the finest places in this marvelous country—will rebuild, the charter companies will repair or replace damaged boats, and the trees will come back. It may take some time, but the islands will regain their former glory. Until then, enjoy this book and the description of a paradise as it was.

To my family and all those who sail with me.

"The pessimist complains about the wind; the optimist expects it to change; the realist adjusts the sails." - William Arthur Ward

1

ISLANDS rise from the sea as you approach them. A smudge on the horizon becomes a greenish lump, then an island with trees. In the Caribbean, the fragrant smell of frangipani blossoms hits you about the same time you see the white, sandy beaches.

The water turns progressively lighter, too. The deepest blue becomes dark green, then jade. When you reach a good anchorage in pale turquoise water, you can see the hard dark green and tan coral heads sticking up from the floury sand below.

And it is good that you can see them.

St. John rose in the early light of a clear Sunday morning and I was glad to spot it. I knew I would—I'd seen that island on my chart for days—but there is far more comfort in sighting land after a long sail than there is in watching your position advance toward it on paper.

I'd spent three months sailing my thirty-nine-foot boat from California, most of it with fair winds and favorable seas. The last two weeks, however, had been tough. After six days on a comfortable broad reach, the wind clocked around and dealt me eight solid days of beating into a stiff wind that never quite turned into a gale. I was bone-weary, sleep deprived, and eager to see Al.

Al is a well-educated, barely house-trained, short brown bear of a fellow. He is generally quiet and moderately principled. My friend and new business partner, he'd flown to the British Virgin Islands three months earlier to find a dive shop for us to buy. It was the dream job he'd always talked about. The dream he'd talked me into.

Tortola began its steady rise from the sea an hour after St. John. By the time Norman Island appeared on the horizon, I'd already reviewed the cruising guide and prepared *Figaro* for landfall. The Customs and Immigration office would be closed so I could either pay the exorbitant after-hours fee or anchor out in the harbor and sit in my cabin until a customs officer came in on Monday morning.

After fourteen solid days and nights at sea, I was ready for some human contact and looking forward to a long swim and some solid ground. But the Scotsman in me wasn't about to pay an onerous after-hours fee. I chose the third, somewhat less legal, option of ignoring Customs and turned ten degrees to port.

With over twelve hundred nautical miles under my keel since leaving Panama, another five to Jost Van Dyke wouldn't kill me. Keep quiet, stay under the radar, and blend in with the hundreds of chartered sailboats that ply the local waters. Nobody would be the wiser.

An hour later I dropped the sails, fired up the diesel engine, and powered the last few hundred yards into White Bay. The bay nestles up to a narrow scimitar of pure white sand wedged between blue Caribbean waters and steep green hills covered in manchioneel trees and coconut palms. A shallow reef protects the anchorage. Safe and comfortable, a guy could spend days there just relaxing. I needed one night and a cold beer.

I slipped *Figaro* in behind the reef on the east side and set her anchor in hard sand below eight feet of water. I tucked a few bills into the front pocket of my swim trunks and dove in.

It was a couple hundred yards to the beach in front of Henry's Good-Time Bar and Restaurant, and I let the long, steady strokes unwind the muscles in my shoulders and back while I reflected on the trip behind me. The last stretch of solo sailing in a three-month-long escape from California was over, and it felt good to have my boat at anchor and my body in the water.

Two weeks at sea had ruined my land-legs, but the fine, warm beach sand felt good under my feet as I walked unsteadily past the coconut palms and sea-grape trees to the little restaurant. Henry's was constructed of rough boards that somebody had painted a vivid shade of turquoise and then covered with seashells arranged into unusual shapes. Artful.

A barefoot, middle-aged black man in faded brown shorts and a sparkling white linen shirt sat on a bench in front of the bar reading a newspaper. He looked up from the paper and smiled as I walked up.

"I'm Henry. We've got fresh grouper and conch fritters tonight for dinner. Best on de island."

"No, thanks," I said. "Just something cold to drink."

He gave the sigh of the disappointed entrepreneur.

"It's an honor bar, mon. If you can make it, you can drink it. Just write it down on de bar tab and pay before you go."

"Got any cold beer?"

"In de fridge, mon."

He turned back to his paper. Dried palm fronds hung above the door to the bar. I had to duck to get in. Nautical flags and yacht club burgees hung from the ceiling. Seashells, license plates from a dozen countries, and old T-shirts signed by their former owners covered the walls. A few pictures of lesser celebrities smiling with Henry hung behind the bar. A newer sign advertised free wireless internet access.

The room itself wasn't much larger than my old office at the naval base, but, with one older couple and two very cute girls occupying the only tables, it was considerably more crowded. One of the girls was a brunette on the short side of twenty with large, glossy brown eyes. The other was a younger bleached blonde with a tattoo in the small of her back. Depending on the observer's philosophical point of view, the tattoo could have been either some sort of tribal design or a bull's-eye. She was barely legal and wore a barely legal swimsuit. She could have kept a spare in her cell phone case.

"Like what you see?" said the blonde. She wasn't angry.

"What's not to like?" I said.

"What can't you see?" said her friend.

The blonde's jaw dropped and the two giggled in faux shock.

Whether it's biological compulsion or nautical tradition, sailors fresh from the sea tend to lose all reason when they find themselves near the opposite sex. The girls probably expected me to shake like a dog and roll over on my back. I almost did.

But gentlemen have their limits. So do I. At my age, I limit myself to women. Girls bring the complications that accompany inexperience and youth. And I'm too old for giggling.

I kept a cool head and refused to rise to the bait. Instead, I grabbed an ice-cold Carib from the back of the refrigerator, pulled off the cap with the church key that hung from the wall, and put a couple of bucks in the cigar box that sat on the bar. I smiled at the girls and went back outside to talk to Henry.

Henry's newspaper lay folded on the bench next to him. He sat at a small wooden table with a top made from four large white ceramic tiles. Several brightly colored cards lay face up on the tiles. Henry studied them.

I sat down on a chair nearby, dug my toes into the warm sand, and pulled a fine, long drink from the bottle. The cold liquid washed away some of the salt from my throat and a few hundred miles off the trip.

"Henry, there is nothing like that first taste of beer."

"Yeah," he said. "Nothing like de cold beer after a long trip, eh?"

"Long trip?" I asked.

Henry studied the cards some more. He pointed at a card in the middle of the table. A man poled a small wooden boat through dark water. A half-dozen steel swords pierced the boat's bow.

"You've been on a long, lonely journey, mon." He said it with conviction as he stroked his right temple with a long index finger.

"And you've come here to get away from something painful or difficult. Maybe something dangerous, eh?"

I took another swallow from the bottle. It was almost as good as the first.

"Oh c'mon, Henry. You saw me bring that sailboat into this bay and anchor it by myself. And you can see I've had too much sun and wind, that I need a shave, and that walking straight on land is a bit of a challenge. It's not hard to guess that I just finished a long sail."

"You don't believe in de Tarot." It was not a question. His smile was wide but not happy.

"I believe you've learned to size up the tourists pretty well over the years," I said.

He shook his head from side to side. "You're no tourist," he said.

He got up to greet two middle-aged couples coming from the beach. He reeled them in, told them about the daily special, and ushered them to a table at the restaurant side of the building. I pushed my toes deeper into the sand and took another pull at the bottle. The liquid smoothed a few more of the rough edges off my trip as the sun dropped below the palm trees and fizzled into a postcard-beautiful Caribbean. I finished my beer.

The girls walked out of the bar.

"We're going over to the Soggy Dollar," said the blonde. She shifted her weight from one foot to the other and then back with an effective and well-practiced bit of hip-wiggle. "There's gonna be a dance on the beach around nine," she said. "See you there?"

As tempted as I was, they were both younger than my lower limit.

"Sorry, not tonight," I said. "Henry tells me I've had a long and dangerous trip and that I need my rest."

The brunette laughed. The blonde looked puzzled at first but then smiled. I smiled back. The smile from the fish that gets away. They walked west along the beach and my eyes followed. I thought how nice it would be to dance with the blonde I'd left in California.

Melancholy pressed for another beer, so I went to the fridge, grabbed Carib number two, and put a couple more bucks in the cigar box. The older couple had left the bar so I sat down at one of the now-empty tables. Henry came in and checked the contents of the cigar box. He smiled, grabbed a beer for himself, and sat down across from me.

"Nobody drinks alone in my place," he said.

He tipped back his beer and then dealt two more cards onto the table with a third one below the first two. The last card pictured five guys fighting with long sticks. Henry's eyes narrowed a bit and his voice lowered.

"Oh, you got big troubles coming, mon."

I leaned back in the chair and looked up at the ceiling.

"All God's children gots troubles, Henry."

He pointed at the five guys with the long sticks and poked the card several times with his long index finger. "There is great strife and hard times ahead for you," he said. He poked the card as I drank some more beer. "It's right there in front of you, mon."

This was my first conversation with another human in two weeks. I'd hoped for small talk with a tourist or maybe some local wisdom from a seasoned islander. Instead, this guy threw me the evil eye. He dealt two more cards.

"You carry a big anchor for such a small boat."

"It's forty pounds or so," I said. "Seems about right."

Like this guy had something to teach *me* about sailing?

"A heavy weight in de soul with a long chain."

I drank some more beer. "That sign over there says 'Henry's Good-Time Bar' and here you sit trying to scare away paying customers? It doesn't seem like a very sound business practice."

He put the cards back in his pocket, cocked his head a little to one side, and lowered his voice.

"Man come here to dis island—he no tourist, he no charter—he come alone on his own boat to the BVI. Man your size wearin' nothin' but swim trunks, a tanned hide, and a broken nose? Man looks like he take care of himself, too." He leaned back in his chair. "Alone in dese islands," he said, "that man will find real trouble soon."

"Thanks for the warning, Henry. I'm just here to relax and have a good time. Broken or not, I'll keep my nose clean." I finished the beer and stepped outside onto the beach.

Henry spoke up as I left. "You try to be de good boy, eh?"

I walked back down to the bay shaking my head and wondering why I always ran into the local crackpots. I swam back to *Figaro* through the dark water, showered off the salt, and went below to click on the anchor light. It was seven o'clock and too early for bed so I dug my laptop out from under the chart table and logged on to Henry's Good-Time free wireless internet service.

There were only a handful of emails worth reading. A short, terse note from the blonde in California shared her many frustrations with me and indicated no small degree of finality to our relationship. It wasn't exactly unexpected but the words still stung.

Another, nearly a week old, was from Al. He'd been granted resident status and a government work permit, talked with a few diving operators, and worked out a deal with a guy who was looking to retire. He'd even made a down payment. All he needed to seal the deal was for me to show up with the rest of the money.

I threw a high five to nobody in particular.

The last email, two days old, made me want to throw my laptop against a bulkhead or punch a hole through a door. Al's girlfriend, Liv, reported that he'd been arrested and charged with murder for killing a tourist. Henry's prophecy had some nasty yellow teeth. *Great strife. Big trouble in the islands, mon.* Thanks for the welcome, brother.

Liv had found the best attorney on Tortola and he wanted to meet with me. I replied and asked her to meet me at the West End ferry terminal at nine the next morning. We could meet with the attorney any time after that.

Tired and worn out, I crawled into *Figaro*'s quarter berth, listened to the rhythmic hiss of ocean swells as they washed across the reef, and tried to fall asleep. For two solid weeks, I'd sailed *Figaro* alone and nonstop, making do with forty-minute catnaps. Now, at anchor, I should have hit my berth like a felled tree.

But a fortune teller's warning overpowered sleep. How did he know about Al or why I'd spent three months escaping the problems in California?

He didn't, I reasoned. *Cards couldn't tell him that.*

2

I woke before dawn and scrounged the last of the food out of *Figaro*'s refrigerated icebox. I took my breakfast up to the cockpit and ate it in the gathering light while a few shearwaters and a trio of pelicans dove for theirs outside the reef.

An easterly wind was building, and it foretold a day picture perfect for sailing. A few odd patches of fluffy white cumulus marched west across a sky the color of a robin's egg. As beautiful as the day was, Al—my old friend and new business partner—was in jail and I had to figure out how to get him out. Whatever the second step was, the first was to get into the country legally. I weighed anchor and made way under full sail to the West End of Tortola. The customs office opened at eight thirty and I intended to be their first customer.

The overdressed agent fidgeted in her booth while she reviewed my passport and *Figaro*'s documentation.

"You came here directly from Panama?" she asked.

"Yes, ma'am."

"And where is the rest of your crew, sir?"

"You're lookin' at him," I said.

She stepped outside the office and walked toward *Figaro*. From the dock, she eyed her from bow to stern with a heavy dose of semi-professional indifference. The entire inspection took eight seconds. She returned, flipped through my passport again, and stamped "30 days" on my entry form.

"Enjoy your stay in the British Virgin Islands, Mr. Greene. We do ask that you move your vessel from the Customs and Immigration dock within the hour."

I was in the country fair and square and the authorities hadn't even boarded the boat. There could have been a case of loaded machine guns and twenty kilos of dope aboard and they wouldn't have had the slightest clue. It seemed like an odd way to run a customs office. I thanked the officer and stepped back out into the warm sunlight.

The West End is a sheltered anchorage replete with brightly painted green and blue buildings with orange roofs, red shutters, white balconies, and yellow awnings. The primary colors of a child's finger painting. But the festive shops and stores meant little to me.

I walked back to *Figaro*, cast off her lines, motored into the harbor, and dropped the anchor in thirty feet of water not far from the ferry terminal. I waited in *Figaro*'s cockpit and watched the shoreline for Liv. I didn't have to wait long.

A small blue Isuzu pulled into the parking lot, and a slender woman with fine athletic legs got out and walked to the terminal. Two thick braids of pure blonde hair framed an innocent face dappled with freckles. She was Switzerland's Heidi in a purple T-shirt, faded red shorts, and green flip-flops. Al had a well-documented weak spot for leggy blondes.

I went below and grabbed my day pack and a small wad of cash. I stepped down into *Figaro*'s small inflatable dinghy, fired up its tired outboard, and motored over to the dock near the parked Isuzu. She came back out of the building as I approached her car.

"You must be Liv," I said.

"Are you Sim?" she asked. "Al's partner, eh?"

She spoke in that beautiful British/Aussie/South African accent that I can never quite place geographically. Four days of anxiety showed in her voice.

"Yep," I said. "Have they set bail?"

"No," she said. "I mean, I don't know. I don't know anything." She pulled a bent pack of cigarettes out of her shorts pocket and fumbled one out. "You have a light, luv?"

"Sorry," I said.

"Oh, I suppose you don't smoke."

I shook my head.

"I've been meaning to quit, myself," she said. She broke the cigarette in half and threw it in a trash can by the car. If anxiety was a commodity, she'd be driving up the price.

"How is Al doing?" I asked.

"He's surprisingly calm. Shall we go see him?"

I tossed my day pack into the back seat of the car and climbed into the passenger side. Liv was maybe a couple of years older than me, but the years hadn't damaged much. I did the math in my head and figured she was somewhere around fifteen years younger than Al. The sly old dog.

She maneuvered the car onto the two-lane road past Frenchman's Cay and drove east toward Road Town. She drove the car like she'd stolen it.

"I am so glad you're here," she said.

"Tell me about his lawyer," I said.

"My boss recommended him. He's supposed to be the best solicitor on the island, but we can't meet with him until tomorrow."

"Is he expensive?"

"I think so. Is that a problem?" she asked.

"No, no. With any luck he'll be worth every penny."

Liv entered a roundabout too fast and almost put the little car up onto its two left wheels.

"We're not in any big hurry, Liv. Al's not going anywhere." I held on to a bracket on the dashboard with whitened fingers as the car swerved around narrow, tree-lined corners.

"He's going to be all right, eh?" she asked. "Please tell me it's all going to be okay."

"If he didn't do it, Liv, it'll be okay."

I had tried to sound reassuring. It didn't work.

"Are you mad? Of course he didn't do it. Al is the sweetest, kindest, and most caring person I've ever met. He's a bit of a dag but how could anybody even think that he could kill someone?"

I wondered for a moment if we were talking about the same person.

"So, how long have you known Al?" I asked.

"We met about two months ago, I guess."

Okay, so she didn't know *all* about Al.

"He's a great guy," I said. "And he's helped me out of a jam or two."

She parked the car under a tree on a busy road near the center of town. A white two-story building with forty feet of steel antennae poking into the sky stood across the street. Large black letters over the entrance indicated that we'd arrived at the Road Town Police Station.

"They'll only let one of us in at a time to visit him," said Liv. "And they won't let anybody see him for more than fifteen minutes."

I handed her my day pack. "Please keep an eye on this for me," I said.

I walked across the street and into the air-conditioned lobby. The officer at the front desk wore a light brown shirt with military creases and thick black and silver shoulder epaulets. His black hard-brimmed cap and checkerboard hat band reminded me of a New York City taxi driver I'd seen in an old movie.

"How may I help you, sir?" he asked.

"I'd like to see Mr. Al Higgins, please."

The desk officer asked for my passport, examined it, and picked up a telephone. He told somebody somewhere what I wanted, and another cop walked into the lobby a few minutes later. The new cop fell into the minority of men who are taller than me, but he was at least twenty pounds lighter. He might have been the tallest and leanest policeman I'd ever met. Could have been a decent point guard back in the day. He had a narrow, British face with colorless lips and steel-gray eyes. Thin black hair covered a tall forehead. He picked up my passport and thumbed through the pages.

"You are Mr. Greene?" he asked.

I nodded. A brass name tag over the right breast of his tunic read "D.C. Millet."

"Arrived this morning, did you?" he asked.

"Uh-huh."

"Airline or ferry?"

"I sailed here from Panama," I said.

He glanced up from my passport and looked me over. "Where is your vessel at the moment?"

"West End," I said. "Lying at anchor."

"And what is your relationship to Mr. Higgins?"

"We've been good friends for years."

He thumbed through the pages of my passport again, closed it, and handed it back. "Enjoy your stay in the BVI," he said. "We only allow visits to prisoners on Mondays, Wednesdays, and Fridays."

Another policeman walked in ten minutes later and led me to a windowless room with two steel chairs at a small table in the center. Al sat in one of the chairs. A uniformed guard sat in a third chair in the corner of the room and worked hard to look intimidating.

Al looked about the same as he had the last time I'd seen him, three months earlier. Taller than a fireplug but about the same build and not any softer. His brown, close-cropped hair grayed at the temples. The right sleeve of a sweat-stained yellow T-shirt obscured the upper half of an old-school fouled-anchor tattoo. The wide scar on his right leg peeked out from under the leg of his shorts. There were no handcuffs and no leg-irons. They obviously didn't know him as well as I did.

He didn't get up. I held out my hand and he shook it like he always did. Like he was crushing a golf ball to powder. The guard kept his eyes on us, making certain that I didn't hand the prisoner a weapon. As if Al needed one.

"Good to see you, buddy," I said.

Al nodded. "How was the trip from California?" he asked.

"Good. It was downwind most of the way to Panama. The last two weeks getting here, though, were pretty lousy. Lots of wind and most of it on the nose."

He leaned back and crossed his hairy arms.

"So," I said. "What's going on here?"

He looked over at the guard. "These idiots think I knocked a guy off last week."

"Did you?" I asked.

"Not this time."

"So why are you here?"

"Lars and I were talkin' to a guy over at Cooper Island who runs a small dive shop. You know, making a few connections. Networking."

"Lars?"

"Lars Solberg," he said. "He's the guy who's selling us his dive boat and salvage operation. Wants to retire. Don't you read my emails?"

"Yeah, sorry. Go on."

"Anyhow, we were puttin' a few back at the beach club when this beauty walked over and asked the bartender if there were any cops on the island."

"When was this?" I asked.

"Thursday. About two or so in the afternoon." A fly buzzed over the table. Al caught it in his fist and threw it to the ground. The guard looked up for a moment. "Anyway, this gal had a plastic bag with a guy's passport in it. She told me that she found it floating in the channel and that she wanted to get it to the authorities. I told her that I was headed to Road Town and that I'd take it to the cops for her. So she gave me the bag." He shrugged his shoulders.

"And how does this amount to murder?" I asked.

"There's a little more to it," he said. "The bag had a key in it and inside the passport was a slip of paper with a couple of phone numbers. I tried to call the numbers later that night, but they were disconnected or something. Then I noticed that the key was for a safe deposit box at one of the local banks. So I went to the bank the next day to check it out. You know, maybe find out where this guy lives."

"Sure," I said. "You were just going the extra mile to locate the rightful owner."

Al's eyes went hard.

"Sorry," I said. "So what'd you find at the bank?"

"I found a boatload of cops, Sim. Somebody at the bank must have called the police as soon as I showed up with that key. The cops took one look at the passport and hauled me in here." He lowered his voice and leaned toward me. "But I got the box open before they showed up. You know what I saw in there? A fat wad of cash, Sim. That whole box was crammed full with stacks of hundred-dollar bills."

"I don't get it. How does this add up to murder?" I asked.

He turned his palms up and shrugged. "It seems the passport's rightful owner got whacked on the beach."

"How long ago?" I asked.

"I don't know, but they've been asking me a lot of questions about last Wednesday night."

I shook my head and gave a low whistle. "So the police find a body on one of their well-manicured tourist beaches and you show up at the bank a couple days later with the victim's passport and his safe deposit box key."

"Yep."

"And the box is packed with U.S. currency," I said.

"Uh-huh."

"Circumstantial evidence."

"Yeah," said Al.

"But enough to keep you in jail. And maybe enough to make it stick."

"Thanks," he said.

"Have you got an alibi for Wednesday night?"

Al nodded.

"Then give the cops your alibi. They'll check it out and you're outta here."

He shook his head. "I can't do that," he said. A wry grin swept over his face. "She's married."

"So, you've got a live-in girlfriend *and* a mistress?" I asked.

He nodded.

"And the mistress is married?"

"Call it a mid-life crisis," he said.

"Couldn't you just buy a Corvette? They're a lot cheaper."

Al smiled again. "Not on this island," he said.

"And you won't tell the police about your secret side-squeeze because it would get her in hot water, right?"

"Uh-huh."

I looked over at the guard. He wasn't quite asleep, but he didn't seem interested in us anymore.

"Give the cops your alibi, Al. If it checks out, it ends this thing. You get out of here and we go diving."

He shook his head. A faint buzzer sounded in the room and the guard stirred.

"Sir, your time with the prisoner is up," he said.

The guard got up out of his chair and walked toward us. Al lowered his voice to a whisper. "Sim, there must have been a million bucks in that box."

3

I walked outside into the heat of the day. Liv saw me coming and got out of the car.

"I've got to see him. How is he?"

"He's fine," I said. "Tell him to relax and that we'll be getting him out soon. I need to run a few errands."

"Meet you back here, then?" she asked.

I nodded.

"Cheers," she said.

She walked across the street toward the police station. The view was admirable. I grabbed my day pack and headed the other direction into the busy part of town.

The British Virgin Islands adopted the U.S. dollar as its own currency decades ago and there are thousands of Americans who surreptitiously keep a lot of money here. Most of the banks have become accustomed to large cash deposits and their employees have learned not to ask a lot of questions. The teller was quiet and thorough as he began to open my new account. He completed a small stack of paperwork and looked up with a smile.

"Could you please remove your hat and look directly at me?" he asked.

Small red dots illuminated on two small cameras, each about the size of a penlight, positioned at eye level on either side of the teller window.

"Don't your customers bank here because they want some privacy?"

"Oh, sir, this is not an identification tool. We use it for screening only."

"I'm not sure what you mean by that," I said.

"The cameras measure your facial bone structure; the length of your nose and the distance between your eyes, nose, mouth and ears. The system processes the measurements into a unique digital code and stores it with your account information. The next time you come in, the cameras perform the same measurements and compare against the stored value for verification purposes. It has proven to be quite reliable. We don't save the photograph."

He pressed a button and the two red lights dimmed a bit.

"There," he said. He handed me a safe deposit key. "All done."

"What if I get a haircut?" I asked.

"The system allows for small differences."

"What if I get a nose job or send my brother in here to get something for me?"

He smiled.

"That does happen from time to time, sir," he said. "We usually cooperate with the individual and then call the authorities. They resolve any confusion."

I deposited a couple thousand dollars into my new checking account and left the rest in my wallet for walking around money. I had other plans for the safe deposit box, so I left it empty. I walked out with a small pack of temporary checks, a safe deposit box key, and an otherwise empty day pack. On the way back to the car, I dropped into one of the street-side shops and bought a cell phone. Liv was waiting for me in the Isuzu's driver's seat when I got back.

All the cars on the island were left-hand drive as if they'd been manufactured for the American market, but everybody drove on the left side of the road as if they were in Britain. That put me, as the passenger, sitting on the side closest to oncoming vehicles. It was a bit unnerving and Liz's love for freeway speeds on narrow two-lane streets didn't help. I kept my eyes open and on the road.

A white, mid-sized SUV pulled onto the road behind us as we entered the Road Town roundabout, and a little voice deep inside suggested that I keep an eye on it. I caught glimpses of the SUV in the side mirror as the road twisted and turned.

"Can we make a stop at Nanny Cay?" I asked.

"Sure, what for?"

"I want to ask them about slip fees," I lied.

Liv shrugged and, a few minutes later, pulled off the road toward the Nanny Cay Marina. We circled around the boatyard to a lot near the marina office and parked. I stepped into the heavily air-conditioned office. A woman in her late fifties with dark hair, thick glasses, and thin bones sat behind the counter.

"Do you have any slips available for a thirty-nine-foot sailboat?"

"Monohull or catamaran?" she asked.

"Monohull."

She flipped open a binder on the counter and adjusted her glasses. I found a pair of marine binoculars on a nearby table and looked out the window across the marina to the northwest.

"Fifty-five dollars per day for dockage in the high season," she said.

A white, mid-sized Mitsubishi Montero sat at the edge of the main road about 250 yards away. The driver was male with a fair complexion. He wore a medium-blue polo shirt and dark sunglasses. I didn't see any passengers.

"Thank you," I said. "I'll bring her around tomorrow morning."

"Call us on channel 16 before you arrive and we'll direct you accordingly."

I nodded, put the binoculars back on the table, and walked back to Liv. We passed the parked Montero on our way to the West End and it fell in behind us. I saw no reason to tell Liv about our tail.

"Do you mind if I ask you a few questions, Liv?"

"No, I guess not."

"What happened last Wednesday night?" I said.

"Well, I went to work as usual and finished up around midnight. I got home to Al's house around one or so and he wasn't there. He'd told me that he'd be on Virgin Gorda talking to some folks about a dive shop or some such thing and that he might not make it back until late."

"When did he get home?"

"Sometime before nine the next morning," she said. "That's when I woke up. The dear was in the kitchen cooking me brekkie."

"Is that usual? Him being out late?"

"No, not really," she said. She took a deep breath and let it out slowly. "We'd had a bit of a tiff that afternoon."

"If you don't mind me asking, what were you arguing about?" I said.

"It wasn't so much an argument," she said. "I'm absolutely in love with that man but there's a part of him I can't reach. It's damned annoying and I was brassed-off about it, that's all."

So Liv couldn't provide Al with a truthful alibi. I told her I needed to get some provisions. She drove to the south side of the anchorage, dropped me off behind a small market on the waterfront, and drove back the way she'd come. I didn't look for the Montero; I knew it was there behind me. I walked through the back door of the market, smiled at the woman at the register, and exited out the front of the store near the harbor. I circled around and back out to the road three buildings down. The tail was parked about sixty yards away. I watched the driver get out and walk into the back door of the market.

I hiked about twenty yards up the hill behind the Montero and found a tree surrounded by thick bushes. I sat there and studied the car; local license plate, new tires, no distinguishing marks.

I don't like being followed and I considered looking for the driver and confronting him on the subject. But I was in a new country with a fresh stamp on my passport and didn't need the complications. I sat and waited.

The driver came out along a pathway between two shops a half hour later. He was a white guy with a medium build and a long face topped with short, curly hair. He held a cell phone to his ear and talked as he walked back to his car. He didn't look like one of the local cops but, of course, not all cops do. He sat in the car for another twenty minutes with the engine running and the air conditioning on and the cell phone pressed against his ear. He hung up as he drove away.

I walked back down off the hill, bought a couple days' worth of groceries at the small market, and wondered why the local cops were watching me.

4

I weighed anchor, sailed out of the harbor, and headed into the channel. I didn't like the idea of staying in a spot where strangers knew I could be found so I headed east to another, much less populated, island. An hour later, I motored into a quiet, windless cove and found a good place to drop the anchor. Four other boats shared the small harbor.

I had two fathoms under the keel, but I let the windlass run until *Figaro*'s anchor and all 250 feet of her chain lay on the bottom. Down below, I retrieved the three carefully wrapped packages that I'd hidden under all that chain months earlier and slipped them into my day pack. Three small, precious parcels filled with crisp U.S. currency. The two men who had tried to kill me several months prior no longer needed it—or anything else, for that matter—but a customs officer would certainly suspect its origin if I declared it. Better to hide it where nobody thinks to look.

With the money now stashed in my day pack, I brought in the excess chain and left fifty feet out to hold *Figaro* in place. The hill west of the cove obscured the setting sun and a dark yellow-orange glow suffused the small anchorage. I sat on the cabin top toward the bow and looked at the beautiful water and clear skies and wondered what the hell I was doing there.

I'd burned most of my bridges in Southern California months ago and came here intending to work with my last good friend on earth. Now he was in jail. I thought of two people I could call and then realized the list really boiled down to one. He'd be getting back from lunch about now—given the four-hour time differ-ence—so I went below, grabbed my new cell phone, and dialed a direct line at the Navy base. I knew the number from memory. He picked up on the second ring.

"Master Chief Joe Richardson," he said.

"Hey boss, this is your good buddy, Sim."

There was a long pause at the other end and, for a moment, I wondered about the quality of cell service in the islands. I stepped up into the cockpit to see if that would help the signal.

"Well," he said, finally. "There's a voice I thought I'd never hear again. Where are you, brother?"

He said "brother" like I was from the 'hood, a place he'd escaped by joining the Navy.

"The sunny Caribbean, my friend."

"Did you hear about Captain Overson?" he asked.

I told him I hadn't.

"He put the business end of an M9 in his mouth six weeks ago and messed up his office something bad. NCIS was all over the base like a bad sweater on a hot day. You're lucky you missed it."

"I'd like to say 'I'm sorry,' but you know better than that," I said. "I've got a favor to ask."

"Ask," he said.

"Can you get me some intel on the British Virgin Islands? Crime rate, conviction stats, CIA and State Department fact books? Whatever seems interesting."

There was a long pause on the other end.

"What is going on, Sim?"

"Al Higgins is in jail."

"Bound to happen someday, brother. Just a matter of time."

"He didn't do it," I said.

"Uh-huh. You need anything else?"

"See if you can find anything on a guy named 'D.C. Millet'," I said. "I think the 'D.C.' might stand for 'Detective Constable' or some such thing."

"You want me to order you a pizza, too?"

"Joe, there's something strange going on here and I need to get myself up to speed. I'll owe you big time."

"No kidding," he said. "Maybe I'll come down and visit you someday so I can collect."

"It'll never happen, Joe. Too many beautiful ladies here. Your wife wouldn't like that."

"Yeah," he said. "Well, I'll get back to you."

I gave him my email address and we hung up. I put the phone away and went for a swim in the last rays of sunlight. It was dark when I got back. The stars above were joined by the anchor lights glowing from the tops of the five masts in the cove. I toweled off and sat in the cockpit looking at the lights of Tortola barely four miles away.

The "restful Caribbean lifestyle" I'd been sold on months ago was not proving to be so restful. I sat in the cockpit and wondered what I'd gotten myself into by teaming up with Al.

5

ROAD Harbor lay about an hour to the north. A variety of shipping plied those waters that morning—chartered sailboats, a rusty freighter, a few huge power yachts, and a couple of dive boats— but the channel was wide and I didn't have to bob and weave like a boxer to get there. *Figaro* reached across the channel at hull speed leaping over the short swells like a happy young dolphin. It was the kind of sailing that gives a guy grins.

"Why not keep on sailing?" I said to nobody in particular.

It wouldn't have been hard. Point *Figaro* east, hold a course for St. Maarten, and let Al get himself out of this jam. *He's a big boy and can fend for himself*, I thought. Then I remembered how he'd saved my bacon in California. I owed him big.

Road Town is set within a tall natural amphitheater of steep, tree-covered hills that protects a semicircle of water on the southern shore of Tortola. The town occupies all of the level space between sea and mountain. Perched on the slopes above the town, the brightly-colored homes of well-to-do locals and wealthy absentee owners peer down upon the small city like smiling tropical gargoyles.

A short stop at the fuel dock satisfied *Figaro's* need for fuel, water, and propane. A half hour later, I motored across the harbor into Fort Burt Marina. The marina is horseshoe-shaped with a half dozen long docks on each side and a small office at the base. Tall coconut palms lined the driveway connecting the office with the island's main road. One of the island's smaller charter boat operations occupied most of the slips, but I'd called ahead and they had space for *Figaro* at a reasonable daily rate.

One of the docks swayed as a large islander in brown shorts and a bright red T-shirt walked out to greet me. He wore several gold chains that, back in the eighties, would have passed for a Mr. T. starter set. A four-inch-tall golden "D" hung from the thickest chain. "ALE" was printed in smaller letters on the big "D."

"You gonna be here long?" he asked.

"Only a day or two, Dale."

"How you know my name, mon?"

"Lucky guess."

I threw him my mooring lines and he secured *Figaro* adjacent to a large catamaran. The big boat buzzed with activity as four couples unloaded their luggage and diving gear and made ready for the flight back to their nine-to-five jobs. They'd already had their week in paradise.

"How will you be paying for de slip?" asked Dale.

"You take cash?"

His face grew a wide smile.

"Mon, this island, she take more cash than you can imagine."

A few minutes of spraying *Figaro* with fresh water and scrubbing her deck with a long-handled boat brush removed several weeks of salt from the boat. Once she was clean, I headed to the marina facilities for a hot shower and a shave. It was a sensual experience non-sailors take for granted. Clean shorts and a fresh T-shirt completed the transformation. I was a new creature.

I grabbed my day pack, walked up the driveway to the main road, and hiked into town. I walked into the bank, read the number of my safe deposit box key to the clerk, and smiled for the cameras. She returned with the box and led me to a small room where I could open it privately. I fished the three packages out of my day pack and stuffed them into the box.

I stepped out onto the sidewalk to see the white Montero parked across the street. The curly-headed driver spotted me and we made eye contact. I smiled and waved, but he didn't wave back. Oh well, nothing you can do about an unfriendly cop. I kept walking.

The lawyer practiced from an office on the third floor of a building two blocks from the bank. Liv met me there at the appointed time. A receptionist led us to a conference room with solid mahogany walls and carpet thick enough to drown a mid-sized poodle. We sat in leather chairs at an oak table that couldn't have weighed less than a Dodge truck. Phillips walked in a few minutes later.

At first glance, he looked to be nothing more than a little over six feet of air-conditioned gray suit with wavy hair, a deep crease in his chin, and a chiseled, professional smile. The consummate solicitor advocate of the British legal system. But he was well-spoken, self-confident, and already familiar with Al's legal situation.

"Mr. Greene," he said, "from what I understand, the Royal Virgin Islands Police Force is quite certain that your friend murdered another tourist, a British subject by the name of Bradley Somerset."

Phillips leaned back in his brown leather chair and waited for a response. I didn't have one.

"Have you ever heard of the man?" he asked.

"Not at all," I said.

Liv shook her head.

Phillips pursed his lips and put his hands together, making a tent of his upraised fingers.

"I understand that the evidence is rather incriminating," he said. "Are you quite certain of your friend's innocence?"

"No."

Phillips raised an eyebrow. Liv sat bolt upright in her chair.

"Am I to understand that you believe that your friend may be guilty of this murder?" he asked.

"Of course he didn't do it," said Liv.

Phillips looked at me.

"No, he didn't do it," I said. "He wouldn't have been caught. But I don't generally think of him as 'innocent,' either."

Phillips appeared to be a little shaken at my forthright assessment of Al's character, but not enough to deter him from asking for a hefty retainer. My instincts told me he was worth it, so I wrote the check and gave him my phone number. Liv and I walked back out to her car.

"You hungry?" I asked.

She drove us toward the waterfront and stopped in front of an open trailer painted so bright and garish that you naturally reached for a pair of sunglasses. An older couple sold paper-wrapped meals to hungry locals as fast as they could hand them out. The only things for sale were roti with chicken and roti with goat. I bought two of the chicken and a couple of sodas. We took them over to a bright orange wooden bench overlooking the harbor.

"Do you mind if I ask you a few questions?"

She shrugged as she bit into her roti.

"How'd you meet Al?" I asked.

"We met over in Trellis Bay at the full moon party a couple months ago. I was there with some girlfriends and one of them introduced me to Al. He was funny and a good dancer. I took a fancy to him."

I took a bite of the roti. It was good. Time to venture a guess.

"You're an Aussie, right?"

"Kiwi, mate. I'm from New Zealand. Are we just having a yack or are you interrogating me?" she asked.

"Sorry. Bad habit, I guess."

"You're a cop, eh?" she asked.

"Used to be. When I was in the Navy. I'm just trying to understand things so I can do my best to help Al."

The eyes relaxed. She ate some more of her roti.

"How well do you know Al?"

"What do you mean by that?" she asked. "I know all about him."

"You've known him a couple of months, Liv. And you told me yesterday that there was part of him you that you couldn't reach. Has he told you much about his past?"

"He told me he'd been a college professor. He taught history, right? And he just retired from the university three or four months ago."

I nodded.

"I think he was in the Navy before that," she said.

"Did he tell you what he did in the Navy?" I asked.

"He taught people to SCUBA dive, didn't he?"

I nodded. She knew what he wanted her to know and he *had* been an instructor at BUD/S. He had done other things for the Navy before that. It wasn't my job to tell her about his Silver Star and Purple Heart or how he'd earned them. Some of those details were still Uncle Sam's secrets, anyway.

"Well," I said, "what more does anybody need to know?"

She smiled, leaned over, and gave me a kiss on the cheek.

"Thanks for tea, luv, but I've got to run. Shall I pick you up in the morning to go see Al?"

"Sure," I said.

"Cheers, then."

She walked back to the car and soon disappeared down the road at flank speed.

The bank clerk had recommended a chandlery along the waterfront and I set off to find it. Some say that cruising is merely fixing a boat in exotic locations. They're right. The sea will corrode, waterlog, and beat to pieces any man-made object placed in or near it. Every long passage with *Figaro* generates a new list of things to be fixed or cleaned or maintained. It's the price of living aboard. I pay it gladly.

The list was mercifully short this time and the chandlery stocked everything *Figaro* needed, albeit at living-in-paradise prices. I loaded my daypack with motor oil, filters, a tube of grease, and a package of marine epoxy.

The previous day's provisioning had been light so I walked over to Bobby's Marketplace. Caribbean Christmas music—Santa Claus playing steel pan drums—blared over an outside speaker system. Four older local men sat on a long bench outside talking, smoking, and laughing. A car pulled into the parking lot as I walked toward the store's open doorway. I looked over my shoulder to see the white Montero stop at the far end of the lot about thirty yards away. So the cops wanted to know where I bought my groceries? I waved again and walked in.

A large woman stood at a cash register and joked with a coworker. A few other people roamed the aisles. Quiet afternoon.

"I don't have a car," I said. "Do you deliver to Fort Burt Marina?"

She smiled and nodded toward a skinny fellow sitting on a short stack of empty pallets and reading a book.

"Julian here, he drives the shuttle," she said. "He'll take you to Fort Burt. No charge."

Julian looked up from his book, nodded at me, and smiled. Bob Marley replaced steel-pan Santa over the store's sound system as I grabbed a cart and headed down the aisles. Food wasn't as cheap in the Caribbean as it had been in Central America, so I kept it to the basics: rice, bread, beer, eggs, cheese, fruit, fresh vegetables, and more beer. The local rums looked tempting, but hard booze and I don't mix well. Practicing restraint, I bought two cases of Coronas and a small sack of limes. Sailors need limes. They prevent scurvy. They go well with Corona beer, too. To ensure adequate variety in my diet, I picked up a case of Caribs.

The four locals that had been smoking and laughing outside walked into the store while I was in the meat section considering some overpriced sausage. They were in a hurry and had somber looks on their faces. One of them closed the sliding door behind him and sat down next to Julian, shaking his head. Four syncopated popping sounds—sounds all too familiar to me—came from the parking lot. Instinct and training kicked in and I headed toward the door. Julian looked up and shook his head. One of the other fellows shrugged as if nothing could be done. I stopped and walked back to my cart.

Sirens drowned out Bob Marley a minute later. The woman at the cash register was quiet and rang my groceries without a word or a smile. Julian opened the door and pushed the cart toward a light gray minivan parked next to the store. He didn't look out into the parking lot.

Two police cars, blue lights flashing, stood at the far end of the lot. Two uniformed officers looked inside the Montero and examined the ground nearby. A third picked up a few brass casings with bare fingers. Another talked to two local women. The top of a curly head leaned against a shattered car window. Blood spatter clung to the inside of the car's windshield.

None of the policemen approached us or asked us if we'd seen anything or if we knew the victim. Nobody bothered us at all as we loaded my groceries into the minivan thirty yards away.

6

"THAT sort of thing happen a lot around here?" I asked.

Julian stared straight out the window as he entered the round-about.

"Your friends saw what was going to happen and who was going to do it," I said. "You got any thoughts about that?"

"It don't do to talk about it," he said.

He sped down Waterfront Drive and turned into the marina driveway.

"Whoever it was killed a cop back there," I said. "Most cops take that kind of personally, Julian."

Julian looked at me as if I'd come from outer space.

"You think the guy that got *killed* was a cop? That's rich, mon."

He stopped the van and began to unload my groceries as fast as he could.

"Well, if he wasn't a cop then who was he?" I said.

Julian ignored me and kept unloading the van. I offered him a tip and he waved me off without speaking, hopped in his van, and sped back up the driveway.

I carried my bags to *Figaro*, fit my key into the little brass padlock, and slid the companionway hatch forward. I stowed the groceries in the icebox and cabinets and all the little cubbyholes that *Figaro*'s builder had left for such things. An hour later, I sliced a lime, grabbed a beer, and went topside to think about a curly-headed guy in a white Montero who hadn't really been a cop. Why would some total stranger follow me around in the first place?

Why would somebody kill him in broad daylight with witnesses around? How could the murderer expect to get away with that?

The sun dipped behind Mt. Sage and darkness settled over the marina. Lights flickered on in Road Town a half mile away. A skinny, middle-aged woman with her head wrapped in a red bandana boarded the catamaran next door and began to clean it. She sang a pleasant, quiet song as she wiped the helm's gauges and controls with a piece of an old beach towel.

"New group coming in?" I asked.

She looked over at me for a moment but didn't stop cleaning.

"Tomorrow morning, sir. This is de busy season right before Christmas. We don't get much time to clean the boats up and turn 'em around."

"New Englanders getting away from the snow, eh?"

"So I'm told, sir."

"You been here long on the island?" I asked.

She stopped her cleaning, stood straight up, and put the towel on her hip.

"Been here my whole life, mister. I was born here and I raised two children here."

"Pretty dangerous place to raise kids," I said.

"What are you talkin' about, mister? The BVI 'bout the safest place you could be."

She went back to her cleaning. I wondered if I'd sailed into a culture of denial.

"So where's the prettiest beach around here?" I asked.

"Long Bay by the airport or maybe de Cane Garden. I ain't been to any of the other islands, sir, so's I can't really say."

"Doesn't the charter company ever take you out on these nice boats?"

"Some of the others go out to party at the end of the season," she said. "But I always been afraid of the water, sir."

"I suppose folks born on an island and afraid of the water don't ever get to go anyplace, do they?"

She put her towel down, straightened up again, and smiled at me.

"And I s'pose folks that stay in love with de ocean don't never grow up and settle down, do they now?"

I smiled back at her and shrugged. She went back to her cleaning. Maybe she had a point.

I finished my beer, went below, pulled out my laptop, and checked my email. Master Chief Joe had delivered the goods on the BVI. It took me a few minutes to download the attachments, but it proved to be interesting reading.

A State Department extract estimated the country's population at approximately 22,000 people. Tourism made up forty-five percent of the economy and employed the majority of the country's workforce. There were the usual concerns over drug trafficking and money laundering: concerns shared with most Caribbean nations. Despite those issues, the country had a low crime rate and acceptable conviction rates in most categories. Homicide was the statistical outlier. Eight murders last year but only three convictions. I thought about how Bradley Somerset and the curly-haired guy who had tailed me—two murders in as many weeks—would skew the local cops' stats and how this could affect Al's case. Not good.

I shut down the laptop and thought of my life aboard *Figaro*.

The small, comfortable space below was clean and seamanlike. A place for everything; everything in its place. The only purely decorative feature was a painting on the forward bulkhead that I'd bought in Monterey. A solitary cypress tree gripping a clump of rocks high above a dark blue Pacific Ocean. I never tired of that painting; it spoke to me.

It was late, I'd nearly witnessed a grisly murder, and I wasn't ready for any negative introspection. I slipped into my berth; my refuge in the darkness.

7

SHE lay in the back of a brown station wagon fifty feet away, unconscious and bound at the hands and feet. A short, well-dressed man held a small automatic to her head while another guy, a taller fellow wearing a cowboy hat, pointed a revolver the size of a horse's leg at me.

Helpless.

Then a loud crack and the well-dressed man's head whipped back as he dropped the automatic. A shotgun appeared in my hands, another loud boom sounded, and the taller gunman fell backward into a river. The cowboy hat floated downstream.

I woke up in a sweat and stepped into the galley for a glass of water. It wasn't quite daylight. I slid the companionway hatch open and climbed up into the cockpit. The first rays of morning sun crept around the southern slopes of the hills east of town, and the little marina came to life.

A brown and white cat stalked something into a bush. A half dozen chickens appeared and pecked at bugs or seeds or whatever chickens ate around here. Small fish, none longer than an inch or two, schooled around the marina, breaking the water's surface in pursuit of floating insects. Larger fish stayed a bit deeper eating the small fry that strayed from the school. Everything killing to stay alive. Life requiring death.

I made a fried egg sandwich for breakfast and ate it in the cockpit. A van drove down the marina driveway and disgorged four couples and an impressive store of duffel bags and other luggage.

The group boarded the big catamaran with loud voices and pounded the deck with heavy footsteps.

Liv sped down the driveway a few minutes later and parked next to the van. I locked up *Figaro* and got in the car. Liv blasted back up the driveway.

"Do you have to drive this fast everywhere you go?" I asked.

"Sorry, but I always feel like I'm going to be late."

She blasted into town and parked across the street from the police station. We weren't late.

The cop in the cabbie's hat at the front desk acted like he'd never seen me before. He scrutinized my passport again and studied my face. Ten minutes later, I walked into the same windowless room with the same steel chairs at the same small table. Al and his guard walked in half a minute later. He was silent until the guard moved off to his corner.

"Word is that they're gonna transfer me to Balsam Ghut prison on Monday morning pending trial," he said. He showed no anxiety or concern. "If you can't get me out before then, I'll do it myself." He looked at the guard. "It won't be pretty."

"Hang tight," I said. "We've hired a lawyer."

"Yeah, Phillips came to see me yesterday afternoon. I'm not impressed. He wants me to give them my alibi."

"Sounds like good advice to me," I said.

Al shook his head.

"They might not even believe her."

"Give it a try," I said. "What's to lose?"

"She's married, Sim. And I guess it's a decent marriage. I don't want to ruin it for her."

"There is no guarantee that I can get you out of this, Al. I don't even know where to start."

"Start with the girl on Cooper Island," he said.

"Needle in a haystack."

He turned his head to study the guard. Evaluating the enemy.

"Okay," I said. "I'll find the girl and she'll tell Phillips and the RVIP how you got the passport. All we need is reasonable doubt."

"She was with some older guy. Gray hair, mid-sixties, looks like money comes easy to him."

"So I need to find a cute girl with a rich older man," I said. "Not exactly a rare thing."

"Find their boat, Sim. It's sixty feet of varnished wood; schooner-rigged with dark red sails. A real gold-plater if you ever saw one."

"Shouldn't be hard to pick a boat like that out of a crowded anchorage," I said.

Al was silent.

"You ever run into Bradley Somerset before?" I asked.

"You sound like one of these cops," he said. "I never even heard of the guy until that girl handed me his passport."

"What about those phone numbers?"

"My cell phone might still be in Liv's glove compartment."

"I'll check it out and find the girl," I said. "Any thoughts on where I should look?"

"Virgin Gorda Sound, Peter Island," he said. "The fat-cat hangouts." He thought quietly for a minute. "If I had the dough for a boat like that, I'd drop my hook at the Bitter End in Virgin Gorda Sound. It's a protected anchorage with good bars and restaurants. Posh. You might find someone there who remembers them."

"I'll give it a shot," I said.

"It was all set up," he said. "The boat. The dive shop. I just had to wait for you to bring the money, Sim. But I got greedy and I screwed it up." He looked over at the guard again and chuckled. "Sunday was pretty slow here. Not a lot of cops around. If you can't get me out before Saturday night, then I'll walk out of here on Sunday morning."

The buzzer sounded again and the guard stood up.

"Al, don't do that," I said.

He lowered his voice as he stood up to go.

"Don't worry about me," he said. "Just keep Liv up at the house Sunday morning. I'll be off the island by noon and I'll email you when I get somewhere safe."

We shook hands and I walked out of the windowless room.

I had some time to kill while Liv visited Al so I went back to the desk cop and asked him if I could see the officer in charge of investigating the Somerset murder. He led me to the office of the tall, skinny cop I'd met two days earlier.

Detective Constable Millet sat in a worn metal office chair behind a scratched white steel desk in a sparsely furnished office that struggled to hold us both. Four manila folders lay stacked on the left side of the desk. Two blue pens lined up on the right. There were no family pictures, no souvenirs of past cases, nothing that wasn't police business. A laboring air conditioner droned through the walls.

"How can I help you, Mr. Greene?"

"I understand you're handling the Somerset case."

He motioned with an upturned palm for me to sit and I pulled up an old wooden armless chair. He picked up a manila folder from the stack on his desk, opened it, and thumbed to a page near the back.

"Mr. Simpson Greene. Master-at-Arms, United States Navy. Recently retired after twenty years of service."

His BBC-quality British accent was as sharp and precise as a scalpel in the hands of a surgeon.

"I am here two days and you have a file on me?" I asked.

"We take an interest in Mr. Higgins's visitors. And the internet is a marvelous tool, isn't it? How can I help you?"

"I'd like to help you find Bradley Somerset's killer," I said.

"We've accomplished that already, Mr. Greene."

"Then my poking around won't hurt anything."

Constable Millet smiled and shook his head.

"You have no authority here, Mr. Greene. You are a retired military detective from a foreign country. You are here on a thirty-day tourist visa."

"I don't want to arrest anybody, Constable. I'm just going to look around, keep my eyes open, and ask a few questions. I won't bother anybody."

"It bothers me a great deal," he said. "You have no authority here and I will not tolerate any interference with our investigation."

He glared at me. The stone statues of Easter Island were warm and friendly in comparison.

"Did Al tell you how he got that passport?" I asked.

Constable Millet smiled.

"The mystery woman on the expensive sailing yacht?" he said. "We won't waste any time trying to track down that little piece of fiction."

"Of course not. You don't have the staff to check out every anchorage or follow every lead. That's why you close only three out of every eight homicides."

Millet stiffened in his chair.

"And you got another one slapped on your desk last night. A curly-headed guy outside Bobby's."

"What do you know about this?" asked Millet.

"I walked out of the store last night and saw the body and a bunch of junior officers picking up spent casings with bare hands, fouling up the crime scene."

Millet's eyes narrowed.

"And nobody wants to talk about it," I said.

He said nothing.

"So I'll do my thing and help as much as any retired detective can," I said. "If I find anything interesting, I'll bring it straight to you."

"Anything that tends to exonerate your friend, you mean."

"I'm pretty sure the facts will help him out in the end," I said. "Where and how did Somerset die?"

The tips of his ears reddened.

"I am not in the habit of discussing the facts of a murder with an agent of its most likely suspect," he said.

"I don't want to sound impertinent, Constable, but if Al killed this guy then he could easily tell me how he did it and where. How does it hurt your investigation to tell me something you think I should already know?"

He thought for a minute, stood up, and left the office. He hadn't kicked me out so I waited. He returned and handed me a thicker manila folder.

Bradley Somerset's British passport had been issued in Manchester, England, and he was born the same year I was. But even in his late thirties, the small photo showed a boyish face. Long dark brown curls framed a light complexion with bright blue eyes set just a little too wide. Dressed properly, he could have been mistaken for Gainsborough's *Blue Boy*.

The autopsy photo showed the same boyish face with the curls matted and the open eyes pale and empty.

"Two local fishermen found the body floating in Gravel Bay off Scrub Island," he said.

"Water in the lungs?" I asked. "Foam in the trachea, nose, and mouth?"

"Some water but no foam. He didn't drown. He received two bullet wounds to the chest sometime between seven o'clock and midnight Wednesday last. His body was found Thursday morning and Mr. Higgins was caught rifling through the victim's safe deposit box on Friday."

"Al has an alibi for Wednesday night," I said.

"He has not shared that with us."

"He won't."

Constable Millet's eyebrows rose.

"Do you mean to tell me that he has an alibi that would clear him of murder charges but that he will not use it?" he asked.

"It involves a woman he wishes to protect. That's all I know about it."

Millet smiled.

"Another mystery woman?" he asked.

I shrugged.

"We hope that you enjoy your brief stay in the country, Mr. Greene, but this is not the United States and I will not have you interfering with a murder investigation." He stood, took the file from my hand, and smiled. "I have no reason to charge you with anything at the moment, but if I or any of my officers see you driving a bit too fast, think you've had too much to drink, or even hear that you've picked fruit from somebody else's tree, we will come down on you faster than a pack of hounds on a three-legged fox." He put the folder on his desk and sat down. "And you will *not* be able to interfere with our investigation while sitting on a steel and canvas cot in Her Majesty's jail, Mr. Greene."

I took a pen off his desk, grabbed one of his business cards, wrote my new cell phone number on the back, and handed it to him.

"You can call me anytime you like," I said. "But please, Constable, call me 'Sim.' 'Mr. Greene' was my dad."

I walked down the hall and smiled at the desk cop as I left. He was unmoved. The car was unlocked, so I got into the passenger side, opened up the glove box, and pulled out Al's phone. The little slip of paper he'd mentioned lay underneath it. The paper was pale yellow and water-stained. The words "Liquid A$$et$" were printed in lime green in the top left corner. An artful swoosh of the same cool shade of green underlined the printed logo.

Two phone numbers were written in the middle of the slip in blue ink. There were no country or area codes. Al had said he'd called them without success. I pulled out my cell phone and was about to give it a try myself when Liv showed up.

"He seems so calm today," she said. "So relaxed."

"Maybe he feels good about your choice of attorney."

"Do you really think so?" she asked. "That's such a relief."

"Sure," I lied.

Liv dropped me off outside the marina office. I paid the daily dockage fee and walked back toward *Figaro*. As I climbed the dock stairs to her deck, I noticed a Tarot card leaning against the companionway hatch boards. I stepped down into the cockpit, picked up the card, unlocked the boat, and went below.

It was a nice card. A little bigger than a regular playing card. It featured a painting of a large man with a big "V" over his head sitting on an ornate throne and talking to two other men. It was slick and colorful, even pretty.

But what the hell was it doing on my boat?

8

I grabbed a Coke from the icebox and sat at the navigation table to examine the card. The man on the throne wore a gold crown and a red robe and held an odd multi-headed scepter in his left hand. The two other men were smaller and balding. They appeared to be imploring the man on the throne, but the big guy wasn't putting up with any of their guff. He held up two fingers of his right hand in a gesture that reminded me of when I was a Cub Scout in Bakersfield. The back of the card was blank.

Henry's words came back to me. "You don't believe in de Tarot," he'd said. He was right. Still, I wondered who had left it and why.

I pulled the BVI cruising guide out from under the chart table and slipped the card into it. It seemed as good a place as any to store a new bookmark. I started the diesel, cast off lines, and backed away from the dock. A half hour later, I turned *Figaro* into the Sir Francis Drake Channel and headed toward Virgin Gorda Sound.

Figaro points beautifully when sailing upwind, and her helm balances easily. The sail northeast to the Sound's main entrance was almost straight upwind, though, and I had to spend most of the afternoon tacking back and forth up the channel to get there.

There was little swell in the channel and the wind, appearing stronger for sailing into it, was almost stout enough to justify reducing sail. *Figaro* sliced into the small ocean swells and the water hissed by her hull. I took my shirt off to feel the warm late afternoon sun on my back.

Less than an hour out of Road Harbor, I spotted a big speedboat roaring up my wake. It was an offshore racer that, like a French politician, is two-thirds nose and one-third noise. A great boat to have if you own an oil company. Or if you smuggle drugs.

It was at least two miles away when I first saw it and it brought back an unpleasant memory of a different speedboat in a different channel. Concern turned to annoyance as over a thousand loud horsepower blew past close astern at sixty knots. A smiling buxom passenger, clad in a miniscule bikini, waved with enthusiasm. I smiled back, wondering how such a small amount of fabric withstood the pounding ride of an offshore racer. It was a marvel of modern textile engineering.

Figaro continued on.

Every tack brought us close to either an anchorage or a mooring field—Cooper Island, Fat Hogs Bay, The Baths—and I used my binoculars to look for a wooden schooner with maroon sails. A boat like that would stand out like a lumberjack at a baby shower.

No luck.

A small Tunny took the lure I'd been trolling, and I brought it in, cleaned it, and put the fresh fillets in the icebox. The sun warmed my back, fish bit the lines, and *Figaro*—sails straining in the breeze—dipped her rails into the warm Caribbean. It was everything I loved about sailing.

Nature guards the Virgin Gorda Sound quite well. A long reef, a graveyard for scores of boats over the last few centuries, stretches a half mile across the Sound's entrance. The entry channel, now well marked with green and red buoys, is wide enough to allow even small cruise ships safe entry. Not a great thing, in my opinion.

The Sound is about two nautical miles long and maybe a mile wide. It is almost entirely surrounded by the island of Virgin Gorda to the south and a phalanx of steep islands and rocky reefs to the north, east, and west. Each of the anchorages and marinas received a thorough scan with the binoculars. No wooden schooner.

The Bitter End Yacht Club dominates a tree-covered headland on Virgin Gorda's extreme northeast. It's the last place to buy either a drink or a winch handle before venturing into the open waters of the Atlantic. With several restaurants, a hotel, bakery, laundry, chandlery, a small grocery store, a selection of beach bars, and a gazillion moorings, it is the most developed resort in the Sound, if not the entire country.

Biras Creek is just around the corner and south of the Bitter End. It is a lot quieter and a guy can anchor there for free. Free has always been the right price. I dropped the hook in twelve feet of water near the middle of the narrow channel with an hour of sunlight to spare.

The NOAA weather report from Puerto Rico predicted thunderstorms and strong winds from the northeast. I dug out the weight belt I use for diving, tied some line to it, and strapped it around Figaro's anchor chain. I let it slide down the chain until it was only a few feet from the bottom. The extra weight would make it much harder for strong winds to break the anchor free.

A hard, cool east wind fell upon *Figaro* about a half hour later. I climbed into the cockpit and turned around to see the perfect, beautiful arc of a rainbow framing a dark mass of roiling clouds. A meteorological juxtaposition of heaven and hell. A Caribbean squall. No big deal.

I struggled in the building wind to cover the flaked mainsail and then dogged every hatch on the boat. The first drops of rain washed *Figaro* as I went back down the companionway into the cabin and turned on a playlist of music from my father's generation.

Gregg Allman sang about a stormy Monday as I cooked rice with a slice of lime and sautéed one of the fresh Tunny fillets with some onion. The storm built while I ate dinner below. Wind howled through the rigging and small wind waves slapped at the hull in syncopated rhythm. John Fogerty started singing about a bad moon rising and I turned the music off.

I was warm and dry in the cabin, but there was nothing to do. I'd read and reread all the books aboard and I couldn't force myself to open any of them. Then I remembered the yellow slip of paper I'd found under Al's phone and pulled it out.

I fished my cell phone out from under the chart table and tried both numbers. Both were disconnected lines in the BVI. *But what if the numbers were for people located in another country?* I thought. Working west, I tried both numbers with the U.S. Virgin Islands area code and then tried them again with both of Puerto Rico's area codes. Of the six tries, I connected with a pizza joint in St. Thomas owned by a guy who had never heard of Bradley Somerset and an automobile repair shop in Fajardo that had closed for the evening. The other four were non-working lines.

I thought of listening to some more music or going for a swim but then it occurred to me that Ashley might still be at work in California. Our relationship hadn't ended well and she probably figured she had every reason to hate me. And her email hadn't left much of an opening. Still, I felt like it wouldn't hurt to try calling her again.

9

"COULD you please connect me with that hot blonde in Marketing?" I asked.

"Sim? Is that you?"

Her voice held the rising tone of surprise.

"Handsome sailor boyfriend at your service," I said.

"Some boyfriend you are that drops off the planet without a word," she said. "Did you know that some insurance agent has his ugly powerboat in your slip?"

"I tried to call you a dozen times before I left."

There was a long pause.

"My dad was pretty angry with you," she said. "He assumed the worst, I guess."

"I noticed. Last time I saw him he was beating my Jeep with one of his Japanese fighting sticks."

She laughed.

"Did you get my email?" she asked.

"Three nights ago," I said. "Harsh."

"Sorry. I sent it over a month ago, when I was still angry." She paused. "So, where have you been?"

"Sailing," I said. "South and east, mostly. I'm in the BVI now."

"The BV what?"

"The British Virgin Islands," I said. "East of Puerto Rico. Want to come down and visit? I've got a spare bunk."

She chuckled a little.

"I know all about that 'spare bunk.' So, you're in the Caribbean somewhere? How'd you get all the way down there?"

"I loaded up *Figaro* and sailed her down Baja, past Costa Rica, and through the Panama Canal."

She was quiet. The storm built outside and rain drummed against the cabin top. I looked outside. It wasn't a picture of tropical paradise.

"It's a nice place," I said. "Warm water and cool drinks. Sandy beaches and fair winds. You can fly down here in a day. No strings."

"No strings?" she asked. "Isn't that the problem?"

I didn't have an answer.

"For a while there I thought that we could be, you know, something," she said.

"We were something," I said. "It was a pretty good something, too."

"I meant something steady, something that lasted."

"Ash, I'd clean up *Figaro* and make room for you in a heartbeat. I'd sell her and get a bigger boat if you wanted me to."

"Something permanent, Sim. Something that doesn't float."

The familiar picture of a beige stucco house in a long row of beige stucco houses came to mind. I envisioned a dozen similarly dressed men mowing their similarly perfect lawns every Saturday morning. A drop of sweat rolled down the back of my neck.

"I'm kind of a boat guy, Ash."

"That's not it and you know it," she said. "Look at yourself. You can't settle down. Why don't you have an apartment like a normal person?"

"I guess I'm not normal."

"My dad was right," she said. "He told me months ago you were driftwood. Navy driftwood. He said you'd always be floating from one shore to the next."

Having done exactly that for three months, I could hardly argue.

"You can't build a home out of driftwood," she said.

"I was only asking if you wanted to join me for a nice Christmas vacation."

"I… I don't think so," she said.

There was a long pause.

"I've met another guy," she said.

"That's great," I said.

"Do you mean that?"

"Not even a little bit."

She laughed. It was a pretty laugh, a marvelous laugh. From four thousand miles away it brightened *Figaro*'s darkening cabin.

"Is he a doctor or a lawyer?" I asked. "No, let me guess. He manipulates foreign currencies, right?"

She gave a sigh of distilled annoyance.

"He's a contract fulfillment supervisor for Toyota."

"Well, you'll always have something reliable to drive," I said. "Is he good to you?"

"We've only been dating a couple of months but he's nice and seems steady. I don't think he'll run off on a little sailboat when things get rough."

It seemed best to let that one pass without a response. There wasn't much left to say anyway. The cabin started getting stuffy, and I felt like hanging up and going for a swim.

"Well, I'm glad to hear you're safe and happy," I said.

There was a long pause on her end.

"There's one more thing I need to ask you, Sim. I need you to tell me what happened right before you left."

I thought for a moment. It was a long moment.

"I want to know what happened that weekend," she said.

"I've told you all I can, Ashley."

"There was a tall man in a cowboy hat standing by my car when I left work that Friday night. The next thing I remember is waking up Sunday morning in my apartment with you giving me cold water to drink and asking me if I was all right."

"I remember," I said.

"That Monday, the local paper printed a story about a murder-suicide near the Santa Clara River east of Fillmore. Later, they said the two men who'd died had been involved in smuggling and counterfeiting and organized crime. They had pictures of them on the front page and one of them looked a lot like the guy I saw by my car. A week later, Al sold his boat and then both of you just disappeared."

"I saw the papers, Ash. What do you want to know?"

"I want to know what you guys are running from," she said. "And I want to know how I was involved."

"You were kidnapped by some dangerous people and Al saved your life. Some unpleasant things happened."

"Were you there, Sim?"

"I can't tell you any more than I have," I said. "Just remember, Al saved you from a bad situation and everything worked out all right. Okay?" There wasn't anything left to say. "You're alive and you're happy. I'm grateful for both."

"You mean that?"

"Very much so. Even the part about you finding a nice guy."

"I'm sorry," she said.

"Don't be," I said. "We had some great times. Now hang on to this guy if he's any good. Buy yourselves a little tract house in a nice subdivision, pay your taxes, raise a family of cute kids, and send them off to good schools."

She laughed.

"If it doesn't work out you can always come visit me in the sunny Caribbean," I said. "I'll still have that spare bunk."

"Take care of yourself," she said. "And your cute little boat."

We said goodbye and hung up. I knew it was the last call we'd share and life felt emptier for it.

Raindrops pelted *Figaro*'s cabin and the flash of a distant lightning bolt shot through her ports. I shucked off my shorts, climbed up into the cockpit, and dove over the side into the black water. It

felt good on my bare skin and I thought of a cowboy hat as I floated on my back in the darkness.

Like driftwood.

10

IN spite of the storm and the strong winds, *Figaro*'s anchor held steady. I slept like a dead man, but, unlike Bradley Somerset, I woke up just fine. Morning brought a cloudless sky.

I wanted to go straight over to the Bitter End to ask about a wooden schooner, but it was too early for that. And there was work to do on the boat.

Figaro's little diesel engine—the "iron jib"—needed an oil and filter change. A messy job that was long overdue. Wedged under the companionway, her engine was almost entirely inaccessible and I spent over an hour replacing the oil filter, pumping filthy old oil into jugs, pouring in the new oil, and testing for leaks. I cleaned up the boat, put the jugs into *Figaro*'s dinghy, and put-putted over to the Bitter End to recycle the old oil.

The resort occupies over a mile of the Sound's coastline and I passed thatch-covered cabañas and beachside villas amid mature coconut palms that strained toward the sun from beaches of freshly raked white sand. Chalets and bungalows stretched up the slope of the island amid tamarind trees and frangipani. The yacht club, with its orange-roofed restaurants, cozy bars, and retail shops, lay north of the beach.

Boats of every size, shape, and variety hung off mooring balls or lay tied to piers. Relatively inexpensive sailboats rented by upper-middle class families moored only yards away from the mega yachts of the ultra-wealthy. Amid this sea of white fiberglass, one large power yacht stood out like an embarrassing yellow stain on an expensive turquoise carpet.

It was a pale yellow, 150-foot-long tribute to capitalism anchored only about a hundred yards offshore with her stern toward the beach. As I rounded the yacht on my way to the dinghy dock I glanced at her stern and read the name "Liquid Assets" printed in large lime green letters. A lime green swoosh underlined the yacht's name.

A thin islander about my age sat on a beach chair at the head of the dinghy dock. He walked down as I approached, caught my dinghy's painter, and made it fast to a cleat on the dock.

"Thanks," I said. "Do you know where I could dump some used motor oil?"

"Straight up de path, sir, about forty yards. You'll find de marine service center on your left."

"Thanks."

I walked about halfway there, thought of something, and turned back. I put down the oil, sat down in the chair next to him, and stuck out my hand.

"My name's Sim," I said. "What's yours?"

He offered his hand with some reluctance.

"Well, sir, most folks around here don't generally ask," he said. "Others call me Levon."

"You're the invisible man around here, eh?"

He flashed a wide grin.

"I'm not paid so much to be seen as to be helpful, sir. You need help with dose jugs?"

"No, thanks," I said. We both sat quietly for a moment. "You have a nice view of the Sound from here."

"Yes, sir. Lots of fine boats here in de Sound. Lots of nice people, too."

"You ever see a wooden schooner with maroon sails? Big, maybe sixty feet long, and finished bright?"

"Gotta pretty lady on it," he said.

It wasn't a question.

"It might at that," I said.

"Seen dat boat here two weeks ago. Stayed a couple of days." He stretched his legs out in front of him. "Fine boat. People on it were real nice, too."

"You remember the name?" I asked.

He shook his head.

"No, sir. I don't."

"How about that big yellow yacht out there?" I asked. "How long has that been here?"

He sat up a little straighter and looked around. He wiped the back of his neck.

"Can't help you there, sir," he said. "It don't do to talk much about some things, if you know what I mean. Some folks get picky about their privacy."

I nodded and picked up my jugs.

"But you might find a crew member or two over at the Crawl Pub," he said. "You might talk to them, sir."

I thanked him, walked to the service center, dropped off the dirty oil, and headed to the pub. It was early for a drink, but that wasn't what I was looking for. A guy with dark, slicked-back hair and a miniscule soul patch beard sat at the bar nursing a tall one. He had a tattoo of a small playing card, an ace of spades, on the inside of his left wrist. He wore boat shoes, off-white twill pants, and a pale yellow polo shirt with "Liquid A$$et$" embroidered in green letters over the left breast.

"Buy you a drink?" I asked.

"Not that kinda guy, sport," he answered without looking up from his drink.

"I'm not either," I said. "I'd just like to ask you a few questions about your boat."

"I'm just the cook, man." He looked up from his drink. "You got questions about the boat, you gotta talk to *el capitán*."

"He around?" I asked.

He nodded toward the door as another yellow polo shirt walked in.

"His name is Rick. Knock yourself out, bro."

The guy walking into the pub had the swagger of a man who'd spent a good chunk of his life at sea. He was a couple inches shorter than me, maybe a pound or two heavier, and he had a full five o'clock shadow before lunch. His black hair was short enough to obviate the need for a comb. A little gray crept into his sideburns. His yellow polo shirt had the familiar green lettering.

I walked up and stuck out my hand.

"My name is Sim Greene. Guy at the bar says you're the captain of that big yellow boat out there. I'd like to ask you a few questions if you don't mind."

"Sure, whatever Cookie says, I guess. I'm Rick Schuster."

He shook my hand like he was twisting a screwdriver and pulled me over to the bar with him.

"Let's have a drink or two. We'll put it on the boat's account."

We sat at the bar and I ordered a Heineken. Rick asked for something much stronger.

"I'm trying to find out as much as I can about a guy named Bradley Somerset," I said.

"Can't help you there, friend. Never heard of the guy." A look of concentration fell over his face and his eyebrows nearly met in the middle. "What's this guy got to do with the boat?"

"Probably nothing at all," I said. "But he had a piece of preprinted notepaper with the boat's name on it. Yellow paper with green printing."

"The boss has pads of that stuff all over the boat. Hands it out like it's candy." He shrugged his shoulders. "The guy might have been a party guest or something, I suppose."

The bartender brought our drinks and Schuster launched into his with vigor.

"Your boat been here long?" I asked.

"Not my boat." He smiled broadly. "I just drive it when the boss says 'go.' But we haven't moved an inch in almost two weeks and there's no sign of leaving anytime soon."

"Owner likes it here, eh?"

"Oh, he loves it here," he said. "We come down here every winter 'cause the boss hates snow. But right now we're stuck here at the Bitter End because we lost our first mate." He reached a few feet down the bar and grabbed a small dish of peanuts. "The guy jumped ship and the damned insurance company says the boat is too big to sail without a full crew. It's all hogwash, of course, but we're stuck right here with our anchor in the mud until I hire a new guy."

"Why'd he quit?" I asked.

"He didn't quit. He didn't get fired, either." He paused to take another sip of his drink. "He took off Wednesday night. Said he was meeting a cute rich girl over at Leverick. Must've fallen pretty hard for her, too, because he didn't come back. I had to go over there the next morning to get our yacht tender."

"Weren't you worried about him?" I asked.

"No. He's a big boy. We all joked around about what a good time he must be having, but it's been a week now and the whole crew is madder than hell at him." He took another drink.

"Did he come back and get his things?"

"That's the weird thing about it. He left all his crap in his cabin. Didn't take a damned thing as far as I can tell."

The little voice in my head whispered again. *Wednesday night.*

"What's your first mate look like?" I asked.

Schuster cocked his head and closed one eye halfway.

"I dunno," he said. "I mean, you don't usually think that much about how you'd describe a guy even if you've worked with him for ten years."

He grabbed some more peanuts. I waited.

"Thirty-seven or thirty-eight, I think. Looked a lot younger, though. Not a big guy at all. Five foot nine, maybe. A little bit of a boy-toy for the ladies." He smiled. "I think they liked the curly hair. He kept it on the long side."

The Captain finished his drink and ordered another. The bartender was fast and efficient and placed a four-inch round paper coaster in front of Rick. The coaster featured the image of a white, three-stranded line made fast to a blue dock cleat. The bitter end of the line pointed its whipped end skyward. He placed the drink on the coaster. Schuster tried the drink and nodded in appreciation.

"Did you say he left all his stuff in his cabin?" I asked.

Schuster put the drink down and turned to look square at me.

"You a cop or something?" he asked.

"Retired. I'm trying to solve a problem for a friend."

"Retired? You're younger than I am." He looked like he was sizing me up, then smirked. "I guess I picked the wrong line of work."

"Any chance I can visit your boat?" I asked. "Might be able to figure out what happened to your first mate."

He gave me a look that carried no small amount of suspicion and shook his head.

"The owner's not too keen about strangers on the boat."

"Would he be happier with a half dozen local cops crawling all over it?" I asked. "Interviewing the crew? Dusting for fingerprints? Going through his underwear drawer?"

"You sure know how to play hardball, don't you?"

Schuster charged the drinks to the boat account and I followed him down to another dock where a big yellow yacht tender lay tied. It was one of those large, inflatable tenders with two high-speed outboard motors and a big center console. The kind of dinghy that cost as much as *Figaro* did when she was brand new. "Petty Ca$h" adorned the side of each hull in lime green letters. I detected a common theme.

The ride to *Liquid Assets* was short. Schuster didn't even come close to full throttle. He took me aboard and led me to the crew's quarters in the forward section of the vessel.

"If anybody sees you and asks you what you're doing here, you tell them you're a cop and that you're looking for Derek," he said. "Otherwise, I'll have to toss you overboard."

Schuster left and I started poking around. The first mate didn't rate a private stateroom. He got a lower bunk and a small locker for his personal gear. Clothes, wallet, foul weather gear, a small digital camera. He hadn't packed much, if anything, before leaving the boat. His passport was in a small drawer built into the locker. Derek Brownell was from Quincy, Massachusetts, and born the same year I was. The photo showed a guy with curly brown hair and a boyish grin. Exactly like the passport photo I'd seen in Millet's office.

Another picture of him and a pretty blonde girl sat in a cheap plastic frame at the back of the drawer. I pulled the picture from the frame, folded it in half, and shoved it in my shorts pocket. I thought for a minute and popped the memory card from the digital camera. I slipped it into my wallet. Derek wouldn't miss it.

I found Captain Schuster in the pilothouse.

"How long have you known Derek Brownell?" I asked.

"I dunno. Maybe ten years," he said. "We worked together in the Coast Guard. I brought him on here as first mate a little over four years ago when I got this gig."

"Know anybody who'd want him dead?"

He thought for a moment.

"I think we'd better go talk to Mr. Wells," he said.

11

TERRENCE Wells sat at a desk in the yacht's main salon reading the *Wall Street Journal* on a tablet. I vaguely remembered him as a guy who'd made big money with a software company he'd sold a dozen or so years before. I anticipated that he'd be in his early fifties, but he looked much older. His blond hair was set as though woven in place by spiders. A yellow mustache, thinner than a politician's morals and with matching goatee, framed the edges of a mean little mouth set between distended cheeks. He looked like a big squirrel worrying about a harsh winter.

He wore stone-washed jean shorts, a pale yellow silk shirt, and large white athletic shoes that, on his legs, looked like giant marshmallows stuck on toothpicks. He was as stylish as a middle-aged guy can be when he's trying hard to look thirty years younger.

He glanced at us through half-height reading glasses as we approached, but he didn't stand.

"Mr. Wells, this is Sim Greene," said Schuster. "He seems to think he knows what happened to Derek."

"I don't care what happened to Derek," said Wells.

He waved his hand as if he were shooing away a fly and turned back to his tablet.

"Dude runs off for a week with some cute skirt and leaves us high and dry," he said. "He's fired. Ungrateful little son-of-a..."

"He's dead," I said.

Wells turned back around, rubbed his little yellow goatee, and looked at me as if I were a nasty, annoying insect.

"What are you, some sort of cop?" he asked.

"No," I said. "The local police think a friend of mine killed your first mate. I'm checking into it."

"How come the real cops aren't here?" Wells asked.

"They might not know, at this point, that he was one of your crew. They think he's somebody named Bradley Somerset. You ever hear of anyone by that name?"

Wells thought for a minute and turned to the captain.

"Rick, I think I want to talk to Mr. Greene alone. Would you please excuse us?"

Schuster nodded and went upstairs to the pilothouse. Wells motioned me toward a couch.

"Have a seat," he said.

He set his tablet on the desk and turned in his chair.

"I've never heard of this Somerset guy," he said. "What makes you think he and Derek are in any way related?"

"I saw Somerset's passport yesterday. It had Derek's picture in it. Your first mate created a false identity."

"And the local cops don't know about this?" he asked.

I didn't like the way he said "cops."

"They don't seem to have caught on to it, yet."

"I'd like to keep it that way," he said. "I mean, nobody knows for sure that Derek is dead, right?"

"Not yet," I said. "But I'm going to get my friend cleared of this murder. If it means that I have to tell the local police, so be it."

"I don't want any cops nosing around here."

"They aren't stupid, Mr. Wells. They'll eventually find out on their own," I said.

Wells thought for a few moments.

"You seem to know your way around these things, these criminal investigations," he said. "You sure you're not a cop?"

"Navy cop, if you like. Master-at-Arms. Retired."

I didn't care much for Wells and I liked answering his questions even less. I considered walking out of the room, getting back to my boat, and calling the RVIP. But the little voice wanted to find out more about Derek Brownell.

"I've got a little problem of my own, Mr. Greene," said Wells.

He rubbed his goatee again. I wondered if that was how he kept it thin and scrawny.

"I think I could use somebody with your experience," he said. "Are you available for hire?"

I generally have no interest in the problems of the rich and pampered. I had even less interest in his, but something told me to keep listening.

"That depends, I suppose. And you can call me Sim if you like."

He stood up, walked to the picture windows, and looked out at the blue water of the Sound.

"It's my wife, Sim."

He asked if I wanted a drink. I didn't. He walked over to a large mahogany bar anyway.

"My first wife left me before I made any money," he said. "I bet she's kickin' herself right now."

He chuckled. It was an unpleasant laugh and not the least bit contagious. He picked up a large glass from behind the bar, put a few ice cubes in it, and poured four fingers of Chivas Regal over the ice. He walked back with his drink and sat in a large leather chair facing the couch.

"I met Meghan—she's my current wife—about four years ago at the Kentucky Derby and I instantly fell in love with her. You know that feeling? When you see some girl and you know deep down inside that she's your soulmate?"

I felt like I was talking to an eighth-grader.

"Sounds wonderful," I said. "So, what's the problem?"

Wells looked at me through eyes as moist and shiny as a window in the rain.

"She's younger than I am. Twenty-four years younger," he said. He took a sip of the scotch whiskey. "I think she's seeing other men. Younger men."

It was a common problem but not as common as the suspicion.

"Can you help me find out?" he asked.

"It's not my forte," I said.

"If it's true, I need to know. I need to find out once and for all," he said. "I want pictures I can use in court and I want to know whom she's sleeping with. You're a retired cop. You know how to do that, right?"

I'd never trailed a woman at her husband's request and never thought I would. It wasn't what the Navy trained me to do.

"I'll pay you five hundred dollars a day."

I thought about it. It gave me an excuse to hang around and find out more about Derek Brownell. I could snoop a little and push a little and see who pushes back; maybe find out who killed him. Five hundred bucks a day didn't sound bad, either.

"Do you have a recent picture of her?" I asked.

He got up and went forward to another part of the ship. Wells returned with a framed picture of a young woman with curly blonde hair. She was almost pretty, the chin a tad too square, the jaw pronounced, the teeth a half-size too large.

"Do you need to take this?" he asked.

"No, I'll recognize her. Where is she now?"

"I said something last week that ticked her off pretty bad." He took another long drink from the glass. "So she hopped on a plane to Miami for a little 'shopping trip.' She's supposed to be back on Saturday around two or so."

"Then I'll start looking for her on Saturday afternoon," I said.

I wrote my phone number on one of his little pale yellow notepads. He folded the paper and put it in the pocket of his yellow shirt.

"Call me whenever she leaves the boat. I'll follow her around and let you know what I find, if anything."

"Thank you, Mr. Greene," he said. "I trust that you will be discreet and not mention this to anyone."

"That's one of the things you're paying me for."

"Indeed," said Wells.

He shook my hand. It was a done deal. I was now officially in the employ of Mr. Terrence Wells. I didn't like it.

Wells picked up a phone and spoke a few words. Schuster came back down to the salon and drove me back to the Bitter End in the yacht's tender. Thinking the cook could tell me something about Somerset/Brownell, I went back to the bar. He wasn't there so I walked over to Levon at the dinghy dock.

"You find what you was lookin' for, sir?" he asked.

"More than I'd hoped, Levon."

"There's always more to learn in this life," he said. "You just gotta ask de right people, don't you?"

Levon's face held a knowing look.

"You're a helpful guy, Levon. I like talking to helpful people and, sometimes, I even buy the drinks. Not here at your place of employment, of course. Much too expensive."

He thought for a minute as if weighing the value of a few free drinks over the possible disadvantages of talking to a big, nosy tourist.

"There is a fine bar at Gun Creek," he said. "Reasonable prices. Just up de hill a ways. I sometimes stop on my way home to have a beer and play de dominoes." He thought a little more. "Probably be there myself 'bout seven tonight."

I nodded, got in my dinghy, and headed back to *Figaro*. Phillips' secretary answered on the first ring and transferred me to the good solicitor a few moments later.

"Good to hear from you, Mr. Greene," he said. "How can I help you?"

"You can tell the RVIP to check Bradley Somerset's passport with British authorities," I said.

"Why should they do that, Mr. Greene?"

"Because it's a fake," I said. "There is no Bradley Somerset."

"And how do you know this?" he asked.

"It doesn't matter right now and I'd appreciate it if you didn't tell them I was the one to discover it," I said.

"This could present them with a serious evidentiary problem," he said.

"A pleasant thought, Mr. Phillips. Please let me know how it shakes out."

I gauged the height of the sun over the water and figured I had less than two hours of daylight left. Not a lot of time to work my way much farther down *Figaro*'s fix-it list. I dug out a few tools, pulled her cockpit winches apart, and cleaned the pawls and roller bearings in some solvent. I couldn't finish the job before the sun set so I tossed a couple of old towels over the disassembled winches and cleaned myself up.

It was time to check out a bar at Gun Creek.

12

MY little outboard drove *Figaro*'s dinghy across the glassy waters of the Sound at a dignified and sedate pace toward Gun Creek. I tied off at the dock and walked up the hill toward a group of shops. Levon hadn't told me the name of the bar, but a young boy directed me to a pink and white building with a red roof.

The bar was clean, well lit, and full of locals. The tables were built of heavy wooden timbers. They were strong; they had to be. Three local men played dominoes at a corner table with a zeal I'd never before witnessed. It appeared to be a contest to determine who could slap their domino to the table the hardest. I ordered a Carib from the bartender and sat at a table near the back of the room.

Levon walked in a few minutes after seven, grabbed a beer from the bartender, and sat down across from me.

"Mr. Sim, right?" he asked.

I nodded. He smiled and drank some of his beer.

"Sim, you done found de best bar in all de BVI."

"A lively place," I said.

"That it is, sir. That it is."

"What can you tell me about that big yellow yacht that's anchored off the Bitter End?" I asked.

"You don't mess around, Mr. Sim. You get right straight to de point, don't you?"

I took a twenty out of my pocket, folded it in half, and tucked it under the coaster that held my bottle of beer.

"Time is money," I said. "I don't like to waste either."

Levon reached for the twenty. I put my finger on the bill and shook my head a little from side to side.

"Tell me something first, Levon. Something that is worth the money. Something that will save me time," I said.

Levon smiled.

"That big yellow boat has been dere nearly two weeks, now. The owner almost never leaves the boat, but de crew is always runnin' all over the place drinkin' and doin' whatever they please. They flash money 'round the club like dey all be printin' it aboard ship."

"They get paid that much?" I asked.

"We see lots of big yachts in the Sound, Mr. Sim. None of those other crew members spend money like dese guys."

"Any of them say where all the money comes from?" I asked.

"No," he said. "They just always be drinkin' and eatin' and blastin' all over de Sound in that big yellow dinghy."

The waiter brought Levon another beer and I paid for it.

"Any of the other workers at the Bitter End talk about the yacht?" I asked.

"We stay quiet and we keep our jobs." He took a long drink and thought for a moment. "They were down here last April and one of the waitresses at de club told the manager that one of de crew tried to rape her. Her family was quite upset about it."

"A crewmember? Which one?"

"The one dey call Cookie."

"Anybody call the police?" I asked.

"Yeah, the club manager got pretty upset and called 'em right away. But by the time the police got there de waitress had this big wad of money in her pocket and she wouldn't talk to dem about nothing." He drank some more of his beer. "Heard she got ten thousand dollars to keep her mouth shut."

"Where does a guy like Cookie get that kind of dough?"

"I heard another member of de crew paid her."

"Yacht crew don't keep that kind of money around," I said. "And they don't pay other peoples' debts. Are you sure it wasn't the yacht owner who paid her off?"

Levon smiled and shrugged.

"I'm just a simple island boy," he said. "But that yacht owner is tighter than two coats of paint. He don't even tip de waitresses."

I took another twenty out of my wallet and tucked it next to its brother. Levon wasn't simple enough to avoid noticing. He licked his lower lip.

"I get the feeling that you have a good idea of where that money came from."

"People around here say de boat is runnin' drugs to the states."

The door to the bar opened and a scrawny, young, twenty-something white guy of medium height with long, straight red hair walked in and sat down two tables away from us. He stood out in that bar full of locals like Lady Gaga at a NASCAR race. Conversations stopped and dominoes fell silent for a minute. The redhead's eyes darted back and forth across the room like a nervous rodent. His eyes found us and something registered. From that point on, they spent too much time pointed in our direction.

Levon stiffened and froze when he saw the young man. His eyes moved from the windows to the redhead to the bathroom door and back to the redhead. He wiped his neck with a paper napkin. After a half minute or so, he stood to leave.

"Something wrong?" I asked.

"I gotta get home now, sir."

I nodded at the twenties on the table. Levon ignored them.

"Mon," he whispered. "I ain't told you nothing, okay?"

Levon walked away and out the door, clutching his beer in his right hand. I palmed the bills and sat back to watch the locals at the next table resume their game of dominoes.

The redhead didn't look all that worrisome to me. Levon could have backhanded the kid into next week. But something about the skinny redhead scared Levon.

Red left a few minutes later and I followed him out the door with my beer bottle. Even empty, a beer bottle can be quite useful. He got into a Jeep that was parked across the street and drove up the hill. Levon was nowhere to be seen.

I walked to my dinghy and motored back toward *Figaro*. Her anchor light at the top of the mast traced a gentle arc across the black sky in rhythm with the almost imperceptible swells of the Sound. When I got back, I pulled out my laptop and plugged in the memory card I'd taken out of Derek's camera. The pictures were of boats and islands and pretty girls. A few piqued my interest.

One featured Meghan Wells, sans bikini top, walking alone on a white sand beach and smiling at the camera. The date stamp indicated that he'd taken it over three weeks before. Another, taken two months earlier, showed Rick Schuster and Cookie sitting on and pointing to a large plastic cooler. They were all smiles. The last picture showed the photographer giving a single-finger salute to *Liquid Assets*. It appeared to have been taken from the yacht tender on the day Derek had been killed.

So Derek Brownell didn't much care for his employer and preferred Meghan Wells topless. Big deal. That put him squarely within the majority of American men. But what was the picture of the smiling crew sitting on a cooler all about?

My phone rang. It was Phillips.

"That information regarding the passport was quite helpful to our case, Mr. Greene. We can now post bail for your friend."

"Bail in a murder case?" I asked.

"The only thing that now connects Mr. Higgins with the victim is a picture on a forged document," he said. "He's not exactly 'off the hook,' as you Americans are wont to say, but he is eligible for release on bail. He will not be able to leave the country, of course."

He told me the bail amount and suggested that I meet him at the RVIP station in the morning. He said he would call Liv with the good news and congratulated me again on the progress I'd made in the case. I hung up the phone, shut down the laptop, grabbed an apple, and took it up to the cockpit.

The sky was a pitch-dark dome and the water beneath was a smooth, flat pool of India ink. Pinpricks of starlight shone through the sky and reflected off the thick, dark water.

It was still and quiet and I was perfectly alone. There was no place I would rather be.

13

I rode the morning ferry from the Bitter End to Trellis Bay and caught a cab into Road Town. The young man at the bank smiled and led me to a room where I could access my safe deposit box in private. I picked up one of the wrapped packages, slit it down the side with my pocketknife, and peeled away the duct tape and plastic wrap. The bills were still crisp and fresh after sailing four thousand miles under a wet anchor chain.

I thought about the young bank teller's smile and the curly-headed fellow shot dead in front of Bobby's. I thought about phone calls that could be made to the police or to others and wondered how private my financial affairs actually were. I suddenly didn't feel comfortable carrying around a lot of cash.

I removed the required funds from the package, put the remainder back in the box, and locked it. I handed the box back to the teller and deposited the cash into my checking account. The RVIP would have to take a check.

Phillips met me at the station and the cop in the cabbie's hat directed us to the office where bail could be posted. The girl behind the desk told me the amount and I pulled out my checkbook. A concerned look crossed her face and she picked up a phone. Constable Millet walked into the room a few minutes later. He glanced at me and Phillips and examined the check.

"Go ahead and call the bank, Dora," he said. "We can honor this if there are sufficient funds."

He turned to Phillips.

"Please follow me, Solicitor," said Millet.

The two walked down the hallway toward Millet's office and disappeared. The bank confirmed the funds and Dora filled out the necessary paperwork. There is always paperwork and it's always necessary. Then it is placed into a file and forgotten for eternity. I walked out to the lobby and found Liv. She fidgeted in her chair as if she were waiting for a dentist.

Millet, Phillips, and Al walked into the lobby and Liv almost jumped into Al's lap. We made our way into the parking lot and Al extricated himself from Liv's grasp.

"Sweetheart, I need to talk with Sim alone. We'll meet up with you at the Queen Lizzie for lunch in about twenty minutes, okay? Is that all right with you, babe?"

"Seriously?" she said.

"Please, Liv."

She shook her head, slipped into the driver's seat of the Isuzu, and drove off at an unusually restrained speed. Al and I walked toward the shops downtown.

"Thanks for getting me out of there, Sim. I owe you."

"It's nothing you couldn't have done yourself," I said.

"Maybe, but I would have had to hurt somebody."

"That's not what I meant, Al. You'd have been out days ago if you'd given them your alibi. And we wouldn't have had to pay a lawyer and put up bail. Our investment fund is diminishing rapidly."

"Take it out of my half, Sim."

"It's not about your half or my half," I said. "It's about buying a dive shop. That can't be done in halves."

"It'll work out."

Al turned and walked into a clothing store as we rounded the corner.

"They have a shower in that jail but I've been wearing the same clothes for a week," he said. He picked out shorts, socks, underwear, and a T-shirt. "This is probably a bad time to ask, but could you loan me some dough?"

I handed him my wallet, walked out of the store, sat under a tree, and wondered why I was sitting under a tree without a wallet. Al joined me a few minutes later.

"Did you find that girl I told you about?" he asked.

"No, but I found out who the victim really is and who he worked for. That's a start."

I told him about *Liquid Assets* and Terrence Wells and the boat's rather unorthodox crew. I told him about pictures and money and a bad marriage getting worse. And I told him about Derek meeting up with a cute rich girl the night he was killed.

"Well, there you go," he said. "There's your killer."

"Which one? I see three or four possibilities in that list."

"The rich girl," he said. "The girl with the passport. The one I told you about the other day."

"Maybe. Or it could have been Wells. Or maybe the father or brother or boyfriend of the nearly-raped waitress waited until the boat returned in the winter and killed Derek by mistake instead of Cookie. Or maybe he was killed to cover up a drug smuggling operation. I don't know. I have no idea."

We turned the corner onto Fleming Street and walked toward a larger building.

"Look, Al. All I can do is hang around *Liquid Assets*, watch the boat and this guy's wife, and poke around a little bit. Maybe I'll find something. Maybe I won't. But it's our best shot right now."

"I'm telling you it's the rich girl on the fancy sailboat," he said.

Al headed for the side of the building and we walked up two flights of old wooden stairs to the Queen Lizzie.

"If you want to chase yourself around the islands and check every anchorage for a fancy wooden boat, go ahead," I said. "Maybe you'll find this girl, maybe you won't. But if you do, you should let me do the questioning."

The restaurant was open on three sides, with expansive views of the town to the east, Road Harbor to the south, and Mt. Sage to the west. Large wooden posts held a corrugated metal roof over the customers. The woodwork had been brightly painted at one point, but it hadn't been touched up in quite a while. Much of it was worn and chipped. Island patina.

Wonderful smells slipped from the kitchen and reggae music blared from a massive chrome and plastic stereo in the corner. A dozen large tables in four long rows, each table capable of seating eight or ten diners, covered the bare wood floor of the dining room. Half the tables were occupied by island locals. A good sign.

Liv waved from one of the tables and we joined her.

"Are you okay, luv?" she asked.

"I'll be fine once I get some food in me," Al said. "They don't hang people on this island anymore. They just starve 'em to death."

Liv sat close to Al. Very close. Any closer and she would have been sharing his T-shirt.

"I hope you don't have any plans for this afternoon," she said.

She leaned over and gave Al a kiss that lasted into next week.

"Maybe I should just grab a sandwich and get a cab back to Trellis," I said.

"No, no," Al said. "Stick around."

A short, rotund woman with a round, obsidian face and ivory teeth brought us a bowl of peanuts and left with our drink orders.

"I owe you, Sim," said Al.

Liv gave him another kiss.

"I'm going to run off to the little girls' room and let you boys talk," she said.

She walked away and disappeared into a hallway near the kitchen.

"Nice kid, isn't she?"

"Kid nothing," I said. "She's my age."

Al smiled.

"Ain't it great?" he said.

Our drinks arrived and a light midday rain fell as I drank beer and ate peanuts. Al concentrated on the double-sized Painkiller he'd ordered.

"They always said you were the best detective in that office," Al said. "I hope you haven't lost the touch."

"Give the cops your alibi and you won't need a detective. And I won't need the touch."

He drank some more of his Painkiller and thought.

"What would Liv say?" he asked.

The reggae music emanating from the giant restaurant stereo wound down and a steel pan selection replaced it. Liv returned from the restroom and I figured it would be indelicate to make further entreaties regarding Al's alibi.

"Did you boys solve all of the mysteries while I was away?" she asked.

"We're still working on it," said Al.

I took another drink. The beer was cold and sweet and the color of dry straw. I remembered reading somewhere how the Sumerians had invented beer around 6000 B.C. and that their civilization had survived for over three millennia. Probably the beer.

The waitress came to take our orders. I leaned my chair back against a solid wood railing and listened to the rain on the tin roof as we ordered lunch.

We talked about the dive shop. The dream. Lunch came and it was delicious. Liv kept the conversation light and fun.

I paid the bill, of course, and we walked down the wooden steps and out to the parked Isuzu. An RVIP sedan sat under a tree across the street. Two local cops watched us from the front seat.

"Somebody's not happy you made bail," I said.

"I'm not going back into that jail, Sim If they try to arrest me again, it'll make headlines."

"Just drive carefully," I said.

"You want to see the house I rented?" asked Al. "It's up on the hill overlooking the north side of the island. On a clear day, you can see forty miles of ocean."

"Sounds nice, but I gotta catch a ferry and get back to my boat," I said.

Al and Liv drove me back to Trellis Bay, and I rode the ferry back to the Bitter End. I walked down to the dinghy dock, brought the outboard to life, and motored past the pretty cabañas and the raked sand beaches to *Figaro*.

The towel-covered, disassembled winches glared at me in accusation as I boarded the boat and unlocked the companionway hatch. I greased and reassembled them while thinking about the slight progress I'd made on the case. Al was out and we'd identified the victim. *Big deal.*

The winches spun with no resistance—pawls clicking their metallic tune—and their chrome drums gleamed orange-gold in the setting sun. There is always a feeling of satisfaction that comes when I've completed a difficult or demanding job. If only Al's problems could be fixed so readily.

14

THE dream returned and I woke up in a sweat as the cowboy hat floated down a dark red river. It was three in the morning. I slid the companionway hatch open, climbed up into the cockpit, and went forward on deck to look around. It was a perfunctory task that every sailor does. You reach down and feel the chain to see if the anchor is dragging, you check the reference points ashore that you'd picked out while anchoring to see if you've moved in the night, and you look for loose lines or anything that could chafe or wear through and cause problems later.

There was almost no wind and *Figaro*'s chain hung straight down into the water. The reference points confirmed that she hadn't moved an inch. There were no loose lines. Everything squared away.

The moon, setting behind Mosquito Island, reflected off the still waters of the Sound. I sat down on the cabin top with my legs dangling down into the cockpit and looked west. I could see the white anchor lights of nearly thirty boats sprinkled throughout the Sound. There were a dozen neatly packed together at Vixen Point, another fifteen or so at Leverick Bay, and a couple of strays tucked into Gun Creek. I knew there were dozens more at the Bitter End but I couldn't see them from where I sat.

I went down below, left the companionway hatch open, and crawled back into bed hoping the dreams were over. Sleep came quickly and held me to my bunk until the sun rose high enough to poke its yellow nose through a cabin port and into my berth.

There was no wind in the Sound that morning and *Figaro* appeared to be surrounded by a massive pane of cobalt glass. The glass rippled slightly like an antique window, but it still reflected the images of flying seabirds and the tree-covered hills that encircle the Sound.

I grabbed my goggles and broke the smooth surface with a short dive off the stern. Morning in the Caribbean was meant for swimming and I headed for a point of land about a half-mile west and a little south of *Figaro*.

The water was remarkably clear. Groups of tiny bait fish schooled ten feet below me and large, flat sand banks stretched as far as I could see. Eelgrass poked up out of the sand and random piles of rocks broke up the flats. Young moray eels and spiny lobsters hid in the rocks. A few rays glided inches above the eelgrass looking for the small crabs that forage there.

The bottom dropped to thirty or forty feet as I left the anchorage and approached the point of land. The water became murkier around the point and I couldn't see the bottom. Only a translucent green void lay beneath me.

I got back to the boat with barely enough time to eat some lunch, pick up my binoculars, and dinghy over to the Bitter End to stand watch for Meghan Wells. Levon wasn't there to assist me, so I tied up to the dock by myself and walked to the pub with my binoculars. I felt as inconspicuous as a guy carrying a hockey stick through a hospital lobby.

Another crewman from *Liquid Assets*, wearing the *de rigueur* yellow polo shirt, was eating lunch at a table near the beach.

"Mind if I sit down?" I asked.

"No problem, man."

I took a chair in the shade.

He was an American-born black, lighter-skinned than most of the islanders. A fouled-anchor tattoo peeked out from under the sleeve of his shirt. He appeared to be about Al's age and was equally fit. He had the rough and calloused hands of a mechanic. He gnawed on a ham sandwich between beers and the score, so far, appeared to be beers–3; sandwich–0.

"Nice boat you got out there," I said.

"Not *my* boat," he said. "But I know every nut, bolt, and circuit breaker on that thing."

"Ship's engineer?" I asked.

He nodded and took a bite of his sandwich. He noticed my binoculars and raised an eyebrow.

"Those are U.S. Navy issue," he said. "You a squid?"

"Now assigned to the USS *Loungechair*."

"Did your twenty and got out, eh?" he said. "You must've started young."

"Yeah, but it was a good run." I fingered the binoculars. "These were sort of a last-minute midnight requisition."

He chuckled and stuck out his hand.

"Always good to meet a shipmate," he said. "Folks call me Chip."

"Sim," I said. I looked over at *Liquid Assets*. "Must be a lot of work keeping a boat like that running?"

"Man, that boat nearly runs itself. I'm just a glorified go-fer."

He laughed and shook his head from side to side.

"Tonight, I get to 'go-fer' the owner's wife," he said.

"Doesn't sound like the worst errand."

"Not usually. But her flight got delayed and now she's coming in on the last plane to Tortola, so I gotta go all the way to Trellis and back in that big dinghy in the dark."

"Shouldn't take you more than a half hour each way," I said.

"I don't like driving boats around here at night," he said. "Too many coral heads stickin' up from the bottom for my taste and that channel at Anguilla Point is too damned narrow. I had to do it last week when I took her to the airport and I thought for sure I was gonna hit something. Now I gotta do it all over again."

He took a long pull from beer number three, paused a moment, and then drained it.

"Get someone else to do it," I said. "You're not the only crew on that yacht."

"The first mate used to do all that shuttle stuff," said Chip. "He was supposed to take her to the airport but the dude took off to see some skirt and never came back. Boss got real mad about that. He's still mad."

He finished the sandwich.

"Man, you want something to eat?" he asked. "Won't cost you nothin'. I'll put it on the boat's account."

"Don't want to get you fired," I said. "I heard the owner leans toward the thrifty side."

"You got that right, brother. But don't worry about me." He smiled and leaned back in his chair. "I'm jumping ship."

"Captain Schuster too hard on you?"

"No, Rick's okay even if he did come from the knee-deep Navy," he said. "There's just too much drama on that ship."

"What do you mean?" I asked.

"Everybody walkin' around quiet-like and keeping to themselves. Like something is going on and I ain't supposed to know about it."

Levon's words rang in my ear.

"Something illegal?" I asked.

"I don't know and I don't want to know. All I can say is that I don't want no part of it."

He spun his empty bottle and looked at it as if deciding whether or not to order a fourth.

"Another thing," he said, "is the owner's wife. She's a first-class, grade-A hot pants and the owner ain't got a clue."

He looked around and leaned toward me.

"I think she's dirty dancing with half the crew."

"That can make for some touchy working conditions," I said.

"Yeah, that kinda crap could get somebody killed."

Chip finished his three-beer lunch and got up to leave. I wished him well and watched him walk down the dock. The sun had arced enough during our discussion that I had to move my chair to stay in the shade. I watched the back-and-forth travel of dinghies and the ferry and the seemingly endless play of vacationers in the warm Caribbean.

Schuster and Cookie walked out with drinks from the bar and sat down three tables away. If they saw me, they didn't seem to care. I was about to get up and walk over to join them when they started arguing. It kept me in my chair.

The argument was quiet at first but it grew in intensity to the point that other patrons started to notice. The two of them weren't loud enough for me to hear what they were arguing about but the conversation peaked quickly and culminated in Cookie standing up and loudly telling Schuster to perform a biologically impossible act.

"Hey, get back here, Cookie," said Schuster. "We gotta figure out how to fix this."

Cookie ignored him and walked into the bar.

Schuster shook his head, balled up a fist, and slammed it onto the table top, knocking over his drink. He picked it up, drained what was left down his throat, and stood up to leave. Then he noticed me.

"What are you lookin' at?" he asked.

There are only a few ways a guy can respond to that question. Almost all of them result in a fistfight.

"I'm fine, Captain. How are you?" I asked.

Schuster looked a little confused at first and then sat down at my table.

"Sorry about that," he said. "I'm a little pissed, that's all."

"Dissension amongst the crew? Mutiny?"

"Huh?" he said. "Yeah, I guess."

"Can I buy you a drink?" I offered.

The universal loosener of tongues.

"No, thanks."

He looked over toward the bar and then back at me.

"So what did the boss want?" Schuster asked.

"Who says he wanted anything?"

"I figured since he wanted to talk to you alone, he must have wanted something?"

"Why don't you ask him?" I said.

"Well, he can be a bit touchy about his privacy," said Schuster.

"Hmmm," I said. "People are like that, sometimes."

I picked up the binoculars and glassed the Sound for no particular reason at all.

"So?" he asked.

"Can you keep a secret?"

"Sure," he said.

"So can I, Rick."

Schuster's lips got tight and he took in a deep breath through flared nostrils. I remembered seeing gorillas do that on a National Geographic special I'd seen as a kid. It wasn't flattering.

"Look, fella. I'm the captain of that ship out there and I need to know everything about anything that concerns it," he said.

"You didn't seem all that concerned about the disappearance of your first mate," I said.

"He jumped ship."

"He didn't jump," I said. "Somebody pushed."

He said something that was not entirely in keeping with the unwritten standards of the Bitter End Yacht Club, stood up, and walked toward the dock. A few minutes later, I saw him driving a small gray dinghy, probably the backup yacht tender, across the mooring field toward *Liquid Assets*.

I learned a long time ago that people kill for four reasons: love, lust, lucre, and loathing. The Four L's. Almost every motive boils down to one of them. From what I'd seen in the last couple of days and from what I'd been told by Levon, Chip, and Terrence Wells, almost everybody on *Liquid Assets*, and a maybe a few folks ashore, could have had a reason to kill Derek Brownell. But it was an embarrassment of riches, and almost as bad as having no leads at all.

As late as it was in the afternoon, I had a few hours before Mrs. Wells would return. I glassed the Sound with my purloined military-grade binoculars. The crisp, steady image was a huge improvement over the last pair I'd had. I silently thanked the U.S. taxpayer.

I viewed the activities of the northern part of the Sound in minute detail. Four couples lounged on shaded chaises near the beach bar at Prickly Pear Island and a half dozen snorkelers cruised over a nearby reef. A couple passionately kissed under a tree over a half mile away. I'd never considered that to be much of a spectator sport so I passed on.

Boats entered the Sound past Colquhoun Reef looking for their night's anchorage or, perhaps, a vacant mooring. Though over a mile distant, I could see the boats and the people aboard with crystalline clarity. The view, however, was compressed by the magnification.

Something entered the channel that I didn't quite recognize at first. It was low to the water with a black hull and dark gray superstructure. I focused the binoculars on what appeared to be a blacked-out version of a twenty-five-foot U.S. Coast Guard response boat. It moved forward through the pass and turned toward Leverick Bay. "Homeland Security" was painted in white block letters on the port side of the inflatable hull. It seemed odd to spot one of those in foreign waters.

Four sailboats moved into view and blocked out the big black inflatable. They were headed toward Vixen Point and looked like racehorses nudging each other around the last turn before the home stretch. A fifth boat approached from the rear and nosed into the original pack of four. But the fifth boat was very different.

Where the first four were white sloop-rigged fiberglass charter boats with white sails and blue trim, the fifth boat was varnished wood—finished bright, in sailor's terms—and wore maroon sails on a schooner rig. I smiled and put down my binoculars. Then I picked up my phone and called Al.

"You have any luck finding that wooden mystery boat with the lovely lady aboard?" I asked.

"No," said Al. "I've checked Peter Island, Cooper, Norman. Probably blown a couple hundred bucks in fuel looking for it. Nothing."

"Maybe you should check the Sound," I said.

His voice pitched up a full octave.

"You're kidding me, right?"

"Less than a mile away and getting closer as we speak," I said. "You want me to ask her a few questions?"

His response was graphic and ungentlemanly. "How about I come out there and ask her a few questions myself," he said.

"I'll catch more bees with a drop of honey than you will with a barrel of vinegar, Al."

"Yeah, well that bee has got a stinger so you better watch your..."

"Roger that," I said. "I'll make a full report in the morning."

I hung up the phone, kicked my feet up onto an adjacent chair, and watched the wooden schooner through my binoculars. She turned into the wind a couple hundred yards away and dropped her main and fore sails. I could tell that she was an older design, maybe sixty feet long, and that she had been expertly restored by someone who appreciated gleaming brass and brightly varnished wood. *D'Artagnan* was spelled in gold letters on her aft quarter.

A white-haired gentleman and a much younger man secured the sails to their respective booms as the boat motored at a sedate pace toward the yacht club's mooring field. A slender, dark-haired woman stood at the helm. She maneuvered the schooner's bow into the wind and forward to a mooring, stopping the boat's momentum at the perfect spot so the younger man could reach the mooring pennant with a boat hook. It was not a feat of casual seamanship for a vessel that size.

She shut down the boat's diesel and went forward to double-check the mooring lines. She wore light shorts and a blue- and white-striped long-sleeved shirt reminiscent of those worn by Russian sailors during the Cold War. I guessed she was in her early thirties.

And she was a beauty.

I put the binoculars back in their case and watched *D'Artagnan*'s crew stow their gear and secure the vessel. Minutes later, they stepped down into their dinghy and headed toward the main dock. The two men walked north along the brick pathway toward the resort's reception building.

I followed the woman into the small grocery store.

She was taller than I'd originally thought. Nearly six feet with a deep, well-earned tan and jet black hair. She carried a large canvas tote bag and I watched her for a moment as she selected items from the shelves and put them in the bag. Her movements were graceful. Elegant.

"That is a beautiful schooner you've got out there."

She stopped, turned around, and gave me a broad, welcoming smile. Her deep brown eyes were confident and slightly challenging.

"Thank you," she said. "We launched her this summer and brought her down with the Caribbean rally."

"I saw you bring it in." I said. "Anybody watching could see you know something about handling boats."

She cocked her head a little.

"Thank you," she said. "That's very nice."

"It's only the truth."

I put out my hand.

"My name is Sim Greene," I said. "May I buy you a drink?"

The smile melted. She didn't shake my hand.

"I appreciate the offer but I'm not on the market."

She turned away to continue shopping.

"It's not what you think," I said.

She walked farther down the short aisle.

"I'd like to ask some questions about the passport you found in the channel last week."

She turned around with a look of complete surprise.

"What?" she asked. "The little bag we found off Beef Island?"

There isn't really a nice way to say it.

"The guy it belonged to was killed ten days ago," I said. "I need to ask you a few questions. It's very important."

The brown eyes opened a little wider and her mouth opened a little without saying anything. If she was faking ignorance, it was a good act. I held out my hand again.

"My name is Sim. Can I buy you that drink, now?"

15

WE walked over to the pub and sat down at a table overlooking the mooring field and the Sound. Windsurfers, daysailers, and small catamarans raced back and forth in the late afternoon breeze.

Her name was Marie Tanner. The two men with her were her father, David, and younger brother, Lance. They had sailed their newly restored schooner down from Connecticut for an extended vacation. Money did not seem to be a concern.

The initial shock of hearing about a murder wore off as she talked. She sat back in her chair comfortably and crossed her legs at the knee.

They were fine legs.

"Are you a policeman?" she asked.

"No," I said. "Not anymore."

She raised a long, thin eyebrow.

"Then why are you asking me about a murder and how did you know about that little bag?"

"You gave it to a tough old guy at Cooper Island," I said. "A short, stocky fellow. Could have been chewing on a cigar at the time."

Her eyes lit up. "I remember him. He was very nice; a perfect gentleman."

"He was probably leering at you."

She smiled.

"He was very nice," she said.

"He's a friend of mine," I said. "The local police put him in jail the day after you gave him that bag."

Her mouth did not quite drop open in shock but her eyes opened a little wider.

"They think he killed the fellow whose passport you found," I said. The waiter delivered our drinks. "I'm trying to find out what happened so we can clear him of the charges."

She quietly sipped some of her drink.

"So, how exactly did you come to find that little plastic bag?" I asked.

She relaxed and a wry smile graced her countenance. She re-crossed her legs. I noticed. I had to. I'm a trained observer.

"Is this the part where you mercilessly interrogate me and force me into a confession, Mr. Greene?"

"Actually, I *am* buying you drinks," I said. "You should be batting your eyelashes and calling me 'Sim.'"

Her smile faded and then I noticed the narrow gold ring on the third finger of her left hand. Al wouldn't have noticed. Nor would he have cared.

"Sorry, I'm a little beyond the age of eyelash batting," she said. "But I can tell you where I found the bag."

"Like Mickey Mouse, I'm all ears," I said.

"We were on our way to Cooper Island."

"From where?" I asked.

"Trellis Bay."

She paused to sip some of her drink.

"Dad was sailing the boat and I was sitting forward watching traffic in the channel when I saw a small boat fender floating in the water ahead of us. I wanted to get that fender..."

"She's a real packrat," a male voice interjected.

I stood up and turned around to see the older of the two men who were sailing with her.

"Hi, Dad," said Marie. "Sit down and join us."

He smiled and sat down to my right with his back to the Sound.

"Just go on with your conversation, you two," he said. "I'll catch up eventually."

"As I was saying," Marie continued, "I wanted that boat fender but Dad wouldn't steer toward it so I could grab it with the boat hook."

"She has some difficulty with authority," David said.

Marie ignored him and continued.

"So I hopped into the dinghy and got it myself," she said. "Floating next to the fender was a small plastic bag with a passport and some other stuff in it."

I heard the sound of twin outboards barking into life and looked toward *Liquid Assets* to see Chip idling the yacht's big tender into the Sound. A moment later, he opened up the throttles and the boat skipped across the smooth water toward Anguilla Point at over forty knots.

"Did you open the bag?" I asked.

"Sure," she said. "When I saw it had a passport in it, I realized we should get it to the proper authorities."

"What did you do next?" I asked.

"We sailed on to Cooper Island. When we got there, I went ashore to a small boutique there. I asked the girl at the counter if she knew of a policeman that I could give the bag to and she told me to ask the bartender at the beach club."

"And that is where you met Al," I said.

"Al? Is that your friend with the cigar?"

I nodded.

"I give up," said David. "Someone is going to have to bring me up to speed at this point."

I told him about how and why the Royal Virgin Islands Police had arrested Al. I saw no reason to mention the safe deposit box or the money. David put his drink on the table and sat back in his chair.

"In my profession," he said, "when somebody is asking these types of questions, they are usually doing so from an adversarial position. I think I'd like to know a little bit more about you before this conversation goes any farther."

"What would you like to know?"

"Right now, I don't even know your name."

"My name is Greene," I said. "Sim Greene."

"What? Like 'Bond, James Bond'?"

"No," I said. "That guy drives a million-dollar car, flies planes and helicopters, always has a beautiful woman on his arm, and shoots people while wearing a tux."

"You're not like him?" asked Marie.

"Nah," I said. "I don't own a tux."

David laughed. Marie shook her head.

"Can I speak with my daughter alone for a few minutes?"

"Of course," I said.

I got up from the table and walked over to the bar. The bartender approached. He was a little younger than me, with shoulder-length blond hair and a tan that screamed island life.

"What'll you have?" he asked.

"Beer."

He stepped over to the taps, drew me a glass, and brought it back with a coaster. Based on a lifetime of close observation, I have concluded that there are two types of bartenders: the quiet ones who focus on their job and pretty much leave you alone, and the talkative, friendly folk who want to be your best friend. Mine was the latter.

"Are you thinking of going after that one?" He nodded in the direction of the table I'd just left.

"I haven't thought about it, actually."

"The hell you haven't. Every guy on this island has thought about it."

I laughed.

"She's a regular visitor?" I asked.

"Been here before. Twice in the last couple of weeks, I think. She's on that bitchen wood boat in the mooring field. You can't miss it."

"I've seen the boat. Nice."

"Seriously," he said. "I wouldn't waste a lot of money on her. She's kind of a cold sister."

"Do I look like the kind of guy who's got a lot of money to spend on the ladies?"

"No, brother. You look like a starving sailor who isn't going to leave me a tip. I just can't figure out why you're here paying this much money for a beer."

"Don't let your employer hear you talk like that."

He grinned. Another patron at the bar needed service and he left to gab over there. I drank my beer, ate a few peanuts, and watched the clock behind the bar. I gave the Tanners five more minutes and then waved the bartender back over.

"What are the cold sister and her father drinking?"

He told me and prepped a tray with the two drinks. I paid in cash and left him a nice tip. Starving sailor, indeed.

"Good luck, brother," he said.

I walked back to the table and delivered the drinks.

"I'm sorry if I came off as too, what was your word, 'adversarial'? Perhaps this will help make up for it."

"Thank you," said David. "I have a few questions of my own."

"Shoot," I said. "Figuratively."

"Are you a policeman, Mr. Greene?" he asked.

"No."

"Are you working for the local police in any capacity?"

"No, I'm just trying to help a friend who's in a bit of a bind."

"How long have you lived here in the BVI?"

"Less than a week," I said. "I brought my boat here from California."

"Through the Panama Canal?"

"Yep."

"Did your friend Al help you?"

"No, I came alone. No crew."

David's eyebrows rose a notch.

"Single-handed?" he asked.

I nodded.

"It seems to me that would be both dangerous and uncomfortable," said David.

"It's not so bad. You set the boat up right and she sort of sails herself," I said. "You just don't get as much sleep. And conversations aboard tend to be considerably less stimulating."

"I'm not sure how we can help you or your friend," said David.

"Have either of you ever heard of a man named Bradley Somerset?" I asked.

"We've never heard of him," said David.

"Or Derek Brownell?" I asked.

"No," said Marie.

She turned to look across the Sound. The sun slipped behind Mosquito Island a couple of miles away. I got the distinct impression that I was no longer welcome.

"Would either of you be willing to talk to the local police and tell them how you found that plastic bag?" I asked.

"No," said David. "We're on vacation. We don't know anything about any of the people you've mentioned and we don't honestly know if the bag you describe is the bag we found. You say somebody was murdered but we certainly don't know anything about that. I don't see how we can help you."

The unwilling witness: a problem as old as police work itself.

"I understand your reluctance to get involved," I said. "I only want you to tell the police how Al received the bag and the passport from you."

"I don't see how we can help the authorities in any way," said David. "And I am not willing to involve my family in a murder investigation, especially one being conducted in a foreign country."

I considered telling Constable Millet myself and letting him question the Tanners directly. Then I thought of the level of police work I'd seen outside Bobby's and realized how badly that tactic could backfire.

"You could help," I said. "But I can see why you'd be reluctant. I'll get out of your hair and let you folks get back to your vacation."

I stood to leave and turned to walk back down to the dock. I only got a few steps.

"Hang on a second," said David. "I'd very much like to hear about your experiences sailing alone. How it's done. How you set up your boat and such. Perhaps you could tell us about your trip from California."

Marie shot her father a puzzled look.

"Are you free for dinner tomorrow?" he asked.

I tried to think of something refined to say but hit a brick wall.

"Yeah," I said. "I guess so."

"Come on over to our boat around sunset tomorrow and we'll dine aboard," he said. "I'm ready for a few new stories around the dining table and I'd bet you've got some good ones. Perhaps, you could educate us all about single-handed sailing."

The invitation threw me.

"Sure," I said. "Sounds great. See you tomorrow."

They were nice, respectable, high-class folks on vacation in paradise. Why would they invite a stranger who thought they could be involved in a murder to dinner? I walked out of the club and down to the dock in the darkness trying to figure it out. It hit me as I stepped down into my dinghy. They had just done to me what I'd done to Terrence Wells; continue a relationship with a person for no other reason than to watch them more closely. Clever. I wondered what David Tanner did for a living.

16

I untied my dinghy and motored to a spot near the beach a couple hundred yards south of *Liquid Assets*. It was a good spot hidden beneath palm trees that stretched low over the water. From there, I had a direct view of the yacht's stern and main salon as well as most of the Sound to the west.

I tossed the anchor over the stern and set two of the boat cushions against the bow. Then I lay in the bottom of the dinghy and settled back with my binoculars to wait for the return of Meghan Wells.

The Return of Meghan Wells, I thought. It sounded fearful and ominous, like a 1950s monster movie. The studio would have released *Godzilla vs. Meghan Wells* before the producers realized that Meghan had become the audience's true hero. Next in the series would have been *Meghan Wells and the Moth Monsters*. Later they'd release *The Son of Meghan Wells* after the B-movie actress who played Meghan had gained a pound or two or acquired an unpleasant wrinkle.

You think of strange things when you're lying on your back in the bottom of a dinghy on a dark night with a pair of binoculars on your chest.

I had lain there for nearly two hours thinking of odd horror movies and was starting to feel more than a little stiff when I heard the whine of twin outboards coming across the Sound from my left. I looked over to see the big inflatable's green forward navigation light racing toward *Liquid Assets* from nearly a mile away.

A minute or so later, Chip throttled down and pulled up to the yacht's stern and into the glow of her aft deck lights. I picked up the binoculars.

Meghan Wells stepped onto the yacht as if she were royalty to be welcomed by her subjects. Once she was under the full illumination of the lights on the afterdeck, it struck me that she really *did* look like a B-movie actress from the 1950s. An absolute scream queen. But she wasn't the headline player. She was the one who got killed by the terrifying swamp monster before you finished your first bag of popcorn.

She had a nice, if obviously unnatural, figure. Some surgeon had seen to that. Her white pants were tight enough to look as if they'd been painted on and the purple blouse, worn loose and open to the navel, revealed an ample portion of the surgeon's unencumbered handiwork.

Half her face was obscured behind bleached blonde curls. But I recognized the chin, the jaw, and the oversized teeth from her picture. She chewed gum, which, along with the jaw and teeth, gave her face a pronounced equine quality. The pants and the blouse, however, played to her obvious strengths. A lot of guys might never realize she even had a face. Overall, however, I concluded that if she were Terrence Wells's trophy wife, he hadn't won first prize.

Captain Schuster walked out onto the deck and she threw her arms around him enthusiastically. She did the same for Cookie. Chip carried her bags into the main salon. I wondered how she had treated Derek Brownell.

Terrence Wells met her at the sliding glass door entrance to the main salon with a smile on his face and a drink in each hand. He opened his arms wide in welcome. She flipped her head, tossed the obscuring curls to one side, and walked past him into the salon without stopping. Her part in the B-movie was over for the moment.

Mr. Wells pursed his lips, shrugged his shoulders, and gave the drink to Rick. Chip came back out of the salon and helped Cookie secure the inflatable to the yacht's stern. Somebody turned off the deck lights.

The show was over. There were no credits to keep me in my seat; no music to listen to. I put the boat cushions away, pulled up the anchor, and headed back toward Biras Creek.

The wife is mad at the husband, the husband wants to make up, and the wife is having none of it. Hardly a first. *Lifestyles of the rich and famous? Who cares?*

Figaro was right where I'd left her that morning, tugging lightly at her anchor chain. I unlocked the companionway, went below, and clicked on the anchor light. I leaned back against the cabin and watched the thin nighttime clouds sliding along under the stars, each cloud taking its turn at obscuring and revealing the constellations.

I still wasn't enjoying the thought of spousal surveillance and wished I could quit. But there was something unusual about the owner and crew aboard *Liquid Assets*. As far as I knew, they had been the people closest to Brownell but none of them seemed all that concerned about his disappearance. It was an odd way to treat a shipmate who had been aboard for four years.

17

SOMEBODY left a message on my voicemail while I had my morning mile swim. It was from Wells. He wanted me to call him back.

"Where have you been?" he asked. "I've been trying to reach you for half an hour."

"Swimming," I said. "My phone gets a lousy signal underwater."

"Is that supposed to be funny?"

"I guess not."

"I hired you to do a job and I expect you to do it," he said.

"Fire me if you like," I said.

He paused a moment as if taken off guard.

"I need you to find out if she's cheating on me," he said.

I didn't feel like taking a rich man's guff and I didn't feel like pulling any punches.

"Save your money," I said. "She's cheating on you. I saw her come in last night and I saw how she reacted to you."

"That's not enough," he said. "I want proof. I need pictures."

"Okay," I said. "What did you want to tell me while I was swimming?"

"She's leaving the boat," he said. "She says she's going over to Leverick to shop at the Pusser's store and swim in the pool. I think she's going to meet somebody."

"My job to find out, I guess. Is she taking the ferry?"

"No. The cook has to run an errand and is taking her over in the launch with him. Are you going to follow her?" he asked.

"That's what you're paying me for. I'll call you if I find out anything."

"Get pictures," he said. "I want pictures."

He wished me luck before hanging up but I didn't believe him. Nobody really wants to catch their spouse cheating on them. It hurts too much in a tender place.

I grabbed my binoculars and stepped up into the cockpit. It was only a minute or so before I spotted the large, pale yellow inflatable racing across the Sound toward Leverick Bay. Cookie drove the boat from behind the tender's big center console. The blonde B-movie actress sat next to him. She wore a turquoise halter-necked dress and worked hard to hold a big, floppy white hat down on her head. *Meghan Wells vs. The Wind Monster*. At the speed they were going, they'd be across the Sound in two minutes.

I put on dry shorts, a gray T-shirt, my newer L.A. Dodgers ball cap, flip-flops, and sunglasses and fired up my dinghy's reluctant outboard. My heart was pure and my hands were clean but my aging steed was not so swift. I was twenty minutes behind them by the time I got to Leverick Bay. The big tender was tied up at the T-dock and I motored slowly past it to the smaller dinghy dock near Jumbies Beach Bar.

Leverick Bay is another brightly colored resort that caters to those who have more than a few extra bucks to spend. The small beach is surrounded by pleasant shops, a nice restaurant, some tennis courts, a spa, and a freshwater swimming pool. Pastel colored, red roofed, villa-style guest rooms and suites hang on to the hillside by their toenails to peer out over the swimming pool, the bay, and the Sound.

The pool was right next to the beach bar and Meghan wasn't in it. The Pusser's store was fifty yards up the beach on the other side of the aptly named Restaurant at Leverick Bay. She wasn't there, either.

With no better idea of what to do, I walked back to Jumbies, got a Coke from the bar, sat down at a table in the sand under a gaily colored umbrella, and tried to look like a tourist. From my vantage point, I could see *Liquid Assets*'s dinghy tied up at the T-dock, the main dock connecting it to the resort, and several of the little shops. But I couldn't see either Cookie or Meghan Wells.

A little before noon, I walked past the pool to the Cove Grill and added a sandwich to Mr. Wells's expense account. The specials written on the chalkboard featured a "BVI BLT" and my waitress recommended it. But I had to ask.

"Do people really travel thousands of miles to come here and eat a BLT?"

"Mister, people come here for all kinds of reasons," she said. "No sandwich is going to fully satisfy the soul but our BLT is still pretty damned good."

And it was. I was halfway through it and trying to figure out how the grill's special sandwich spread could be replicated in *Figaro*'s modest galley when I heard high-pitched female laughter coming from one of the hillside bungalows. My eyes focused on a blue and white cottage midway up the hill. The B-movie actress and Cookie, both shirtless, walked out onto the balcony.

I got a better look at Meghan Wells in the harsh sunlight of a Caribbean noon. She looked to be about thirty and slightly less attractive than I'd originally determined. She threw her arms around Cookie and pulled him to her.

I felt no joy as I took the pictures Mr. Wells had said he wanted. They would probably make him unhappy. But they were what he was paying me for.

18

I polished off the sandwich, left some cash for the bill and tip, and walked under the wooden patio cover toward the bungalows. There wasn't any real reason to hide, but there was no advantage to being spotted, either, so I ducked into the dive shop and browsed through a book on Caribbean reef fish while surreptitiously watching the loving couple through the shop's window.

Meghan gave Cookie a long kiss; long enough for me to memorialize it with my camera. She finally let him up for air and went back into the bungalow. Cookie pulled on a shirt and waited for her. She returned fully clothed and walked down the hill and into the Pusser's store.

Cookie picked up a large ice chest that had been sitting outside the bungalow and walked past the laundry and the public showers to a road that seemed to function as the landlubbers' entrance to the resort.

A blue Jeep, one of the longer ones with a small pickup bed behind the cab, stopped on the road beside Cookie and a man got out from behind the wheel. The man was dark ebony like most of the locals, and he was enormous. At least six foot five and somewhere north of 350 pounds.

He would have made a decent run-blocker for any offensive line in the NFL except that he was too old for the job. He had to be pushing sixty. He wore jean shorts, a white T-shirt, and sunglasses that probably cost more than I could get for my lousy outboard. A short salt-and-pepper beard covered his chin and closely cropped, curly gray hair peeked out from under a bright red ball cap with an oblate white "C" on the front. A Reds fan. I suddenly felt conspicuous in my Dodgers cap.

Cookie looked up and down the short street, set the ice chest on the small pickup bed, and opened it for the older man. I couldn't hear any of their conversation from my vantage point in the dive shop but I could see that the big islander was more than a little bit angry at Cookie. Cookie shook his head and shrugged his shoulders and the big guy responded by giving him an open-handed slap that sent Cookie back about six feet on his heels.

He collected himself enough to yell the most common words in a New Yorker's vocabulary. It was loud enough to be heard through the dive shop window and attracted the attention of some nearby tourists. Cookie—adulterer, smuggler, accused rapist—was clearly a class act. I felt like hitting him myself. But it wasn't any of my business. My job for Mr. Wells was done.

I left the dive shop and walked toward the dinghy dock. On the way, I stopped again at Jumbies and ordered another Coke, this one laced with a shot of the local rum.

A half hour later Cookie appeared at the top of the T-dock with the ice chest in his arms and a scowl on his face. He carried the chest down the dock to the big inflatable. It was heavier now and probably filled with steaks that he would later cook for the man whose wife he slept with.

Meghan trotted down the dock with a full shopping bag and a big grin. Cookie helped Meghan into the yacht tender and they roared across the Sound back to *Liquid Assets*.

I stepped down into my dinghy, put-putted back toward *Figaro*, and tried to steel myself for an unpleasant conversation with my employer.

19

LIFE in the Sound was fine outside the big picture windows of the yacht's main salon. A few young couples raced their small catamarans between Saba Rock and Gun Creek. Some teenage boys took windsurfing lessons just off the club's beach. Several chartered sailboats maneuvered for position to pick up moorings to the north of the big yacht. People making the most of a beautiful, sunny day in paradise.

Inside the salon, Mr. Wells sat on the sofa and copied photographs from my camera's memory card to a laptop computer.

"Are you trying to tell me that Cookie is doing my wife?" he asked.

"Or your wife is doing him," I said. "It depends entirely on one's point of view."

He pored over each picture carefully, as if the secret to his failed marriage could be found deep within the pixels. He shook his head a little and the width of the shake increased slightly with each successive picture.

"I can't tell you what happened inside that bungalow, Mr. Wells, because I didn't see it." I couldn't think of any way to make the bad news better. "I took these pictures a couple of hours ago at Leverick Bay. You'll have to draw your own conclusions."

"I already have," he said.

His back was to me, but his shoulders slumped slightly. He closed his laptop and silently disappeared into the master stateroom. I took the opportunity to retrieve the memory card for my camera. He emerged a few minutes later and handed me a yellow envelope.

"This is for your services," he said. "You have completed your task, Mr. Greene. I trust that these pictures and our conversations will be kept confidential."

"You have the only copies of those pictures," I lied. "Unless the police decide that they are going to beat it out of me, I can't think of any reason to talk to anyone about this." I opened the envelope and found three one-hundred-dollar bills. "I thought you were paying me five hundred dollars a day for this job."

"And what did you do, Mr. Greene? A half-day's work? If anything, I have overpaid you."

"You would have preferred I took longer?" I said.

He turned to look directly at me. His eyes were lifeless, cold blue steel. He reached into his pocket, took out two more bills, and handed them to me.

"Fine," he said. "A full day, then. But this buys your silence, too. Good day."

He turned and walked back to the master stateroom.

I folded the bills, stuffed them into my shorts pocket, and walked aft to the stern where I'd tied the dinghy. The outboard fired up with uncharacteristic vigor and enthusiasm, and I motored over to the yacht club.

I felt a little richer but more than a little dirty. My soul needed a stiff drink and a long, hot shower.

20

I made it halfway through my first beer at the pub before I remembered that I was to dine that evening with the Tanner family. My more refined senses suggested that it was bad form to show up soused. Being clearheaded might also allow me to learn more about Brownell's murder. So I limited myself to that one beer.

The angle of the sun told me that I had about an hour before my dinner appointment on *D'Artagnan*. Motoring to *Figaro* to change my clothes only to motor back to *D'Artagnan* didn't make a lot of sense so I walked over to the gift shop to buy a new shirt. I found a short-sleeved, pre-washed Breton Red shirt that fit and that actually looked okay with my L.A. Dodgers ball cap. And it cost half as much as a bottle of good local rum.

The sun kissed the top of Mosquito Island to the west as I walked down to the dock to retrieve my dinghy for the short trip to *D'Artagnan*. When I got there, I saw Marie and her father pulling up in their yacht tender. I threw my old T-shirt into my dinghy and caught the painter that Marie tossed to me.

"Don't tie it off," said David. "Lance isn't quite ready for dinner so I thought I'd send Marie up with you to get us a table. We'll join you in a half hour or so."

"I thought we were dining aboard your boat," I said.

"The captain overruled me," said David.

He smiled and nodded toward Marie.

"The captain?" I asked.

Marie took the hand I offered, stepped up onto the dock, and reflexively smoothed her dress. It was a white sleeveless knee length dress that would have looked beautiful on anybody. On her, it was borderline dangerous.

"That's right," she said. "I didn't feel like cooking tonight and I wasn't about to eat the canned nonsense that either of them would open up. So we are eating ashore."

I tossed the dinghy's painter to David and he motored back toward *D'Artagnan.* I turned around to see Marie already walking along the brick pathway. It was a fine view and I took the time to appreciate it.

She led me to the Almond Walk, probably the fanciest open-air restaurant in the country. One of those places where they set three forks to the left of your plate, two spoons to the right, and an artfully folded napkin on top. A knife gets tossed in there, too, somewhere. Mature coconut palms poked through the thick tile floor every thirty feet or so. Single-globe street lamps from the 1950s gently pressed the darkness out onto the adjacent beach and into the Sound. Tabletop candles flickered amid seashell and flower centerpieces.

The maître d' recognized Marie and led us to a table for four at the edge of the sand, barely inside the lit boundaries of the restaurant. Marie sat in the chair opposite mine and crossed her legs.

"That is a beautiful dress," I said.

I felt dumb-as-a-rock stupid as soon as I'd said it.

"Thank you," she said. The faint glimmer of a smile crossed her lips as she pulled the dress down slightly.

"You have no idea what you are in for this evening," she said.

"A nice dinner?" I asked.

"Perhaps, but with *my* family."

Our waiter, dressed in black pants and a blue and white flowered shirt, moved in to take our drink orders. Marie examined the wine list and ordered something I couldn't pronounce. I asked for a Coke.

"Tonight, you'll be having dinner with a family of Type A personalities. Dad is an 'A'ggressive 'A'ttorney and Lance is a devout alcoholic."

"Devout?" I asked. "Will he try to convert me?"

She smiled.

"My brother was on a bender last night," she said. "I have no idea when he got back to the boat or who finally got him there but he slept all day. Dad's trying to straighten him out, I guess."

"I'm not in any hurry," I said.

"I'm just saying that dinner tonight might not be all that pleasant."

"I've been eating my own cooking for over three months. Mostly rice and beans and canned goods with the occasional grilled fish. Tonight, I'm being treated to dinner and drinks at what is probably the finest restaurant in the country. All of that in the company of a beautiful woman."

"Whom you think may have killed somebody," she added.

"Whom?" I said. "Wow, whom says that?"

"An educated woman."

"Well, I am neither of those," I said.

The smile returned. It was almost too wide. Almost. Candlelight danced in the dark brown iris of each eye. I got the feeling that a guy could get lost in those eyes.

The waiter brought Marie's small glass of wine and my large tumbler of Coke and we talked about boats. She'd been sailing since she was eight, had either skippered or crewed on everything from the smallest pram to the largest maxi racing yachts, and had taken second place in the ICSA Women's National Sailing Championships while attending Brown University. Impressive.

Her father and brother arrived as I finished my Coke. I stood to shake David's hand and realized that Marie's younger brother was tall, nearly my height, but that he had to stretch some to get there. Other than sporting a different color polo shirt, he was dressed exactly like his father. Same shorts, same brand of leather boat shoes, same golf cap.

He looked to be in his mid-twenties and he seemed oddly self-satisfied. He was full of the baby-soft snobbishness of an over-privileged youth that had never done anything approaching manual labor. The frat boy who wouldn't consider ordering a beer without an umlaut. A guy who'd been born on third base but had grown up thinking he'd hit a triple.

He tilted his head about fifteen degrees to the right and stuck out a thin, soft hand.

"I'm Lance," he said. His voice carried a hint of aristocratic whine. "Are you the fellow who thinks we killed some guy?"

David dropped his eyes and shook his head maybe half an inch in each direction. Marie shot her brother an icy look. I took his hand, crushed it easily, and held it a bit too long for his comfort.

"And it's good to meet you, too," I said.

We sat down and the waiter returned to take the rest of our drink orders. Marie had barely touched her wine and declined. David ordered an Old Fashioned. Lance got creative.

"Gimlet," said Lance. "And tell the bartender I want Gordon's. The good British export stuff. Not that crap he gave me last week that was brewed in some Dominican bathtub."

Who says you can't buy class?

My Coke was gone, so I ordered something that had been lurking near the bottom of my to-do list for several years: a Daiquiri with ice and a splash of grapefruit juice. I read somewhere that Hemingway drank these in Cuba and I'd decided years ago to try one if I ever got to the Caribbean. I suppressed the urge to demand that my drink only be stirred counter-clockwise.

The waiter left. Lance turned to me and tried a second time.

"So who is this dead guy, anyway?" he asked.

"Oh, stop it, Lance," said David. "You are being extraordinarily annoying."

Lance faced his dad and jerked a thumb in my direction.

"Who is *this* guy to ask us questions?" he said. "Why don't you fly one of your partners down here and put him in his place?"

"Lance, I haven't accused anybody of anything," I said. "I'm not even a cop."

"You're not a cop?" he asked. "Then who is paying you to annoy us?"

"I'm not being paid. I'm doing this for a friend."

"What?" he asked.

"A friend. They are the people we in the lower class keep around to comfort us in our poverty."

Lance gave me a steely-eyed stare through half-closed eyes as though he were a pouting teenager. Marie and her father looked away as if Lance and I weren't there.

"I'm sorry," I said. "You three have every right to enjoy a nice dinner ashore without me mucking it up."

I stood up to leave.

"Please forgive my son's poor display of manners," said David. "I'd very much prefer if you stayed and had dinner with us."

The drinks arrived and I felt awkward standing there so I sat back down.

The waiter took his time describing the evening's specialties as well as the West Indies buffet. The buffet sounded too good to pass up and we each opted for that.

Lance drank a third of his Gimlet and commented favorably on the bartender's skills. David slouched in his chair, crossed his thin legs at the knee, and rested his chin on a tent made of his fingers.

"I'd like to hear about your sailing adventures," he said.

"There's not that much to talk about," I said. "*Figaro* is set up for single-handing. It's really a piece of cake once you get used to it."

I had some of my drink. Hemingway had excellent taste.

"Which one is your boat?" Marie asked.

She turned to look out across the Bitter End's mooring field.

"You can't see her from here," I said. "She's anchored at Biras Creek."

"And you sailed her to the BVI alone?" David asked. "From California?"

I told them about the trip from California to the tip of Baja, then down Mexico's mainland to Costa Rica and Panama. David asked a lot of questions about the passage through the canal and the subsequent windward beat to the British Virgin Islands. He was adept at throwing in the odd personal question as if it were unintended. I recognized the pattern and let the attorney complete his informal deposition.

"You make a credible witness, Mr. Greene."

I was sure there was a clever response but I couldn't think of it, so I smiled. David finished his drink.

"Let's visit the buffet, shall we?" he said.

Tables of West Indies fare were set under a large, open gazebo. There were grilled shrimp, sword-fish fillets, steaks, roast pork medallions with mango salsa, rice and peas, curried vegetables, conch fritters, and johnnycakes. A dessert table offered bread pudding, Key lime pie, and large servings of apple and carrot cake. You didn't have to be a Mensa member to realize that we were eating considerably better than most folk in the West Indies.

Marie and I returned to the table first and sat down. She sat back in her chair and crossed her legs at me again.

"Do you see now what I meant about having dinner with my family?" she asked.

"Your dad can cross-examine me all he likes. I don't have much to hide."

"He's intolerable," said Marie.

I had a bite of roast pork with mango salsa and realized how much I had missed meat during the long sail. Marie picked at her food, occasionally eating a small bite.

"How do you handle sail changes, cook, sleep, maintain a proper watch, and navigate when you're single-handing?" asked Marie. "You've only got two hands."

"It's a smaller boat so it has smaller sails; nothing I can't handle by myself. All of her lines are led aft to the cockpit, she balances nicely under sail, and I've got some good self-steering gear to man the helm. That frees up time for other things. I sleep in catnaps. I even have time to check the fishing lines."

Lance and David overheard my answer as they returned.

"Do you catch any decent fish?" asked David.

"Dorado and tuna, mostly. Sometimes I'll hook a wahoo or a Spanish mackerel."

"I never catch a thing worth eating," said David. "Worst luck in the world. I'll snag a bluefish once in a while, but I can't stand the taste so I throw them back. I'd love to catch a tuna."

"What kind of tackle are you using?" I asked.

"I've got a tuna rod and a nice reel with eighty-pound test line. The best you can buy. But I have the worst luck."

"You must be using the wrong lure," I said.

"Your type of sailing sounds quite rigorous," said David.

"It's not that much different from you bringing your boat down from Stamford," I said.

David chuckled. "I didn't bring her down," he said. "Marie sailed her from Stamford with Lance and a few temporary crew."

Lance had a piece of swordfish on a fork and pointed it at me.

"I'm sorry about being so aggressive with you earlier," he said, "but I am very concerned about this murder issue."

He said it as though he were parroting phrases he'd learned at one of those negotiation seminars that are advertised in the back pages of an in-flight magazine.

"A guy was killed the day before you found his passport," I said. "Or it was one of his passports, anyway."

"One of his passports?" asked David.

"The one you found was for somebody named Bradley Somerset," I said. "He was also known as Derek Brownell. The victim had a passport for that name, too."

I picked up Hemingway's favorite drink and drained it. *Sucker knew how to drink.*

"Derek Brownell?" asked Lance. "I know a Derek Brownell. He crews for one of the mega yachts around here."

21

THICK tangible silence surrounded the table. David turned directly to Lance and broke it.

"How exactly do you know this person?" he asked.

Lance ignored his father's question and turned to me.

"We can't be talking about the same guy," he said while shaking his head. "I had drinks with him a couple of weeks ago."

"He was killed a few days later," I said.

Lance shook his head.

"What do you remember about him?" I asked. "What did he say?"

"I met him over at the Willy-T. He said he crewed for one of the big yachts."

"When?" I asked.

Lance thought a moment.

"It was Sunday," he said. "Two weeks ago, exactly."

He turned to his father.

"You remember when we were anchored at Norman Island?" asked Lance. "It was Sunday night. You were on a call with one of your partners and Marie was reading a book. I was bored out of my skull so I took the dinghy over to get a drink at that floating bar. It is called the Willy-T, right?"

"Yes. Tell me about him," I said. "Tell me anything that comes to mind."

Lance shook his head.

"Lance," said his father. "It is imperative that you tell us everything you know."

"There's nothing to tell," he said. "He was acting like a big shot and buying everybody drinks. And totally working the girls, you know. Nobody complained, though."

"How many people were at the bar?" I asked.

"I dunno," he said. "Fifteen or twenty people. Four or five were from the same ship, I think. They all had matching yellow polo shirts."

"You said he was acting like a big shot," I said. "In what way?"

"Like I said, he was buying all the drinks. It must have cost a load but he didn't seem to care."

"What makes you say that?" asked David.

"He was flashing a wad of hundred-dollar bills. He told everybody he'd won the lottery and had money to burn."

"Why would anyone crew on a yacht if they'd won the lottery?" I asked.

"Well, we were all pretty loose," said Lance. "I mean there wasn't a lot of analytical thinking going on. He got pretty gassed and said he wanted everybody to remember his name. I mooched drinks for a couple of hours."

"My brother the beggar lush," said Marie. "How dignified."

"He's really dead?" asked Lance.

"Did he say what boat he was crewing on?" I asked.

"No," said Lance. "One of the other guys mentioned a big power yacht."

He thought a minute. It took considerable effort.

"He and the rest of the crew took off in one of those giant inflatable dinghies, though. The kind that have two outboards. It was yellow, too, like their shirts. It shouldn't be hard to track something like that down."

I didn't bother to tell him that there was a big yellow inflatable tied to a big yellow mega yacht only a couple hundred yards from his father's boat.

"There is one more thing," Lance said. "He told a bunch of the guys there that he was doing the yacht owner's wife. He said she was a real looker and wanted to leave her husband for him."

Marie stood up.

"I am going to the ladies' room," she said. "I would appreciate it if you 'gentlemen' would conclude your coarse discussions prior to my return."

She turned and walked toward the clubhouse.

"Miss Sensitive High-Class has spoken," said Lance. He looked at his glass, noticed that it was empty, and stood up. "I'm going to the bar for another drink."

David reached for his Old Fashioned and downed about half of it. We sat and listened to the hiss of small wind waves breaking on the beach a few yards away. David peered out into the Sound.

"My family is on a well-deserved vacation, Mr. Greene. I don't want my kids dragged into a messy criminal investigation."

He turned from the Sound to face me.

"My wife was diagnosed with cancer about a year ago," he said. "She passed away in June. My two children are all I have left and you need to understand that I will not allow them to be involved in any kind of foreign entanglements."

I didn't have a clever answer or compelling argument.

"Marie is the second most charming woman I have ever known," he said. "Bright, good looking, and over-educated just like her mother. Lance, however, is a complete and utter disappointment. But they are both mine—all that I have—and I will vigorously protect them."

He drained his drink and stared back out into the Sound. After a few minutes of quiet he flagged down a waiter and ordered another. A stiff breeze blew through the restaurant. Wide palm fronds rustled above and candles flickered on the tables below.

"Tell me about your boat," I said. "Marie said you launched it this summer."

He leaned forward and stared directly into my eyes.

"The boat is nothing," he said. "It's wood and brass and varnish. It is a meaningless object." He reached across the table and grabbed my arm. "I don't want my kids involved in any police matters. What you know about my family, this Derek Brownell guy, and my son's source of free booze on a Sunday night stays right here. Do you understand that?"

"I'm not a cop, David, and I don't report to them," I said. "But my best friend is their number one suspect right now and I am going to find out whatever I can and do whatever needs to be done to clear him."

The waiter brought David his fresh drink. He smiled and thanked the young man. The smile left his face and he slouched back into his chair as the waiter turned to leave.

"I appreciate your loyalty to your friend," he said. "But Marie and Lance have nothing to do with this. What you've heard from them tonight is all there is to it. There's nothing more."

He downed a quarter of the drink.

"You're probably right," I said. "And I can't think of any reason to talk to the local cops about your family."

"Mr. Greene, I can be the best friend you will ever have. Or I can be your worst enemy. It's entirely your choice." He stood, smiled broadly, and shook my right hand while patting me on the shoulder with his left. "Just keep my family out of this."

David left the Almond Walk, stepped into the darkness, and walked south toward the dock. And I was alone. Sim Greene, the life of the party.

I walked over to the dessert bar, took two slices of Key lime pie, and walked back to the table. I put one of the plates on the table in front of Marie's chair. Hope may indeed triumph over experience.

It did; Marie returned a few minutes later.

"So what happened to Dad and Lance?" she asked.

"Are you asking me as a trained investigator?"

Marie smiled and waited.

"Lance went to get another drink," I said.

"Like he needs that," said Marie.

"I suspect it may be a lengthy quest. Your father, on the other hand, decided to go back to the boat."

"How was he?" Marie asked.

She asked the question as though I were now party to a family secret.

"He misses your mother and he worries about his children," I said.

She broke off a piece of Key lime pie with her fork and nibbled it.

"Dad is a different sort of guy," she said.

"Seems okay to me," I said.

"He's the managing partner of a large Wall Street law firm. He's got a lot of money, more than he could ever spend. And he got it the old-fashioned way."

"He inherited it?" I said.

"Funny," Marie said without smiling. "He earned it, actually. Every shiny, thin dime. He specializes in securities litigation. You know, derivative lawsuits?"

I shook my head.

"Anyway," she continued, "he's the most self-assured and self-confident person I have ever known. He's the lawyer everybody fears."

She took another small bite of pie.

"When Mom got sick a little over a year ago, his self-confidence began to suffer," she said. "Badly."

She waved her fork gently in the air.

"There he was," she said, "this great, powerful attorney, and there was nothing he could do to save his wife. It was the first time he'd come up against a problem that couldn't be bullied, bought, threatened, or negotiated away."

"A hard lesson to learn at his age," I said.

"There wasn't much left of him by the time we buried Mom. This sailing trip was to give him time off to recover."

The sound of small waves beating against the beach, the smell of frangipani on the sea breeze, and the taste of Key lime pie were a sensual combination hard to duplicate. For Al's sake, I tried to focus on the immediate problem.

"You, on the other hand, seem to be faring much better," I said.

"My self-confidence was tested years ago," she said.

She turned to look out into the darkness much as her father had.

"It survived," she said.

Further inquiry did not appear to be welcome.

"Pretty good pie, isn't it?" I asked.

She nodded her head and smiled.

"Pretty good pie," she said.

22

WE finished our desserts and the waiter took our plates. Marie flushed slightly when he returned and placed the bill in front of me.

"Dad should have taken care of that," she said. "He invited you to dinner and I'll not have you paying for it."

I opened the little plastic folder and raised an eyebrow at the amount. It was an involuntary reflex, like pulling your hand off a hot stove.

"It's probably a good thing he didn't see this," I said. "We'd still be looking for a defibrillator."

Marie laughed and people sitting at adjacent tables smiled. I pulled out the cash I'd earned by filming the Meghan Wells Show and put some into the plastic folder.

"My wallet is on *D'Artagnan*," she said. "But if you can give me a ride back to the boat I'll repay you for dinner tonight."

"How would you get back if I didn't take you?" I asked. "Swim?"

"Been there, done that."

We walked in the darkness to the dinghy dock, found mine, and untied it from the jumble of tangled dinghies.

"How's Lance getting home?" I asked.

"One of his drinking buddies will probably bring him over. And it will be late and he will be loud and he will sleep in his clothes."

"He'll grow out of it."

"We're still waiting," she said.

When we reached *D'Artagnan*, Marie ascended the boarding ladder with a practiced grace. I climbed up the ladder like a trained ape, tied my dinghy's painter to a stern cleat, and stepped down into the cockpit under the bimini.

A few minutes later, David Tanner climbed up into the cockpit from the cabin with a half-empty highball glass. He nestled it into a cup holder attached to the helm and pulled out his wallet.

"Marie tells me that I stuck you with the dinner bill," he said.

The word "stuck" sounded more like "schtuck."

"She is not too happy with me for that," he said.

"It's no big deal."

"An embarrassing oversight on my part," he said.

He pulled several hundred-dollar bills from his wallet.

"I gather that this will cover it?" he said. *Thish.*

He handed me the money and sat down across from me.

"Thanks for dinner," I said.

David took a drink from his glass.

"I'm sorry if I came on a little strong about this murder investigation," he said. "It's just that I can't stand the thought of my children getting involved in a police matter. Especially in a foreign country without constitutional protections."

A light tropical rain swept across the bay, but we were well protected under *D'Artagnan*'s bimini. Marie came up from the cabin wearing light-colored warm up pants and an oversized Brown University rugby shirt. It would have looked frumpy on anybody else. She sat down next to her father.

"Sometimes I get a little brash," David said. "I hope I didn't offend or alarm you."

"I'm not that easily alarmed, David."

He smiled and wagged his head back and forth.

"Iron nerves forged by the loneliness and hardship of single-handed sailing, no doubt," he said.

Shingle-handed shailing. Marie noticed and patted his arm.

"No more dangerous than Marie bringing this boat down to the BVI," I said. "Sometimes having crew aboard is worse than being alone."

Marie shrugged and David emptied his glass.

"Dad," she said. "I think it's time for bed."

"I should probably be going, too," I said.

"No, I'm not sending you home in the rain," said Marie. "Stick around a bit. I'll be back in a minute."

David mumbled something and Marie helped him back down into the cockpit. The rain fell harder. It made low thumping sounds on the bimini and clattered noisily on the teak decks. The anchor light at the top of the mainmast clicked on and Marie returned to the cockpit. She sat across from me and tucked her legs under her.

"So, does your husband ever join you on these little sailing trips?" I asked.

"What?"

A puzzled look crossed her face for a moment. Then she felt the ring on her finger and laughed.

"Oh, this thing? I only wear it to ward off the weirdos and drunks," she said. "It's like garlic to a vampire."

She took the ring off and put it in the front pocket of her warm ups.

"That depends entirely on the vampire," I said.

She smiled and the rain stopped. It was a coincidence. It had to be.

"I actually was married about ten years ago," she said. "It only lasted a couple years."

"I'm sorry."

"I'm not," she said. "I was too young for it and he was more interested in money, anyway."

"Fool," I said.

She smiled again.

"And you?" she asked.

"I tried it once but it didn't take. I was at sea for a ten-month tour and she got pregnant halfway through it."

"Uh-oh," said Marie.

"Yeah. And I don't even believe in *mental* telepathy."

She laughed.

"I figured she wanted out of the marriage and she agreed."

"Is that when she broke your nose?" she asked.

"No," I said. "That is a memento of younger, more foolish, years."

"So, how'd it happen?" Marie asked. "I mean, if my asking doesn't bother you."

"There was a bar near Pearl Harbor years ago that hosted round-robin boxing matches. They had a ring and gloves and a bell and everything. Unless there was a clear winner by knockout, the guy with the loudest applause won."

"Sounds a bit primitive," Marie said.

"More than a bit. But that's what sold the drinks, I guess. Anyhow, a sailor from another ship, a southpaw, set me up pretty well one night and threw a left hook that came out of nowhere. That one punch broke my nose and put me on the canvas."

"That's awful," she said.

"I got up before the count, though, and kept at it."

"Who won?"

"I think I did," I said. "But it may have only been because I had more of my crew there to cheer for me."

"You won?" she asked. "Weren't you hurt?"

"All fights hurt," I said. "Even the ones you win."

"Yes, I guess they do at that," she said.

The cockpit was dark enough that I couldn't see her eyes. My loss.

"So, here we are in the Caribbean on a beautiful wooden boat," she said. "Both divorced, both injured, and both recovered."

"Here we are."

It was as close to clever as I could get.

She thought quietly for a minute.

"Do you have a girlfriend?" she asked.

"I did."

"Was it serious?"

"I thought so," I said.

"What happened?"

"She passed away quite suddenly," I said.

Marie gasped.

"How awful," she said.

She pulled her legs out from under her, leaned toward me, and put her hand on my arm.

"That must have torn you apart," she said.

I nodded.

"When did she, uh, pass away?"

"About fifteen minutes ago," I said.

It was dark and I couldn't see much of her deep brown eyes, but the whites got a little bigger and her mouth dropped open just a little.

"You," she said as she pointed her finger. "You are a filthy dog."

"Woof."

She threatened me with a closed right fist.

"Oh, c'mon now," I said. "There's only so much a guy's nose can take."

She laughed, stood up, and walked over to the ship's companionway.

"Well, look at that," she said. "The rain has stopped and you can go home to your boat now."

"Probably a good idea," I said. "But I would very much like to see you again."

She stood with her mouth closed tightly, her eyes narrowed. She nodded almost imperceptibly.

"There is a dinner-dance tomorrow night at the club," she said. "And I am a little tired of attending these things with my father and brother. Another face might make things a bit less boring."

"Sounds like fun to me," I said.

"It's not formal or anything," she said, "but if you do happen to have something nice to wear, well, tomorrow night would be the night for it."

"No baseball cap?" I asked.

She shook her head.

"See you around sundown at the club?" I asked.

"Don't you ever wear a watch?" she asked.

"Can't stand the tan line."

I got up, untied my dinghy, and stepped down the ladder. It occurred to me that I should contact Constable Millet and share what I had learned about the passport floating in the channel, Derek Brownell, and the wad of C-notes that he flashed at the Willy-T.

But the little voice inside told me not to. There was too much of the Somerset/Brownell story I didn't know yet. Marie, her father, and Lance fit in there somewhere but I had the feeling that the RVIP would run like poorly shod draft horses over the facts until any tracks worth following were obscured by clumsy police work.

The little voice has saved my bacon more than once and I've learned to trust it. I decided to keep the Tanners out of it.

23

I started my morning swim a little earlier than I had the previous two days. The water was just as clear, the baitfish schooled below me again, and the large, flat sand banks still stretched as far as I could see. The eels, lobsters, rays, and crabs were all in attendance. I got my arms and legs moving in a steady cadence and let my mind relax and move little pieces of information around like a jigsaw puzzle. There were a lot of little pieces. And darn few corners.

I rolled the pieces over and tried to arrange them into different combinations but no matter how hard I tried, I got the strongest impression that half the pieces were missing; lost under the furniture somewhere.

When I got back to *Figaro*, I showered off the salt, cued up the Allman Brothers on the stereo, and made some breakfast. I considered the messy job of cleaning and greasing the rest of *Figaro's* winches but quickly and bravely put it off.

I hopped in the dinghy and motored over to the Bitter End. I needed to pick up some wire ties to tame some cables that had come loose in *Figaro's* engine compartment, and I thought it might be smart to stop in and see Terrence Wells. I had a few more questions about Derek Brownell.

Chip met me at the large yacht's stern, took the dinghy's painter, and tied it off as I killed the engine.

"You better wait here," he said. "I'll go get the captain."

Schuster showed up a few minutes later.

"What do you want?" he said.

"I'd like to talk to Mr. Wells."

Schuster bent down, untied the painter, and threw it back to me.

"He's not taking visitors today," he said.

"Could you ask him? He might want to talk to me."

"No," said Schuster.

"Can you talk to me about Derek?" I asked. "I've got a few more questions."

"Nobody on this boat has anything to say to you about Derek or anybody else, sailor. Turn that thing around and make some wake."

I brought the dinghy motor back to life and headed to the club. A helpful islander in yacht club uniform met me at the dock.

"Is Levon around today?" I asked.

"Levon been gone a couple days now. Can I help you, suh?"

"I guess not."

I walked up to the small chandlery and bought the wire ties. I went into the pub and asked the bartender if he could tell me anything about Derek Brownell or the crew from *Liquid Assets*. He declined. I bought a Coke, took it out to the patio, and sat at a table in the sunshine. A light breeze rustled the coconut palms overhead.

"I understand that you have some questions about some of our guests."

I looked up to see a fellow about my age in blue shorts and a white polo shirt. He sat down at my table.

"I'm Ross," he said. "I am the assistant manager at the club. How may I help you, sir?"

"A fellow was killed almost two weeks ago," I said. "He was the first mate on *Liquid Assets* over there. I understand that there was some trouble last April between a crew member from that boat and some of your staff."

"That was a long time ago, sir. There was a concern expressed by one of our staff and the police were called to investigate. They determined that no charges should be filed. I understand that the matter is closed."

"I'm just trying to find out if there's any connection between this incident and the murder," I said.

"Are you with the police, Mr.….?"

"Greene," I said. "No, I'm not with the police. I'm providing some informal investigative support."

Ross looked confused for a moment.

"Mr. Greene, it is club policy to discuss police matters only with the local police," Ross said. "I'm sure you understand that our guests do not wish to be disturbed by such news or events. That applies to our staff, as well."

"I understand."

"Then I will leave you to enjoy the sun and our facilities, Mr. Greene."

He stood up to leave.

"I have just one more question, Ross. Why isn't Levon at the dinghy dock?" I asked. "Day off?"

"Mr. Baptiste has been replaced," he said.

"Replaced?"

"He stopped showing up for work. Now if that is all you require, I must return to my responsibilities. Good day, Mr. Greene."

I finished my Coke and walked down to the dock. On the way back to *Figaro*, I decided to motor over to Gun Creek and see if anyone there could tell me how to find Levon Baptiste. I walked up the hill to the pink and white building. Two islanders played dominoes in the corner and the bartender watched a small television while drying glasses. I sat at the bar and he walked over.

"How can I help you, mon?" asked the bartender.

"Do you know Levon Baptiste?" I asked.

"Fella come here most nights for de dominoes," he said.

"I'm trying to find him. I owe him some money."

One of the domino players overheard me.

"You can give me de money, mistah. I give it to Levon when I see him next, eh?"

The other player and the bartender laughed.

"I ain't seen him here for a couple of days," said the bartender. "Maybe he sick."

"Anybody around here know where he lives?" I asked.

"Spanish Town," said one of the players. "I don't know where but he always catches a ride with someone to Spanish Town."

I put a couple of bucks in the tip jar, walked back to the dinghy dock, and motored back to *Figaro*. Schuster and Wells wouldn't talk to me, the Bitter End's management didn't want me nosing around there anymore, and Levon had disappeared. Leads were drying up.

It was time to call Al.

"So did you beat the truth out of her?" he asked.

"Gentle persuasion and unfeigned affection seem to be working quite well at the moment."

"Funny, Sim. She could be the killer, you know."

"Something tells me it has more the do with the big motor yacht," I said. "The crew throws around too much money, they all seem to hate each other, and the owner is a first-class weirdo. There is something illegal going on that involves that yacht and the owner or some of the crew or all of 'em. I just can't put my finger on it, yet."

"Illegal?" asked Al. "Like what? And how does any of this help me?"

"I'm not sure, Al. It's something well beyond the normal infidelities of the rich and bored. There are too many pieces to the puzzle. There might even be more than one puzzle."

Al was quiet.

"How are you doing on your side?" I asked.

"It's weird," said Al. "Nobody will talk to me. It's like I'm branded. The whole country thinks I killed someone and nobody wants to get involved."

"What does Phillips say?" I asked.

"He tells me to lie low and keep my nose clean. Typical lawyer-speak."

"It's not the worst advice," I said.

"I can't just stay home and play solitaire on the kitchen table, Sim. You gotta understand that."

"Uh-huh."

"And there's somebody following me," he said.

"The RVIP? Tell Phillips to make a complaint and get 'em off your back."

"Oh, I don't care about the cops," he said. "They're easy to shake loose. There's somebody else, though. I don't know who it is but he's better at following me without being too obvious about it."

"Are you worried?" I asked.

"Not really. It's just annoying as hell. And I'd kinda like to know who he's working for."

"You're just tired of sitting around waiting for me to dig up something, that's all." I said.

Al was quiet.

"Use your alibi, Al. You get clean off the case, we get back our bail money, and we go to work."

"Nope," he said.

"Are you afraid of losing Liv? It's not like you've ever been tied to one woman. At least, not as long as I've known you."

There was a long pause at the other end.

"I told her yesterday morning," he said. "I told her all of it."

"How'd that go?" I asked.

"I figured I'd be ducking dishes all day."

"You weren't?"

"No, it's worse than that," he said. "She was hurt. Seriously hurt. She didn't want to talk to me at all."

I wasn't about to get involved in Al's domestic squabbles. I'd already traveled well beyond the requirements of friendship in trying to track down a killer.

"Well, sit tight and let me work it from this end for a while," I said. "There are some loose threads I need to yank on."

"Watch yourself, Sim. Don't get yourself hurt."

"Don't worry about me," I said. "This isn't the first game I've pitched in the majors."

I hung up and watched seabirds dive on baitfish near the edges of Biras Creek.

24

THE sun approached the horizon and I realized it was time to shower, shave, and dig out my best threads for the club's dinner-dance. My blue oxford-cloth shirt and khaki twill pants that I'd stored in the forward locker were still dry, clean, and holding a noticeable press. Not bad given the damp marine environment.

I cuffed up the pant legs, tucked my nice leather boat shoes into the bow of the dinghy, and slowly motored to the Bitter End as the sun gave way to the full moon. I secured my dinghy, uncuffed my trousers, slipped on my shoes, and walked along the boardwalk to the restaurant.

The boardwalk was lined with brightly burning tiki torches. The sound of a local dance band, augmented with steel drums, filtered through the coconut palms from the Almond Walk. It was quintessential Caribbean music, the kind that tourists expect to hear at a place like this, executed at a calm and relaxing pace. It was a beautiful and magical night for those who could afford it.

I found Marie alone at a table for four and saw David talking to some friends a few tables away. I looked around for Lance but didn't see him. I sat down across from Marie.

She wore a white dress with spaghetti straps that perfectly contrasted with her black hair and deep tan. There were light green vines and small pink roses embroidered from just above her knees to slightly below her waist. She looked like she'd stepped out of a catalog. A very fine catalog.

And she wasn't wearing her gold ring.

"You forgot your garlic necklace," I said. "Decide to give the local vampires a shot tonight?"

"My neck's not all that tasty."

"I'll be the judge of that," I said.

She smiled.

"Track down any killers today?" she asked.

"No," I said. "Too busy. Went for a swim, almost overhauled my boat's winches, and talked to my friend Al about you."

"I thought I felt my ears burning," she said.

"Probably too much sun."

David returned from his visit and grabbed my hand.

"Good to see you, Sim," said David. "Very good to see you again. Let me get you a drink."

He motioned to the waiter and sat down. David was the epitome of old-school high-end recreation in khakis, a light blue LaCoste polo shirt, and a navy Greek fisherman's cap. There wasn't the slightest indication that he'd had too much to drink the previous night.

"Sorry, again, about last night," he said. "Damned inconsiderate of me walking off and sticking you with the bill."

"You paid me back, Mr. Tanner. It's all good."

"David. Please, call me David," he said.

The waiter arrived and I asked for another one of Hemingway's favorite daiquiris. One wouldn't kill me.

Lance returned from wherever he'd started drinking. From the looks of it, he'd started pretty early. He'd departed from the prior day's rich dad/rich kid uniform and was now the essence of midtwenties cool with a three-day growth of beard, white pleated pants, shirt open at the neck, ivory linen jacket, and a white fedora with a wide black hatband. And he wore John Lennon sunglasses at night. I half expected him to pull out a saxophone and belt out the Dick Parry solo from Pink Floyd's "Money."

"I hate to ask an extraordinarily indelicate question," Lance started, "but, uh, are you hanging around here and following us around in hopes of tying us all to a murder?"

"Nope. I came here to fix stuff on my boat and rest up from too much sailing alone," I lied. The waiter returned with our drinks and I took a sip from Papa's favorite. "Anyway, the RVIP's case has a couple of holes in it and Al's got a good lawyer in Road Town. I'll let the fellow earn his fee."

Dinner was ordered and served and was delicious. The conversation was light and pleasant and did not include references to dead guys or passports in the channel. Nobody but Lance got drunk and he was only borderline obnoxious. It almost felt as though I were on vacation with friends.

The club staff cleared an area for dancing and the band started playing less reggae and more danceable tunes from the 1970s. Several couples took the cue and moved in to occupy the floor. Two older couples moved gracefully, if slowly, in half-time to their children's music. A twenty-something couple gyrated with enthusiasm while a middle-aged couple performed the high-school hang.

The band started their version of Chicago's "Colour My World," and a few more couples got up to enjoy the slow song of the set.

A fellow with a thin face and long, straight hair got up, drink in hand, and approached our table. Except for his light blue linen jacket and lack of sunglasses, he could have been Lance's fashion twin. Or the drummer for a 1980s hair band. He was older than Marie's father but confident in the quality of his anti-wrinkle treatments.

"My name's Richard," he said to Marie. "Would you care to dance, little lady?"

"Oh, I'm sorry," Marie said. "I'm here with my fiancé and I promised him the first slow dance tonight. I am sure you understand."

Disappointed, Richard excused himself and walked over to the bar. I got up and helped Marie out of her chair. David chuckled as she took my arm and we walked to the dance floor.

"Fiancé?" I said.

"It was frying pan or fire," she said.

"I'm flattered."

I was not a stranger to dancing but this was the first time, as far as I could remember, that I'd danced with a woman anywhere close to my height. She fit comfortably in my arms and she knew how to dance. It may have only been perfume, but the smell of jasmine and lavender filled the air.

"You come here often?" I asked.

Her smile was broad and her eyes laughed.

"Only with my fiancés."

"Last night, I was a filthy dog," I said. "I think I'm enjoying the promotion."

The song was short and ended much too soon. To make up for it, the band worked in another slow piece with almost no break.

"We could dance this one, too," Marie said.

"We'd be stupid not to."

"You dance well," she said. "Like you don't care who's watching."

"I'm dancing with you; nobody is watching me."

She moved closer and I had difficulty breathing. It felt like somebody had knocked the wind out of me but had done it so gently that I couldn't rightfully object.

The song ended and I caught my breath.

Walking back from the dance floor, I noticed that Lance was sitting with Cookie and Rick Schuster at a table bordering the shadows. Back at our table, David had exchanged places with mine.

"Dad?" asked Marie.

"I thought you might like to sit closer to your fiancé," he said.

A broad smile illuminated his face. Marie's eyes narrowed. I helped her to her seat and sat down next to her.

"You two looked like you were enjoying yourselves," said David.

"I'm not complaining," I said.

"It's good to see Marie having a nice time," said David.

Marie stiffened at the remark but her father didn't notice. It was an excellent time to change the subject.

"I'd still like to hear about your boat, David. All I saw last night was the cockpit."

David sat back with the drink in his hand, and a smile crept over his face.

"Okay," he said. "She's fifty-seven feet on deck with another four feet of bowsprit. Red mahogany over oak frames. I found her in a shipyard where she'd been wasting away on the hard for at least a dozen years. The owner had been a client of our firm for some time and when he passed away I decided, more as a favor to the widow, to take a look at her. I made the mistake of taking my wife with me."

He stopped for a moment and swallowed.

"Lorraine fell in love with her lines," he said. "I bought *D'Artagnan* on the spot for pocket change."

He took another drink.

"I imagine the restoration cost a bit more," I said.

"You have no idea," he said. "She had no engine or spars. All of her systems were horribly outdated, completely rusted out, or missing entirely. I think the yard workers had been cannibalizing her over the years. By the time we got her, she was little more than a bare hull. But she really did have great lines."

He paused and looked out over the sound. We could see *D'Artagnan*'s anchor light where she lay at her mooring.

"Luckily, almost all of her frames were sound and most of the planking was good," he said. "But every screw and bolt had to be pulled and replaced. We tracked down some vintage spars and had them refinished and modernized. Interior, fixtures, plumbing, and electrical systems are all brand new. We even installed electric winches and a bow thruster. It took three solid years to bring her back."

"Long time," I said.

"Too long," said David. "She was supposed to be a gift to my wife. She loves…"

David paused and then corrected himself.

"She loved sailing far more than I ever have," he said. "By the time the boat was finished, Lorraine wasn't well enough to go out on her beyond her initial sea trials. I only wish I'd spent more time…"

He stopped mid-sentence, took another drink, and turned to look back out into the darkness of the Sound. Marie patted his arm again.

"Dad," she said. "Don't do this to yourself."

I couldn't see his eyes. I didn't want to. A few minutes passed without talking. David took a deep breath and let it out slowly.

"I'm sorry, Sim," he finally said. "I'm not being very good company, I'm afraid."

"No worries," I said.

"I think I'll go back to the boat if you two don't mind," he said.

He stood up, finished the last of his drink, and turned to me. There was a smile on his face.

"Oh," he said. "I took the liberty of paying the bill in advance this time."

Marie pushed her chair back and began to get up.

"I'll go back with you, Dad."

"No, no," David said. "You two stay and enjoy yourselves. Sim, could you please make sure that Marie gets back all right?"

"Of course," I said.

Marie shook her head. I could tell she wanted to follow her father.

"Don't worry about Lance," said David. "He can fend for himself. Or, at least, he might give it a try sometime."

25

DAVID walked away from the club and onto the path toward the dinghy dock.

"Dad's going back to the boat to cry his eyes out," said Marie.

"Part of the healing process," I said.

"What do you mean?"

"Tears, sweat, the ocean; it's all salt water. It's all healing."

Marie thought for a minute and finished her drink.

"Well, I'm not crying or sweating tonight," she said. "Let's go find a beach."

We walked south from the club and onto one of the small beaches beyond the dock. It was far enough away to enjoy a break from the crowd but close enough that we could still hear the music. I slipped off my boat shoes and cuffed up my pant legs. Marie carried her sandals in one hand and walked out into the water until the little wind waves broke against her calves.

"So, your father is a highly venomous New York attorney and your brother is an amateur drunk working toward semi-pro status. What do you do?" I asked. "When you're not sailing your dad's boat."

"That seems a bit harsh about Lance," she said.

"But accurate," I said. "And the question you just ducked was about you."

"I teach tenth grade English."

"You teach tenth grade English on a wooden schooner?" I asked. "You must be teaching Lance."

She laughed.

"I teach barely post-pubescent kids in Stamford," she said. "And I dearly love what I do. But I decided to take the year off after Mom got sick. I guess the whole family is on a bit of a sabbatical right now."

"I didn't get that option."

"You lost a parent?" she asked.

"Both," I said. "And two little sisters."

"Is this another joke?"

"No," I said. "A trucker fell asleep and crossed the double yellow line."

"Your whole family?" she asked.

I nodded. She put her hand on my arm. It was warmer than I'd expected.

"I can't imagine anything more awful," she said.

It was like someone had slipped truth serum into my drink. I never talked to anybody about my family, but there I was opening up and sharing feelings and emotions that I'd buried nearly two decades ago.

"I was two years into the Navy, in the middle of a tour at sea, and about a thousand miles south of India when it happened. The captain broke the news to me."

"How did you deal with it?"

"I don't know that I ever did," I said. "I mean, you don't just 'deal' with something like that. At least, I don't know how anybody does."

"How do you feel now?" she asked.

"It still hurts at times. There are times I want to make that call on Mother's Day or buy my dad a fishing lure for his birthday. My sisters were both very beautiful and sweet. I should be playing on the floor with their kids after Christmas dinner."

We walked quietly along the beach.

"I'm sorry," I said. "This has got to be depressing the hell out of you."

"No, that's okay."

Marie thought for a moment.

"Does it get better?" she asked. "Over time? That is something that I think about quite a lot."

"For me, the sense of loss doesn't really go away," I said. "But I remember the pain less often. And other good things come along to fill in the empty spaces."

I saw a piece of driftwood and found it oddly offensive. I picked it up and tossed it as far as I could into the Sound. A seabird squawked and flew off.

"So what did Lance do before his sabbatical?" I asked.

Marie stopped and turned to face me.

"You're still working on this murder case, aren't you?" she asked.

"Uh-huh."

"And you're trying to find out if Lance is involved somehow."

"Or if he knows something that might help," I said.

Marie gave out a short laugh. Her hair flew in the breeze and moonlight reflected from her dark eyes.

"For a while there, I was under the impression that we were a man and a woman discussing life and walking barefoot on a beach in a tropical paradise," she said.

"Aren't we?"

"Well, yes, I suppose. I mean, here you are in the moonlight with a reasonably attractive woman and you're still focused on doing your job."

"True," I said. "Except that you're considerably more than reasonably attractive. And it's not my job anymore. It's my best friend's life that's at stake."

Marie sat down on a bench situated under a palm tree near the shore, tucked her knees up to her chest, and put her arms around her legs.

"I have to work on Al's case," I said. "I owe it to him."

I sat down next to her. Another couple walked down the sand toward us holding hands. They continued past the bench and into the palm trees until we could no longer see them in the moonlight. We sat there for a few minutes and listened to distant music from the club band over the hiss of gentle waves lapping on the beach.

"Do you get lonely on your boat?" she asked.

"Oh, yeah. But I don't have much time to feel lonely. Navigation, sail changes, keeping watch. There's a lot to do. Still, there are times when I'd rather be someplace else with another person. I suppose it'd be a little easier if I had cable TV."

Marie laughed again.

"And where there are no alternatives," I said, "there are no problems."

Her broad smile returned and shone in the moonlight. She stood and walked down to the water's edge. I joined her.

"There are alternatives," she said.

A ferry boat droned slowly past, headed toward the main dock. It left a small wake that caught and swallowed the three-inch swells that lapped at our ankles. The piece of driftwood washed back up onto the beach and I thought of what Ashley's father had said about me several months and over four thousand miles ago.

The club band started another slow number in the distance. I imitated the voice of a much older man in a blue linen jacket.

"Would you care to dance, little lady?" I asked.

Marie chuckled. I held her in my arms and we danced slowly in the sand while the waves washed our feet. She laid her head on my shoulder and gently, effortlessly, knocked the wind out of me again.

Without warning, Marie turned her head and kissed me. I was back in junior high school riding my bicycle six miles on a Saturday morning to kiss Annette King under the apple tree. I pulled my left arm tight into the small of her back and the kisses became deeper and more passionate as our bodies moved with the slow

Caribbean music. When the music stopped, Marie put her hand on my face and stroked my cheek.

"Where is your boat?" she asked.

"A few hundred yards down the beach. Then a hundred yards into the bay."

She kissed me again lightly. I wanted to speak but my throat tightened.

"We could go back and get my dinghy," I croaked, "if you'd like to see my boat."

She leaned up slightly to whisper in my ear.

"Or we could swim to it in the moonlight," she said.

"We'd get our clothes soaked."

"Not if we left them on the beach," she chuckled.

My breath left again and the sailor's urge took over.

"The obvious solution," I said.

The band started up again and we danced another song. The moonlight glinted off her hair. The song ended and she pulled away. I held on to her hand.

"I should probably check on Dad," she said.

A friend of mine who sold used cars once told me that the best weapon in his arsenal was what he called the Take-back: "Maybe this car isn't right for you." He said it turned tire kickers into buyers.

"No moonlight swim?" I protested.

"I know it's not fair. I mean, it was my idea," she said. "I'm just worried about Dad. I should really check on him."

"Can I get a rain check?" I asked.

She smiled.

"Maybe," she said.

We walked back up the beach toward the dinghy dock.

"Ready to tell me about Lance?" I asked.

Marie groaned and shook her head.

"What's to tell? He was a normal kid growing up," she said. "He got a bit surly in high school, but who didn't, right? Then he went to Princeton for a couple of years and became a real jerk before dropping out. He probably smoked a lot of pot. I don't think he's ever had a job until last year. Now he tells us he's building an internet-based import-export business of some sort."

"Is it successful?"

"I don't know," she said. "He flies out to visit manufacturers in other countries, attends meetings with business partners we've never met or even heard of, and talks about cash flow problems and new investors and a growing economy."

"It sounds like he must be making a little money," I said.

"I think Dad is quietly funding his little pipe dream."

Another couple walked toward us and hurried past. Probably on the way to their bungalow.

"It is so wrong for you to be a tenth-grade English teacher," I said.

Marie turned to me with sharp eyes.

"What makes you say that?" she asked. "I absolutely and completely love what I do. And I do it well."

"I had Mrs. Peterson for tenth-grade English," I said. "She was a great teacher. But if she'd looked anything like you, I wouldn't have learned a thing."

Marie's smile returned.

"I might have stayed up all night but I certainly wouldn't have gotten any homework done," I said.

"You're awful," she said. "Awful but funny."

We walked up the short stairs to the dinghy dock.

"I'd like to go sailing tomorrow," she said.

"You've certainly got the boat for it."

"No, not on *D'Artagnan*," she said. "I want to take something smaller around the Sound. Maybe go north out past Saba Rock."

She stepped down into my dinghy. I untied it from the dock and started the little outboard.

"We could rent a catamaran," I said, "or one of the larger racing dinghies, if you like."

Marie smiled again as I drove her out to *D'Artagnan*. I didn't think I'd ever get used to that. As we approached the boat, she turned and kissed me. It wasn't casual or hurried. It was gentle and full of promise. I watched her as she gracefully boarded the boat. It was all I could do to keep from chasing her up the ladder.

"Don't get a cat," she called down. "I want to make a picnic. We can have lunch on a secluded beach."

"The wind picks up around one or so,' I said. "That's the best time for sailing."

"Pick me up at noon, then."

Fifteen minutes later, I was in *Figaro*'s cockpit looking at the full moon directly overhead, drinking a beer, and feeling a little like a tenth-grader who couldn't sleep.

26

LIKE most boats her size, *Figaro* is never entirely at rest. Even at anchor she is constantly moving, if only a little. The wind gently pushes her to port or starboard while even the smallest swells in a protected anchorage will rock her back and forth.

I have grown used to her dance and I generally sleep through it. Unless she makes an unfamiliar move or an unusual noise. Such a move or noise could be caused by a shift in the wind, an increase in wave action, or a dragging anchor. It's rarely a big deal but it sometimes drives me from my berth to let out more anchor chain or reposition the boat in the anchorage to find better holding ground.

The creak from *Figaro*'s boarding ladder woke me instantly and I lay still in my berth. The boat was quiet but *Figaro* listed slightly to port as someone silently placed his weight on the cockpit coaming.

I sat up in my berth, reached for the empty beer bottle I'd left on the floor, and grabbed it by the neck with my right hand. I quietly dropped to one knee. The moon was bright and two wet bare feet stepped noiselessly down the companionway steps. Above the feet was a hand carrying a pistol.

I smashed the wrist above the pistol with the bottle and then, with my left fist coming all the way up from the floor, planted a solid uppercut on the intruder's chin. The gun fell to the cabin sole and slid under the chart table while my uninvited guest went down hard in the galley and hit his head against the steel safety bar in front of the oven.

He lay still so I picked up the pistol and put it on the chart table. I grabbed my red-bulbed flashlight from its holder and took a look at the intruder. It was the same skinny young guy with the long red hair who'd walked into the bar at Gun Creek and scared off Levon.

I reached back over to the chart table and grabbed the package of long plastic wire ties I'd left there. One wire tie around each of Red's wrists and a third wire tie joining them made an effective set of makeshift handcuffs. I crafted another set for his ankles.

The gun was a Colt .45 model 1911 semi-automatic pistol. A classic military sidearm and an old friend. There were seven rounds in the magazine and one in the chamber. The thumb safety was off. I clicked it on.

Red lay unconscious as I searched him for a wallet or some other identification. He had nothing on him but an extra magazine for the pistol. Seven more rounds. His shorts and T-shirt were wet with saltwater, indicating he'd swum the short distance from shore. He didn't look particularly strong, but I felt like being on the safe side so I covered the makeshift handcuffs with duct tape. Elbows can be highly effective weapons, so I taped his together. Three strips of duct tape went over his mouth to keep him quiet.

My guest regained consciousness a minute later and mumbled through the duct tape.

"Be quiet," I whispered. "Or I'll put you back to sleep."

He lay there quietly, breathing softly through his nose, his eyes wide. I held the gun in my hand, clicked off the flashlight, and sat down in the salon staring at the companionway and the shaft of moonlight which illuminated it. I was in control of the situation down below in the cabin, but I had no idea who, if anyone, waited on shore.

The luminous hands on the ship's chronometer indicated that it was two in the morning. Popping up into a moonlit cockpit could earn me a bullet in the head from an unfriendly party on the shore. I'd never hear the shot that killed me.

I waited in the dark cabin watching my uninvited guest and listening for any unusual sounds. Two hours later, I crept up the companionway into the cockpit. There were no lights on the beach, no strange boats, no vehicles parked on the small path near Biras Creek. My visitor didn't seem to have any friends waiting for him in the moonlight.

I slipped the heavy Colt into my shorts pocket, started up *Figaro*'s little diesel, and winched up the anchor. We headed west out of Biras Creek and into the Sound. Once out of the anchorage, I went below, pulled my unwanted guest to his feet, and heaved him up into the cockpit. Red winced as I tore the duct tape from his mouth.

"Who are you and why are you on my boat?" I asked.

He glared at me defiantly.

I slapped him with an open hand on his right cheek. It shocked him and some of the defiance wore off. I slapped the left cheek hard enough to sting my hand. Red gasped.

"Who are you and why are you on my boat?" I asked.

Red spit in my face. I grabbed a towel off the lifelines and wiped off the spittle.

"Okay, hard ass. Have it your way," I said.

I opened up the lazarette and pulled out the twenty-pound Danforth that I occasionally use when *Figaro* needs a stern anchor. I unshackled the nylon rode and wrapped the remaining anchor chain around my guest's ankles. I made sure he saw the anchor in the beam of the flashlight. Then I clicked it off.

"What are you doin', man?" he asked.

His eyes were wide.

"You're an okay swimmer with a loaded pistol and an extra magazine," I said. "Let's see how you do with forty pounds of anchor and chain."

I maneuvered the boat out of the Sound north through the gap in Colquhoun Reef and turned west toward the Sir Francis Drake Channel. The full moon dropped into the Caribbean as the faint morning twilight began to illuminate the intruder.

"You're crazy," he said.

"I'm crazy mad, you skinny little bastard."

Figaro continued due west. I went down below, grabbed my chart, and brought it back up to the cockpit. I scanned it with my flashlight and found an area with some depth. I pointed at it with my finger.

"Right there," I said. "When we find eighty feet in the channel you're going for a swim."

The depth sounder showed fifty-seven feet in large, red numbers that glowed in the darkness. Red tightened his jaw and scowled at me. Minutes passed and the numbers on the depth sounder steadily increased in two- to three-foot increments. Red scraped his lower lip with his teeth and looked for a way out as we entered deeper water. He tested the wire ties and duct tape. At seventy-three feet, his poker face cracked and he folded his hand.

"Okay, man. I'll talk. Don't throw me in," he said.

"Too late, brother."

I let him stew a while. The urge for self-preservation tends to lubricate the tongue. Maslow's hierarchy of needs was now working for me. He became frantic.

"I'm serious, man. I'll tell you anything," he begged. "Don't drown me."

"Okay, fella. I will ask you some questions and you will answer me immediately and truthfully. I've heard plenty of lies in my line of work and I'm good at picking them out. You lie to me and you'll go for a swim with that anchor."

His mouth opened and his eyes implored. He nodded his head quickly.

"What's your name?" I asked.

"Ronnie Thomas. Please don't drown me, man."

"Why were you on my boat? Were you going to shoot me?"

"I wasn't gonna shoot you, man," he said. "I was only looking for the three packages you got."

"What packages?"

"You took three packages from Brownell before you killed him," he said. "I was just supposed to find them and bring 'em back."

"You brought a gun," I said. "It was fully loaded with a round chambered. You brought an extra magazine. You were going to shoot me."

"No, that wasn't it," he said. "The lights were out on your boat. You didn't even have an anchor light on. I thought you were gone."

"I'm not buying it," I said.

He knew I was going to toss him and he started to cry.

"Tell me the truth, you little bastard."

"I only wanted the packages," he said. "That's God's honest truth. I swear it."

"What's in the packages you wanted?" I asked. "Drugs?"

"I don't know," he said. "The man said he wanted the packages. He gave me the gun and told me to get 'em off your boat."

"What man?" I asked.

"He'll kill me if I tell you."

"Ronnie, you've got a tough choice to make and you have less than one minute to make it."

I looked at the depth sounder, put the engine in neutral, and stood up to undo the pelican hooks on the starboard lifelines.

"You know what happens when you drown, Ronnie? You hold your breath as long as you can but your lungs ache for air. They burn until you can't take it anymore, and then your lungs take over and they suck up water. The air left in your lungs mixes with the water and your chest muscles churn it all into a red, bloody froth that fills your mouth and nose. You're awake while all this happens and it takes some time to die that way."

He swallowed hard.

"We've got eighty-three feet here," I said. "Decision time. You can either tell me who put you up to this and I'll let you off at Trellis Bay or you can keep your mouth shut and try to hold your breath all the way down to eighty-three feet."

It wasn't that tough a choice.

"Jimmy Cattrel," he said.

I refastened the lifelines.

"Did he tell you to kill Levon?" I asked.

"I never killed nobody."

"Why was he so scared of you over in that bar at Gun Creek?"

"All the locals know my boss," he said. "Everybody is scared of him."

Once he got started he couldn't stop talking. He told me about Jimmy Cattrel, all about his own life, anything and everything else he could think of. It was a complete brain dump from a small brain. I finally got sick of listening to him, retaped his mouth shut, and put my stern anchor away.

We motored through the darkness for another hour until we reached Marina Cay. I found an empty mooring, put a line through the pennant, and stepped back aft to sit in the cockpit. Ronnie stared at me as dawn approached.

The sun rose over Trellis Bay as I thought about Jimmy Cattrel, who, according to Ronnie, was a big, tough, old black guy who drove a long blue Jeep.

27

AL picked up on the second ring and I told him about the morning's events. His proposed solution had been my first impulse but Ronnie *had* told me what I wanted to know and I didn't really want to lose a perfectly good stern anchor. Al agreed to my suggested alternative.

I'd promised the little jerk that I'd let him off at Trellis Bay so I motored the half mile south. I pulled out my rigging knife as we entered the bay and Ronnie's eyes nearly bugged out. I shook my head and cut the wire ties and duct tape that secured him. He rubbed his wrists as *Figaro* powered past the numerous sailboats and smaller power yachts in the crowded mooring field.

"You call the police on me, man?"

"No," I said. "You answered my questions, so I'm letting you off at Trellis like I promised."

"No hard feelings, eh?" he said.

"I didn't say that. I didn't say that at all. Truth is, if you ever see me again, you oughta run as fast as you can in the opposite direction."

I stepped closer to him for emphasis.

"Because if I see you first, Ronnie—and I don't care where we are or who I'm with or who is watching—I will beat you to death with whatever is handy. Have you got that straight?"

He swallowed hard and nodded. I reached down and grabbed him by his shirt and shorts and heaved him overboard. He swam for the shore, swearing at me in clever combinations as if it were his sole creative outlet and his greatest source of pride.

It was early in the morning, and most of the crews aboard the boats in the bay were still snug in their bunks. A Labrador on the deck of a big catamaran woke up at the sound of Ronnie's effusive anger and barked in response. A barking dog is a highly effective security measure, so I grabbed a vacant mooring next to the big dog's boat. It seemed like the perfect place to leave *Figaro*.

I had some time so I stripped the Colt down to its component parts, cleaned it thoroughly, and oiled it. I cleaned the ammunition with fresh water and oiled the two magazines. The pistol felt good in my hand, but a lot of countries, including the BVI, do not allow such weapons on board. I decided not to tell them and stowed my newly acquired armament in one of *Figaro*'s hard-to-find little hidey-holes. After locking up the boat, I climbed into the dinghy and motored to the bay's little dock.

It had rained at Trellis Bay during the night and drops of water slipped off the fronds of tall coconut palms as I walked along the beach to a small restaurant on the south side. I bought a large cup of hot coffee and a copy of the local paper and took both to an old wooden table on the beach about fifty yards from *Figaro*. If anybody else decided to come aboard while I waited for Al, I'd know about it. I sat down, dug my feet into the cool, damp morning sand, and opened the paper. I sipped some of the coffee. It was much better than I'd expected. Of course, I'd been up since two in the morning and my standards were somewhat relaxed.

Levon's picture was on the second page. The article stated that Levon Baptiste, father of three, had gone missing. He'd had been seen departing the ferry at Gun Creek on Thursday night but hadn't been seen since. The article made me wish that I'd tossed Ronnie in at the eighty-foot mark.

Al walked up with his own cup of coffee, sat down, and tossed his feet into the chair opposite him.

"You want breakfast?" he asked.

"I've been up since two in the morning dealing with that little jerk. I want lunch."

"Well," he said, "I hope you're in the mood for eggs."

I went back to the paper and read more about Levon.

"I followed that skinny little turd to an apartment in Road Town," Al said.

"Somebody pick him up? He couldn't walk that far."

"He hitched a ride. He was outta there so fast he never even looked to see where you parked your boat."

Al sipped his coffee and chuckled.

"Nice throw, by the way. You cleared the lifelines and splashed him ten feet from the boat."

"I was a little ticked," I said.

He chuckled again.

"Did you really think that runt was gonna kill you?" he asked. "I've seen more meat on a chicken wing."

"He brought a forty-five with him," I said. "That evens things out some."

Breakfast arrived and it was impressive. I was hungrier than I'd thought and dug into the large omelet. Between bites, I told Al about Levon, Derek, a wad of cash being flashed at the Willy-T, and the drama unfolding aboard *Liquid Assets*. I also told him the details of the early-morning boarding and how I'd interrogated Ronnie with a depth sounder and a Danforth anchor.

"So why did the kid come out there?" asked Al.

"Some guy named Jimmy Cattrel wanted some packages off my boat," I said. "You ever hear of the guy?"

There was a flicker of recognition in his eyes.

"Never heard of him," Al said. "But I'll bet Millet has. You want to ask him?"

It seemed to be the smart thing to do and I felt like doing something smart.

We finished breakfast and Al drove me to Road Town. I thought about Marie, who expected to see me at noon in a sailing dinghy. I figured I should call her to explain why I wouldn't be there. That would also be the smart thing to do. And it would have been possible if I'd gotten her phone number.

Al decided to wait in the car when we got to the police station. I couldn't blame him. I walked past the front desk and straight into Millet's office.

Detective Constable Millet sat at the same spartan desk in the same worn chair. The same stack of files lay on the left with the same pens to the right. A cup of tea stood sentinel as the only added feature. He studied the contents of a file and barely looked up when I sat down in the old wooden chair.

"How can I help you, Mr. Greene?"

"Somebody boarded my boat very early this morning and threatened me with violence," I said.

Millet looked up from his paperwork momentarily and went back to the file in his hand.

"The sergeant outside can take your complaint," he said. "Good day."

I did not leave.

"I think it has something to do with this Somerset murder," I said. "I thought you might be interested."

"Inebriated tourists board other people's boats by mistake every night in this country," he said. "Sometimes people get upset and make empty threats. It is hardly a remarkable occurrence. And we have already solved that murder."

"The guy wasn't drunk," I said. "He was stone-cold sober. Said he was trying to collect some packages for a guy named Jimmy Cattrel."

Millet stopped reading when I said the name.

"You ever hear of the guy?" I asked.

Millet put his folder away and stared at me.

"Yes, I know Mr. Cattrel," he said. "I know him quite well. He was my boss."

28

"HE is a prominent businessman and a respected former officer in the Royal Virgin Islands Police. And he was my friend, too," said Millet. "However, I fail to see how his business is any of yours, or, for that matter, any of mine."

"As I told you, Constable, he sent somebody to my boat to threaten me with violence."

Millet smiled, leaned back in his chair, and clasped his hands behind his neck.

"You aren't interested in this at all," I said.

Millet flashed a wry smile.

"Message received and understood, Constable. I'll get out of your hair or, at least, your office."

"Excellent," said Millet. "Good day, Mr. Greene."

I got up to leave and opened the door to his office.

"Oh, there's just one more thing," I said. "As you already know, there is no Bradley Somerset and that British passport you showed me was a fake. The victim's real name was Derek Brownell. And he was an American, not British. Former U.S. Coast Guard, in fact."

I tossed the picture of Derek Brownell and the blonde on Millet's desk and he picked it up. The smile dropped. I thought of telling him about *Liquid Assets* and Terrence Wells but decided to let him do some police work of his own.

"You could probably check with your Customs and Immigrations offices to find out how and when he entered the country," I said.

Millet was silent. He did not look pleased.

"I just thought you might like to know, Detective."

I walked out of his office and down the hallway to the door. Al's car was parked at the next block so I walked over and hopped in. He started up the little Isuzu and pulled into traffic toward town.

"Take me back to Trellis Bay," I said. "I'm not leaving my boat there overnight."

"Millet tell you anything about Cattrel?" he asked.

"He says Cattrel is a former cop turned successful businessman. A pillar of BVI society."

Al made a grunting sound as he entered a roundabout and turned the car back toward Trellis Bay.

"You believe that?"

"I believe Millet couldn't care less what Cattrel does to us," I said. "But that kid was telling me the truth and I'm going to find out why Cattrel sent him to my boat in the wee hours of the morning."

"How's he connected with the dead guy?" Al asked. "What's he got to do with my case?"

"He wants something Derek had. Some packages. Who he is and what he wants could lead us to the murderer."

"A wild good chase."

"Maybe," I said.

"What about the girl?" asked Al.

"She's clean and I'm pretty sure her father is, too. The son is a wild card, though. He's got something going with that big yacht's crew and I don't see any reasonable explanation for it."

"Don't be so sure about that girl, Sim," said Al.

I looked over at Al. His teeth were set hard. Arguing with him once he'd made up his mind was like preaching tolerance to a terrorist. An effort doomed to failure.

"So the kid brought a forty-five with him, eh?" asked Al.

"Uh-huh. With a full magazine and one up the pipe; hammer back and safety off. He had a spare magazine in his pocket."

"The kid thought he needed fifteen rounds?" said Al. "Seriously?"

"I am rather formidable."

Al entered the dirt parking area near the dinghy dock and pulled the car into the shade of two coconut palms. We both got into the small inflatable and motored over to *Figaro*. I tied the dinghy off to the stern and went forward to the companionway. The short length of monofilament fishing line that I'd stuck into the hatch boards was still there. Nobody had been below in my absence. I unlocked the hatch, stepped down into the cabin, and sat at the salon table. Al followed.

"I think I'll motor over to Marina Cay for the night," I said. "Tomorrow, I'll sail her to a spot where I can lie low for a while."

"While I find out what I can about Cattrel?" asked Al.

I nodded.

"Have you still got any government connections back in Port Hueneme?" I asked.

He shook his head.

"None that would know anything about this guy," he said. "You?"

"Same problem."

"What about that ICE guy?" he asked.

"Bartholomew?"

"Yeah, that's the guy," said Al. "From what you told me, he was pretty happy about the way things turned out in California. If he can't help, he'd at least point us in the right direction."

I tilted up *Figaro*'s chart table and dug amongst the odds and ends that had accumulated there over the years. I picked up the cruising guide to move it out of the way and the big, colorful playing card slipped out onto the floor.

"What the hell is that?" asked Al.

"A Tarot card. Somebody left it on my boat a couple of days ago."

Al picked it up and examined it closely.

"This is big stuff in the Caribbean. Magic, fortune telling, that kinda voodoo nonsense. I didn't think it had much hold in the BVI, but..."

"Why would somebody leave it on my boat?" I asked.

"Beats me," said Al. "A curse or a spell or something. Have you pissed somebody off, lately?"

I thought about Henry on Jost Van Dyke.

"Maybe I should have ordered the fish," I said.

Al muttered something about crazy single-handed sailors, and I went back to looking for what I needed under the chart table. Toward the back under the ship's documents was a plain white business card with the blue and white logo of the United States Department of Homeland Security.

"Here it is," I said. "I'll give him a call tonight."

I grabbed my roll of charts and the cruising guide and laid them on the salon table.

"Any idea where I should hide *Figaro*?"

Al thought for a moment, unrolled the chart, and spread it on the table.

"Either Anegada or Little Jost Van Dyke," he said. "Anegada's way out there all by itself, thirteen miles or so north of Virgin Gorda. There aren't a lot of fancy things out there and not everybody on vacation wants to sail that far. Horseshoe Reef to the south is pretty bad and the harbor entrance is tricky. That weeds out a lot of the tourists."

"Sounds like the spot for me."

He pointed at a quarter circle of blue on the chart.

"Tuck her right in there behind Pomato Point," he said. "Stay west of the moorings and anchor out. Folks on the island will figure you don't have any money and nobody around here pays the slightest attention to a guy without dough."

"*Figaro* draws about five feet," I said.

"You'll find some patches of deep water between the mooring field and the point," he said.

He rolled up the chart and handed it back to me.

"Find out everything you can about Cattrel," I said. "Where he lives and who with, what he does, where his office is, anything you can think of. Then give me a call. I'm not going to let you get stuck in Her Majesty's prison."

"That *is* a motivating factor," he said.

The cabin was a little stuffy and I wanted to keep my eyes on the shore anyway, so we went back up into the cockpit. We talked a little about California and our ideas about a diving business and then the conversation lagged. There was a lot of heavy quiet in the cockpit.

"You ever think of taking another shot at marriage, Sim?"

It was a question entirely out of left field and it took me by surprise.

"Yeah, I guess so," I said. "A couple of times, maybe. But every time I got that close to a woman I always got the impression that I was missing something she needed. That I had to be a lot more than what I am."

Al nodded.

"I'm getting that feeling about Liv," he said. "Like I could maybe stick with one woman. For the rest of it, you know."

I felt like telling him to take an aspirin and to call me in the morning, but my better instincts prevailed.

"Isn't she still mad about your alibi?" I asked. "The one you won't tell the cops about?"

"That's it, I guess. She forgave me. I don't think I've ever felt that before. It's a good feeling."

"That's great, Al. Let's concentrate on keeping you out of prison so you can keep that option open, okay?"

He laughed.

"Then I guess I'd better get going," he said.

We motored back to the dinghy dock and I dropped him off. His little Isuzu left the parking area trailing a plume of brown dust as I headed back to *Figaro*. I tied off the dinghy, started the diesel, and powered out of Trellis Bay. Three hundred years earlier, this bay had been a refuge for local pirates who only left its safe confines to plunder heavily laden Spanish galleons. Today, I was leaving to keep from being plundered.

It was a short sail back to Marina Cay, and the shadows cast by the setting sun raced to cover the mooring field. I picked up a mooring, unwrapped the last fish fillet I'd stored in the icebox, and grilled it with some canned pineapple slices. I ate in the cockpit and thought about a redheaded killer, Constable Millet, Derek Brownell, and Her Majesty's prison. I thought about Liv and how Al was feeling about her. How weird was that? And I thought about Marie.

The last rays of the sun disappeared over Great Camanoe Island to the west and plunged the mooring field into near darkness. A commercial airliner, one of the smaller turboprops that comes in every couple of hours from Puerto Rico, appeared out of the west over Tortola and set itself up for a landing at the airport a half mile away.

A fresh batch of tourists to be housed, fed, tanned, entertained, and supplied with authentic Caribbean trinkets before the long trip home. Most stay a week or less. Very few go to prison.

I looked at the time on my cell phone and subtracted four hours. Frank Bartholomew was still on Uncle Sam's dime in California. I dialed his number.

29

"SPEAK."

"It's me, Frank. Your old buddy Sim Greene."

He was silent for a long moment.

"So, how are the British Virgin Islands this time of year?" he asked.

"How'd you know I was down here?" I asked.

It was more than a little disturbing to have a federal agent know so much about my life.

"Edward Stevenson."

"Is that name supposed to mean something to me?" I said.

"Doesn't it?" he asked.

I had no idea what he was talking about.

"There are a lot of folks here in the department who are wondering if you've gone to work for the other side," he said.

"I've never heard of this Edward Stevenson guy and I honestly don't know what you are talking about, Frank."

"One of our guys, Sim. He sent his partner a cell phone picture of you walking out of a bank in Road Town. You want to tell me why he found you to be so interesting?"

"I don't have the slightest idea," I said. "Why don't you ask him?"

"Because he is lying in a morgue in Virginia right now. His funeral is on Thursday. Maybe you'd like to show up. His wife and two little kids will be there."

There wasn't anything to say to that.

"A bunch of my colleagues will be there, too, and they'd love the opportunity to ask you a few hard questions about what happened," he said. "Word is that DHS now has a team in the BVI looking for you. I'd advise you to cooperate if they succeed."

I thought about the blacked-out Coast Guard response boat.

"Did this Stevenson guy have a long face and curly brown hair?" I asked. "Did he drive a white Montero?"

"I have no idea what he was driving," said Frank. "But your description isn't far off."

"I got here eight days ago. Early Monday morning. Some guy with a long face and curly brown hair followed me around in a white Montero that afternoon. He picked me up again on Tuesday. I never spoke with him or even got within twenty yards of the guy. I figured he was a local cop."

"Why would a local cop follow you around?" he asked.

"No reason at all. Anyway, he followed me to a grocery store in Road Town Tuesday afternoon and was gunned down in broad daylight while I was inside filling up a cart in aisle nine."

"Go on."

"The locals saw it coming," I said. "A bunch of them walked into the store and closed the door behind them less than a minute before he was shot. They all acted like they knew what was going to happen, and nobody wanted to talk about it afterward."

"What were you doing in that bank, Sim?"

"Opening up a checking account, Frank. Is there something wrong with that?"

"You know what those banks are used for, don't you?" he asked.

"Sure. They're used by foreign corporations who want to park their profits in a tax haven and they're used by American citizens who want to cheat the IRS. Occasionally, a guy like me stumbles in who only wants to open up a local checking account."

"Did you forget money launderers and drug smugglers?" he asked.

"Frank, since the last time you saw me I have sailed a small boat from Oxnard to Mexico to Costa Rica to Panama. I rested on the Caribbean side of the canal for a couple of weeks but then sailed straight to the BVI. Do you honestly think I smuggled drugs *out* of the United States?"

He was silent for a while.

"You once told me that you thought I was a pretty good investigator," I said. "Would you like to know what I observed at the crime scene?"

"Absolutely."

"Okay, then."

I told him where Stevenson parked outside Bobby's, the descriptions of the locals I saw walk into the store, and the number of gunshots I heard. I told him about the cops coming and the fairly slipshod investigative procedures I observed.

"None of this is particularly helpful," said Frank.

"There is one more thing. The shuttle driver—his first name was Julian; I didn't get a last name—was very close-lipped on the trip back to my boat. I asked him about how his friends knew what was going to happen and who he thought did it. He wouldn't talk. I thought at the time that your guy was a local cop, and I suggested that the RVIP would turn Julian's little island upside down looking for a cop killer. His response was a little weird."

"What'd he say?"

"As I think back on it, he may have implied that the killer, not the victim, was a cop," I said.

Frank was quiet for a few moments.

"You got anything else?" he asked.

I heard some relaxation in his voice, as if he believed me.

"I've got some questions for you," I said.

"Yeah," he said. "That's right. You called me."

"You ever hear of a guy down here named Jimmy Cattrel?"

"No. Should I?"

"He sent a kid to my boat in the middle of the night with a pistol," I said. "I get the feeling that he is some sort of local badass."

"And I am supposed to be the repository of knowledge regarding the world's population of badasses?"

"I figured somebody in your circle of friends—DHS, ICE, DEA—might know something."

"I'll check into it," he said. "You want me to call you back at this number?"

"Please."

I thought for a moment.

"Frank," I said. "I've told you everything I know about your guy's death. I'm not holding anything back on that. If I find anything else out, I'll bring it straight to you."

He was quiet for a moment.

"I appreciate that, Sim."

We hung up and I went topside to look around for a blacked-out boat full of angry federal agents lurking in the darkness. I didn't see one, but it didn't mean they weren't there.

The sun was down for the count and so was I. It had been too long a day and I wanted to sleep soundly, confident that I would not be disturbed by nighttime intruders. I took three boxes of treble fishhooks out of my tackle box, emptied them into my hand, and arranged the hooks along *Figaro*'s side decks, cockpit seats, and companionway. Any uninvited barefoot visitors would be unpleasantly surprised.

I also tucked the .45 under a spare cushion in my berth.

The wind picked up and sang in the rigging, and raindrops hit the deck as my head hit the pillow.

30

A good breeze crept in behind the early morning squalls and *Figaro* tugged at her mooring. I had nearly thirty miles to put under her keel before reaching my destination, so I cast off the mooring line, raised the mainsail, and headed west to the narrow passage between Little Camanoe and Great Camanoe Islands. I continued along the northeastern shore of Guana Island sailing a route that shielded *Figaro* from any prying eyes that might have watched us leave. This added nearly two hours to my route but gave me some assurance that anyone watching *Figaro* would have a tough time predicting my destination.

Satisfied that unwanted onlookers had been led astray, I turned hard to starboard and headed toward Anegada. The harbor's entrance buoys lay over eighteen miles to the northeast and almost straight into twenty knots of wind. No sailboat can sail directly upwind but *Figaro* can work her way there by pointing about forty degrees off the wind and tacking toward the destination.

I put a reef in the main, furled the jib some, and set Kyle to steer the boat on a starboard tack so I wouldn't have to spend the entire day at the helm. Kyle—the self-steering contraption I'd installed on *Figaro* years ago—is a concoction of ropes, wind vanes, and gears that keeps the boat on a constant course relative to the wind. The solo sailor's third hand.

I rigged one of my favorite fishing lures to *Figaro*'s trolling line as she headed into deeper and darker water. A ten-inch plastic squid I called Big Pink. It rarely failed me.

We made a little over six knots in the fresh breeze. I did a little mental math and figured that the trip would take us four hours with the necessary tacking. That would put us in the harbor around two that afternoon. About halfway there, the fishing rod bent aft and line sang off the reel. I disconnected Kyle and turned *Figaro* into the wind, grabbed the rod, and reeled in a fair-sized dorado. I poured a shot of rum into its gills and the fish died instantly. An object lesson I could have benefited from in my youth.

I sliced up the dorado and put the fillets into the icebox. Having restocked the larder, I turned *Figaro* back onto the desired course and consigned Kyle back to steering duty. He wasn't the best conversationalist I'd had aboard as crew but he didn't complain, never got tired, and never talked back to the captain. Compared to the rest of my friends, he was remarkably low-maintenance.

I thought about Marie and mentally kicked myself for not getting her phone number. It would have been nice to have the option of apologizing for missing yesterday's sail and picnic. And it is considered good form in the profession for a homicide detective to know how to contact a suspect. At least I knew her name and her boat. Small comfort.

The island of Anegada sort of sneaks up on you. The tall casuarina trees look like a gray-green fuzz on the horizon from about five or six miles away. Shorter bushes and mangroves fill in the gaps as you get closer. The island is surrounded by Horseshoe Reef on three sides and the narrow entrance to the harbor is marked by a few carefully placed buoys.

Sailors straying from the channel or pointing too far east in their approach run the serious risk of running aground. The cruising guide suggested that villagers had done well over the last couple hundred years or so by salvaging wrecks impaled on Horseshoe Reef. Supposedly, some of the villagers had been more intent on salvaging valuables than saving the crew.

I found the entrance buoys, entered the channel, and motored *Figaro* past the few shore-side shops and restaurants. A dozen or more sailboats occupied the deeper water of the mooring field, but I continued northwest to Al's recommended anchorage. The shallow water there was as clear as rippled glass, and I saw large fields of eelgrass stretching all the way to Pomato Point.

A small, isolated patch of sand lay halfway between the shops on the shore and the point. I dropped *Figaro*'s hook and dug it in. Diving on the anchor, I realized that there was little more than a foot of water between *Figaro*'s keel and the bottom. Given the shallow water and the eelgrass, it was unlikely that I would have any close neighbors.

It had been a long day in the hot sun, and I needed a long swim. I walked ashore when I reached Pomato Point and sat down on warm sand the color and texture of powdered sugar. I lay back and worked the problems in my mind a bit. A dead federal agent, a midnight intruder with a pistol, a big yellow yacht with more than its share of onboard drama, a dead first mate floating in the channel, and a detective constable who didn't seem to care all that much.

What had I gotten myself into and how did I get this big red target painted on my backside?

The narrow entrance channel was plainly visible from my spot in the sand. I looked south as I sat up and saw a large wooden schooner with maroon sails working its way through the red and green buoys.

31

I swam back to *Figaro* and grabbed my binoculars. By that time, *D'Artagnan* had picked up a mooring off Setting Point near the other boats. I watched Marie and her father stow gear and furl the sails. I reached for the VHF radio to call her but realized that the party-line nature of that device would defeat the purpose of my sailing there in the first place. I was supposed to be hiding. I clicked the radio off.

D'Artagnan's dinghy motored to the dock and I watched David and Marie go ashore and walk to one of the island's restaurants. I fought the urge to join them.

I dug into the lazarette and pulled out the small barbecue that locks on to *Figaro*'s stern pushpit. Dorado sizzled on the grill as I peeled a ripe mango. A cold Corona rounded off my dinner. The shadows in *Figaro*'s cockpit lengthened and a young islander walked out on the beach and lit oil torches on the shore near the restaurant.

The coconut palms on the beach stretched out in the wind and an early evening squall set down on the anchorage. The little storm was full of loud, hard rain that forced me below and washed the salt off the boat. It seemed at that moment that while so many of my old friends had found permanent moorings—marriage, children, career—I had spent my own years struggling into safe harbors right before the big storms blew in.

The sun went down hard and left the anchorage completely dark except for the lights of moored sailboats and the flickering of beachside torches. The rain pounded down. With nobody around to complain about it, I stripped and climbed into the cockpit *au naturel* to shower off in the warm, fresh rain. It was a marvelous feeling. One of sailing's simplest pleasures.

The squall blew itself out, and island music played across the anchorage from a big stereo at the restaurant. A dinghy left the dock, headed toward the mooring field, and stopped at *D'Artagnan*. The boat's cabin lights turned on. Shafts of warm light beamed through the vessel's ports and played on the water.

I put on a clean shirt and shorts, grabbed a paper bag and a couple of things I'd meant to give David, and stepped down into my dinghy. I motored to the small hotel on Setting Point and paid the manager way too much for a bottle of eight-year-old port. David had turned on the cockpit lights and was reading a book under *D'Artagnan*'s bimini. He looked in my direction as my dinghy got closer, but his night vision was shot and he couldn't see me.

"Ahoy," I said.

"What? Hello. Is that you, Sim?" asked David. "What in the world are you doing here? Come aboard, come aboard."

I tossed him the dinghy's painter and climbed up the boarding ladder with my paper bag and the bottle of port.

"I saw you pull in and decided to bring over some grog for the crew," I said.

Marie came up the companionway and sat down in the cockpit across from me.

"Are you here to continue with your merciless interrogations?" she asked.

Her voice was more than cool. Roald Amundsen would have shivered.

"Just a neighborly visit," I said.

"I'll go below and get some glasses," said David.

Marie waited until her father went below.

"Dad and I had a wonderful picnic yesterday."

"Sorry about that," I said. "Something came up and I had to deal with it. I would have called you, but I didn't have your number."

"It must have been very important," she said. "Blonde or brunette?"

"Redhead, actually."

Marie's eyes narrowed and her mouth became thin.

"Probably a lot younger than me," she said.

"Mid-twenties, I'd guess."

Her nostrils flared slightly.

"He swam out to my boat in the middle of the night with a loaded pistol," I said.

Marie's eyes widened.

"What are you talking about?" she asked.

"Some guy swam out to my boat with a gun only an hour or two after I left your boat the other night."

"You're joking," she said.

"I'm not joking. He boarded my boat while I was asleep and came below."

"With a gun? My God," she said. "What happened?

"I disarmed him and convinced him to tell me who put him up to it."

"What do you mean you 'disarmed' him?"

"I took the gun away," I said.

Marie's face was a blank screen.

"Don't look so surprised," I said. "Did you think all I could do was dance?"

"What are you doing here?" she asked.

"Al and I figured it would be best for me to hide until we figured out why somebody is sending gunnies out to shoot me."

"Did you go to the police?" she asked. "They need to put him in jail. And the people who sent him, too."

"Yeah, I told them. They didn't seem to be particularly interested."

"That's crazy," she said. She stood up, walked over to my side of the cockpit, and sat down next to me. "That's their job, isn't it? To serve and protect?"

"These aren't television cops, Marie. These guys serve their own interests first. Right now, they think my best friend is a murderer. And they think I'm running around muddying their waters and trying to confound their legal system. At best, they think I'm lying to them. At worst, they're being paid off by the guy who sent the redhead."

Marie shook her head.

"That's crazy," she said again.

David came back with three wine glasses and opened the bottle of port. He informed us that it was a good vintage. I agreed wholeheartedly as if I'd known all along.

The sky cleared from the previous squall, and we could see the pinprick lights of Virgin Gorda thirteen miles to the south. David handed out the glasses and poured the wine.

"This is excellent," he said. "Where did you get it?"

"At that little hotel over on the beach," I said.

"You have excellent taste, Sim."

I nodded as if I knew something about the subject. I didn't want to admit that most of the wine I'd drunk had come out of a box kept on top of the refrigerator.

"Thanks," I said. "Here's something else for you."

I handed him the bag. He returned a puzzled look.

"Open it," I said.

David reached in and pulled out three fishing lures. One was about six inches of bright pink plastic with a hook buried in a skirt of shredded foil toward the end. The other two were small, white plastic cylinders, each equipped with squid-like eyes and smaller hooks.

"Use the little ones around the islands for jacks and tunny. Save the big one for bluewater passages where you might hook a tuna or a dorado."

A broad smile crept over his face.

"Thank you," he said. "That was very thoughtful of you. I'll let you know if my luck changes."

He went below to stow the lures.

"So, where's Lance?" I asked Marie.

"He flew to the Dominican Republic yesterday."

"Scouting for a shortstop?" I asked.

Marie smiled.

"No, he's meeting with some manufacturing interests on the island," she said.

"All the great jobs go overseas, don't they?" I said. "So, what is he having manufactured?"

David returned from below as I asked the question.

"It is still in the start-up phase, I believe," said David. "I don't think he wants to talk too much about it until he can bring products to market."

I had a lot of questions about Lance, but the Tanners didn't want to discuss him or his business. Instead, David told me more about his boat. Nearly sixty feet of classic wooden boat finished bright with more varnish than I'd ever want to brush during my lifetime. Everything topside was either oiled teak, polished brass, or varnished mahogany. The ship's compass sat in a brass binnacle atop a solid mahogany post. It looked like it could have come off a whaling ship a century and a half ago. Everything looked as if it had been built in the late 1800s. Except that it was all new.

The rain returned and played a heavy staccato on the bimini.

"Let's go below and get out of this weather," said David.

We stepped down the companionway and the appearance of antiquity fell away like French soldiers guarding Paris. Modern low-voltage lighting illuminated a bright and airy cabin. A modern galley with granite countertops stood to port while a high-tech navigation station with all the state-of-the-art doo-dads sat to starboard. A salon table of figured maple appeared to burst into flames, and a large oil painting of waves beating against a rocky coast hung on the forward bulkhead. We sat in the salon and David described the different types of wood, the fixtures, and the various systems installed on the boat. He was proud of his vessel and with good reason.

When the wine ran out, David produced a bottle of Kirsch brandy and three of those fat-bottomed stemmed glasses that cultured folk hold in upturned palms between their middle and ring fingers.

"I decided that outwardly she would appear to be a faithful restoration," he said. "But I also wanted a completely modern and comfortable sailing vessel. What do you think?"

"She's gorgeous," I said. "Pure craftsmanship. How does she sail?"

"Wonderfully," said Marie.

She used the word as if she were describing an object with feelings and emotions. We talked of boats and sailing. David's vision of a life at sea was quite different from the reality I experienced.

"What brings you to Anegada?" David asked. "It's a little off the beaten path."

"I'd heard it was peaceful and very quiet," I said.

"Have you ever been to Loblolly Bay?" Marie asked.

"No," I said. "This is my first time here."

"It's on the far side of the island," said David. "Fabulous snorkeling. Marie and I are going there tomorrow. You must join us."

I thought about that. Anybody working for the bad guys would be looking for a lone-wolf sailor. A trio of tourists would go relatively unnoticed. And it gave me another chance to be with Marie.

"Sounds like fun," I said. "Count me in."

"Wonderful," said David. "Meet us on the dinghy dock around nine or so. We'll take a taxi, do some snorkeling, and have lunch over there."

David yawned.

"I think this brandy has made me a little sleepy," he said. "I'll turn in a bit early if you two don't mind."

He went forward to his stateroom.

Marie swirled the last of her brandy in the bottom of her glass. It was an elegant movement that came naturally to her. She finished her drink and put the empty glass on the granite countertop. She sat on the port settee across from me with her hands in her lap.

"Last night, I was impossibly angry at you for standing me up," she said.

I leaned forward and touched her hand.

"I'm very sorry I missed that picnic," I said. "There is nothing I would have rather done. But it couldn't be helped."

She looked back up at me with a little bit of fire in her eyes.

"What makes you think *you* can solve this murder?"

"I don't *think* I can solve it," I said. "I know it. I have to know it."

"Somebody is trying to kill you, Sim."

"It's part of the territory," I said. "When you dive into the ocean, you give up your spot at the top of the food chain. You know there are sharks in there with you. But you either accept the risk or you stay out of the water."

"Like I said, last night I was impossibly angry at you. But if you don't show up tomorrow morning, Sim, I will be impossibly worried."

She moved to sit down next to me on the starboard settee. She turned her back to me, put her legs up on the cushions next to her, and turned until her arms were around me. She nearly lay in my lap.

"Maybe I should keep you here to be certain," she said.

She kissed me lightly, the taste of fine brandy on her lips.

"Any chance of claiming that moonlight swim tonight?" I asked.

"You just finished telling me about giving up my spot in the food chain to sharks," she said. "*Maybe* some other night."

The kisses were light and unhurried. Passionate but patient.

"I'm really starting to like this, Marie."

"I can tell," she giggled.

"Hey, that's not fair."

The antique ship's clock chimed an early-morning hour.

"So," I said. "Which one is your stateroom?"

"All the way forward." She kissed me again. "Where I can hear the chain if the anchor drags."

"Of course," I said.

A few minutes passed.

"I bet it's beautiful," I said.

"The anchor?" asked Marie.

She smiled and that made it hard to kiss her.

"Your room," I said.

"It is quite nice," said Marie. "And right next to Dad's."

She smiled again.

"Oh my, look at the time," she said.

"I suppose I'd better be getting back to my boat."

Marie stood up, told me to stay where I was, and went forward to her stateroom. She returned a minute later with a folded piece of notepaper. It smelled faintly of lavender.

"We're well into the twenty-first century," she said, "and I have a phone."

I put the notepaper in my shirt pocket.

"I'll see you on the dock in the morning," I said.

"That will be nice," said Marie.

"You wouldn't prefer that I stay here?" I asked.

"It isn't the time or place, I'm afraid."

I stepped up the companionway and into the cockpit. Marie called after me.

"Please call me if you can't make it tomorrow," she said. "Then I can be angry at you instead of worried."

I laughed and climbed down to my dinghy. The rain had stopped but the wind still blew in gusts from the northeast. *Figaro* rolled slightly at anchor, her masthead light winking at me with each delicate movement.

She wasn't much compared to *D'Artagnan*. Small, white, fiberglass, with aging systems and the barest of conveniences. But she was mine and in thousands of miles at sea, she had never let me down.

I tied the dinghy to a stern cleat, went below, and crawled into my berth. I remembered the note Marie had given me, got out of bed, and found it in my shirt pocket. I breathed in the smell of lavender as I opened it. A phone number was written in beautiful feminine handwriting with a heart-shaped happy face underneath the number. I tucked the note into the space under the hinged chart table and grabbed my phone.

"Hello?" she said.

"I just wanted to say good night," I said. "And to see if I still have a rain check on that swim."

She laughed lightly.

"Good night," she said.

32

TOO much hard liquor the night before reared its ugly head and I woke up with the squabbling of seabirds in my ears. A flying fish had miscalculated in the dark and had landed in the cockpit. Two shearwaters fought over the small carcass. They flew off when I climbed up the companionway. The toughest bird got the little fish. The other screamed of life's injustice.

The sun stung my eyes and the light breeze made my hair hurt. It was the not-so-gentle reminder of the old days when mornings with a bad head were the norm. I made a renewed resolve to stick with beer; the sailor's beverage that is never purchased but can only be rented.

The red blinking light on my cell phone indicated a received voicemail. It was from Al. Like most messages from him, it sounded like somebody reading a telegram.

"Sim. Got some info for you. Coming out tonight after dark. Put two white lights in your rigging."

I climbed out of the cabin into the early-morning sun, dug the mesh sack of snorkeling gear out of *Figaro*'s deep cockpit locker, and tossed it into the dinghy.

Marie and David were already on the dock when I got there. Marie wore a big white sunhat and a turquoise wrap-around skirt over her swimsuit. They looked into a box that hung in the water at the edge of the dock. Some of the largest lobsters I'd ever seen slowly climbed over each other trying to find a way out of their watery prison.

"Lunch?" I asked.

"Probably," said David.

He hired a taxi and we hurtled down Anegada's only paved road at an alarming pace toward Loblolly Bay. Most of the islands in the BVI are mountainous, volcanic creations reaching into the Caribbean skies. Anegada, however, is little more than ten miles of beach sand covered in coconut palms, sage, and loblolly. Its tallest point is thirty feet above sea level.

Loblolly Bay is a mile-long semicircle of fine sand that stretches into a pool of transparent, turquoise-tinted water. Ocean waves travel thousands of miles across the Atlantic to crash onto the barrier reef protecting the bay.

The locals have primitively developed it for tourists. They built a restaurant and bar out of concrete blocks and put up some palm frond umbrellas over a few rough wooden benches. A concrete walk connects the taxi area with the beach and the restaurant.

Only a few small groups of tourists were on the beach and the three of us didn't have to walk far to find a nice spot to ourselves. Marie's blue one-piece swimsuit was designed more for swimming than impressing guys on the beach. I was still impressed.

We entered the bay and snorkeled over sand banks, rock outcroppings, and groups of large brain coral. Sea fans stretched out under the glassy water. Triggerfish, puffer fish, and sergeant majors swam among the hard and soft corals while lobsters and moray eels hid among the rock outcroppings. A few conches shuffled across the sand flats.

I couldn't help but notice that Marie was as elegant in the water as on land. A hawksbill turtle popped up from a sand bank to catch its breath and Marie chased after it. She was a fine swimmer and was closing in on it when the hawksbill casually stroked its paddle-shaped front legs and glided away. Marie didn't have a chance.

"You're a pretty good swimmer," I said. "But you're not that good."

"I suppose you could have caught it?"

"Nope. She was born on the beach. I was born in a hospital."

"How do you know it's a she?" asked Marie.

"I don't think a 'he' would try very hard to get away from you."

She laughed, splashed some water at me, and swam away. After an hour or so of snorkeling, we walked to a nearby restaurant. The place was an open-air affair with a large post-and-beam roof to protect us from the hot tropical sun. A gentle breeze blew between the posts. The smiling waitress brought us our drinks, took our lunch orders, and disappeared into the kitchen. Marie excused herself to the ladies' room. David didn't waste any time with formalities.

"This might be extraordinarily premature of me but are you pursuing my daughter or is your interest in my family simply a part of your murder investigation?" he asked.

"I haven't told the police anything about your family, if that is what you are worried about. There hasn't been any reason to."

"You haven't answered my question," he said.

"David, I am going to find out who killed Derek Brownell and why. I don't think Lance killed him, but he knows something about it and I need him to tell me."

"Lance is just a kid," said David.

"Yeah, I know. He's an irresponsible party hound; a ship without a rudder. But he also knew the victim and he still hangs around with the victim's fellow crew members."

"Circumstance," said David.

"And then the three of you find the victim's passport the morning after the murder," I said.

"Coincidence," said David.

"Which does occasionally happen," I said. "But in my experience, a coincidence is a rare enough occurrence that it justifies professional skepticism."

David turned his head to look outside the restaurant at the transparent water over the reef.

"Okay, let's address the first part of my question. Is there something going on between you and my daughter?" he asked.

"I don't know," I said. "But if there is I'm not entirely against it." He smiled.

"I'm not sure I am, either," he said. He smiled again and took a sip of his drink. "I'll get Lance to talk to you."

Marie came back from the ladies' room and our waitress delivered our lunch. Each of us was served a large lobster sliced down the middle, cooked over an open pit grill, and bathed in butter. I was glad I'd skipped breakfast.

We walked back to the beach after lunch. David stretched out on one of the umbrella-shaded benches to take a nap, and Marie and I walked farther along the bay. Her hand felt good in mine. We sat together looking toward the clear water.

A young family walked past us and into the bay with their snorkeling gear. The father, about my age, patiently taught his young daughter how to breathe through the snorkel. The mother and son swam out to a nearby rock outcropping.

"Ever wish that were you?" asked Marie.

"What?"

"Do you ever wish you hadn't gotten divorced? That you'd stayed together and had a family?"

"Not often," I said.

I sensed some shared regrets.

"There are people who wish they were dolphins," I said, "only because dolphins look like they're always smiling. So they naturally think dolphins know the secret to happiness."

"And?" she said.

"How many people find it? How many know what it would look like if it landed in their laps?"

"The mass of men leading lives of quiet desperation?" she asked.

"Precisely," I said. "But happiness turns out to be a lot of hard work. 'Man is the artificer of his own happiness.'"

Marie cocked her head a little. "So, you're a Navy cop with a broken nose who sails the oceans alone and reads Thoreau?"

"An ex-Navy cop," I said. "And, yes, I can read. Surprised?"

"A little, I guess. I suppose I figured you were just tall and good-looking."

"And a great dancer," I said.

"And that."

We sat quietly and watched the young family pursue the same fish, turtles, and conches that we had chased while ocean waves crashed against the barrier reef a half mile away.

"What do you think about me?" she asked.

"I think you're beautiful and funny and smart and a pretty good sailor," I said.

"Pretty good?"

"I watched you bring a big boat into a crowded mooring field. You did a fine job, too. But I've never sailed with you."

"Yet," she said.

Marie snuggled under my arm and laid her head on my chest. I ran my hand slowly through her raven-dark hair and tried to breathe casually.

"You are a very nice man, Sim. Why couldn't I have met you ten years ago?"

"You might not have liked me ten years ago," I said.

"Maybe it's never too late to meet nice people," said Marie.

I sat quietly with nothing clever to say.

"Why don't you just run away from this place?" she said. "Forget about this murder and get away from the BVI. We could meet up in Anguilla or St. Maarten."

"Too many people think they can solve problems by running away from them," I said. "It doesn't work."

Marie sat up straight and looked into my eyes.

"But somebody tried to kill you and the police are on their side," she said. "Sometimes you've got to think of yourself."

"I am thinking of myself. Al is my friend and I help my friends. I wouldn't feel right about myself if I abandoned him."

"What are you?" she asked. "Some sort of knight in shining armor?"

"Well, the armor is a bit bent and tarnished," I said.

She sighed.

"I'm staying to help Al," I said.

"Have you ever wondered if you can be too loyal?"

"It is one of my many faults."

David woke up, walked over, and said we needed to get back so they could sail *D'Artagnan* through the channel and make it to their next anchorage before dark. We walked back to the taxi and rode the solitary track of concrete back to Setting Point. David got into their dinghy and started its engine. Marie turned to me and we kissed goodbye.

"Are you going to be around here long?" I asked.

"A week or so," she said. "Maybe less."

"I'll call. I promise."

We kissed again and she stepped down into the dinghy. I watched them motor back to the large wooden schooner.

I clambered down into my own dinghy and pointed it toward *Figaro.* I realized that I cared a great deal for Marie and wondered if it might be too much, too soon. I sat under the bimini to escape the sun and watched David and Marie prepare *D'Artagnan* for their afternoon sail. They cast off their mooring, motored through the channel, and hoisted sail. The fresh breeze filled the blood-red sails and carried the big schooner south toward Tortola. *Figaro* suddenly seemed small, empty, and old.

I picked up Jack London's *Cruise of the Snark* and read about his travails with a wooden boat a hundred years ago. By Jack's account it cost much more than he'd budgeted, never sailed properly, leaked constantly, and carried a balky engine that served mostly as additional ballast. But it took Jack and his wife across the Pacific to unspoiled islands and new cultures that they experienced together.

Figaro didn't leak, her systems were reliable, and she sailed beautifully. But I sailed alone.

My phone rang and buzzed on the chart table, disturbing my self-indulgent melancholy as the last rays of sunlight disappeared beyond the horizon.

I recognized the number.

33

"SPEAK to me, Frank."

"I wasn't so sure I'd find anything useful on Jimmy Cattrel," he said, "but I checked a few databases and made a few phone calls. He's a local tough guy; *the* local tough guy. He is rich, connected to some bad Venezuelan families, and meaner than a sack full of rattlesnakes. And not the least bit reluctant to kill."

"Great," I said.

"DEA wants his head on a stick. It seems that he was mentioned in some phone calls they were monitoring, so they sent an agent down to investigate. The agent flew in on a Tuesday morning two months ago and disappeared before lunch. They're sure Cattrel is responsible."

"But they thought I killed Edward Stevenson?" I asked.

"Yours was the last picture he sent them. They figured you were working for Cattrel. That assessment has changed."

"Why?"

"They received additional information from another local asset," he said. "They confirmed you were inside the store when Stevenson was shot in the parking lot. The consensus of opinion is that Cattrel ordered the hit and you happened to be there by coincidence."

"So DHS isn't looking for me anymore?"

"We've called off the big dogs, Sim."

"Do you have enough to arrest Cattrel?" I asked. "Can you get him extradited?"

"The guy is connected down there," he said. "Totally untouchable."

"So what do you think he wants with me?" I asked.

"Yeah, we're sorta wondering that ourselves. I'm guessing it's not a good thing."

I couldn't think of anything else to ask him.

"Can't you just order up a drone strike or something?" I asked.

Frank chuckled.

"Not in our *own* hemisphere," he said. "While tempting, it would be mighty hard to explain to the locals."

"You could blame it on an asteroid or something," I said.

"You might want to sail that little boat of yours someplace else," said Frank. "If that guy wants you dead, it'll wind up getting done."

"I don't think so."

"Your self-confidence, though admirable, might be horribly misplaced," he said. "Let me know if you need anything else, though. We are highly motivated to assist."

"Will do," I said.

"Good luck."

We hung up and I wondered why a big, mean, untouchable guy would be interested in me. My thoughts were interrupted by the sound of a high-powered speedboat approaching the island. The boat shut down its throttles and idled past the channel buoys with its navigation lights off. I watched as it approached the mooring field. Five minutes later it was tied up to *Figaro's* starboard rail.

"Very discreet, Al. I don't think anybody more than five miles away could have possibly heard you."

"Gimme a break. I borrowed it on short notice, and—" Al threw a grin a mile wide—"this thing is scary fast."

"And very efficient at converting fuel into noise."

"I'm thirsty," he said. "Let's go ashore."

"There's beer on the boat," I said.

"I may want something a little more potent," he said. "And I want it with dinner."

He hopped in my dinghy and started the outboard. I went below, found my cruising guide, and locked up *Figaro*. The dinghy laid a slow wake toward the dock and the restaurant beyond it.

"There aren't many locals who want to talk about Cattrel," he said.

"Frank Bartholomew came through," I said.

Al listened as I recounted what the ICE agent had told me.

"I found his office in Road Town," said Al. "I drove down there and parked outside to get a look at him. Big black guy. Really big. Probably got three inches and over a hundred pounds on you. Mid-sixties, I'd guess."

"Salt-and-pepper beard?" I asked.

Al stared at me.

"I saw him at Leverick Bay a couple of days ago. Big, old, and mean. Drives a blue Jeep."

"Maybe on Virgin Gorda," said Al. "On Tortola, he's got a dark blue Lincoln and a driver."

We finished our dinghy ride to the dock and tied up in the middle of a half dozen other inflatables. I noticed a lot of vacancies in the lobster box as I walked by.

The oil torches burned bright along the beach in front of Squatter's Restaurant. A lovely island woman in a purple and red batik skirt and a T-shirt the color of a robin's egg led us to a table on the sand and told us about the night's specials.

"We'll start with two beers, please," said Al.

A barefoot, middle-aged islander in shorts, a white linen shirt, and a San Francisco Giants ball cap came out of the kitchen and walked toward the cash register at the front of the restaurant. The room was dark but there was something familiar about the man. He finished his business at the cash register, turned, and walked toward us.

"Henry," I said.

He looked up at me when he heard his name, and he gave a wide, knowing smile.

"De sailor with de broken nose," he said. "Welcome to Anegada."

He reached a thin hand toward his shirt pocket.

"Another reading of de cards, mon?"

"No, thanks," I said. "In fact, if you pull out another one of those nasty cards I'd be tempted to feed it to you sideways."

Al looked amused. Henry lowered his hand, obviously disappointed.

"Mon, dere is nothing to hurt you in de cards," he said. "Tarot is only knowledge of de future."

"I think I'd rather not know," I said. "And I've had enough of your cards."

I opened up my cruising guide and fished out the extra Tarot card.

"Do you want this one back?" I asked.

"That is not from my deck, mon."

"You didn't leave this on my boat a couple of days ago?"

"No, mon. Why would Henry do that?" he asked.

"What does this card mean in your Tarot?" I asked.

"That depends," said Henry.

He picked up the card and examined it closely. Deep furrows stretched across his forehead.

"This card is de Hierophant. In this deck he is de pope; he is divine. Its meaning depends on how you received it. How was it presented to you?"

"I found it on my boat leaning up against the companionway," I said.

He held the card on the table so that it stood upright.

"Was it dis way or was it upside down?" he asked.

"That way."

The furrows eased.

"In the upright position, dis card symbolizes kindness and wisdom. It is a card of protection. Somebody wanted to protect you from something, I think."

"Can it mean something else?" I asked.

"Upside down or facing away from you, it means cowardice, hatred, no conscience. It's a very bad card that way."

He paused a moment and seemed to shrug off a nagging thought.

"But you did not receive it like that, mon. All is well. Enjoy your dinner."

Al sat back in his chair, cocked his head a fraction of an inch, and squinted at Henry as he walked back to the kitchen. The restaurateur and fortune teller came back a minute later with two icy cold Caribs.

"Martin?" said Al. "Tommy Martin?"

Henry stopped in his tracks about ten feet away.

"You mistaken, mon. Ah'm Henry."

"Henry, my ass," laughed Al. "You're Tommy Martin, Petty Officer Second Class, U.S. Navy. We were on the *Spruance* together in the Med."

Al paused a moment and lowered his voice.

"And we'd all heard you were dead," said Al.

Henry's eyes quickly darted left and right as he walked toward us and put down the two bottles. He licked his lower lip and rubbed his chin with his right hand.

"Dere must be a mistake, mon," said Henry. "But if you gentlemen can give me a minute, ah'll join you so's we can talk."

Henry turned around and walked to the kitchen.

"You want to tell me what's going on here?" I asked.

"I'm not really sure," said Al, "but I'd swear that guy is an old shipmate."

Henry returned a few minutes later with another beer and a bowl of peanuts. But he'd left his bright Caribbean accent in the back room and had picked up some low-voiced South Central L.A. on the way out.

"Mah man, Al. Good to see you after all these years," he said. "But don't be callin' me Tommy 'round here, okay? That dude disappeared ages ago."

The Caribbean lilt returned.

"Ah'm Henry now," he said.

"Well, Henry, this is Sim Greene. He's also ex-Navy and a he's good friend of mine. And what do you mean by 'disappeared'? A guy doesn't just disappear these days."

Henry shrugged.

"Before I got a chance to leave the Navy," Henry explained, "my wife left me. And she left me with nothin' but an order to pay alimony. She garnished my paychecks to the point it hardly made any sense to stick around."

He paused to drink a little of his beer.

"So the next time I got leave, I went back to L.A. to see my folks. I stayed a couple of days with them, packed a few things, and drove south into the *Estados Unidos Mexicanos*, brother."

"I didn't know you could speak Spanish."

"I couldn't. Hell, I thought *quesadilla* meant 'What's the deal?'"

Al laughed.

"But I hit the border and just kept on going. Mexicali, Rocky Point, Guaymas, Mazatlan, Acapulco. Somebody stole the car in Acapulco so I hopped on a bus. I lost my passport in Mexico City."

He shrugged his shoulders again.

"Henry got himself a new one," he said.

He drained the bottle with a long, slow drink. He waved his hand at one of the ladies who waited the tables and held up three fingers. I sat quietly.

"So how many pesos does it take to get a new Mexican passport?" asked Al.

"Surprisingly few, my man." Henry kicked his feet up on a nearby chair and leaned back. "Surprisingly few."

The waitress brought us fresh bottles and took away the empties.

"After that, I headed east to find a job on the beach. A boat in Yucatan needed crew. I hopped boats to Cayman, Jamaica, Cuba, Haiti, and finally landed here in the BVI. Been here ten years, mon. I got this little restaurant and another over in White Bay runnin' fine and makin' me a little cash money. Even do a little magic here and there for the tourists."

"Okay," I said. "Try and do a little magic for me right now. Ever hear of a guy named Jimmy Cattrel?"

Henry swallowed involuntarily and his eyes went wide. His voice dropped at least three clicks of volume.

"Keep your voice down, mon. Cattrel's got ears and he's got 'em everywhere," said Henry. "It ain't healthy to talk about the man."

"Who is he and what's his game?" asked Al.

"He used to be a cop. Toughest cop in the islands. Born here and raised by a fine woman who never had nothin'. Now he's got money. Loads of it. And he lives high."

"How did he make all this money?" asked Al.

"Nobody knows for sure, man. But everybody knows better than to ask. Word around the islands is that three big, tough white guys came down here a couple years ago from Philly and started askin' lots of questions about him and his business. They got on the ferry to Virgin Gorda to pay him a visit. They never got off. That's all I know, man."

"Why would he give a gun to a bad little boy and tell him to board my boat?" I asked. "To kill me?"

Henry turned to me.

"Man, if Cattrel wanted you dead, then you wouldn't be here talkin' to me and drinkin' my beer," he said.

Rain pattered on the tin roof. A group of tourists, loud and wet, walked into the restaurant antsy for their lobster dinners. Lightning flashed through the coconut palms to the north.

Henry got up to leave.

"I can't talk about the man no more," he said. "Just talking about him scares me white. You want dinner? Lobster and rice is on the house, mon. But I never talked to you about nobody."

"Thanks," said Al. "Thanks for the info."

"What you talkin' 'bout, man? I ain't never even seen you."

Henry went back into the kitchen.

Lobster is delicious even if you eat it twice a day. Mine should have been marvelous, but my appetite had been compromised. Al and I ate in silence. We didn't get a bill but Al left a big tip for the lady in the purple and red skirt before we walked back to the small dock.

We motored slowly back to *Figaro*, pulled the dinghy onto her foredeck, and buttoned her up. She would be at anchor on her own for a few days. We hopped into the speedboat and gurgled out of the anchorage, past the red and green buoys, and into the open channel.

Once in the channel, Al opened up the big twin inboard engines and the boat punched a fast, noisy hole through the night toward Road Town. It had taken me the better part of a day to sail from Tortola to Anegada. The return trip took barely a half hour.

We tied up the boat at Fort Burt and Al drove east through Road Town and up a winding road to his house overlooking Josiah's Bay. There we began working on a plan to find out more about Jimmy Cattrel.

34

FINDING out where Cattrel lived didn't take long because Frank Bartholomew had emailed me the guy's address on Virgin Gorda. Having accomplished so much that night, we slept in the next morning. There was no reason not to; we had all day to drive into town and pick up the few things I would need that evening.

The chandlery sold me a small waterproof duffel, a tiny handheld VHF radio, and a pair of cheap miniature binoculars. A thrift store supplied the clothing and a nearly worn-out rucksack, Bobbie's sold me a tube of black mascara at an outrageous price, and a real estate agent gave us a very detailed street map of Virgin Gorda. I already had a .45 with an extra loaded magazine.

The hardest part was waiting for the sun to go down.

We left Road Town about a half hour after sunset. The speedboat didn't have a stealth mode so we blasted along toward Virgin Gorda Sound with both engines in full voice. I readied my gear and opened the mascara. I threw away the brush, squeezed the tube, and smeared some of the black makeup onto my face. It wasn't military-grade camouflage by a long shot, but it broke up the outline of my face and reduced my chances of being spotted in the dark.

The narrow channel into the Sound past Anguilla Point is a shallow entrance used mostly by the locals and always used at slow speed. It is rarely used at night. The waning moon had not yet risen and there were no lights on either of the beaches that front the channel. Al slowed the boat down to a crawl as we approached the entrance and we coasted carefully across black water under an ink-dark sky.

"You sure you don't need me?" asked Al.

"Extraction only."

"I'd rather be on the ground," he said.

"Sorry."

Al clicked off the navigation lights.

"I'll drop the hook at Gun Creek," he said.

"Sounds good. If you don't hear from me before zero-five hundred, then you need to bug out."

"I'll be waiting," said Al.

"That's the hard part, isn't it?" I said.

"Ain't that the truth?"

I slipped over the side with the waterproof duffel and side-stroked toward the shore. Al continued through the channel into the Sound at a sedate pace. The speedboat's navigation lights clicked on as it entered the Sound.

The little cove on the north shore of Virgin Gorda west of the point was a short swim from where Al had dropped me off. I walked up the small beach and into the trees where I opened the duffel and changed out of my swim trunks into the old jeans, black long-sleeved T-shirt, navy blue beanie, and worn tennis shoes I'd bought at the thrift store. I put the pistol in my pocket, shouldered the rucksack, and started hiking up the hill to the paved road.

I climbed up the steep hill with the brush and the trees fighting me all the way. Being quiet takes time, so it took me over an hour to reach the road.

Twigs cracked to my right as I approached the road, and I quickly pulled the pistol, dropped to one knee, and held my breath. Something moved in the tangle of bushes ahead of me and jumped through the brush. An island goat and her kid clip-clapped across the asphalt. I let out my breath, put the gun back in my pocket, and got out the map.

Cattrel's home sat on the Atlantic side of another hill about a mile and a half farther east. The road would get me about two-thirds of the way there, so I broke into a comfortable jog and followed the asphalt ribbon as it wound through the trees and bushes.

The glare of headlights peered around a corner up ahead, and I ducked off the road behind a thick stand of trees. A small car sped past followed by two teenage kids on a loud scooter. Darkness returned and I stepped back onto the road.

Ten minutes later I left the paved road and followed a narrow dirt track that led to a water tank. The last quarter mile of my approach was slow going through the thick brush and trees west of where I had figured Cattrel's house should be.

It was nearly nine o'clock when I finally wedged myself under the low branches of a short tree on a knoll above the first small group of homes. I watched the moon rise out of the Atlantic and gradually illuminate the Caribbean. I pulled the small binoculars out of the rucksack and scanned the houses below me.

The four homes down the hill were first-class villas sharing a long road that circled among them. They had been built with a lot of space between them with a few stands of indigenous trees shielding each house from its neighbors. Each home overlooked the Sound to the northeast, the Atlantic Ocean to the southeast, and a string of older houses that stretched down toward a beach.

The two houses to my right were dark and appeared to be empty, but the other two were lit and occupied. The dark form of a long Jeep slept quietly under a dimly lit carport next to the third villa.

The lights were on in Cattrel's house, so there was nothing to do but wait and hope I'd get a chance to carry out the plan. It wasn't a complicated plan. Simple burglary. And I could wait until four in the morning if I had to.

I got comfortable and glassed the area There were no guards, no tall fences, no big dogs, nothing out of the ordinary. He was either D.C. Millet's squeaky clean businessman, pure as the pow-dered white sand in front of the yacht club, or he was the DEA's evil but overconfident bad guy.

Either way, it was a beautiful spot for an upscale home. The lights and tiki torches of the Bitter End Yacht Club were dim pin-pricks from nearly three miles away. A small cruise ship anchored off Vixen Point did its best to illuminate its portion of the Sound. The red and white navigation lights of a freighter several miles out in the Atlantic indicated its northerly course.

Not a bad view for a retired cop.

The lights began to go out one at a time at a quarter past ten. A tall woman with long blonde hair and fine features exited the door near the carport and walked toward the Jeep. She was well dressed for a late Friday night on the town. I guessed that she was close to my age; maybe a few years younger. The big man himself followed her out, helped her into the passenger side of the Jeep, and got in the driver's side. A moment later, the car backed down the drive-way and turned onto the road to Spanish Town.

I used every bush, tree, and rock I could find for cover as I passed through the last hundred yards to Cattrel's house. I pulled a new headlamp that I'd equipped with red bulbs from the rucksack and put on a pair of old, worn cotton gloves. A brief examination revealed that there was no alarm system.

The door adjacent to the carport was securely locked, but a kitchen window around the side opened with mild, if firm, en-couragement. I swung my legs over the windowsill, clicked on my red-bulbed headlamp, and started my tour of Cattrel's home.

It was a beautiful home decorated with modern furniture and expensive artwork. The air conditioning droned on in earnest and I involuntarily shivered from the artificial cold.

I'd searched a lot of buildings a lot of times while on the Navy's dime. Houses, sheds, garages, offices. There is a procedure, and once you learn it, it becomes second nature. Like riding a bicycle.

Cattrel's home was nice but fairly standard in layout. What could have been intended for an extra bedroom appeared to be Cattrel's home office. Unlike the rest of the home, it was sparse and entirely businesslike. It seemed to be the best place to start. There was a two-drawer filing cabinet, a small desk supporting a laptop computer docked to a large monitor, and a bookcase with a large selection of uninteresting titles on investment management and real estate.

I turned on the laptop. It was password protected. No surprise there. The filing cabinet was unlocked and a brief review of the files inside it revealed no obvious skullduggery. The man appeared to be a wealthy retiree with a simple real estate portfolio and a variety of other safe investments.

I began to think that maybe Cattrel *was* just a wealthy retired cop with a short temper and a bad reputation. Maybe Ronnie had lied about him to keep from drowning. Perhaps Henry had only heard a few trumped-up rumors or had been putting us on for giggles. Maybe the DEA and the other feds had him all wrong and I was on a wild goose chase.

But when I manipulated the catch mechanisms behind each file drawer and pulled the drawers out of the filing cabinet, I found a ledger book and a small computer thumb drive sitting on the carpet. Clever.

I examined the ledger. It was unreadable. Entries made in block letters accompanied columns of numbers, but the words appeared to be in a code. I shoved the ledger and the thumb drive into the rucksack.

The moon rose farther above the Atlantic and cast a pale light through the windows of the home. It took a few minutes to put everything back in its place and to remove all evidence of my visit. That done, I walked back to the kitchen for my exit. I heard the sound of a key entering the lock to the side door as I walked into the room. I clicked off the headlamp, laid the rucksack on the floor, and crouched low behind a kitchen cabinet.

The side door opened and a gray hand reached into the room to turn on the kitchen lights. I grabbed the wrist with my left hand and pulled hard as I swung with my right fist toward where the face would be.

I connected hard with the first punch and threw two follow-up hits. The wrist and arm went limp and the figure fell to the floor. I pulled the .45 in a reflexive movement, but the thin man lay on his back unconscious.

Moonlight streamed through a window and fell across Ronnie's face. I thought about Levon's disappearance and his worried family and considered some unpleasant options for the redhead. After a few moments of personal reflection, I put the pistol back in my pocket, pulled out my knife, and cut the sash cords from the kitchen blinds. I used them to tie up the little creep. It wasn't turning out to be his week.

Confident that he was in no position to either follow me or cause me any trouble, I slipped out the side door and into the night. The hike back to Anguilla Point was uneventful. There were no cars on the road, no mother goats, and no reasons to pull the pistol from my pocket. Just the steady drone of the high-pitched, insect-like mating calls of the island frogs punctuated by the occasional shriek of a night bird. I wondered if the birds made that noise out of fear, to talk with other night birds, or while feeding on island frogs. I didn't hear the surf until I was nearly back to the little cove where I'd left the duffel.

I peeled off the dark clothes and put on my swim trunks. Looking at the moon, I put the long-sleeved T-shirt back on, grabbed the little handheld VHF radio, and tuned it to the prearranged channel. I looked at my watch. Almost two in the morning.

"Hey, Pete. You still awake over there at the *Flying Low?*"

There was a short pause before Al's voice came back.

"Is that you, Phil?" asked Al. "The party's just getting started, man. Come on over."

"Okay, buddy. See you in about fifteen minutes."

"See you then," said Al.

I clicked off the radio, tossed it into the duffel, and secured the waterproof flap. I peeked out from the trees to see if there was anybody or anything around. There wasn't.

I carried the duffel across the sand and waded into the waves. The water was warm and I kicked toward the center of the channel while pushing the duffel ahead of me. When I got to a good waiting spot, I tucked the buoyant duffel between my legs and rode it to keep my head above the water.

Green and red navigation lights entered the channel a few minutes later. The boat was several hundred yards from me when the lights flashed off and on for two long flashes and then two shorts. I responded with three flashes from my red headlamp.

Al maneuvered the boat toward me and his thick, bear-like arms reached out and grabbed the duffel. I pulled myself into the speedboat's cockpit.

The trip to Anegada took barely twenty minutes. While en route, I shoved the clothes I'd worn to Cartrel's house into a rock-weighted onion sack, wrapped it all up securely with duct tape, and tossed the whole mess into ninety feet of water. No point in leaving any evidence.

The big speedboat lumbered into the harbor and pulled up next to *Figaro* a little before three in the morning. I hopped onto my boat with the rest of my gear, and Al idled back out of the harbor. Once past the entrance buoys, he gave the powerful twin engines full throttle and turned due south for the big island. The roar of the speedboat permeated the air for several minutes until it finally faded away into the darkness of the Sir Francis Drake Channel.

I went below, turned on the cabin lights, and opened the stolen ledger.

35

I read through the rows and columns of block letters and tried to find some meaning in Cattrel's entries, but I couldn't figure out the code. I fell asleep on *Figaro*'s port settee and didn't wake until after noon.

The ledger made no more sense in the sunlight than it had in the wee hours of the morning and Cattrel's thumb drive was password protected. It seemed as if the adventure had gained me nothing more than lost sleep and sore knuckles.

I'm no good at breaking codes and I can't crack passwords. But I knew someone who had spent a lot of time on Uncle Sam's dime doing both. I grabbed my cell phone.

"Al, you got any idea where Jack Penn is these days?"

"The Cracker?" he asked. "I haven't kept up with him. Last I heard he transferred to Naples, Italy, but that was eight years ago."

"You got any plans today?" I asked.

"Lars wants me to help him with a deepwater salvage project tomorrow so I'm going over later to help plan the job. I also thought I might sleep off last night's party"

Some party.

"Do what you can to find Penn for me, okay?" I asked.

"I can try," Al said. "What for?"

"I'm bringing in *Figaro* this afternoon. I'll tell you all about it when I see you."

I got off the phone, weighed anchor, and piloted *Figaro* out of the anchorage. The northeast trade winds were strong and *Figaro* fairly flew on a broad reach. Al met me at the Ft. Burt marina.

"Jack's still with Naval Intel," he said. "He works out of the Mayport office in Jacksonville. You gonna call him?"

"He's that close? Maybe I'll visit him. But I need to make some copies first."

Al drove us to a copy shop that was locking up for the night. A ten kept them open long enough to make three copies of Cattrel's ledger.

When we got back to Al's house in the hills, I used his computer to see if I could get a flight to Jacksonville. The only option was an early-morning flight with two stops and layovers in Puerto Rico and Miami, but where there are no alternatives, there are no real problems. I bought the round-trip ticket.

While I wrangled airline schedules, Al wrestled with some frying pans and produced something a guy might call dinner. We ate it on the patio deck that overlooked Josiah's Bay, a crescent of white sand a half mile away.

Torches on the beach below flickered like fireflies in the dark. A slight breeze, barely strong enough to keep the evening bugs at bay, came in from the north and brought the smell of rain. Forty miles away, shafts of lightning punched at the inky darkness of the horizon.

I showed Al the ledger and handed him the thumb drive.

"You think the Cracker can get into this thing?" Al asked.

"You know he hates being called that," I said.

"He's not listening," he said. "At least I hope not."

We laughed knowing that if anyone could tap into a private conversation from thousands of miles away, it would be Jack Penn.

"Even if he cracks that code and that computer thingy, Sim, what are you gonna do with it?" asked Al. "Turn this Cattrel guy in? Big deal. The guy is connected. Probably makes direct deposits to the RVIP officer's fund. And how is this gonna keep my neck out of the noose?"

"We need to find out who killed Somerset," I said. "If Cattrel did it, case solved. If he didn't do it, then he might help us find out who did. This could be leverage. Motivation."

The breeze died down and the creatures of the night came to life. Insects pursued us in earnest and we retreated indoors.

Al stayed up to watch the news on television and to wait for Liv to get home from work. I was still tired from the prior evening's outing and ambled down the hall to the bedroom Al had assigned me.

Through the large window looking north I saw the lightning strikes of rain squalls battling for territory beyond the horizon. Nature in all its fury. I stretched out on the bed and thought of Marie for the half second it took to fall asleep.

36

THE ticket agent led us out the door and onto the tarmac toward a small twin-engine plane that probably took its maiden flight during the Nixon administration. Javier introduced himself as the pilot. There was no copilot, and every seat was a window seat. Piston engines howled as we climbed off the runway and clawed our way to cruising altitude.

Minutes later, Puerto Rico appeared as a green hump surrounded by a blue sea. Details materialized as we approached the big island. The green trees reluctantly gave up space for ugly boxes that housed a growing population. Some of the boxes were nice. Close to the beach. Surrounded by golf courses with freshwater pools nearby and docks for yachts. But they were still boxes.

The boxes grew uglier and closer together as the plane approached the airport at San Juan. During the last half minute before touchdown, all I could see beneath us were three-story rectangles surrounded by hot asphalt parking lots and clotheslines.

I had to change planes again in Miami, and the layover there was long enough for a late lunch and a phone call to Jack Penn.

He must have been promoted a couple of times since I'd worked with him last, because his office phone was now two receptionists deep and they even answered on the weekends. The last of his gate-keepers needed my full name, spelled slowly, before I could be transferred to Jack's cell phone.

"Sim Greene?" asked the familiar high-pitched voice. "The same Sim Greene that I drove home so many times because he could barely walk from the bar to the car?"

"Yep," I said. "The same one who helped you out of that little situation involving that girl who…."

"Let's not get into that bad little memory on this particular phone, shall we?" he said.

He paused a moment.

"So why are you calling my office number on a Sunday afternoon?"

"I'm on my way to Jacksonville right now," I said, "and I'd very much like to see you. My flight gets in a little before eight. Can you pick me up at the airport?"

"You sound like somebody who wants something."

"You want to talk about it now?" I asked. "On this phone?"

"Probably not," he said. "Has this anything to do with Al Higgins? I hear he's been calling all over the planet trying to find me."

"Uh-huh. I'll tell you more about it tonight."

He was quiet.

"Jack, I am asking for the absolute smallest of favors," I said.

"You have no idea how many times I have heard that from guys like you." He paused a moment as if he were weighing alternatives. "I'll be in a brown Crown Vic."

There was still an hour to kill before boarding my flight to JAX. The newsstand and magazine racks offered the usual drivel from a cultural wasteland. The tourist shops offered more of the same in the form of shot glasses, T-shirts, coffee mugs, and snow globes. I asked the lady behind the counter if they had a "Cuba Si! Castro NO!" T-shirt, but she wasn't amused. They probably wouldn't have had my size anyway.

The flight to Jacksonville was uneventful. A quiet, smooth ride in an airborne cattle car. Outside the terminal, a brown Ford Crown Victoria screamed "unmarked cop" to interested bystanders.

"Did you get promoted or something?" I asked. "This looks like a company car."

"You know I'm not a field officer," he said. "I picked this up at a government surplus auction."

Jack hadn't aged much in the eight years since I'd last seen him. A nearly-bald, short guy with half-glasses that sat on a face full of hard planes and sharp angles. I tossed my small duffel in the back and hopped in the passenger seat.

"Can I buy you dinner?" I asked.

"I already ate."

He said it in a perfunctory way that sounded like he wished I would stop bothering him.

"You been working hard, Jack?" I asked.

"Not on anything I can talk about with a civilian," he said.

Civilian. He spoke the word with no small amount of disdain.

"So are you going to tell me why you left the Navy?" he asked.

"You're Intel. You tell me?"

"I heard you killed at least two people," he said. "Maybe as many as six. Some seem to think it was all done in self-defense—the preferred supposition among your superiors, by the way—but others aren't so sure. In any case, your CO let you go with full retirement and you buzzed out of Oxnard before anyone who cared much about the details could ask. I also heard you destroyed evidence."

"Wow, I should be in jail," I said.

"But you're not."

"And how does Intel explain that?"

"Word is there were no witnesses, that the world was measurably improved by said killings, and that the local cops more or less approved of the end result." He turned off Highway 95 toward the Dames Point Bridge. "A clever man such as myself might also think you were holding something over your CO's head."

"Where do you guys come up with this stuff?" I asked.

Jack looked over and smiled.

"It's a gift," he said.

Jack drove past a phalanx of the usual fast-food places and strip malls that line the roads leading to Naval bases and pulled into an immense parking lot. The lot surrounded a large complex of two-story brick apartment buildings that might have been built during the Eisenhower administration. Jack's apartment was a short walk up metal stairs to the top floor. He clicked on the lights, showed me to a comfortable chair, and retrieved two cold beers from the kitchen.

"Is this how Naval Intelligence now interrogates us non-military combatants?" I asked.

"We've used other methods."

The barest smile graced his lips.

"Gitmo?"

"Yeah," he said. "I was there in the early days when we were getting some useful information from those guys." He paused to drink his beer. "The data quality dropped after a couple of years and I was transferred here to work on more pressing projects."

"Don't tell me about it, Jack."

"Couldn't if I wanted to." He thought for a half minute. "So why did you leave?"

"Let's just say it was a mutual conclusion drawn by my CO and me."

Jack shrugged. "Fair enough," he said.

He thought hard about what to say next.

"I'm going to be straight with you, Sim. I'm not jazzed about guys who ditch the Navy the way you did and I don't like Al Higgins at all. I never have. His methods were always crude and, in my opinion, illegal. I was glad to see him get out when he did."

"Purple Heart, Silver Star," I said. "And a brace of others they couldn't give him because the missions weren't on the books."

"Okay, he deserves respect for that," he said. "The point is, I don't like whatever it is that I feel I'm getting dragged into right now. But I owe you, Sim. And I repay my debts."

"Thanks," I said.

"So why are you sitting here and drinking my beer?"

"Do you still crack codes these days?" I asked.

His eyes opened wide. "What the hell are you into, Sim?"

I told him about Al, the RVIP, Bradley Somerset, my uninvited midnight guest, Edward Stevenson, and Jimmy Catrell. I pulled the flash drive and a copy of the ledger from my duffel and handed it to him.

"Have you got the original?" he asked.

"Sure," I said.

I handed him the ledger I'd pulled out from under Cattrel's filing cabinet. Jack left the room and returned wearing a pair of latex surgeon's gloves. He examined the ledger slowly; turning the pages as though each were as fragile as onion skin. He looked at each page from several different angles. He held them up to the light and examined them with a jeweler's loupe. He finally closed the book and laid it on his coffee table.

"No hidden watermarks, nothing fancy," he said. "I can work from a copy."

"Good," I said. "The rightful owner probably wants his original back anyway. They tell me he's prone to violence."

Jack rolled his eyes. "Don't talk to me about 'rightful owners,'" he said. "I'll let you keep track of those little details."

He picked up his copy and examined it. He made notes on a yellow legal pad.

"I'm also going to call you once in a while to check in," I said. "It'll be every day at first."

Jack stared at me. His mouth opened slightly.

"You're in that deep?"

"If you don't hear from me for a couple of days…"

"I got it, Sim. If it comes to that," he said, "I know exactly whom to give this to."

I looked around at Jack's apartment. There wasn't much furniture. It was definitely a single man's digs. One wall supported a few aged photographs. Jack Penn graduating from college three decades ago. Jack Penn in dress whites receiving an award from an admiral. Jack Penn in a small boat on a river fishing with a nephew.

Other walls featured some stock posters of San Francisco, a Mediterranean village perched on rocks above an impossibly blue sea, the Eiffel Tower at night, and, oddly, a gray storm developing over the Royal Observatory at Greenwich, England. The view out the window was dominated by another apartment building in the same complex. There wasn't the slightest indication of female influence.

I leaned back in the chair and kicked my feet up onto a coffee table that looked like it had been made out of a hatch from an old sailing ship.

"So you think you can crack it?" I asked.

"It looks like a fairly simple code," he said. "It probably won't take me more than a couple of hours. The flash drive could take longer, though, especially if I have to physically open it."

"There's one more thing," I said.

"What's that?"

"Remember a guy named Terrence Wells from ten years ago or so?" I asked.

"The software guy? He's a billionaire, right?"

"Seems pretty well off," I said. "He's got a big yellow yacht down in the Virgin Islands."

"That's the guy," said Jack. "He sold his company for something close to a billion dollars right before the last big crash. Must have made a killing back then."

"Figuratively speaking?" I asked.

"Of course," said Jack.

"There's also a kid in his mid-twenties named Lance Tanner. His dad is David Tanner, some big-time Wall Street lawyer. Lance seems to be a high-class bum."

"That's three things," said Jack. "Not one."

"A mere technicality," I said. "I want to find out if any of the three-letter agencies you deal with have any of these guys on their smoky little radar screens. It would be great to know why, too."

"Of course," he said. "Just think of me as your own private research librarian in the spook business."

"I owe you, man."

He turned his attention back to the ledger.

"You prepaid years ago," he mumbled.

37

JACK didn't have a spare bedroom, so I slept on the couch. He left for the office before I woke so I called a cab for a ride to the airport. Breakfast was a fried egg forcibly introduced to a stale bagel.

Like the trip to Jacksonville, the return to Tortola was broken into three legs and two layovers. But the layovers were mercifully short. At least, they were supposed to be.

A TSA Agent stood at the top of the ramp visually scanning the passengers as we walked off the jetway in San Juan. Her eyes fixed on me the same way a Brittany spaniel's will lock on to a hiding pheasant. I looked around for some hunters but didn't see any.

"Will you come with me, Mr. Greene? There seems to be some difficulty with your luggage."

I looked down at my duffel and didn't see any problems with it. I had no other luggage. I thought of simply walking away from her but reflected on the enforcement power of the TSA and the consequences of noncompliance. At a bare minimum, I'd miss my flight if I challenged her authority and upset her. I shrugged and followed.

She walked with me down toward the baggage claim and stopped at an unlabeled door. She swiped a card key past a reader on the wall, opened the door, and led me down a brightly lit hallway. Another pass of the card key unlocked another door that opened into a small interview room with a table and three steel chairs.

"Please sit down, Mr. Greene. If you will please give me your claim check, I will collect your bags and bring them to you."

"I didn't check any bags," I said.

She was not the least bit surprised.

"Oh," she said. "There must be some mistake, then. Please wait here while I look into it."

She left me in the room, and I heard the door lock behind her. The room was clean and spare. No windows or two-way mirrors. Two fluorescent fixtures recessed in the ceiling. A locked steel door. I was being detained for somebody higher up the food chain.

Two fit guys walked in about ten minutes later. They both wore dark suits, white shirts, conservative ties, and sensible business shoes. The kind of shoes a guy could run somebody down in if they had to. One of the men was about my age and the other was maybe ten years older. I was certain I could handle the guy my age; not so sure about the older fellow. He had that look. The Special Forces look.

The younger one carried a small blue gym bag. They weren't TSA and they wore no visible badges but they were definitely federal. Their demeanor implied unbridled power.

"How are you, Mr. Greene?" asked the older one.

He extended his hand. I did not.

"A bit annoyed at the moment," I said.

The older one, the spokesperson, took the chair directly across the table from me. The younger one sat to his right.

"We apologize for the inconvenience," said the spokesperson.

"Don't apologize for what you meant to do," I said. "Why am I here?"

"We'd like to know who you were visiting in Jacksonville."

"Who said I was visiting anyone?" I asked. "And who wants to know?"

The older one nodded and paused for a moment as if he were testing the words he wanted to speak. He reached into his pocket, pulled out a wallet-size picture, and handed it to me.

"We understand that you were one of the last people to see this man alive," he said.

I looked at the picture and nodded.

"I saw him pull into a parking lot as I walked into a supermarket in Tortola. Forty minutes later, I walked outside to find some local cops plowing around the crime scene like draft horses."

They had a lot of questions about the murder outside Bobby's and I answered every one truthfully. There was no reason to hold anything back. The younger one took a lot of notes. The older one seemed satisfied with my answers.

"We understand you've been asking some of our colleagues about Jimmy Cattrel," he said. "We'd like to know why."

"He sent somebody with a gun out to my boat several nights ago," I said. "I thought it might be prudent to inquire about the fellow. So I asked a friend to ask a friend."

He smiled as if he'd already spoken to Frank.

"Do you think Mr. Cattrel was trying to kill you?"

I shrugged.

"If so, he failed," I said.

"What do you know about him?" asked the younger one.

"I hear he's a bad fellow."

They both nodded. The older fellow reached out for the picture and I handed it back to him. He put it in his shirt pocket and thought for a moment as if choosing his words with chopsticks.

"We understand that you killed two people in California, Mr. Greene."

Technically, I'd killed four, but I didn't feel the need to correct them.

"Am I under arrest?" I asked. "If so, then read me my rights, cuff me up, haul me off, and get me a lawyer. If not, then I've got a plane to catch to Beef Island."

"You're not under arrest," said the older one. "And we only want a few more minutes of your time. You see, we want you to catch that plane."

"Do either of you guys have any identification?" I asked.

The younger one smiled.

"Who do you think we are?" asked the older one.

"Mormon missionaries?" I asked.

The younger one put his gym bag on the table and unzipped it. He pulled out a medium-sized rectangular box and lifted the lid. Inside was a Beretta M9 with a threaded barrel, a silencer, and two fifty-round boxes of nine-millimeter ammunition; probably subsonic. The kind that works well with a silencer.

"Do Mormon missionaries carry these?" he asked.

"Probably not," I said.

The younger one closed the box and pushed it across the table toward me.

"We'd like you to take this, Mr. Greene. And we'd like you to use it on Jimmy Cattrel."

I thought about it for a moment.

"And I'll just walk past BVI Customs this afternoon with that in my duffel?" I said.

"There is a very tall customs officer on duty all day," said the older one. "Probably got an inch or more on you. He is balding and will have two stripes on his shoulder boards. You'll want to get in his line at the airport. He will be watching for you and he won't look very deep into your bag, Mr. Greene."

"Who the hell do you guys think you are, British Intelligence or something? You think I have two confirmed kills and so now I qualify to be one of your 'Double-0' agents? Sod off."

"We are American, Mr. Greene," said the older one. "And we thought that your interests and ours might be advanced with a measure of mutual assistance. You have demonstrated the ability to kill and, presumably, the motivation to stay alive. We'd like to supply the means to assist you in doing both."

I thought about the offer and the debt I would incur by accepting it.

"I don't want a license to kill and I don't need your gun," I said. "I need to make my flight."

They stood and I walked to the door. As I stepped out, the older one turned and handed me a card.

"My name is Spencer," he said. "Please call me if you change your mind."

It was a white card with blue lettering. It had the same look and feel of every other business card I'd seen from a federal agency. But there was no seal, no three-letter agency's acronym, and no address. Only a first name and a telephone number with a 202 area code. Washington, D.C.

Curious.

38

THE plane from San Juan to the BVI jumped and fell in the unstable late-afternoon air and the pilot had to dodge a few squalls along the way. We landed just before sundown.

I passed through Customs and Immigration without a hitch. The tall, balding agent seemed to recognize me and processed my paperwork quickly. He was polite and kind and had almost nothing to say as he stamped my passport and ignored my duffel. I wondered if he had the slightest idea of what I wasn't carrying.

I grabbed my bag, walked out past the tourism agent and the rental car office, and found Al waiting in his little blue Isuzu.

"How's Jack?" he asked.

"He doesn't like you."

Al laughed loud and long. "I guess he wouldn't, would he?" asked Al.

Al drove across the small bridge that links the island to Tortola. He was still laughing.

"That little guy sure can carry a grudge, eh?" he said.

"And he might give us what we need to get you off the hook, Al."

Al thought for a minute.

"Then I should probably get around to apologizing to him, shouldn't I?" he said.

"Couldn't hurt," I said.

Al raced the little car into Road Town and over to Fort Burt Marina as the sun set. He was late to meet Liv for dinner—I was not invited—so he dropped me off at the marina entrance in the darkness.

I grabbed my duffel and walked down the palm-lined driveway toward *Figaro*. One of the local scrap cats jumped out of the cockpit as I walked down the short dock to my boat. The wind shifted to the north and the breeze drifted across the cockpit. The smell hit me all at once. It is something that cannot be forgotten no matter how hard you try and I immediately knew what the cat had been investigating. I pulled a small flashlight from the boat's pilot locker.

Somebody had tossed an old tarp into *Figaro*'s cockpit. Under the tarp, they had carelessly left a skinny young man with long red hair. Even though this wasn't my first time, I still had to force back the gag reflex. The Caribbean heat is not kind to the dead.

Ronnie lay with his left cheek against the floor of the cockpit. His stringy red hair was matted in blood over his right temple, barely obscuring a small entrance wound. I didn't want to see the exit wound, so I replaced the tarp, walked to the air-conditioned marina office, got a cold Coke out of the vending machine, and called the RVIP.

Two officers and their squad car showed up in a screech of gravel minutes later as if dinner up the street had been disrupted by the call. I hadn't even finished my Coke. I pointed my boat out to them and went back inside to sit down and finish my Coke. Another squad car showed up about five minutes later and one of the officers, a young one, walked into the office. He was there to make sure I didn't kill anybody else. He must have felt the need to be useful, so he pulled out a small notebook and asked the usual questions. Name, address, phone number, and, of course, why I'd killed the victim.

"I didn't," I said. "But if you don't mind, I'll save the rest of my answers for Constable Millet. I am tired and bore easily with the sound of my own voice."

I stood up to get another Coke. The young officer tensed, ready to respond to a threatening move.

"You'd do well to cooperate with us, sir, and answer my questions now," he said.

I laughed as I remembered having said that myself to a witness when I was much younger.

"You're right, officer. It's time to come clean."

I took my Coke back to the couch under the air conditioner and sat down.

"I killed that guy this morning in Jacksonville, Florida. Then I shoved him into my carryon, snuck him past TSA, and boarded three separate airplanes. It was very messy. The dude bled all over the place. I landed here an hour ago and walked right past Customs with his legs sticking out of my duffel bag right there. Then I tossed him into the cockpit of my own boat and called you guys."

The young officer had stopped writing halfway through my confession.

"Did you get all that?" I asked.

He put the notebook back in his pocket and walked out of the marina office. I called Al, told him about the evening's surprise, and asked him to pick me up after dinner. I also looked at the marina register to see what boats had come and gone since my flight to Jacksonville.

Satisfied with what I'd learned, I picked up one of the glossy sailing magazines that caters to wealthy dream-sailors, glanced through a review of a gorgeous new million-dollar sailboat, and read a technical article about how to download weather data to a computer tablet.

Constable Millet arrived in his cruiser a half hour later with a police van close behind. Two uniformed officers fell in step behind him with an empty body bag. The officers returned from *Figaro* a half hour later with the bag—now much heavier—and loaded it into the back of the van. Millet walked into the office and leaned against the wooden railing that, when the office was busy, separated the charterers from the office staff.

"Can I buy you a Coke?" I asked.

Millet ignored my smart aleck question.

There is never a good reason to not tell the police something they already know or will soon find out. They will figure out you knew it and hold it against you.

"I flew in from Jacksonville a little over an hour ago and found him in the cockpit of my boat," I said. "I think he's an American named Ronnie Thomas."

"How do you know this man?" asked Millet.

"I wouldn't really say I knew him. He was the kid who boarded my boat last week."

Millet was silent.

"Don't you remember, Constable? I walked into your office last Tuesday morning and told you how this guy boarded my boat and threatened me. You didn't seem too worried about it."

Millet pulled out a small notepad.

"That kid told me he worked for a guy named Jimmy Cattrel," I said. "I mentioned that little detail to you and you said it was none of my business."

"Mr. Cattrel is a respected businessman," said Millet.

"If you say so. That kid told me he worked for Cattrel and boarded my boat on his orders. You might ask your respected businessman if he knows anything about the killing. I certainly don't."

"We know Mr. Cattrel quite well and do not believe that he could be involved in this case," said Millet.

"Well, neither am I."

Millet made a few notes. I thought about Millet and Cattrel. It changed things if they wore the same jersey.

"Can you account for your actions since Saturday night, Mr. Greene?" he asked.

"I sailed my boat here Saturday afternoon from Anegada, had dinner at Al's house, and bought a round-trip airline ticket that night. I flew out Sunday morning to Florida and got back an hour ago. I found the body where you saw it and called you guys. I've been sitting in this office since that time."

Millet wrote silently.

"He was shot while I was in Jacksonville," I said.

Millet looked up with a furrow in his brow. The furrow disappeared.

"I keep forgetting that you were a detective in the U.S. Navy," he said. "Your professional opinion notwithstanding, our coroner will determine the time of death."

I shrugged.

"Please tell me about your flight yesterday," he asked.

"It was a little bumpy and the peanuts were stale."

Millet smiled.

"Why did you go to Florida, Mr. Greene?"

"To visit an old friend," I said.

"You only stayed one night? Why is that?"

"It was only meant to be a short visit," I said. "He wanted to talk about a possible business venture, but it didn't sound as good to me in person as it had over the phone. I politely declined the opportunity and came back first thing this morning."

Millet stared at me. It was the stare that was supposed to make me crack. It bore no fruit.

"Do you have anything else to tell me?" he asked.

"He wasn't killed here," I said. "There isn't enough blood to begin with and no blood spatter at all in the cockpit. Just some secondary pooling. Whoever it was shot him somewhere else and dumped him in my boat."

Millet held up a small clear plastic evidence bag holding a Tarot card exactly like the one I'd found leaning against *Figaro*'s companionway the previous week.

"Do you know anything about this?" he asked.

It didn't seem smart to tell him that the card's twin was being used as a bookmark in my cruising guide. I shook my head.

"Where'd you find that?" I asked.

"It was under the body."

Headlights turned onto the marina driveway from the main road.

"Who shot him?" asked Millet. "Your friend Al, perhaps?"

"Ask him yourself," I said.

I nodded toward the driveway as Al's car pulled into the gravel lot. He got out of the car and walked into the office.

"Good evening, Constable."

"Good evening, Mr. Higgins."

The office was suddenly much cooler, but it wasn't because of the air conditioning. I sat back down on the couch to read more from the glossy sailing magazine.

"Mr. Higgins, can you account for your actions since Saturday night?" asked Millet.

"Uh-huh," said Al.

Silence enveloped the marina office.

"Then please do, Mr. Higgins."

"I went to bed late Saturday night and woke up early Sunday morning to take Sim to the airport," said Al. "I had breakfast with my girlfriend and then she drove me over to Lars Solberg's shop at the east side of the harbor."

"We are familiar with Mr. Solberg," said Millet. "What was the nature of your business with him?"

"He needed help with a salvage job on a sunken charter boat over near Jost Van Dyke," said Al. "We spent the morning loading lift bags and diving gear into his boat and getting out to the site. She was in about sixty feet of water and it took the two of us all afternoon to get the bags placed and the air lines run to a buoy."

Millet took notes as though he understood what Al was talking about.

"By the time we finished prepping her there wasn't enough light left to start the refloat so we went over to Great Harbour, dropped the hook, and spent the night drinking at Foxy's."

"You were at Jost Van Dyke all last night?" asked Millet.

"Yep," said Al. "You can ask Lars."

"And what did you do today?" Millet asked.

"I don't honestly remember getting back to Lars's boat last night but that's where I woke up this morning. We went back to the salvage site, hooked up the compressor, floated the boat, and passed her off to a tug. Then I got back home, picked up Sim at the airport, and dropped him off here."

Millet wrote some more in his notebook and then turned to me.

"You're not planning on leaving the country again, are you, Mr. Greene?" asked Millet.

"Not anytime soon," I said.

"Good," said Millet. "We may wish to ask you some follow-up questions."

Millet walked out of the office. I finished my Coke and phoned the marina's manager. He showed up almost immediately.

"Somebody left a very nasty mess in the cockpit of my boat," I said. "Did you see anybody hanging around last night who could have done it?"

"No, sir," he said. "We used to have a security guard here at nights but we've never had any problems. We had to let him go when the economy slowed. If you wish, I can ask the staff in the morning if any of them saw anybody near your boat."

"Well, like I said, it's a very nasty mess." I pulled two twenties out of my wallet. "Could you please get someone to clean the cockpit and topsides for me?"

The manager took the bills and nodded. I wondered how much would make it to the cleaning crew. Al and I stepped out of the office and the last of the RVIP cars pulled out of the gravel lot as we reached his car.

"What's going on?" asked Liv.

"Somebody left a dead body in Sim's boat," said Al.

"Oh my God," she said.

I squeezed into the back behind the driver's seat and Al started up the car.

"Do you think Phillips might still be in his office on a Monday evening?" I asked.

Al called the attorney's phone number and he picked up. He agreed to meet us but said he could only spare a few minutes given the late hour. We drove to Phillips's building, and the three of us walked up the metal stairs to the third floor and punched the doorbell. Phillips met our ring, led us into his office, and locked the outer door. Al asked Liv to wait in the reception area and she protested mildly. Al and I followed Phillips into his private office.

"Gentlemen, I don't generally stay this late beyond regular business hours. How may I help you?" asked Phillips.

I reached into my duffel and tossed the flat brown paper bag onto the desk in front of him. He reached inside the bag and pulled out a stack of papers held together with a binder clip.

"That, Mr. Phillips, is a copy of a ledger kept and written in code by Jimmy Cattrel. I don't have the code yet, but I think it contains details of criminal activity."

Phillips' eyebrows rose and his lips pursed. The whites of his eyes enlarged noticeably.

"Do you know who Mr. Cattrel is?" he asked.

"Supposed to be a tough rich guy," said Al. "People we've talked to describe him as the devil incarnate. I take it that we are supposed to fear him as such."

Phillips nodded slowly.

"He has money and influence," he said. "Some say it comes from a connection to organized crime. Some say it's because he was an officer in the Royal Virgin Islands Police and they are protecting him. I don't believe the latter and nobody has proven the former."

He paused a moment as he looked at the ledger. "Are you suggesting these papers could do that?"

"Beats me," I said. "All I want you to do is hold on to that copy. If something happens to me or to Al, I want you to give it to the most trustworthy person you know. Somebody who'd be willing to see Cattrel prosecuted."

Phillips nodded again.

"Is Cattrel the kind of guy who'd shoot somebody and dump the body in Sim's boat?" asked Al.

The lawyer's eyes widened a millimeter or two and he swallowed involuntarily.

"Please tell me what happened," he said.

"Somebody left a body in the cockpit of my boat last night," I said. "Cattrel is on my short list of possible malefactors."

"Malefactors," said Al.

Phillips picked up the ledger again and looked at it.

"You said something about a code?" he asked.

"Somebody is already working on that," I said. "Just hang on to that copy. If you don't get a phone call every day from either Al or me, then give it to somebody who cares, okay?"

Phillips nodded, put the ledger in the bottom drawer of a filing cabinet, locked it, and led us out of the office.

39

"FEELING a bit like a target?" asked Al.

We were sitting on the deck behind his house again. The oil torches on the beach below flickered in the cool ocean breeze. A few pinpricks of light shone from Guana Island to the north. Beyond that, it was eight hundred nautical miles of blue water to Bermuda. Bear sixty degrees west and you'll hit the Turks and Caicos after four hundred miles of open ocean. There wasn't much land north of this island. Nothing but water. Beautiful, empty water.

"I'm thinking I should have stayed in Costa Rica or the San Blas Islands and kept all the money," I said.

Al chuckled.

"You know, I never once worried about that," he said. "Avarice is not in you."

We sat quietly for a moment.

"So what do we do now?" asked Al.

"I think I'll take *Figaro* back to the Sound and hole up for a while," I said. "Swim and read and poke around. Maybe stumble over a killer."

"Poke around?" asked Al. "What for? Cattrel's our man."

"And why exactly is that, Professor Higgins?"

He hated being called that.

"He dropped that kid in your boat, didn't he?" asked Al.

"Maybe."

"Maybe? Are you kidding me?"

"Ok, probably," I said.

Al smiled and shook his head a little.

"He killed that Brownell guy, he killed that kid, and he's going to kill you," he said.

"Ok, let's give it an eighty percent chance he killed Ronnie," I said. "That doesn't mean he killed Brownell. Where's the link? If there is one, I haven't seen it. And Cattrel could have killed me a long time ago if he'd really wanted to."

"You don't think he sent the redhead out to your boat to kill you?" asked Al.

"No," I said. "Why would he go to all that trouble to kill me on my boat? If he's as bad as everyone says, he'd have a gunnie walk up to me in the dark and put a bullet in my ear."

A large power yacht motored into sight from the west and headed toward the north shore of Guana. Its lights glared across the water.

"Anyway, I'm going back to the Sound and I'm going to find out who killed Derek Brownell. We still need to get you off this murder charge."

"Aren't you going to ask me to give the cops my alibi?" asked Al.

"I seem to remember having already tried that. It didn't work."

Al didn't offer a response.

"You still want to live here?" I asked. "I mean after all this garbage with the RVIP and this thug Cattrel and all the lawyers and crap?"

"There's decent money to be made in salvage diving and scuba tours around here. And the weather's nice." He thought a moment. "And Liv's here."

"You weren't exactly a one-woman man back in California," I said.

He smiled.

"Nothing quite so constant as change, eh?" he said.

By the time our conversation tailed off, it was past time for bed. I woke up late the next morning with a raging hunger. Nobody else was there to stop me, so I raided the refrigerator and made a breakfast of scrambled eggs and fried plantain and ate it on the deck. The sky was a bleached sapphire and the sun shone as if the day were hopeful and filled with promise.

I remembered my promise to Jack Penn, dialed his number, and left a voicemail message to let him know that I was alive and well and waiting for a solution to Cattrel's code

Al returned and we left to go check on *Figaro.* The road from Al's house wound its way up a couple hundred yards to a steep ridge that separated the north and south sides of the island. At the ridge road you could turn left to Fat Hogs Bay or right to the street that circled back down Sabbath Hill to Baugher's Bay and Road Town. The air was unusually clear and the view to the south of the ridge was impressive. I could see the topmost hump of St. Croix fifty miles to the south.

We turned right and drove down through town and on to Fort Burt.

Al parked at the marina office and I walked over to *Figaro,* where the same sassy cleaning woman with the red bandana that I'd met two weeks earlier scrubbed my boat with a brush and a piece of an old beach towel.

"Dis fish blood is mighty hard to lift off dis boat of yours," she said. "Next time, you slosh a little rum in its gills and it'll die right quick. Less blood on de deck."

"It wasn't a fish," I said.

She dropped her eyes to the ground.

"De others say you killed a man right here where I'm standing."

"Somebody else killed him," I said. "I found the body last night."

"Ah'm doin' my best to clean off de poor man's blood, sir."

"I appreciate it."

She went back to scrubbing the cockpit coamings.

"I checked the register yesterday. You were here Sunday night getting a boat ready for the next charter, weren't you?" I asked.

"Yessir. Cleanin' up a boat for a new group."

"Did you see anyone near my boat?"

She shook her head and dropped her eyes again. I pulled two more twenties out of my wallet.

"I'd like to spend the night on my boat but it's still too much of a mess for me. Can you have it clean by dark?" I asked.

"Yessir," she said. "I can do that."

She reached for the money and I held on to it.

"You saw somebody here Sunday night," I said. "Somebody who didn't belong in the marina."

She nodded.

"Who was it?" I asked.

"I don't remember his name," she said, "but he used to play with my son when deys both kids at school. He a big man, now. Taller than you and heavy. Looks mighty strong. I saw him get into a truck 'bout ten o'clock and pull outta de lot. I dint see him near your boat, though."

"How old is your son now?"

"He's twenty-six, sir. Works over in Anguilla as a bartender. Very successful boy."

I stepped aboard *Figaro,* walked down into the cabin, and fished the Tarot card out of my cruising guide.

"You ever see anybody around here with one of these?" I asked.

She looked down at the deck.

"That is mine, sir."

"What's it doing on my boat?" I asked.

"That is de card of protection, sir. We heard about your friend's problems and de man who wants to hurt you. I put de cards there to protect your boat."

" 'We heard'?" I asked. "What do you mean 'we'?"

"It is a small island," she said.

A small island populated with invisible men. The men and women at the bottom of the economic ladder who clean houses and boats and restaurants. Invisible people with ears and friends and things to talk about. And fear of the police.

"I guess the cards couldn't protect Ronnie Thomas," I said.

I handed her the twenties, thanked her, and walked back to the marina office. Al sat under the air conditioner reading a diving magazine.

"Everything shipshape?" he asked.

"Not quite."

"Then let's go see our new business partner," he said.

Two businesses, actually. Blue Water Salvage and the Caribbean Dive Center shared an old rust-colored building on the east side of the harbor.

A tall, blond, shirtless man walked out of the building as Al parked the car. His hide was the deep brown color you see on sailors, lifeguards, fishermen, and other candidates for basal-cell carcinoma. Bright green eyes peered over high cheekbones. A straight mouth stood vigil above a square jaw. He would have looked at home in a Viking helmet. I guessed him to be somewhere north of Al's age.

Al introduced us and Lars showed us around the shop. Diving gear hung from hooks on the walls, columns of scuba tanks lined up near a large compressor system, and a series of closet rods held wetsuits and rash guards. An adjacent room housed open-bottomed lift bags, air drills, lengths of chain, mooring balls, and long, tube-shaped pontoons. Hundreds of feet of coiled air hoses hung on the wall near a pair of portable gas-powered air compressors. The place looked more like a warehouse than a dive shop.

"I'm guessing you don't get much walk-in business," I said.

Lars laughed.

"No walk-ins," Lars said. "We only build moorings, raise boats, or take people scuba diving. And even that is only rendezvous diving. I bring the boat to the customer."

We walked out to the dock and looked at the boat. It was little more than twenty-four feet of patched and painted worm-rotted wood. A cracked windshield protected a small cabin from the elements. Two Johnson outboards old enough to collect Social Security hung off an added-on metal transom.

"She'll haul ten divers, twenty tanks, and all the gear they'll need," said Lars. "Take those tank racks out and you can fit the salvage and mooring gear."

Lars and Al talked about diving and clientele and advertising while I poked around the boat and quietly confirmed its unseaworthy status. By the time I was done, my neck hurt from shaking my head.

We were both hungry when we left, and Al drove to the roti shop Liv had taken me to two weeks ago. I felt adventurous and ordered the goat. It was delicious.

"We're not paying much for that boat, are we?" I asked.

"He's throwing it in," said Al.

"We should throw it away."

"It'll do until we can afford a new one."

I ate some more of my roti and thought about how to ask the obvious question.

"Can we pull this off?" I asked. "The dive shop?"

"Once we get the bail money back, we'll have enough to make the first three quarterly payments," said Al. "The next three will need to come out of profits."

The San Blas Islands suddenly sounded even better.

"Then we need to get that bail money back," I said.

"And sailing back to the Sound is going to make that happen?"

"Unless you're going to give the cops your alibi," I said.

Al turned back to his roti without a response.

40

AL dropped me off at the entrance to the marina and took off to pick Liv up from work. The sun had gone off to hide somewhere in the Orient, and I walked in the dark toward *Figaro* between the coconut palms lining the driveway.

I saw a sudden movement at the edge of my peripheral vision and felt a hollow thud near my left ear. My knees buckled and somebody pushed me off an eight-story building into pitch darkness. But it made no sense at all because there weren't any eight-story buildings on this island.

Much later—it felt like weeks had passed—my right eye opened to see a dull and dry, sepia-toned marina wrapped in thin gauze and lit by orange-brown streetlights. The roar of an ocean gale blew inside my skull. It was my own shallow breath.

"Hey, mon. What you doing down there?" said a low voice.

I tried to pull myself up from the brown grass but I had no arms. My legs were great timbers, waterlogged from decades of floating at sea. Driftwood. I felt myself being picked up and turned to look at a large golden "D".

"What's the matter, mon? You don't smell drunk."

Feeling came back to my right shoulder, elbow, wrist. I felt myself being pushed into a standing position and my eyes slowly focused on large, fuzzy, twisting shapes. They swayed and danced until the eyes focused and the twisting shapes morphed into the fronds of a coconut palm.

"Thanks," I said. "I think somebody hit me."

"You be all right in a minute. Dale gonna help you."

I felt myself being maneuvered into a chair and resting my head in my hands with my elbows on my upper legs. I waited a few minutes for my head to catch up. A wave of nausea built up from a wind-driven following sea and broke over me.

"You all right, mon?" asked Dale. "You need something to drink?"

"Some water, maybe. Just water."

Dale left and returned a few minutes later with a cold bottle of water.

"Somebody hit you, mon?"

It hurt when I nodded.

"You want me to call the police or somethin'?" he asked.

"No," I said. "I'll be fine. No police."

My duffel was on the ground. I reached over and unzipped it. Nothing had been taken. The ledger was still there.

"I think I'm okay, Dale."

He helped me stand up. The earth was on a slow spin cycle and the marina lights blurred from the movement.

"You need help to your boat, mon?" he asked.

I leaned against a palm tree and took a few long, slow breaths.

"No, I think I'm all right now," I said.

Dale handed me the duffel and I walked toward where I thought *Figaro* should be. On the way, I took a quick personal inventory. Wallet, watch, and cell phone were still in my pockets. No keys.

When I got to the boat, I found that somebody had unlocked *Figaro* and tossed her like a Caesar salad. The cabin was a mess. It was a midshipman's locker with everything on top and nothing handy.

Burglary victims are universally filled with a feeling of violation. It is as old as the species. Neanderthal man probably got testy when somebody swiped his good skinning rock. Somebody had knocked me out, taken my keys, and rifled through my boat. I stood in *Figaro*'s cabin filled with the visceral desire to cut the hides off the creatures that did it.

My watch told me I'd lost nearly an hour. My cell phone told me that I'd missed a call from Al.

"Where have you been, Sim?"

"Lying in the grass," I said. "Somebody conked me on the head."

"I'll be down in twenty minutes," said Al.

As far as I could tell, nothing had been stolen. The keys were stuck in the companionway padlock. Even Ronnie's .45 automatic was still in its hiding place. But it looked like everything else had been opened, picked up, inspected, and tossed on the cabin sole. It took me the better part of an hour to clean up the cabin and put things away even with Al's help.

I slid the companionway hatch closed, locked up the boat, and hoped that these measures would, at least, keep out the casual burglars. Al drove me to his house, where I went to bed and fell asleep with a tender head.

The sun was higher than usual when I woke and the late morning was clean and bright. Liv called us to "brekkie" in her lovely accent and brought out baked plantain, tropical fruit salad, and inch-thick slices of sweet coconut bread with lime marmalade.

"Where did you learn how to cook like this?" I asked.

"Cooking's what pays me passage, Sim. I've put tea and brekkie on the table from New Zealand to Cuba."

"Can you do that on a thirty-nine-foot sailboat?"

"Hmm," said Liv. "How about fresh mahi-mahi over coconut rice?"

"Heaven help me," I said. "I'm in love with a Kiwi."

Al reached over and gave Liv a squeeze.

"You go find your own piece of heaven, sailor. This one's mine."

"Have you got a sister?" I asked.

Liv laughed as she walked back to the kitchen.

"I suppose I'm destined to remain a single-hander," I said.

Breakfast ended too soon as Al had to take Liv to work before noon. My head still hurt, but I was worried about my boat and hitched a ride with them back to the marina.

They dropped me off at the entrance again, and I was careful and wary as I made my way through the coconut palms to the marina. When I got to *Figaro*, I found two big local guys standing on the dock, arms folded, leaning heavily against my boat's toerail.

The deep, visceral anger I'd felt the previous night returned, and I marked them as the creatures that had jumped me and violated my boat. I wanted their heads on a wall.

The bigger of the two was a tall, acne-scarred black fellow in a dark blue muscle shirt. He had a few inches on me and looked every inch a weightlifter, bulky and strong. He probably figured he could break me like a toothpick. The other guy was also heavily-muscled but was, for lack of a better word, squatty.

The tall one had been elected spokesperson. He talked slowly and deliberately as though speaking were a newly learned skill. It made me wonder if the squatty guy was mute.

"De Boss wants to talk to you, mon," he said.

"Then tell him to get his ass down here, Dimples."

The big guy's eyes went wide and his brow creased. He stood up to grab me but I planted a straight right into his jaw before he got his arms unfolded. The punch moved his head a little to his right, so I followed with a left hook and threw it at the moving head to catch him below his right eye. That put a few stars in his skull and knocked him back against *Figaro*. He grabbed her lifelines to keep from falling into the water.

Squatty was slow in stepping up to the plate, but he got around to it. He reached into his pocket for something, and I hit him straight on the nose with a left jab. The nose broke and started to bleed. He tried to get his hands up, but I followed with a fast right cross and left hook combination that folded his legs beneath him. He didn't get up. He didn't try.

Dimples recovered his balance enough to throw a right round-house at me. It was as slow as a locomotive in a switch yard. I ducked low inside it and put two quick punches into his kidneys and backed away. A grunt came from deep inside him as he re-loaded his swing.

"A little tougher than lifting weights, eh?" I said. "I guess most of the little boys you scare don't fight back."

He didn't answer. His eyes were on fire. I felt the anger and the hot rush of adrenaline that flows through a man during a fistfight. My lungs sucked up gallons of air and my knuckles felt like iron hammers.

I backed down the dock toward *Figaro's* bow and picked up a big fishing sinker somebody had left on the dock box. The smooth piece of lead felt as good and as solid in my palm as a ten-dollar roll of quarters.

Dimples followed me and swung faster with his right. I pulled back and turned with the punch but not quite enough. He caught my jaw with a glancing blow, and shafts of searing hot light momentarily burned through the back of my skull. I'd have gone down badly if he'd hit me square.

As his momentum swung him around, I recovered and hit him in the right eye with another left hook. He spun toward me and I planted my right fist, enhanced by the big fishing weight, firmly into his gut.

I couldn't tell if it had been a late breakfast or an early lunch but Dimples left it on the dock, crouched on his hands and knees. I considered place-kicking his testicles from the rear for the extra point, but he passed out before I could line up properly.

Dimples's wallet was in his back pocket, and a brief examination produced half a dozen business cards from a local company called Blue Water Investments. I took one of the cards.

Both of the local bad boys were done for the moment, so I boarded *Figaro*, stuffed what I needed into my rucksack, and re-locked the boat. I called Al and told him of the morning's festivities. He said he'd be there in a few minutes.

I walked back to the marina office and told the manager about the mess I'd left on their dock. He shrugged.

"I'm very sorry, sir," he said in a cool British tone as if he'd just told me the bar was out of gin. "Would you care for me to call the police, sir?"

I shook my head.

The marina office stocked bags of ice to sell to their charter groups. I bought one and shoved my hands into it to slow the swelling of my knuckles. The Coke I bought was cold enough to form ice crystals on the top layer when I opened it. I drank it fast in the air-conditioned office but it didn't help much. I was still white-hot angry.

Ten minutes later, a car crunched the gravel outside of the office and Al walked in.

"See any trash on the dock?" I asked.

"They're gone," he said. "Let's get out of here."

41

AL drove me into town. I gave him the address on the card.

"Blue Water Investments?" he asked. "That's Jimmy Cattrel's company."

"No surprise there. Time to meet the big man himself," I said.

His office was in the most modern building in Road Town. I climbed the steps two at a time until I came to the third floor. I entered the reception area and walked past the girl at the desk toward the only other door in the office.

"Excuse me, sir, but you will have to wait until I ask Mr. Cattrel if he can see you," she said in a very proper British accent. "He is a very busy man."

"He's expecting me," I said as I opened the door and walked into his office.

He reached into a desk drawer as I closed the door behind me. I pulled Ronnie's .45 from my pocket.

"Uh-uh," I said.

His hand froze but he turned to look at me.

"Don't even think about it," I said. "Nobody is that fast."

He carefully closed the drawer and put his right hand on the desk.

"Now the left hand," I said. "Be careful, I am in an exceedingly bad mood right now."

I sat down in the chair across from his desk.

"I heard you wanted to see me, Jimmy.'

"Mr. Greene, is it?" he said. "I wasn't expecting you so soon."

Cattrel was much better dressed than when I'd seen him last. He wore a tan linen suit with an ecru shirt open at the collar. His short gray curls and salt-and-pepper beard framed a strong and confident face. He appeared to be the consummate distinguished businessman.

Except for the eyes. The eyes were pools of liquid hate.

"You don't know who you're dealing with, Greene."

His voice was low, guttural, and filled with malice. Like Paul Robeson singing "Old Man River" while sharpening a machete.

"I know enough," I said. "I know you sent your boy Ronnie to kill me on my boat a week ago."

I laid the .45 down on the small side table next to me. The speakerphone on his desk came to life and the receptionist's shrill British voice rang through his office.

"Mr. Cattrel, should I call Germaine to come in and remove your visitor?" she asked.

"Like that's going to happen," I said.

"That won't be necessary, Dede," Cattrel said.

He turned from the speakerphone to face me.

"Mon, I didn't send de white boy to kill you," he said. "I told him to get me my money. That was before I found out you put it in de bank."

He sat back in his chair and put his hands in his lap. I didn't like the move and picked up the .45 again.

"I still want my money," he said.

I pulled the ledger out of my duffel with my left hand and tossed it on his desk.

"Who'd you send last night?" I asked. "Another stupid kid? Whoever it was didn't even look in my duffel. He just tore my boat apart without finding what you wanted."

Cattrel picked up the ledger, examined a few of the pages, and set it to the side of his desk.

"Yeah, I figured you took this, mon," he said. "And I be glad to get it back, too. But it don't mean nuthin' to you or anybody else. And I didn't send anyone to find it."

"Why'd you kill Ronnie and toss him in my boat?" I asked.

"I have not killed anybody."

"A witness saw your slow fat boy toss him in my boat."

"What witness?" he asked.

"I'm holding the gun so I get to ask the questions."

His nostrils flared and his lips pulled back into an unpleasant grin.

"Ronnie s'posed to guard my place. Instead, he be up in the bushes smokin' fatties while you bust my house pretty as you please. I don't put up with that nonsense."

"So you killed him," I said.

"No," he said. "Germaine takes care of that for me. He enjoys that kind of work. And he won't like that you called him a 'slow fat boy.'"

His voice lowered to a growl.

"And I am still wanting my money," he said.

"I don't have it," I said. "But I'm making a few guesses about where it comes from. What do you get? Four percent for making it legit?"

"Dead men tell no tales, friend. Dat's still true in these islands."

"I have no interest in telling tales," I said. "And you should wish me a long and pleasant life."

"Why is that, mon?" he asked.

"Because there's a duplicate of that ledger and copies of your secret computer files being held for me by a U.S. Naval intelligence officer," I said. "If he stops getting phone calls from me, he'll forward his copy of that ledger and those files to a very close friend of his at the DEA. Between the two of them, they'll find somebody who can figure out your little code and put an end to your fun and games. And I hear there are folks in the DEA who have a score to settle with you."

Cattrel sat back in his chair and folded his arms. The hatred in his eyes cooled slightly. A dispassionate cobra.

"You don't know what you're talkin' 'bout, mon," he said.

"Like I said before, I have no interest in telling tales and I couldn't care less about your money. I just want to know who killed Bradley Somerset."

"You mean Derek? Who you trying to kid, mon?" he asked. "Your friend killed him and took de money. My money. And then you used some of that cash to bail him out of jail."

"Nope," I said. "I used my own money."

"Yeah, sure, Mistah Greene. And Terrence Wells is your butler, too, eh?"

He laughed loud and strong. I watched his hands and the drawer.

"You bring that tired, leaky old sailboat to de islands and I'm supposed to think you've got the dough to hire a man like Phillips?" he said. "And then you got even more money to post bail for your friend? Brownell stole that money from me and a lot more to go with it. I want it back."

"Why didn't you take it back when you killed him?" I asked.

"I didn't kill him," laughed Cattrel. "I didn't have him killed, either. I didn't even know who de guy was until I found out he lifted over two million dollars off my courier. Then your friend comes along, pops him off dead, and walks off with de money."

"Brownell had a safe deposit box loaded with cash," I said.

"Yeah, I know all about that," he said. "De RVIP has it and that money gone for good, maybe. But dere's a million bucks missin' and nobody be accountin' up for it. That million ain't coming out of my percentage, Mistah Greene. I want my money and I want it now."

"I'll let you know if I ever find it," I said.

I picked up the .45, stuck it in my pants pocket, and walked out.

42

THE Isuzu pulled up as I walked out of the building.

"Cattrel says he didn't kill Derek," I said.

"Uh-huh."

Al turned the car toward the harbor. He spent a lot of time scanning the rearview mirror.

"He says Derek skimmed two million dollars from his cash pipeline," I said.

Al shook his head.

"There wasn't that much in his safe deposit box," said Al.

"He says only half of it was in that box. He thinks we have the other half."

Al parked the car in a small lot overlooking the harbor south of the cruise ship dock.

"The only way Cattrel would know that is if he had a friend in the RVIP," said Al.

We bought a couple of sandwiches and some Cokes from a shack near the road and took our lunch down to the harbor. I gave Al the rest of the details about my meeting with Cattrel. He listened quietly while he ate his lunch.

"So there's a million bucks missing," he said.

"If we're to believe Cattrel," I said.

"And he thinks we've got it?"

"Uh-huh."

"You want to know what I think?" asked Al.

"Sure."

"I think the Grenadines are beautiful this time of year," said Al. "Or maybe St. Eustatius. That's a very quiet island. Almost nobody goes there. It would be a great place to hide out for a few months."

"What are you talking about?" I asked.

"Cattrel is going to pop you, Sim. And he might try to pop me, too. So you get on *Figaro* and set sail for somewhere else. Anywhere else. Because he will kill you, brother."

"Unless you kill him first, right?" I asked.

Al shrugged and sipped his Coke.

"I think you're being a bit premature, Al."

"Was I 'premature' three months ago?" he asked.

I thought about the cowboy hat and the river.

"No, you were right on time."

The low bellow of a ship's horn drifted into the harbor from the east.

"You pulled Cattrel's chain, Sim. And you pulled too hard. Think about it. You broke into his house, you stole his secret files, and then you just now walked into his office and stuck a gun up his nose. How do you think he's gonna react?"

"I think he wants his money," I said.

A cruise ship poked its nose around Prospect Reef, blew its horn again and turned toward Road Town. Three thousand tourists armed with hard currency waiting to descend on the island. It was the economic equivalent of the invasion of Normandy. And the locals were just as happy to see them.

We could see the commercial docks where our new dive shop was located across from the cruise ship facilities. A large yellow yacht tender shot out of a small marina near those docks with both outboards at full throttle. It was only about two hundred yards away from us, and I could see the familiar yellow polo shirt of a *Liquid Assets* crewmember. I wasn't sure but it looked like Rick Schuster, and I wondered why the ship's captain was running errands on the inflatable.

Al brought me back to the issue at hand.

"Cattrel has got to be madder than a hornet," said Al. "Do you think for one minute that those guys who knocked you on the head and broke into your boat wouldn't cut you up for fish bait if he asked?"

I thought about that for a minute and another piece of the jig-saw puzzle rotated and fell into place.

"Cattrel's people didn't sap me. And they didn't break into my boat, either," I said.

"What makes you think that?" asked Al.

"He knows I opened a bank account and dumped a wad of money into it. He knows which bank and he knows the account number. He probably found all this out after Ronnie's little swim or he wouldn't have sent him out to *Figaro* in the first place."

"Unless Ronnie was supposed to shoot you," said Al.

"Why would Cattrel want to break into my boat? What's he hoping to find? He knows the money isn't there."

"Maybe he was looking for the ledger," said Al.

"It was in my duffel. They could have taken that anytime without having to break into *Figaro*."

"So who tossed your boat, Sim? And why?"

"I...I don't know."

"You're gonna have to either skate out of here fast or kill Cattrel. There's no third option."

It wouldn't make sense for Cattrel to come after me given the likelihood that Jack Penn would share his copy of the ledger with the Feds, but Al could be right. Some guys let pride overrule their own sense of self-preservation.

"Well," I said. "Let's burn that bridge when we come to it."

I finished lunch and then made my daily call.

"Penn here."

"Jack, this is Sim. Just checking in with you."

"Glad to hear you're still around," he said. "That code was pretty simple, by the way."

"You cracked it?" I asked.

"Easy peasy. Check your email. I sent you the details this morning."

"Thanks, man. I owe you."

"Yes," he said. "You do."

The *Cloaca of the Seas* tied up to the pier and a stream of tourists poured out. They formed up in brightly dressed assault groups and began their march up the concrete dock. We retreated to the Isuzu before the invasion could begin in earnest and drove up to Al's house on the hill.

I checked my email, saw one from Jack, and opened it immediately. He'd cracked the code in less than two hours on a slow Tuesday. Attached to the email was a printout of the code key and the first page of the ledger in deciphered form.

His informal search for records of interest among various agencies regarding the Tanners and Terrence Wells came up negative. They were, in his professional estimation, very boring, if wealthy, people.

He also wrote that he had found a single word printed in code at the top of the ledger that had no independent meaning. On a hunch, he had tried it as the password for Cattrel's flash drive. The hunch played out and he had copied the hidden files and attached them to the email. I stored the files to Al's computer and sat down to translate more of Cattrel's ledger.

43

AL took Liv to work as I continued deciphering Cattrel's ledger. The files on the flash drive were more in-depth records containing names, dates, dollar amounts, account numbers, and his contacts in both North and South America. Money laundering, plain and simple, and it looked like I had everything a prosecutor could want to build a case. But I had the distinct feeling that this truth was only a small part of a larger puzzle. Nothing I'd seen in the ledger to that point explained Derek Brownell's murder or gave me anything solid that would get Al off the hook.

A cold pork chop beckoned from the fridge. I nuked it in the microwave and ate it with some leftover fruit salad and orange juice. My breakfast was interrupted by the sound of a car crunching the gravel in the driveway. Detective Constable Millet and two officers got out of an RVIP cruiser and walked to the front door.

"How can I help you, Constable?" I asked.

"We'd like to speak with Mr. Higgins. May we come in, Mr. Greene?"

"Al's not here. Should I call Phillips first? He may wish to join us."

"There won't be any need for your solicitor, Mr. Greene," said Millet. "The Crown has dropped all of the charges against Mr. Higgins."

It took a moment for the news to soak in.

"Are you kidding me?" I asked. "What happened? Did somebody walk in and confess?"

"No, Mr. Greene. Somebody contacted our attorney general and presented her with a believable alibi for Mr. Higgins. The Crown has dropped the charges and you and your friend have the Crown's sincerest apologies."

"That's great news," I said. "But why not just call Phillips? Why come all the way up here to tell me?"

Millet looked a little chagrined.

"I understand that you have been conducting inquiries at the Bitter End Yacht Club, Mr. Greene, and I have a few questions for you. May we go inside?" he asked.

I opened the door and led the constable and his officers to the living room.

"Have a seat, gentlemen, and I'll join you in a minute," I said. "I need to make a quick phone call."

I stepped out the back door onto the deck, dialed Al's phone, and told him the news. His response was both joyful and profane.

"I'm on my way up," he said. "I've got a few things to say to that constable."

"Let's try to stay on good terms with him, Al. We may need his help someday."

"I'll consider it," he said.

I hung up and walked back into the living room.

"You had some questions," I said.

"A little over a week ago you came into my office and mentioned a fellow that had boarded your vessel. He was killed last weekend and left on your boat."

"I've already told you all I know about that," I lied.

"Not many tourists expire while visiting the BVI," said Constable Millet. "When they do, it is usually the result of a heart attack or a drowning or a car accident. The murder of a tourist is extremely rare, one or two a year at the most. But since you and your friend arrived, five tourists have been murdered. Derek Brownell, a fellow named Stevenson, Ronnie Thomas, and now two more."

"Kind of blows your stats," I said.

"The last two, a man and a woman, were found very early this morning floating a hundred yards off the dock at Leverick Bay. Both shot multiple times in the chest."

"Have you identified them?" I asked.

"Not yet," said Millet. "The woman was tall, thin, and blonde. Mid-thirties. The man appears to be about the same age and dark-haired. A playing card was tattooed inside his left wrist. Both were naked."

A chill ran down my spine like a slowly evaporating drop of liquid nitrogen.

"The card was an ace of spades," I said.

Millet cocked his head a bit but said nothing.

"And he was the cook onboard the motor yacht *Liquid Assets*," I said. "They called him 'Cookie'; I never got his real name. I'll bet next week's rent that the woman is, or was, Meghan Wells, the yacht owner's wife."

"And you know this how?" Millet asked.

The little voice deep inside told me to trust him, but I had residual doubts.

"I met Cookie at the bar at the Bitter End Yacht Club," I said. "I saw him some time later with Meghan Wells. They were, uh, quite close."

Millet thought for a moment.

"And wasn't Derek Brownell a crewmember for *Liquid Assets*?" asked Millet.

"Yes," I said.

Millet stiffened slightly.

"I would very much like you to tell me everything you have learned about that vessel and its crew, Mr. Greene. Everything."

It was against my life's experience to trust him, but I had to listen to the little voice. And I had a few questions of my own. Al's car pulled into the driveway, and the two officers walked to the door to see who it was.

"There are some things I can tell you, Constable."

I nodded toward the two officers standing near the door.

"But I am only going to tell *you*," I said.

Millet hesitated, then told the officers to wait for him at the car. They left as Al walked in. He sat across from Millet.

"The charges against me are dropped?" asked Al.

"Yes, Mr. Higgins." Millet said. "And you have the Crown's sincerest apologies."

Millet extended his hand. Al looked at it.

"It wasn't exactly a holiday in that jail of yours."

"Again," said Millet, "I apologize."

Al looked at Millet's outstretched hand and shook it.

"Sim said something about an alibi," Al said.

Millet cleared his throat.

"Apparently, an individual has come forward who can account for your actions during the entire evening and well into the morning in question."

"Who?" asked Al. "Who called you?"

"This person called our attorney general's office and is, apparently, well known to her. I was asked not to inquire further." He appeared to be uncomfortable with the subject. "And so I shall not."

"So it's over?" Al asked. "Just like that?"

Millet nodded. Once.

"Hot damn," said Al.

He clapped his open palms against his knees as he stood up. He looked two inches taller as he walked into the kitchen.

Millet sat back in his chair, crossed his legs, and looked at me. I told him what I knew about *Liquid Assets* and Terrence Wells and how he had suspected his wife of being unfaithful. I told him Wells had employed me to follow his wife and that I'd seen her exit one of the villas at Leverick Bay with Cookie. I also told him about Cookie's confrontation with Jimmy Cattrel outside the dive shop.

Millet stiffened like he had before when I mentioned Jimmy Cattrel.

"While we are speaking so frankly, Detective, can you tell me what is going on between Jimmy Cattrel and your department?" I asked.

"There is nothing 'going on' between Jimmy and my department," he said. "He was my boss up until his retirement five years ago. And he was a good friend."

I was wondering why the little voice was telling me to trust Millet when Al came out of the kitchen. He carried a tray with a white porcelain teapot, cups and saucers, milk, and two mugs of hot coffee. Millet's eyes widened slightly and a thin smile graced his lips.

"Well, stone me," he said. "You Yanks have Earl Grey."

I was shocked. In the dozen or so years I'd known Al, I'd never seen him with anything less potent than imported beer. Even his coffee usually had a kicker of some sort in there. The shock must have shown in my face.

"Liv drinks tea and it's rubbing off," Al said. "She is a civilizing force."

Millet sat up in his chair, stirred milk into his tea, and complimented Al on his excellent taste. I shook my head and grabbed a mug of coffee. We took our tea and coffee outside onto the deck.

"Retirement around here must be generous," I said. "Cattrel's got a big house in an exclusive area and a nice office, too."

"He is a respected investment manager," said Millet.

"That's a load," said Al. "The guy launders money for drug traffickers and for the families who supply them."

The assertion didn't raise so much as an eyebrow.

"We have never had sufficient evidence to prove that," said Millet.

"I do," I said. "But I can't give it to you."

Millet's eyebrows now rose to form dark question marks as he sipped his tea.

"If you have such evidence," he said, "it is your duty to turn it over to the Crown."

"Cattrel's got an informant in your office," I said.

"What makes you say that?" asked Millet.

"He knew how much money was in Brownell's safe deposit box," I said. "He also knew I hired Phillips and bailed out Al. He assumed that the money came from Brownell and that there was more of it hidden on my boat. Later, he found out that I have a bank account here in the BVI."

Millet looked into his tea thoughtfully.

"He wasn't guessing, Constable. Somebody went through your files and told him. That somebody is on your staff, and that's why I had to speak to you alone."

Millet thought quietly to himself.

"We have heard some rumors and I have had my suspicions," he said. "But we have never had a shred of evidence. Nothing strong enough to support prosecution."

"I've got his records, Constable. Computer files and a ledger book in his handwriting. I can bring you a copy tomorrow. But I need to know if you or any of your officers broke into my boat to search it last night."

"Certainly not."

Righteous indignation permeated his voice. So if the RVIP didn't bust into *Figaro* and Cattrel didn't need to, then *who did?*

Millet poured himself another cup of tea and added more milk. I got out of my deck chair, leaned on the railing, and looked out across the water to Guana Island. My cell phone rang, and I walked inside to answer it.

"Dad says I need to talk to you about Derek."

Lance's voice held an odd mixture of fear and youthful boredom.

"That'd be nice," I said.

"I'm flying in from San Juan in a couple of hours. Can we meet at the airport around three?"

"I'll be there," I said.

He hung up and I walked back to where Millet and Al talked.

"Were all five victims shot with the same pistol?" I asked.

"Actually," Millet said, "Mr. Brownell was shot in the chest with two nine-millimeter hollow point bullets, Ronnie Thomas and the other American were killed with thirty-two-caliber shots to the head delivered from close range, and both of our latest victims seem to have been killed with multiple shots from a thirty-eight, or so it appears. We don't have a completed ballistics report yet on the last two."

"As long as you're satisfied that we didn't do it," said Al.

Millet finished his tea and set the cup back down on the tray.

"Completely," he said. "Now, it seems that I should locate this yacht and conduct some further investigation."

He thanked us for the tea, apologized once more to Al, and walked outside to his car and the pair of officers. A few minutes later, we heard the RVIP cruiser pull out of the driveway and turn down the hill.

"What do you think of that guy?" asked Al.

"He seems like an honest fellow doing a tough job," I said.

"That guy sticks me in the pokey for a week and then wants to apologize."

"Given those facts, I probably would have done the same thing."

"Thanks."

"The rich kid has something to tell me about Derek," I said. "Could be useful."

"When?"

"He's flying in at three and wants to meet at the airport. Can you come along and watch my back?" I asked.

"Let's make it quick. Liv gets off at five and being a free man again makes me want to celebrate."

We hopped into Al's car and blasted down the hill toward Road Town.

"I don't think I'm ever going to get used to sitting in the passenger side of a car and being in the middle of the road," I said.

"Couple of months in this country and you'll be driving on the left like a pro," Al said. "Until then, you're just another dangerous American."

As we came down Sabbath Hill toward Baughers Bay and rounded a corner, I noticed a faded red Suzuki Samurai with tinted windows parked under a tree on a dirt side street. It didn't belong there.

"I think we have company," said Al.

44

"RED Suzuki?" I said.

"Yeah," said Al. "Same guy followed me around last week."

I looked through the right-side door mirror.

"Not trying to be very discreet, is he?" I said. "I thought you said he was good at it."

Al laughed and continued driving at a normal pace. His eyes looked up into the rearview mirror occasionally, but he never moved his head. When we got to the Blackburn highway, Al made the left turn toward the airport.

"Well?" I asked.

"Looks like there are two of them in the car this time. They're still behind us but they're hanging back some."

I pulled the .45 out from under the seat and jacked a shell into the chamber. Al drove on toward Fish Bay and then made a sudden sharp left turn up a narrow paved road that led away from the coast and up into the steep hills.

The road meandered up the narrow canyon and the foliage on both sides grew high and thick. We couldn't see the guys behind us as Al negotiated the corners, but then again, they couldn't see us either. We had no way of knowing if the Suzuki had followed us up the hill or not.

Al rounded a sharp corner and stopped. I got out and stepped behind two big trees at the side of the road. Al continued up another fifty feet, cranked the wheel hard to the right, and stopped the car broadside to any traffic that might be following us up the road.

As Al got out of the car, the red Suzuki rounded the corner and skidded abruptly to avoid hitting the Isuzu. Both doors opened.

The driver had long, dark dreadlocks and about eight inches of dark, frizzy beard. He looked like Rasputin would have if he'd been black, smoked ganja, and listened to reggae. Dimples was the passenger. Being roughly the same size and shape as the Samurai, getting in and out had to have been a major technical accomplishment. They walked toward Al.

I quietly walked up behind them and stood next to the Samurai, shielding myself with the open passenger door.

"Hey, mon," said Rasputin to Al. "We gonna talk to you."

"Go ahead and talk," I said.

They turned around and saw the .45 pointed at them.

"Speed kills," I said. "Don't make any sudden moves."

Al walked around his car toward them.

"Put your hands behind your head and interlace the fingers," he said.

They did so and Al patted them down, relieving each of a pistol. He also grabbed their wallets, cell phones, and car keys. I escorted the two men to the side of the road and told them to sit. Al parked the cars.

"You gonna kill us, mon?" said Rasputin.

He looked nervous. Worried that the pretty girls, the rum, and the fine, carefree Caribbean lifestyle was about to end. Dimples didn't seem to care. The only thing bothering him was a small lump under his right eye where I'd hit him. And that didn't seem to bother him much.

"Only if I have to," I said.

Al sat in the Isuzu with the car door open and leafed through their wallets.

"The big one with the bad complexion is Germaine Walker," he said. "The guy with the dreads is Rudy Archer."

"Did Jimmy Cattrel send you?" I asked. "Why?"

"We ain't tellin' you nothin'," said Rudy.

"What about you, Germaine?" I asked.

He stared at me with cold, empty, impassive eyes. Sharks have those eyes.

"You guys don't have to cooperate," said Al. "We can do this the hard way." He reached into the Isuzu's glove compartment and pulled out a military combat knife. "And I kind of like the hard way."

In a move nobody saw, Al flashed the knife under Rudy's chin and pressed the sharp gray blade against his throat. Rudy let out a yelp.

"Answer the man's questions," said Al.

Rudy almost broke. He swallowed and felt the blade against his Adam's apple. He wanted the knife away from his throat. He wanted to tell us. He wanted all of this badly but he looked at Germaine and clamped his mouth shut. A flick of Al's wrist and Rudy would have bled out in less than half a minute. But Rudy didn't say a thing.

Al moved the blade from Rudy's neck, backed away, and held one of their pistols in his right hand. He turned to Germaine.

"What about you?" Al asked.

"I got nothin' to say," the big man said slowly.

I motioned with my pistol.

"Walk up that road," I said. "Both of you."

"You'll shoot us in the back," said Rudy.

"There's a thought," I said. "Start walking. I might only shoot you if you turn around."

Germaine shrugged his shoulders and headed up the road in big, slow strides. Rudy caught up with him, and I watched them both walk up the road and around the corner.

Al and I pushed the red Samurai off the road. I watched it roll down the hill and land upside down in a deep ditch against a small stand of trees. It would probably stay there under the branches until the combined forces of salt air and tropical rain eliminated it one square inch of rust at a time.

"We didn't make the smart play, Sim."

"How's that?" I asked.

"We should have shot them both and stuck them in the car before rolling it in the ditch."

"Maybe so."

We got back into Al's car and headed toward the airport. One of the pistols we'd taken was a cheap version of a .38 caliber service revolver. The other was a silenced .32 automatic. I put them both in Al's glovebox.

"You still think Cattrel won't kill you because you've got copies of his ledger and computer files?" asked Al.

"My prior convictions are now considerably more fluid."

45

"YOU'RE late," said Lance. "And who's this guy?"

"His name is Al and he's been trained to kill in seven languages."

Al glared at him. Lance responded by looking confused and then swallowing nervously.

We walked the several hundred yards from the airport to Trellis Bay and sat down on a bench in front of one of the tourist shops.

"I don't want to talk with him here," said Lance.

"I'll take a walk," said Al.

Al got up and walked down the beach. I watched him lean against a coconut palm twenty yards away and surreptitiously scan the shops, the beach, and the tourists walking up and down the sandy beach path. His right hand held one of the pistols in his shorts pocket.

"Okay, what have you got for me, Lance?" I asked.

He looked around and swallowed again.

"I don't want to get involved in whatever is going on with this murder and…"

"Just tell me what you know, Lance. Everything you know, everything you've heard, everything you've been told by anybody else," I said.

A drop of sweat slid down his forehead.

"Okay, I met that big yacht's crew over at the Willy-T that Sunday night like I told you."

"Who was there? Who exactly?"

"You know, that Derek guy," he said. "And a guy they called Cookie and another guy named Rick. There were two others who were drinking with us but I didn't talk to them much and I didn't get their names. And there were four couples from a charter group or something. I never talked to them."

"Go on," I said.

"So Derek and Rick and Cookie and I were just talking over drinks, you know, and I mentioned my import business. I guess I oversold it. You know how guys talk in a bar."

He hadn't shaved in a few days, and he rubbed the stubble on his face.

"Anyway, I told them I had some hot products that I was bringing to the U.S. market to sell over the internet and that I was looking for some money people who wanted to make a good return on their investment. I was hoping they'd set me up with their boss."

"But they wouldn't?" I asked.

"No, Derek and Rick both said they were personally interested and didn't want to involve Wells."

"How about Cookie?"

"He couldn't have cared less," said Lance. "After a minute or two, he walked away to drink with the others."

"So what were Derek and Rick interested in?" I asked. "What specifically?"

"They said they had some money, some 'retirement funds' that they wanted to invest. Rick was asking about my business plan and did I have a distribution channel and stuff like that. It sounded like he knew what he was talking about. He was asking all the right questions."

"What was Derek saying?" I asked.

"Not much," said Lance. "He drank a lot and listened to Rick ask the questions."

"How much money are we talking about, Lance? Did you guys talk numbers at all?"

"Yeah," he said, "but I finally figured out they were blowing smoke at me, and I gave up on them."

"What makes you say that?" I asked.

"Rick was saying that he and Derek could each put in over half a million dollars and that they wanted a big chunk of the company in return. I guess I was a little drunk, so it took a while for me to realize that they were putting me on. I mean, how are a couple of deck apes going to raise half a million each for an investment? It's ridiculous."

"Ridiculous," I said.

Lance was quiet.

"Why are you talking to me, Lance? Why are you suddenly being so helpful?" I asked.

He looked out toward the bay for a few moments, shrugged his shoulders, and turned back to look at me.

"I don't know," he said. "My father trusts you and he asked me to call you. He doesn't want us involved in a murder investigation, and he thinks you'll keep us out of it." He pulled a handkerchief from a pocket and wiped his neck. "And my sister seems to like you, too."

Well, well.

"They've dropped the charges against my friend, Lance. I've kept your family out of it so far. There's no reason to drag any of you into it now."

"It's over?" he asked. "Your buddy's off?"

"Uh-huh."

"Then why are you still interested in all this?" he asked.

"Habit, I guess."

He sat quietly on the bench.

"Are you being completely straight with me, Lance?" I asked.

He nodded.

"Is there anything else you need from me?" he asked.

"Can you think of anything else?"

"Nothing much, I guess. Rick did say they wanted to keep it quiet. They didn't want the rest of the crew to find out about it."

"But Derek didn't say much at all," I said.

"No, he didn't really. It was later that night that he loosened up and started talking about hitting the lottery and scoring with his boss's wife."

Lance turned quiet. He hoped I'd run out of questions. I still had a couple.

"I saw you talking to Rick and Cookie at the Bitter End Monday before last. What were you talking about?" I asked.

"I needed that money," Lance said. "I still need that money. I was trying to see if Rick was still interested. Cookie just happened to be there."

"Even though you thought it was ridiculous."

"I really need the money, man."

"Why not hit your dad up for it?" I asked.

"He says he's done funding my 'pipe dreams.' He thinks I should go out and get a job."

"It's not the worst advice," I said.

He stroked the stubble on his face again. It wasn't much. If he ever tried growing a beard, crop failure under the cheekbones would limit him to a Fu Manchu.

"What did Rick say about the investment opportunity?" I asked.

"He was great guns for it at the Willy-T, but by the time we met up at the Bitter End, he was all negative. Wouldn't give me the time of day."

"Maybe he'd lost his investment pool," I said.

"Nah," said Lance. "He never had one."

46

AL didn't want to be late picking up Liv, so he drove with all the reserve and professionalism of a Parisian taxi driver.

"I've been thinking about yesterday's conversation over lunch," I said. "Maybe you're right. Maybe we should think of bugging out of here."

"Those guys back there got you spooked?" he asked.

"Like you said, Al, we made the wrong play."

"Yeah, did you see the look on that big guy's face?" he said. "He didn't bat an eye when I put the knife on Rudy. He'd kill you before breakfast and then shoot the cook because his eggs were cold."

"I say we pick up Liv and go sailing tonight."

"Let's talk her into it over dinner."

We were a few minutes late, but any annoyance Liv might have harbored evaporated when Al told her the murder charges had been dropped. She agreed that a celebration was in order.

Al drove up to the Ridge Road and then down into Cane Garden Bay to their favorite beachfront restaurant. Our table was tucked between a lush tropical garden and one of the prettiest sugar-white sand beaches I'd ever seen. The beach was narrow, and our table was only yards from the wavelets that rolled onto the sand.

A dozen chartered sailboats tugged at their moorings a hundred yards off the beach to the northwest, and several dinghies shuttled their occupants to and from the island. A few surfers worked an overhead break on the reef a quarter mile beyond the mooring field. High slate-gray clouds with sharp, chrome-plated edges obscured the sun. Rays of golden light fanned out to the ocean from behind the clouds.

It was an idyllic setting, but all I could think about was a big, dumb killer being driven around in a small car by a reggae Rasputin.

"You're not especially talkative tonight, Sim," said Liv.

"I'm thinking about what to do now that Al is off the hook," I said. "Maybe we should take a little cruise on my boat. Get away for a few days."

"No, you guys buy that diving operation from Lars and get to work on building your business," she said. "That's what you should be doing."

"He's worried about the guy who killed Derek Brownell," said Al.

"Who cares?" asked Liv. She put her hand on Al's face and stroked his cheek. "The police know Al didn't do it. And that's all that matters, eh?"

"There might be a few complications," said Al.

"You'd better tell her," I said.

"Tell me what?" said Liv.

"There is a local gangster and we managed to get on his blacklist. Sim and I think that the three of us ought to take a few weeks off. Maybe sail to St. Martin or someplace until things cool down."

"Oh, c'mon," said Liv. "It's all over and done with. The local coppers can take care of their little gangsters."

The waiter's arrival cut the debate short. Al and Liv ordered appetizers to go with their Reggae Sunsplash and Island Cooler tropical drinks. I sipped a Coke and moved a few puzzle pieces around in my head. Part of me wanted to know who killed Derek Brownell and who broke into my boat. Another part of me knew I had to stay away from Jimmy Cattrel. All of me wanted to meet up with a tall and leggy lady sailor.

The band kicked in over at the other side of the restaurant around the same time our appetizers arrived. The coconut shrimp and conch fritters were good and the music wasn't too loud, but I wasn't enjoying it at all.

"This is the life, eh Sim?" asked Al.

"Very nice," I said.

The Caribbean sun dropped out of the clouds and kissed the ocean south of Jost Van Dyke. The surfers left the break one by one, and the flames of barbecues began to flare on the sterns of some of the moored boats. A waiter walked along the sand and lit the beachside torches, adding ambience to the little restaurant.

"You guys start your celebrating," I said. "I need to take a little walk. Whistle for me when dinner arrives."

I walked south along the beach out of the glow of the torches. About fifty yards down, I found a piece of driftwood that vaguely reminded me of something. I picked it up and continued walking.

Large stone steps led from the trees and across the beach into the water. I sat down on one of them and looked at the piece of wood, polished smooth by years of saltwater, wind, wave, and tide.

"I'm more than driftwood," I said to nobody in particular.

Or am I? Who knows? I might never know.

But the more immediate observations and questions overpowered the uncomfortable introspection. Cattrel had killed Ronnie and, probably, Stevenson. He may have killed, Cookie, too. Or maybe Germaine did it for him. Neither would have hesitated to kill Meghan Wells if she had been in the wrong place at the wrong time. But who killed Brownell and why? Cattrel didn't do it. He thought Al had killed Brownell while robbing him.

Brownell's passport was picked up off Beef Island, but his body was found floating off Scrub Island. Why were the body and passport found miles apart? And why did somebody break into *Figaro* and not take anything? Millet hadn't done it and Cattrel didn't need to.

I tossed the driftwood into the water and watched it bob forward in an animated way and then float dead out into the wavelets. Its movement in the water reminded me of a body in miniature, face down in the ocean swells. But it was much more rigid and, of course, quite a bit smaller. It was more like a small boat fender. The thought recalled an earlier conversation. I dialed Marie's cell phone.

"Hi sailor," I said. "Where are you tonight?"

"Moored at Cooper Island again," she said. "Are you done with your 'investigation' yet?"

"Well, there's good news and there's bad news. The good news is Al's been exonerated. The bad news is that a few other complications have popped up."

"Well, why don't you uncomplicate things and pop up over here?" she said.

"That sounds nice," I said. "Irresistible, in fact."

"Then stop resisting."

"Okay," I said. "Remember that little boat fender you told me about, the one you found with the passport?"

"Uh-huh."

"Do you still have it?" I asked.

"It's in the lazarette," she said.

"I want to see it. Will you be at Cooper tomorrow?"

"Probably," she said.

"Okay," I said. "Maybe I'll see you tomorrow."

"I'd like that."

The tone in her voice suggested that I'd like it, too.

We hung up and I walked back to our table at the edge of the sand. Al sat alone working on a fresh island drink and digging his toes into the sand. He had a huge smile on his face, like I might have to carry him to the car later that night.

"Where's Liv?" I asked.

"She trotted off to the little girl's room."

His eyes sparkled with new life in the pale gray irises.

"What's up?" I asked. "You've got that big grinning happy porpoise look on your face."

"I've made up my mind, Sim."

"About what?"

"It's the real deal," he said. "I'm going to ask her to marry me."

His words took a minute or two to sink in, and when they did I still couldn't quite get my head around them. It was as if he'd told me the world was flat or that Armstrong hadn't walked on the moon.

"You still with me, Sim?"

"Yeah, sure," I said. "You're gonna marry Liv. That's great."

"Why shouldn't I? She's a great lady and I'm not getting any younger."

"There's no reason not to, I guess."

"What do you mean 'you guess'?" asked Al.

"Nothing. Seriously, it's great," I said. "It's just that I always saw you as being the ultimate lone wolf."

"Maybe I'm growing up," Al said. "I mean, how many Friday nights have I spent at a bar pretending to have a great time drinking myself silly and hitting on pretty girls who weren't interested? And when I'd find one that was interested, I'd find out she wasn't very interesting. Maybe I'm a little tired of struggling through a conversation afterward."

"Some guys think of that as being a high-quality problem," I said.

"Not me," he said. "I'm tired of waking up alone and I don't want to wake up with a stranger."

"I hear you. Been there once or twice myself. For me, it comes as a heavily-armed attack of hormones that I mistake for love. It makes me do stupid things."

He shook his head.

"Nothing stupid here," he said. "I've reached the point in life where I can ignore all the fireworks. Listen, I've finally found a good, smart woman, and if I don't hold on to her, I'll regret it the rest of my life."

There was no point in arguing. Al was a big boy fully capable of making his own decisions. And a closed mouth gathers no fist.

"Liv and I really know each other, Sim. She knows my faults and doesn't judge me for them. I can be completely honest with her. She forgives me. No façade, no faking it. Life is just a hell of a lot better when she's around."

"I'm happy for you, Al. I really am," I said. "It just came as a bit of a surprise, okay?"

Al had a sip of his drink.

"Don't tell me you haven't thought about it yourself," he said. "Do you really like crawling into an empty berth every night?"

I thought about that. It wasn't a new thought.

"Are you going to ask her tonight?" I said.

"Maybe. I really want to talk her into getting out of here with us on *Figaro* and holing up for a while until this Cattrel thing blows over. You sure you can handle two passengers?"

"No problem," I said. "Plenty of room. When do you want to leave?"

"Right after dinner. We can head out to one of the other islands for the night, check out of Customs tomorrow, and then head for St. Martin or Anguilla. Anywhere we can hide out for a while."

"I'll call Phillips tomorrow and tell him to hang on to the bail money for us and to turn in the ledger to the RVIP," I said. "That'll throw a tomcat right into the middle of Cattrel's pigeons."

"I'm glad you're okay with all this, Sim. You're a good friend."

"Now, you're getting mushy," I said. "You better have another drink."

Al smiled and looked for the waitress. The area around us was quiet with couples here and there enjoying gentle conversation in the torchlit outdoor restaurant. The fronds of coconut palms rustled above us in the gentle breeze and the torches flickered. They heightened the illusion of remoteness and peace in a tropical paradise. A marvelous evening in one of the most beautiful parts of the world.

A high-pitched scream pierced the dark Caribbean night and shocked the beachside restaurant with a high-voltage burst of fear. It instantly registered in the eyes of the other guests. A second scream joined the first.

47

AL and I ran toward the source and found two lady tourists sobbing, an older man struggling to punch numbers into his cell phone, and a woman on the floor of the lady's room in a pool of blood. She had been an attractive blonde woman, a year or two younger than me, and well dressed. Taller. There was something familiar about her.

Her head hung unnaturally to one side, her eyes wide open in the surprise of sudden violent death. A long, curving gash stretched from one long black earring all the way across and under her jaw to the other side. The face pale and wax-like. A short and bloody wood-handled carpet knife lay on her chest. It was a gruesome scene. It was meant to be so. A message.

"Danique Cattrel," said Al. "Jimmy Cattrel's wife." He took in a deep breath and let it out slowly. "My alibi."

I suddenly recognized her as the tall, younger woman that got into the blue Jeep that dark night on Virgin Gorda. Al's admission raised a lot of questions, but it wasn't the time to ask.

We looked for Liv, but she wasn't in the ladies' room. The laughing and drinking Al of ten minutes ago was now stone-cold sober; his gray eyes now cold, metallic, and dangerous. He disappeared toward the kitchen and returned with a flashlight.

Al clicked it on and followed a bloody half-footprint outside the building. It was a large footprint. The trail disappeared in the middle of the parking lot where a car had waited for the killer. He quickly and methodically examined the parking lot, looking under and around parked cars while working his way toward the lot's entrance.

I looked the other direction. My eye caught a slight movement in the darkness of the trees about forty yards away. A glint of light reflected off a lens or a piece of metal or glass or something shiny in a spot where nobody had any business being.

I slipped into the shadows, away from the lights and the torches and the very shocked and nervous tourists, and walked toward the far end of the parking lot. Stepping down toward the beach, I turned right and continued on in the shadows until I was behind whomever had moved in the darkness and cast that reflection.

It was a local kid, a boy too young to drive. The jar in his hand was nearly empty.

"You saw it happen," I said.

He jumped straight up but only about three feet.

"No suh," he said.

The kid nervously put a lid on the jar and tried to leave. I grabbed him by the arm. He shook like a fresh tuna caught on the gaff.

"Calm down," I said.

I sat him roughly on the ground, kneeled down next to him, and grabbed the jar. The kid's breath smelled of bad alcohol. He looked around for a means of escape. There wasn't one.

"My dad makes it behind the house," he said. "He don't always count the jars right."

"I don't care about that. You saw a car idling over there in the parking lot a few minutes ago. Some people ran to it and the car left in a hurry. Tell me about it."

He swallowed and looked at the ground.

"I didn't see nobody," he said. "I didn't see no car."

"Yes, you did," I said. "If you tell me everything you saw right now, I won't tell a soul. If you don't, I'll hold you up by your ears and give you to the cops as a witness. And everybody on this island will know you saw it go down."

His head sunk to his chest without a sound. Tears dripped onto his shirt.

"Those men'll kill me if they find out I saw it."

"Tell me what you saw and I'll let you go," I said. "Nobody will know about it. Not the bad men; not the police."

He thought for a few moments and opened up. The kid worked at the restaurant cleaning dishes, bussing tables, whatever the boss needed done. He'd snuck off into the trees during his break to gag down a little homemade hooch.

He pointed at one end of the parking lot.

"A man was leaning against a white car in the lot over there," he said.

"Who was he?" I asked.

"A bad man. I've seen him before but I don't know his name."

"What did he look like?" I asked.

"About as tall as me and real skinny. He's got dreads and a long curly beard with a big pointy nose stickin' out of it. And he was lookin' all 'round the lot real nervous."

Rudy.

"Another man whistled from over there near the bathrooms and the skinny man got into the car and drove it to the middle of the lot with the lights off," he said. "Then a big man came running around the building carrying a blonde woman. He had his hand over her mouth but she bit him or something."

"What happened next?"

"She tried to get away but he hit her with the back of his hand and she went limp. The big guy put her in the back seat of the car and got in next to her. They took off down the parking lot and 'cross the small bridge. Then I heard the screaming."

The boy hadn't gotten a good look at the large man, but the description he gave would only fit the big killer with the bad complexion.

"I knew I should run away," he said, "but the feet wouldn't move. Are you going to tell anyone, mistuh?"

"Not a soul."

I let the boy go, and he disappeared into the trees. He wasn't heading back to work.

When I got back to the ladies' room, there were two more men calling the police on their cell phones and several others trying to calm those who had found the murdered woman. Al stood well outside the circle of people surrounding the body.

"Where the hell have *you* been?" he asked.

I jerked my head toward the beach and Al followed. We stood under the trees near the water well away from other ears.

"I found an eyewitness. Cattrel's two boys took Liv. They took her alive."

Al nodded. He was calm and completely focused.

"The message is obvious," said Al.

"Leverage against the ledger?"

"Not so much," said Al. "He wants me. He's Belisarius."

"What are you talking about?" I asked.

"Flavius Belisarius, the last real Roman general. Eastern Roman Empire; sixth century. His wife Antonina cheated on him with Theodosius. The affair made Belisarius look weak to his troops, so he retaliated. In his business, Cattrel can't risk being made to look weak. So he killed Danique. And now he wants me."

A crowd had gathered, and the restaurant manager tried to get the people to go back to their tables and enjoy their drinks and the Caribbean ambience. Some of them did.

"He wants you, too," said Al. "And the money he thinks we have."

How do you want to handle this, Al?"

"No cops. No noise. We take care of it ourselves."

His voice was cold and the meaning was clear.

The RVIP showed up, and the senior officer recognized the victim immediately. He quickly called it in and four other officers responded within minutes. They questioned everyone at the restaurant until past midnight. Neither of us mentioned Liv. As far as we could tell, the RVIP didn't have the slightest clue she'd been kidnapped and there was no point in telling them. An ambulance took the former Mrs. Cattrel away, and two old island men began to clean up the ladies' room.

"Haul away the corpse, mop up the pretty tile floors, and tomorrow's just another day in paradise," said Al.

I didn't have an answer. I walked toward Al's car.

"Leave it, Sim. They could be in the trees beyond the bridge with shotguns waiting for a blue Isuzu to fly by."

I found an unlocked yellow panel van in the parking lot. Al walked back to his car to get a few things while I got to work on the van. A tool box in the back yielded up a flat blade screwdriver and an adjustable wrench. I used the fat side of the wrench to hammer the screwdriver into the ignition on the steering column and then adjusted it to turn the screwdriver like a key. The van started up and Al got in.

"They teach you that trick in your part of the Navy?" asked Al.

"High school in Bakersfield."

Al checked all three pistols—all were loaded—and handed me Ronnie's .45. He held a pistol in each hand as I drove out of the parking lot and across the bridge. We didn't see any thugs with shotguns or automatic weapons. That, of course, didn't mean they weren't there.

"The house is too dangerous," I said. "We'll take *Figaro* out tonight and drop the hook at Peter Island."

Al shook his head.

"Not yet," he said. "We need some intel and I think I know where to get it."

48

AL told me where to drive, and I parked the van down the street from a small apartment building in Road Town. I picked up the .45.

"This is where your redhead came after you dropped him in Trellis Bay," he said.

We climbed the steps to the second floor. Al examined the door to one of the apartments for a few moments, stepped back, and kicked it directly below the handle. The door jamb shattered and shards of wood shot into the apartment. We walked in.

A tall, skinny local fellow sitting on a couch in front of a TV made a bad decision and reached for a pistol sitting on a coffee table. Al shot him in the arm with the silenced .32. The man yelled in pain and Al slapped him across the face.

"Shut up," said Al. "Or I'll put the next one up your nose."

The man sat there open-mouthed holding his arm. I walked through the small apartment checking the bedroom, bathroom, and kitchen.

"Clear," I said.

"Go down and wait in the car," said Al. "Text me if you see anybody on their way up here."

I walked out and down the steps to the van. There wasn't much traffic that time of night. A small motorcycle blatted past. Three dogs with a pack mentality ran down the street hunting something; probably anything.

Al came down about ten minutes later and walked over to the driver's side.

"I'll drive," he said.

I moved into the passenger seat, and Al slipped in behind the wheel. He put the silenced automatic on the engine cover between us.

"Liv is at Cattrel's place on Virgin Gorda," he said. "He's got a few of his men up there with him guarding her."

"You sure?"

"Pretty sure," said Al. "That fellow didn't want to say much. I had to get a bit creative."

"Creative?" I said.

He shrugged and turned onto the main road.

"Any chance that guy'll call Cattrel or his friends in the RVIP?"

Al looked at me and shook his head.

"This is an all-or-nothing mission," he said. "I'm not leaving any enemy soldiers alive on this battlefield."

Al drove through town at a relaxed pace. No reason to draw any attention.

"This van will be hot in less than an hour, Sim. So I need to get you back to your boat, dump this thing in town, and walk over to the ferry dock. I'll take the first boat to Virgin Gorda."

"She might not be alive, Al."

"She's alive," he said. "Cattrel wants his million bucks back and he very much wants to kill me. You, too. He wants to draw us both in, Sim, and Liv is the only bait that can do that."

Al entered the roundabout and turned toward Fort Burt.

"But he won't be expecting a rapid response," said Al. "People fear him. He's used to them hiding out or trying to run away. He'll think we're no different, so he'll give his people on Tortola a day or two to find us. If that doesn't work, he'll send one of Liv's fingers to Phillips hoping that will bring us in. Or maybe an eyeball. I'm not going to wait around for that."

"I want in," I said. "I want a piece of this. Let's both take that ferry."

Al was quiet as he drove toward the marina.

"Aren't we in this together?" I asked. "I know the house and the approach. And there's going to be a bunch of them guarding her."

"He's looking for two people. Two sets of footprints, two voices, a recognizable team. I'm not going to give him that edge."

He drove halfway down the driveway and stopped. I pulled out my pistol, stepped out of the car, and looked around.

"I'll do my recon in the morning," said Al. "You sail to the Sound tomorrow and I'll call you when I have a plan."

Al covered me from the van as I walked to the slip. I held the pistol low by my right leg. There were no attackers, no tough guys, nothing bad waiting for me in the darkness. I checked the boat carefully before getting onboard. It was locked up and unmolested. The halyard I'd laid casually across the companionway hatch hadn't been moved. I unlocked the companionway, started the engine, and cast off the mooring lines as Al drove the yellow van back onto Waterfront Drive.

The cruise ship blew its horn and powered slowly out of the main harbor a half mile away as I motored out of the marina. At least fifteen stories tall and a thousand feet long, it commanded the attention of any mariner at sea. High-intensity lamps bathed the waters in front of the ship in blue light and every deck emanated stark, bright incandescence. Strings of red and blue lights led from the bow up to the forward antenna structure, aft toward the tall ship's exhaust funnels, and back down to the fantail.

Three thousand people aboard that ship. Three thousand happy tourists enjoying *their* Caribbean. The one that comes with freshwater swimming pools, a spa, and dinner at the captain's table. *Their* time at sea with 24-hour internet, e-mail, and movies on demand.

It was nearly three in the morning when I reached Salt Island. The day anchorage near the abandoned village was empty, and there was hardly a breath of wind. I dropped the anchor in twenty feet of water and stepped down into the cabin. I was bone tired, but sleep didn't come easily.

Al was walking into a trap.

Mom had taught me to pray when I was a kid, but I gave up on the family religion shortly after a trucker crossed the double yellow line. Prayer hadn't been a part of my life since then. That night I gave it another try.

49

I woke to an almost windless Friday morning with a nagging question in my head. Why would someone break into *Figaro* and not take anything? I started looking around. Something had to have been taken or moved or altered, and knowing what it was might tell me who had broken in and why.

After an hour and a half of poring through bookshelves, lockers, ship's stores, and the wet locker, I opened up the chart table and felt that something was missing. It took me a minute to realize that the little slip of yellow notepaper from *Liquid Assets*, the one with the two telephone numbers written on it, was gone.

Why would somebody want that? Because they wanted the phone numbers? Because it tied Brownell to the yacht?

I checked the dialing history on my cell phone. The two numbers I'd dialed in multiple area codes two weeks earlier were still there. Batteries and cell phones die at the worst times, so I grabbed the nearest thing at hand, a nautical chart of the area, and wrote the numbers in the margin.

The fact that Brownell's body and his passport were found so far apart nagged at me, so I spread the chart out on the salon table and got out my cruising guide. A table in the back detailed the prevailing currents around the islands. A strong current flowed between Great Dog Island and Virgin Gorda. A portion of that current hugged the southern shore of Great Dog. As it approached the eastern end of Scrub Island, the current split into two legs; one that turned south toward Beef Island and another stronger one that flowed toward Goat Harbor.

Items floating in the main current would drift toward the split. Lightweight items likely to be blown by the northeasterly winds—a boat fender and a plastic bag, for instance—would be pushed toward the southern leg. A body might not be so affected by the wind and could be carried north to Goat Harbor by the stronger current.

Derek Brownell, the boat fender, and the plastic bag could have fallen into the water at the same spot south of Great Dog and then been separated by the wind and the currents. It was a working hypothesis, but I felt like I was trying to shoehorn the facts I had into a plausible theory.

Rick Schuster had told me that Derek went to meet a girl at Leverick Bay that night. Leverick was inside Virgin Gorda Sound and entirely unaffected by these currents. Had this girl killed him and dumped his body off Great Dog? Why would she toss his fake passport and a boat fender in with the body?

I grabbed my binoculars and stepped up into the cockpit. The day was clear, and moderate winds built from the northeast. Wispy clouds floated through the warm air like dismembered cotton balls.

The mooring field at Cooper Island was only about a mile and a half away. I glassed it and saw *D'Artagnan* hanging from her mooring directly upwind from my position. Even though it was perfect sailing weather, there was no time for tacking back and forth. I motored toward *D'Artagnan*.

While en route, I picked up my cell phone and called Jack Penn. He picked up on the second ring.

"You didn't call yesterday," he said. "I was getting worried that I'd have to turn that ledger over to the DEA."

"Feel free, my friend."

"I thought you were using it as leverage."

"The gloves are off, Jack. Fire for effect," I said.

He promised to get the ball rolling from his end and wished me luck.

The big wooden schooner rested at one of the southernmost moorings in Manchioneel Bay; I dropped *Figaro*'s hook about fifty yards downwind. When I looked up after setting the hook, I saw Marie motoring over in her boat's dinghy. Nice.

"Permission to come aboard," she said.

"Absolutely."

She climbed up the stern ladder and put her arms around me. It was good and it was warm and it felt real.

"Oh, that feels nice," I said.

"Are you staying the night?" she asked.

The question held promise.

"I'd love to, but I can't," I said.

She pulled back a little and studied my eyes.

"What's wrong?" she asked. "You look worried. Are you all right?"

"I'm okay," I said. "But something serious has come up with Al, and I need to deal with it."

"I'd rather you stayed here."

She traced a finger down my right cheek and onto my neck.

"We could have dinner tonight at the restaurant and then go for a walk on the beach," she said. "Maybe, later, we could go for that swim."

"That's much nicer than anything I have planned, but we'll have to settle for lunch," I said.

"I can settle, I suppose. And I have a little surprise for you."

She stepped back down into the dinghy and pulled a small white vinyl boat fender out of the forward compartment.

"Is this what you were looking for?" Marie asked.

The fender was about four inches in diameter and maybe a foot and a half long with molded eyelets in each end. Too small to be used by anything bigger than a runabout. A pale yellow stripe cir-

cled the middle and a three-foot length of white double-braid nylon line hung from one eyelet. A red tracer ran through the line.

"It can't possibly be that important," she said.

"It gave me an excuse to see you, didn't it?"

Marie smiled. We got into her dinghy and she piloted it to the
beach club where we ordered lunch.

"I think this is our first meal together without Lance or your father around," I said.

"They're diving over the Rhone today." She thought for a moment and then raised an eyebrow. "Are you still investigating the
Tanner family?"

"Like I said last night, they've dropped the charges against Al."

"So it's over?" asked Marie.

"That part is."

A smile crept across her face.

"I think I'll miss your interrogations," she said.

"No," I said, "those will continue unabated."

She smiled again. Sunlight filtered through the palm fronds. A
cool breeze wafted through the beach club. The waitress brought
hot conch fritters. Many things were right with the world. There
was no point in bringing up things that weren't.

My cell phone rang.

"Sorry," I said. "I have to take this."

Marie shrugged.

"We still on for tonight?" said Al.

"Sure," I said. "Should I bring anything?"

"The party's going to be up near the Sound. You might want to
take your boat there and pick a quiet spot to hole up near Gun
Creek."

I could hear him unfolding a piece of paper in the wind.

"You still have that map you got from the real estate agent?" he
asked.

"Uh-huh."

"Take your dinghy to Gun Creek and walk up the street toward Spanish Town. There's a bend in the road with lots of trees about half a click up from the last shop. Meet me there at oh-two-hundred and go dark."

"Got it," I said.

"If I'm not there at oh-two-hundred, then sail off to somewhere more restful and have a good life."

"I'll see you tonight."

"Roger that," he said.

I hung up and put my phone back in my breast pocket.

"So what isn't finished?" asked Marie.

"What?"

"You said that they dropped the charges against your friend and that 'that part' was finished," she said. "So what part isn't? What keeps you from staying here?"

"A few complications," I said.

It was an exercise in extreme understatement.

"What kind of 'complications'?" she asked.

"Just a loose end or two," I lied. "A few pieces of the puzzle that I haven't yet found. It'll all be wrapped up in a few days, though."

"And what happens after that?"

She speared a conch fritter with her fork and nibbled on it.

"I don't know," I said. "Day sailing in the Sound, a picnic, and a swim. Some intense questioning over dinner and drinks."

Tropical birds sang in the trees.

"You could quit now," she said. "Ignore the complications and call it finished. Maybe we could go sailing for a few days on your boat."

"How would Lance and your dad get along without you?"

"That's their problem."

"You have no idea how tempting that is," I said. "But I need to ride this thing out. Al is still in a bit of a fix and he needs my help."

We walked back to the dinghy dock. Her hair blew and glistened in the wind as she took me back to *Figaro*.

"Can I call you in a couple of days?" I asked.

"Maybe. One of dad's clients has an estate in the Turks and Caicos and he's invited us there for Christmas. Immigration is closed on Sunday, so Dad is saying that he wants to clear out tomorrow. My phone might not work when we get there."

"I'll find you," I said.

Marie kissed me, got back in her dinghy, and motored back to the big schooner. I thought about the alternatives for a few moments, then weighed *Figaro*'s anchor, raised the main, and headed back out into the channel.

50

I could have motored all the way to the Sound if I'd had to, but I won't endure the noise and smell of a diesel engine if I can avoid it. I prefer sailing. And I had time. Once out of the lee of Cooper Island I unfurled *Figaro*'s genoa on a starboard tack and set Kyle to steer a course past the southeastern shore of Beef Island, where Marie had found Brownell's passport.

The apparent wind was north of east and felt stronger because we were partially headed into it. *Figaro* was nearly close-hauled, but she bit hard into the wind, rose over the swells easily, and made good progress. Now and then a wave would rise up onto the port bow and sluice down the lee side of the deck to wash overboard.

I sat on the windward side of the cockpit and kept a watch for other vessels while Kyle steered without complaint. It was a good time to call Phillips. After the usual folderol of justifying both my existence and my reason for talking to an attorney, the firm's receptionist connected me with Al's good and proper solicitor.

"The prosecution tells me that Mr. Higgins is no longer a suspect," he said. "Do you have any idea why?"

"They were cowed by your superior legal skills?" I suggested.

"Hardly."

"I understand that Al was enjoying the company of a female the night of the murder," I said. "Apparently, the lady contacted your attorney general and claimed that Al's companionship had lasted late into the morning."

"She must be a trusted person. Someone whom the government knows well."

Knew well.

"In any case, I am told that you can now retrieve Al's bail money," I said.

"That has already been accomplished, Mr. Greene. Where should I send the funds?"

"Hang on to them for a while. I may be traveling out of the country for some time."

"We can certainly keep the funds in our trust account for you if you wish. Is there anything else I can assist you with?" he asked.

"You can turn that ledger over to Constable Millet."

"Are you quite certain you want to do that, Mr. Greene? It puts you squarely on the wrong side of Jimmy Cattrel. That may not be the healthiest place to find oneself."

"I'm already there, Mr. Phillips. It's time to get the ledger to the authorities. I know tomorrow is Saturday, but could you get it to Constable Millet tomorrow morning?" I asked. "It needs to go directly to him. Nobody else."

"Of course," he said.

I thanked him, hung up, and dialed Millet's number at the station. The receptionist transferred me and he picked up on the first ring.

"Danique Cattrel was murdered last night, Mr. Greene. And I understand that you and your friend were there."

"Sheer coincidence, Constable."

"There is no such thing in my world," he said. "I have instructed my officers to bring you and Mr. Higgins in for questioning. Where may we locate you?"

"That won't be necessary, Constable. One of Cattrel's underlings did it. Probably on Jimmy's orders. Please don't ask me how I know. Would you now like the evidence that will put him behind bars?" I asked.

"Bring it down to my office anytime, Mr. Greene."

"Nope," I said. "Too busy sailing right now."

"It would be much easier for all of us if you and Mr. Higgins would turn yourselves in," said Millet.

"Mr. Phillips will have the evidence delivered to you in the morning. It's got everything you need to put Jimmy Cattrel in Her Majesty's Prison for a very long time."

Millet paused for a few moments.

"My sources tell me that Jimmy Cattrel wants both of you dead," said Millet.

"My dad used to say that you can tell a lot about a man by the enemies he makes."

"Does this have anything to do with Mrs. Cattrel's murder?" he asked.

"Al was having an affair with her," I said. "She was his alibi. She called your attorney general. Cattrel found out and killed her. Now he's after Al and me."

Millet was quiet for a moment.

"You were right about Mrs. Wells and Jared Payne, by the way," he said.

"Jared Payne?" I asked.

"Mr. Wells's cook."

"Did you find anything on his yacht?" I asked.

"Blood," said Millet. "Mr. Wells did his best to clean it off his yacht tender but it showed up clearly last night under the ultraviolet."

"You've identified the blood already?" I asked.

"The results are expected later this afternoon, but it doesn't matter. Mr. Wells has already confessed to killing both of them and is now in custody."

"He'll lawyer up on you," I said. "Better get all you can from him now."

"He told us that the three of them were in the yacht tender two days ago and that he'd confronted them with the details of their affair."

"I take it that Mrs. Wells was not sufficiently contrite."

"Apparently not," he said. "He shot them both, stripped them, and dumped their bodies in the Sound." He was quiet for a moment. "I suspect that I am going to 'owe you one,' as you Yanks are fond of saying."

"I'll try to think of something."

"Don't get carried away," he said.

We hung up and I kept sailing. One of the nice things about single-handed sailing is the amount of time you can spend thinking. Lately, I'd been thinking a lot about Marie and about not sailing single-handed. But now I thought of Terrence Wells, his murdered wife, and the unfortunate cook.

Wells had spent ten or twenty times more on that big yellow boat than I would earn in my lifetime. Wealth had brought him a great deal of comfort but little happiness. Now his pride and temper would cost him the rest of his life in a Caribbean prison.

And what about Meghan Wells? Money, clothes, and travel had not made her happy. Was her happiness found only with other men? Did she want to hurt her husband or was it merely an afternoon's diversion? The reasons don't matter much once they lay you out on a cold steel table.

Figaro headed toward the Sound and Kyle could not have cared less. He steered his course depending entirely on the direction of the apparent wind. But where was I headed?

51

TWO more tacks and a couple of hours later, I approached the east end of Scrub Island not far from where Brownell's body had been found. The sun set and the wind died with it. The swells, too, subsided into low rollers. I started the engine, furled the genoa, and turned on the running lights. I sat in the red glow of *Figaro*'s instruments and motored toward the Sound.

The shortest course to the entrance at Colquhoun Reef would have been between the three Dog Islands, but it was nighttime and I didn't feel like threading my boat through that narrow channel and adding unnecessary drama to a short passage in the dark. I chose a course south of Great Dog.

If my theory concerning the local currents was correct, Brownell had been dumped overboard somewhere in this area. But, of course, only the killer knew for certain.

As I passed Great Dog, I focused on the red glow from *Figaro*'s GPS unit and watched the numbered coordinates for latitude and longitude change as the vessel moved through the smooth water. At one point, the coordinates on the display seemed strangely familiar, and I pushed the "man overboard" button to save the location. It was an instinctive reaction; a reflexive response to a quiet urging from the little voice.

Darkness fell hard over the islands before I reached the channel. I picked out the lighted red and green buoys that marked the passage through Colquhoun Reef and carefully piloted *Figaro* between them and into the Sound.

The lights on *Liquid Assets* were not as bright as before, but she could still be seen anchored in the same spot off the Bitter End Yacht Club. Probably not moving anytime soon, either.

The spot I'd taken nearly two weeks before in Biras Creek was occupied by a small ketch, so I had to anchor farther out this time. I was more exposed in this new spot, but anybody with a gun would have to swim a lot farther to reach me.

I turned on *Figaro's* anchor light and sat in the cockpit with my back against the cabin top. The ink-dark waters of the Sound reflected the anchor lights of the boats moored at its edges. A few other boats, running lights moving along the dark Sound, hunted about for a place to drop the hook.

The hard wind and bright sun had burned me that afternoon, so I shucked off my shorts and T-shirt and dove off the stern. Some sailors will swear that sharks come out at night to feed but I'd decided a long time ago that the sharks were always there and that the worst of them walked upright and on shore.

No sharks got me during the short swim, so I climbed back into the cockpit, showered off the salt water, and toweled myself dry. I realized that I'd forgotten to turn off the instruments after anchoring and silently cursed the wasted electricity. As I stepped down into the cabin, I remembered the GPS and the man overboard button. I retrieved the stored coordinates, wrote them down on some scratch paper, and switched off the instruments.

My phone buzzed on the chart table and I recognized the number from California.

"Is that you, Sim?"

"Frank," I said. "Always a pleasure. What can I do for you?"

"You can get your sorry ass out of the British Virgin Islands," he said. "If you place any value on said ass."

"Why would I want to do that? It is beautiful here."

"That guy you asked about. Jimmy Cattrel? I just got a call from a guy in the department who's been reviewing some cell phone interceptions. He thinks Cattrel is going to take you out along with that old tough-guy buddy of yours."

"Any idea why?" I asked.

"We're not sure what your connection to all this is, but Cattrel is getting some heated phone calls from a Venezuelan family. A powerful Venezuelan family. The calls involve a large chunk of money that has gone missing."

"None of that involves me."

"You might not think so," he said. "But you are getting the blame and you are now a target." He paused for a minute. "An associate on the East Coast said some fellows met with you in Puerto Rico a couple of days ago and offered you some assistance."

"Yeah, they did. It was nice of them to think of me. Where'd they get the idea that I was qualified to help them in their efforts?"

"I might have given them that idea," he said. "You should have taken them up on their offer."

"Whatever," I said. "How old is this information you've given me?"

"Yesterday," he said. "Day and a half, maybe."

I thought how nice it would have been to have had that little bit of intel a day and a half ago, but there was no point in mentioning the last twenty-four hours to a guy in law enforcement. Especially since so many laws had been and were about to be broken.

"Okay," I said. "Al and I will slink off to some other island and let you professionals deal with these drug lords."

"Good idea," he said.

"You know how I have this habit of giving you information that helps you run down bad guys in the States?" I said.

"Habit? Since when is *once* a habit?"

"Well, now I have something more for you. Electronic files," I said. "Lovely electronic files filled with incriminating information."

I told him about the nature of the files and the level of detail. He gave a low whistle and mentioned how certain federal agencies would love to see them.

"Can you email those files to me?" he asked. "I'll make sure they get to the right people."

"Will do. And feel free to take all the credit yourself."

"You'd rather stay under the radar?" he asked.

"That is a big 'affirmative', Frank."

"Okay, send them off. Can you do one thing for me, though?"

"What's that?" I asked.

"Stay away from Cattrel," he said. "He's bad news. The worst. Just sail off to some other country, and keep your broken nose clean."

I agreed to give it a try, hung up the phone, and stared out the companionway into the darkness.

Too late for that.

52

I dug under the chart table and found my diving watch; the black one with the luminous hands. It was ten o'clock and I had a few hours left to get ready. I rummaged around in the forepeak and found a dark blue pullover sweatshirt and some black jeans. I put on the jeans and tossed the sweatshirt into the cockpit.

The spare magazine for the .45 was in *Figaro*'s little hidey-hole. I ejected the ammunition, counted it, and reloaded both magazines. I slipped the pistol and the spare mag into my jeans' pocket. I pulled some crackers out of one of the lockers and some hard cheese out of the icebox. I took both up into the cockpit where I could wait out the clock.

The Sound was dark and quiet with only a slight breeze coming in from the east. I wondered if Liv was still alive. I thought of Marie. I ate a cracker and some cheese. I checked my watch. Ten thirty. Time flies.

At one in the morning I cocked a round into the .45's chamber, clicked on the thumb safety, and tucked it back into my pocket. I picked up the sweatshirt and motored *Figaro*'s dinghy over the still waters of the Sound toward Gun Creek. I killed the outboard about two hundred yards north of the dinghy dock and rowed the rest of the way.

I walked past the empty restaurant and the closed shops. Dominos were still slapping the table at the bar where I'd talked with Levon, but nobody saw me as I walked past. I continued on up the road and put on my sweatshirt as I approached the bend and the trees Al had described.

The road was quiet and empty. The hands on my watch read two in the morning. I wondered where Al could be.

And then he was standing right next to me.

"I think it'll be easier than I originally thought," he said.

"How do you do that?" I asked. "How do you just pop up out of nowhere like a ghost?"

He chuckled quietly.

"Years of expensive training," he said. "Your tax dollars at work, my friend."

We walked along the road like two guys working their way back home late after a Friday night on the town. Quiet and unhurried.

"Another mile or so," he said. "But let's take our time. I want to hit them around oh-three-hundred."

We continued walking up the road. We were quiet and relaxed. We weren't trying to be invisible; only unremarkable and easily forgotten. We passed a few dark houses and saw nobody. Not much went on in this part of Virgin Gorda after two in the morning.

"I've been watching them a good part of the day," said Al. "Cattrel came up in that big blue Jeep around eleven this morning and packed some things. Rudy drove him and that big, quiet guy away in the Jeep around noon. Rudy came back alone an hour later. I think that big guy is some sort of bodyguard."

"How many are there?" I asked.

"Only five," he said. "I almost didn't bother to call you but I figured it was better to be safe than sorry. And it is a hostage situation. Not a lot of room for error."

"I got a call from Frank Bartholomew this evening."

"And what do the *federales* have to say?" asked Al.

"He said they intercepted some cell phone calls," I said. "There is some discord between Cattrel and his Venezuelan masters. Cattrel blames it all on you."

"Great."

"Frank thought we should know that Cattrel doesn't like us very much."

Al chuckled.

"There's nothing like getting intel a few days late."

We walked along and I soon recognized Cattrel's neighborhood. We moved into the trees and slowed our pace. Al led me to a spot at the edge of some tall bushes about two hundred yards from the house. The hill I'd walked down the previous week stretched up to our left and Cattrel's house stood directly in front of us. Lights were on in the kitchen and living room. A shallow gully stretched from our position to the house. There was no moon.

"They've set a little trap for us, but it's not a very good one," said Al. "There's a guy with an Uzi sitting under a tree in the front yard of the house. He's watching the main road. There are two more guys up on that hill with AK-47's watching the back. They're complete amateurs, though. You'll see them in a minute."

I studied the hill and saw the orange glow of a cigarette being puffed in the dark. Another one farther away along the hill's ridge glowed a half minute later.

"Bad habit," I said. "Not healthy at all."

Al smiled.

"Rudy and some other guy are in the house with Liv," he said.

"You sure she's in there?"

"I saw her through the living room window when Cattrel was here this morning. I couldn't tell what he was yelling at her but I saw him slap her across the face a couple of times."

"And you didn't kill him right then?" I asked.

"I'm a professional, Sim. It was broad daylight with bad odds. I'll concentrate on taking him out once Liv is safely away from here."

Al looked at his watch.

"Two forty," he said. "These guys text each other every thirty minutes on the quarter hour."

"You're sure about that?"

"I've been watching them for over five hours."

"Okay," I said. "What's the plan?"

He reached into his pocket, pulled out the silenced .32 automatic, and handed it to me.

"Can you shoot straight with a silencer?" he asked.

I nodded.

"Have you got that forty-five on you?" he asked.

I handed him Ronnie's pistol and the spare magazine. He checked it over quickly and slid it into his pocket.

"Work your way down that gully," he said. "Take your time. On the off-chance that one of these guys on the hill takes a shot at me, I want you in place by the carport. If Rudy or the other guy comes out of the house, take him down quietly. I'll join you when I'm done with the sentries."

Al disappeared into the trees without a sound and I crawled down the gully toward Cattrel's house. There wasn't any noise; nobody came out into the carport. Al joined me at 3:05.

"The boys on the hill are no longer a factor," he said.

It was a matter-of-fact statement with only a hint of pride. Like announcing that he'd finished painting a bathroom.

"I'll take out the guy in front and then we can draw the other two out of the living room away from Liv."

"How?"

"The master electrical panel is on the other side of the house. I'll kill the power. When the lights go out, start the Jeep and flip on the headlights. The keys are in it. The sound of the Jeep starting will draw both of them to this side of the house. I'll go in the front door and get Liv."

"What do you want me to do with the other two?"

"Don't kill them both unless you have to. I have some questions to ask."

He disappeared into the dark and I stepped over to the Jeep and waited. The lights in the house went out a few minutes later and loud, agitated talking came from inside the house. I heard a cell phone ring way up on the hill. Nobody answered. I started the Jeep, turned on the headlights, and slipped back into the darkness behind the carport.

Footsteps sounded in the house by the kitchen door, and a tall local guy came out the kitchen door with a short-barreled shotgun. The man looked around and swung the shotgun. He turned toward me, and my training kicked in. I double-tapped the trigger and put two rounds in the ten ring. He dropped the shotgun, fell to his knees, and collapsed on the concrete next to the Jeep. The kitchen door slammed shut from the inside. I picked up my spent brass and stepped back into the darkness to wait for Al.

He came out the kitchen door with Liv about five minutes later and headed toward the Jeep. Liv was alert but a little unsteady on her feet. Al had his arm around her. Her left cheek was bruised and swollen, but there was fire in both eyes.

"Wait here," he said. "I need to ask a few questions and tidy up a bit. Shouldn't be long."

He disappeared back into the house. I helped Liv into the Jeep.

"Are you okay?" I asked.

"No," she said. "But I will be."

Al was back in less than ten minutes. He climbed into the back of the Jeep.

"Get us back to Gun Creek," said Al.

I drove down the street we'd walked up. Normal speed. Nothing loud or unusual to annoy the locals. I parked in a stall near the dock, and Al and I helped Liv into the dinghy. Al went back to the

Jeep and wiped off fingerprints. I mounted the oars when he returned.

"Use the motor, Sim," Al said. "Nobody is following us and oars look suspicious."

With three people in it, the little rubber boat was at maximum capacity and considerably slower than usual. But the Sound was calm and we made the trip to *Figaro* without incident. Al climbed out of the dinghy first, and we both helped Liv onto the swim step and into the cockpit. Al helped her down into the cabin while I tied off the dinghy and went forward to check *Figaro*'s anchor. By the time I could join Al down below, Liv was asleep in the forward stateroom. Al helped himself to a beer from the icebox.

"I didn't hear you shoot Rudy in the house," I said.

"I haven't pulled a trigger all night," he said.

He reached into his jacket and pulled out his military combat knife.

"No sense disturbing the neighbors if I don't have to," he said.

He washed the knife in the sink, put it back into its leather sheath, and picked up his beer.

"There are a couple things you might like to know," he said. "Cattrel didn't kill Brownell and his guys didn't break into your boat, either."

"Are you sure of that?" I asked.

Al gave a faint smile.

"Pretty sure," he said. "I asked Rudy. I think he was honest with me. He was highly motivated."

Al drained the bottle.

"Don't worry," he said. "No witnesses, no fingerprints, no evidence."

He looked very tired but very relieved.

"Take the quarter berth and get some sleep," I said. "I'll stay up in the cockpit tonight."

I took a pillow with me and stretched out on one of the long seat cushions. The sliver of a crescent moon rose and pushed away some of the darkness. Lumpy clouds marched across the sky doing their best to keep the moon from seeing the horror on earth.

53

THE sun woke me like a church bell on a quiet Sunday morning. Except it was Saturday. I woke up momentarily confused and wondering if the previous night's activities had been only a horrible dream. No such luck.

I crept down below to check on my guests. They were both still asleep, so I grabbed an apple and a Coke and stepped back up into the cockpit for breakfast. I ate it with my back against the bulkhead and my eyes on the Sound to the west. A few small racing catamarans jockeyed for position and sliced the smooth water between Gun Creek and the Bitter End. A half dozen cruising boats sailed or motored in and around various anchorages. Life in the Sound went on unaffected by murder, kidnapping, and smuggling.

The companionway steps creaked.

"Did I really sleep five whole hours?" asked Al.

"Feeling like a new man?"

He nodded as he stepped into the cockpit, bottle in hand.

"You're running out of beer," he said. "That's a lousy way to run a boat."

"It's a wonder she doesn't sink."

He nodded.

"Liv still asleep?" I asked.

"Yep. She can sleep all day if she likes," he said. "She probably ought to. Our ride won't be here until dark anyway."

"So you've already made arrangements to hide out somewhere until the authorities reel in Cattrel?" I asked.

Al nodded. "Sort of," he said. "I only need to hide Liv until it's all over."

He took another pull from his beer.

"Rudy told me that Cattrel keeps a second home on Guana Island," he said.

I took another bite of apple.

"That's where he is now," he said.

"How is Liv reacting to all this?"

"They weren't very nice to her. Kept her tied up and blindfolded and slapped her around some. I guess she nearly bit off Germaine's finger the other night."

We were quiet for a minute. I could tell he was planning something.

"Phillips has probably given Millet the ledger by now," I said. "They might be picking up Cattrel as we speak."

He shrugged. "Could be," he said. He drank the beer. He acted as if he didn't care what Millet did or what happened to Jimmy Cattrel.

"You got everything under control?" I asked.

"As much as I ever will," he said.

"Mind if I go for a swim?"

He shook his head.

I grabbed my goggles and went for the familiar swim to the little point of land a half mile south. The sun was high in the blue Caribbean sky and the water was clear. The fish, rays, crabs, and lobsters were still there. A pair of young sea turtles ate eelgrass.

The door to *Figaro*'s forward stateroom was closed when I got back, and I could hear Liv crying softly. Al's voice was near her and low. I turned on the stereo to give them some privacy.

The little voice reminded me of some GPS coordinates, and I dug out my chart for the BVI, the piece of scratch paper I'd written on, and my parallel rules. I penciled in a small cross at the spot on the chart corresponding to the latitude and longitude coordinates I'd written down.

I'd motored over that little spot of saltwater south of the Great Dog the previous night. It was fairly close to the island, at the edge of the current, and pretty much in the middle of nowhere. Great Dog Island was uninhabited. There were no tourist traps or restaurants nearby. It wasn't even close to a decent overnight anchorage.

Why was this important?

I felt uncomfortable listening to Al and Liv in the forward stateroom; out of place on my own boat. So I put the charts away and went back up to the cockpit.

The noonday sun beat down on *Figaro* with purpose, and I decided it was time to pull the awning out of the lazarette and set it up over the cockpit. It took twenty minutes to unroll it, lay it out, and attach it to *Figaro*'s standing rigging, but the resulting shade was well worth it.

I lay down on the cockpit cushions under the awning and tried to read some more Jack London. Jack and his wife and crew were in the Solomon Islands dodging headhunters and cannibals. It was hard to believe that the savagery he described as commonplace occurrences took place only a hundred or so years ago. Then again, given my recent experiences with Rudy, Germaine, and Cattrel, civilization might not have made all that much progress. Today's cannibals simply didn't bother to eat the people they killed.

It was a warm day and I'd had a long swim. Al was out of trouble, Liv was safe, and Cattrel would soon be behind bars. I should have been calm and content and able to enjoy a good book in the shade on a warm day. But somebody unknown had killed Derek Brownell and probably meant me harm. The little voice kept nagging me about a meaningless bit of ocean near a worthless lump of earth called Great Dog Island.

I dialed Constable Millet's number, and the receptionist put me through to him.

"I'm glad you called," he said. "It's all resolved. It appears that Mr. Wells also killed Derek Brownell."

"He confessed to that, too?"

"No," he said. "He has a lawyer now who effectively prevents him from telling us anything productive. But we've taken blood samples for all three victims—Mrs. Wells, the cook, and Derek Brownell—from that yacht tender of his. We're now satisfied that Mr. Wells killed Derek Brownell."

"Why?"

"I'm not sure I understand you, Mr. Greene."

"Why did Wells kill him?" I asked.

"Jealousy?"

"There's more to it than that," I said. I was certain of it.

Millet was silent.

"Have you picked up Cattrel yet?" I asked.

"We are still examining and decoding the ledger. If it says what you claim it does, then we should have enough information by tomorrow morning to make an arrest."

"Just grab him and get it over with," I said. "I'm tired of feeling like I have to hide from one of your former cops."

"We will take whatever steps we deem necessary once we are satisfied that we have sufficient cause," said Millet.

"It's your island, I guess. I figured getting that ledger to you this morning would put him out of circulation."

"It very well might, Mr. Greene," he said. "And, yes, it is our island."

He hung up.

I looked out into the Sound again. It was afternoon and the breeze had picked up, rolling and pushing the water into miniature versions of ocean swells. A few of the small catamarans, cruising boats, and water taxis were still out there. Everybody in the Sound enjoying the blissful, joyous, and comfortable life of the relaxed tourist.

Everybody but me.

I closed my eyes and tried to take a nap, but the little voice spoke louder of charts and paper and Great Dog Island. I went below again, grabbed the BVI chart, and took it up into the cockpit. I stared at the place *Figaro* had passed over yesterday and the coordinates. Then I glanced over at the phone numbers I'd written in the margin.

There were similarities. The three-digit prefixes of the phone numbers were embedded within the coordinates I'd plotted on the chart. I stared at the two pairs of numbers for several minutes working it out in my head.

I wrote a "1" in front of the first phone number and a "6" in front of the second. With those additions and a change in punctuation, "847-8275" became 18°47.8275' North latitude and "446-0314" became 64°46.0314' West longitude.

Pieces of the puzzle that had languished at the edge of the table for weeks moved slowly into place. Jimmy Cattrel thought Brownell had pilfered cash from Cattrel's money laundering operation. It was a lot of cash. He figured that Al had killed Brownell, had taken the money from him, and had given it to me to hide on *Figaro*.

Days before Brownell was killed, Rick told Lance they had a load of dough to invest in his business. Derek disappeared and then, suddenly, Rick acted like he didn't have any nest egg at all.

So what if Brownell took Cattrel's cash, hid it underwater, and wrote the coordinates from a GPS unit on the slip of note paper from *Liquid Assets*? He left off the leading digit of each number—he knew the cash was hidden in the vicinity of Great Dog Island—and disguised the remaining digits as telephone numbers. Clever. He stuck the note in his alter ego's passport and put that, along with a safe deposit key, into a plastic bag.

I entered the new coordinates into *Figaro*'s GPS, saved them as a waypoint, and plotted the position on my chart. It was nothing more than an "X" off the southwest point of Great Dog, but "X" marked the spot.

I considered yelling "Eureka" or "By Jove" or otherwise sharing my new theory with Al but decided not to bother my two guests. I folded up the chart, tossed it onto the table down below, and laid down for a nap in the shade of the awning. The little voice quieted down. I was on the right track.

54

FOOTSTEPS on the companionway woke me, and I noticed that the sun had traveled quite a bit to the west during my nap.

"You mind if I whip up something to eat?" asked Al.

I told him I didn't and listened to what sounded like the opening and closing of every locker, drawer, hatch, and door on the boat. Twice.

Al hummed while making dinner and Liv said little. What she did say was so quiet I couldn't make it out. Al reached up from the galley and handed me a sandwich and a glass of water.

"Water?" I asked.

"No other options, Captain."

I could almost hear him shaking his head.

It was an ugly sandwich. Shredded leftover barbecued fish mixed with mayo and incongruous clumps of diced pickle. This was spread between two slices of almost-too-old bread. Ugly but delicious, it filled the hole in my gut.

I got the distinct impression that Al and Liv still had lots to talk about, so I dove over the side, swam to shore, and sat in the sand under a palm tree. I laid my head back against a rock and looked up into the sky between the palm fronds, trying to reason out the circumstances of Brownell's murder.

The murder that started all the problems. I thought long and hard and worked to narrow the field of suspects. It was a short list, and it didn't include either Jimmy Cattrel or Terrence Wells.

Al rescued me from too much thought by popping out of the cabin and waving for me to come back. It was a short swim. He tossed me a towel as I climbed the boarding ladder.

"Liv seems pretty quiet today," I said. "She okay?"

"Not great. She went back to sleep just now, but it was ugly stuff yesterday. She's tough, though. She'll get through it."

"I've been thinking about heading over to St. Maarten," I said. "You guys want to come along? Getting away from here might help."

"Liv's passport is at the house," said Al. "And it's too soon to go back there. I've made other arrangements for Liv until Cattrel is gone."

"You need me to take you anywhere?"

Al shook his head.

"The cops will have Cattrel bagged in a couple of days," I said. "You want to just hang out on *Figaro* with me until he's in jail?"

"No," he said. "We'll be out of your hair after sunset."

Al went back down below and crawled into the V-berth next to Liv. I stayed topside and read more of London's *Snark*.

The sun dropped behind Mosquito Island and the Sound fell into darkness. I put the book away. Minutes later, I saw red and green navigation lights heading toward Biras Creek.

Al must have heard the boat's engine. He appeared in the companionway with the .32 automatic in his hand. A small cabin cruiser barely twenty-five feet long pulled up alongside and Al disappeared below. Henry stood behind the wheel.

"Reading any cards tonight?" I asked.

"I'm just looking for my man Al," he said.

The Caribbean accent was gone for the night.

"Right here," said Al.

He helped Liv up the companionway and aboard Henry's boat. He turned to me and spoke under his breath.

"Cattrel is down six men right now, but he is still alive," he said. "And he still wants both of us dead. You might want to lie low for a couple of days."

I nodded.

"And it'd probably be better if you hadn't seen us at all today or yesterday," he said.

"Seen who?"

He nodded.

Al hopped aboard the little cabin cruiser, and Henry pulled the boat away. I was alone again. I opened up the chart table, found my phone, and dialed Marie's number. The call shunted to a soulless recording that told me her phone was out of the service area.

There wasn't any food on the boat, I was tired of swimming back and forth from Biras Creek, and I wasn't in the mood for music or reading. There was nobody to talk with and nothing aboard *Figaro* needed fixing. And I was out of beer.

55

ABSENT a compelling reason to get up early, I slept in. I didn't have to go to work and I didn't have to walk the dog. There weren't any kids to get off to school and I didn't need to pay a mortgage. But I did feel some urgency to call the cops.

"Have you arrested Cattrel, yet?" I asked.

"Eager to come out of hiding, are you?"

I could hear the smile behind Constable Millet's voice.

"As a matter of fact, yes," I said.

"You needn't wait much longer. It is Sunday and Mr. Cattrel almost always attends church in Road Town. We plan to pick him up before noon."

"I'll feel lots better when he's behind bars," I said.

"We'll call you when it's over, Mr. Greene."

"Thanks," I said.

I thought for a moment and decided to throw Millet an extra bit of information that might save him some time.

"I don't think Wells killed Derek Brownell," I said.

"We are fairly certain of it," said Millet. "As I told you, Mr. Brownell's blood was found on the yacht tender."

"Brownell was shot with a nine-millimeter, wasn't he?" I asked. "But that's not what killed Cookie and Mrs. Wells, is it?"

"We are of the opinion that Mr. Wells could probably afford several guns," he said.

Millet's voice sounded testy. There was no point in being smart about it and getting him mad, so I dropped it. It wasn't my issue anyway.

"You're right," I said. "I'll stay out of your hair."

"While I've never quite understood that particular example of American idiom," he said, "I am quite relieved to hear you say it."

"Message received and understood, Constable."

We hung up and I decided to celebrate Cattrel's impending arrest by having an early lunch at the Bitter End Yacht Club. I weighed anchor, motored *Figaro* the few hundred yards to the BEYC, and took a guest slip.

As I walked down the dock toward the shore, I saw *Petty Cash* lying at the dinghy dock. It had three small white boat fenders. Each fender had a pale yellow stripe around the middle and hung from a white nylon line with a red tracer.

Sometimes the light bulb casts a gentle, warming glow and sometimes it flashes like lightning. I forgot about lunch and went looking for Rick Schuster.

He sat alone at the clubhouse bar working diligently on a tall drink. I sat down beside him and grabbed a handful of peanuts.

"Hey, Rick. How's it goin'?" I asked.

He looked at me cockeyed.

"Greene, right?"

"Sim," I said.

"Yeah, yeah," he said. "Sim, the retired sailor. The ex-navy cop. The guy who can't mind his own damned business."

"Guilty as charged."

He took another sip from the tall drink and softened.

"You hear about Wells?" he asked.

"Uh-huh."

"Ain't that somethin'?" he said. "Killed his own wife and Cookie, too."

"That's something all right."

Rick shook his head back and forth.

"Who'd have thought the boss man would gun down Cookie and the missus?"

He tossed down more of his tall drink.

"Who'd have thought," I said.

Rick looked at me again with no small amount of disdain.

"So what do you want?" he asked. "You still lookin' for free drinks on the boat account?"

I let him have that one. It isn't all that awful to let a guy think he's clever before you drop a bomb on him.

"Rick, I think I know how your first mate died, and I think I know why that big yellow inflatable of yours is missing one of its little boat fenders."

His mouth dropped open about a half inch and his eyes opened wider.

"I also think it was you who hit me on the side of the head with that lead fishing sinker Tuesday night," I said. "And I think it was you who tossed my boat. All that work and the only thing you found was a little piece of yellow note paper."

"What are you talkin' about?" he asked.

I got up and walked over to the bartender and ordered a Coke. I wasn't in a big hurry, and I wanted the captain to stew a little. The bartender handed me the glass, and I walked back to where Rick sat. His eyes were the size of saucers.

"What are you talkin' about, man?" he asked

I drank some of the soda and waited a minute. It was the right moment. It was time to cast out the line. The one with the baited hook.

"I know where Brownell hid the money," I said. "The money you and he skimmed off Cattrel and his clients. I know where he put it and I know you haven't found it."

Schuster licked his lower lip and swallowed. He was mouthing the bait. Time to set the hook.

"It's still there, Rick. Still there and just waiting for the two of us to go out there and get it."

I drank a little more soda.

"You interested in a split?" I asked. "Could give us both a Merry Christmas, eh?"

Schuster looked around the room and swallowed. There was a British couple sitting at a small table near the door and two small families sitting at tables near the windows. The bartender was at the other end of a thirty-foot-long bar talking to an overweight man in a flowered shirt, Bermuda shorts, and black socks inside new leather boat shoes.

"We can't talk here, man," he said. "Cattrel and the cops have got ears all around this place."

None of the people in the room looked remotely like ears.

"Where do you want to talk?" I asked.

"You got your boat with you?" Schuster asked.

I nodded.

"Take it out of the Sound and head due west north of the Dogs," he said. "I'll come find you in an hour or so."

Schuster went back to his drink, and I walked out of the bar. He'd bitten hard on the bait. Now I just had to reel him in.

56

I bought a ready-made sandwich and a six-pack of Caribs on my way back to the guest slips. I pulled *Figaro* away from the dock, raised the main, and motor-sailed toward the Colquhoun Reef entrance. Once out of the narrow entrance channel, I unfurled the genoa, let the main out on the port side, and killed the engine. I set Kyle to steer the boat on a course due west.

I stepped down into the cabin and pulled the .45 out of its hiding place. I went back up to the cockpit, checked the pistol's magazine, and chambered a round. The pistol fit nicely into one of *Figaro*'s little open cockpit lockers near the helm. I covered it with a small towel and ate my sandwich.

The noonday sun would have been hot but for the strong east wind. It came over the starboard quarter and sent *Figaro* almost dead downwind at nearly six knots. I would have normally rigged a line from the boom to the port toe rail to prevent an accidental jibe, but I didn't bother as I figured that we wouldn't be on this heading for long.

Schuster showed up about a half hour later in the big yellow dinghy. He came up on the port side, threw me a line, and hopped aboard. I tied the line off to a cleat and he sat down in the cockpit opposite me.

"What the hell were you talking about back there?" he asked.

"Drug money," I said. "You've been using Wells's yacht to run illicit cash from New England to the BVI for a Venezuelan family. Every winter when Wells decided he'd had too much snow.

Where'd you hide it? In the engine room? Wells wouldn't ever look there."

"Pantry," said Rick. "Cookie had a special spot for it hidden under some sacks of potatoes."

"How much did you bring in, Rick? Ten million a trip? Twenty? That would be easy to hide on a yacht that size. And who would suspect a software billionaire of smuggling cash back to the cartels' money man?"

He leaned back and smiled.

"Wells didn't have a clue," said Rick.

"Just you and Cookie and Derek, right?"

Rick nodded.

"You delivered it to a local guy, a big tough ex-cop named Jimmy Cattrel, for him to launder and manage," I said. "Most of the money arrived according to plan, and the three of you got to keep a bit for yourselves. But then you and Brownell started slicing a little more off the top. It wasn't so much that Cattrel would notice right away, but over the years you two accumulated a hefty chunk of dough. A couple million, maybe three? You even talked about investing some of it. Laundering it yourself, I guess."

"I don't know where you get all that from but go on," said Schuster.

"You'd served with Derek for a long time in the Coast Guard and you trusted him," I said. "But money wears away at friendship and trust. Derek rented a safe deposit box in town and started hiding his share of the money from you. But then one day he decided that his share wasn't big enough, so he planned to make one last grab at the gold. He decided to take another million off the top and disappear leaving you holding an empty bag. He probably figured Cattrel would kill you for it."

Rick shrugged.

"So he packed that last carton of cash onto that big inflatable and told the rest of the crew he was going to see a girl," I said. "He wasn't going to come back, so he took his fake passport and the safe deposit box key and took off."

"You got all the answers, don't you?" said Rick.

"He didn't have enough time to take the cash into Road Town and stick it in a safe deposit box. The word would get out to Cattrel's people and he'd get caught if he stuck around."

"I never told Cattrel," said Rick.

"He couldn't count on that, though. He'd have to catch the last plane out at the last possible minute. So he planned to hide that money on the way to the airport and fly out of the country on his fake passport. He probably figured he could come back a couple of months later, probably by boat, to pick up the hidden cash and to empty the safe deposit box."

"Buried treasure, eh?" said Rick.

"Read some history of this place. It's not exactly a novel concept."

"Yeah," he said. "Pirates."

A small, short-barreled automatic appeared in his hand. Ronnie's .45 lay under a towel near my right thigh, but I'd been too confident and too slow.

"So where's the money?" he asked

"Put that thing away, Rick. We're in this together."

He cocked the hammer back.

"Where's the money?"

"You should know. The answer's on that piece of yellow note paper you took from my boat."

"Those phone numbers?" he said. "They're disconnected."

I shrugged.

"Start talking," said Schuster.

"Four score and seven years ago our fathers brought forth…"

"Shut up," he said.

"You told me to start talking," I said.

"Get your hands on the wheel where I can see them," said Schuster.

"Relax, Captain."

I reached down, disconnected Kyle, and steered the boat due west. Dead downwind.

"I want you to get your money back and I want to help you get away from Cattrel," I said. "All I'm asking is that I get a reasonable piece of Brownell's share for my trouble."

"Tell me where the money is," he said.

"When Brownell left the boat that night he drove that big dinghy to a spot south of Great Dog Island. He dove over the side and hid the money somewhere underwater."

"Now you're on the right track," said Schuster. "Keep going."

"Then he came back up, toweled off, and got dressed. He heard another boat coming toward him in the dark, but nobody is supposed to anchor there overnight. It's not protected. He probably thought it was a curious park ranger or a local islander offering a tow, so he put out the boat fenders. Those little ones with the yellow stripes."

I pointed at the fenders on the inflatable.

"He didn't know it was you in the small dinghy motoring up to him in the dark," I said. "It's just a theory, but it's one that fits the available facts."

"You got any more facts for me?" he asked. "Like where the money is?"

"I don't know how much the two of you talked that night on the water or what about," I said. "But I think he was holding a small plastic bag at the moment you shot him."

"A plastic bag? What the hell are you talking about?"

"He had a bag in his hand," I said. "And when you shot him and he fell off the boat, he grabbed at one of those little striped boat fenders. Probably a reflex action. It didn't help him, though. He was dead before he hit the water."

"Tell me about the bag," said Schuster.

He waved the gun at me.

"It was a little plastic bag," I said. "It had a fake British passport in it and a safe deposit box key."

"Yeah, yeah," said Schuster. "I heard all about the box. What else you got?"

"Not much. You probably searched the inflatable pretty thoroughly looking for the money, but you didn't find it. If you had, you wouldn't be out here with a gun in your hand."

"Go on," he said.

"Once you heard that somebody else got picked up by the police, you didn't bother trying to explain it to Cattrel," I said. "Why go to the trouble? You figured he'd blame it on the poor sap the RVIP snagged and that Cattrel would leave you alone."

Schuster nodded and smiled.

"So you think he hid it underwater, eh?" he said. "Where's it at?"

"Put down the gun and we can talk," I said. "Maybe we can figure out a reasonable split. I've done a lot of work on this project and I deserve a finder's fee."

He smiled, walked over with the gun in his right hand, and slapped me across the face with his left. Then he laughed and sat down on the starboard side of the cabin top with his feet hanging down into the cockpit. He kept the gun aimed at my chest.

"Are you blind or something?" he said. "I am holding all the cards in this game." He waved the gun from side to side. "This one here's an ace, and I know exactly how to play it. Where's the money, sailor?"

"What's our deal?"

"You want a deal?" he asked. "I got a deal for you. How about I shoot off one of your kneecaps and ask again?"

"Be reasonable, Schuster. You shoot me and you'll never see a dime of that money."

"I think you'll tell me right before you lose the second kneecap," he said.

An ocean swell slightly larger and a little steeper than most of the others lifted *Figaro*'s stern and I jammed the wheel hard to port. The wind caught the back of the mainsail and the thick aluminum boom swung across the cockpit.

Schuster raised the gun and pulled the trigger as the boom hit him in the shoulder. Something tugged at my left arm as the swinging boom threw Schuster to *Figaro*'s starboard side deck. He dropped the pistol and it slid into the cockpit.

The jibe put *Figaro* on a port tack. The backwinded genoa heeled the boat over about thirty degrees in the strong winds and tossed me into the cockpit from behind the helm. From that position, I couldn't reach the .45.

Schuster moved to grab his pistol and I hit him square in the jaw with an uppercut that should have paralyzed him. He shook it off, grabbed one of *Figaro*'s winch handles, and swung it at me like a police baton.

I pulled my head back and felt the wind on my forehead as the heavy end of the winch handle swished past. The swing moved Schuster to his left and I hit him twice in the neck and once in the kidneys.

Schuster's gun slid across the cockpit floor and I moved toward it. He swung around again with the winch handle, and this time he connected with my left arm above the elbow. The entire arm went numb from the impact and I fell back behind the wheel.

Schuster dropped the winch handle and grabbed for his gun as I reached under the towel for the .45 with my right hand. Time slowed to a crawl as Schuster raised his gun and turned toward me. I watched my gun rise in slow motion and heard the thumb safety click off as I wondered which one of us would fire first. Instinct and training kicked in as I aimed for the center of body mass and double-tapped the trigger. The two hollow-points landed within an inch of each other in the center of his chest. A look of stunned surprise washed over his face with the sudden realization that he'd lost the draw. The look faded fast.

The pistol fell from his hand into the cockpit and his body fell over *Figaro*'s lifelines into the warm Caribbean. I didn't throw out a life ring. It wouldn't have made any difference.

My left arm was completely numb from the shoulder down. I pulled off my T-shirt to assess the damage. One of Rick Schuster's last acts on earth, the pulling of a trigger, had carved a nine-millimeter trough across the outside of my left arm three inches below the shoulder. It bled fairly well, so I tied the shirt around it as a makeshift bandage and turned my attention to *Figaro*.

I turned her into the wind, hauled in the mainsheet with my good arm, and set Kyle to keep *Figaro* hove-to.

Schuster's body floated face down in the water about fifty yards away.

I stepped down the companionway and fished a cold beer out of the icebox.

57

I seriously considered the option of tossing the .45 over the side, setting *Petty Cash* adrift, and sailing on my merry way to Jost Van Dyke for a week of rest and relaxation. I could have a cold beer and some fresh grouper at Henry's Good-Time Bar and Restaurant. Maybe let the RVIP sort it all out on their own. But there was the risk that somebody would have seen me at the bar with the late Rick Schuster.

I called Constable Millet.

"Yes, Mr. Greene. How can I help you, now?"

He seemed slightly annoyed at the telephonic intrusion.

"You can come out here and pick up a body," I said.

"Another one?" he roared.

"The guy who killed Derek Brownell," I said.

He muttered a few coarse British epithets that I recognized and a few others that were new to me. I let him get it out of his system.

"Where are you?" he asked.

"About two miles north of the Seal Dog islands," I said.

I gave him my latitude and longitude from the GPS. He asked me to repeat them and I did.

"I'll be out there within the hour," he said.

Figaro needed very little tending to maintain her position, and I used the time to break out my first aid kit and put a proper bandage on my arm. Thirst was getting to me so I got another beer out of the icebox and sat in the cockpit watching Schuster's body float nearby. He wasn't getting away.

The nine-millimeter pistol lay in the cockpit where Schuster had dropped it. I left it there. I left the .45 on the cockpit seat next to me. A couple of chartered sailboats passed between *Figaro* and the Dogs. Reflected sunlight momentarily glinted from one of them, and I realized I was being watched through binoculars. I waved. I smiled. I drank some more beer.

Not long after that, a power launch made the turn around the end of West Seal Dog Island and headed directly toward me. Twin bow waves peeled off as it approached. I soon recognized Constable Millet standing next to the launch's helmsman.

Millet and another officer stepped aboard *Figaro*. I pointed off to port where Schuster's body floated, and Millet sent the launch to retrieve it. He sat down in the cockpit across from me while the other officer examined the area and bagged the two pistols.

"Well?" he asked.

I showed him my arm and described how I'd confronted Schuster in the bar and how subsequent events had unfolded. He had some questions about the .45, and I told him how Ronnie had brought it and I had kept it. I told him about Cattrel, the ledger, the smuggling of money, and the skimming that Brownell and Schuster had done.

I told him how *Figaro*'s intentional jibe had given me the momentary advantage I'd needed. I showed him the blood-soaked T-shirt and told him about the onboard fight but saw no reason to mention my hypothesis of where Brownell's hidden money might be located.

"What made you think Schuster killed Brownell?" asked Millet.

"Derek's passport was found floating in the channel the day after he was killed," I said.

"By the mystery woman?"

"As it turns out, this mystery woman not only exists but is also very lovely."

Millet raised an eyebrow.

"Floating next to the passport was a small boat fender with a yellow stripe around the middle," I said.

I nodded toward the big yellow yacht tender tied to *Figaro*'s stern.

"You told me yesterday that the yacht tender had Brownell's blood on it," I said. "That same yacht tender has three boat fenders and all three feature a yellow stripe around the middle."

"I don't see a connection," said Millet.

"There was a fourth fender."

I reached into the lazarette and pulled out the fender Marie had given me. Millet compared it to the others on the inflatable and nodded.

"Also found by the lovely mystery woman," I said.

"Go on," said Millet.

"Schuster told me a couple of weeks ago that Brownell had gone to meet a hot date that Wednesday night—the night he was killed—and that Brownell had disappeared and left the tender at Leverick Bay. He even complained about having to go to Leverick to pick it up the next day."

My mouth was dry. Millet waited patiently while I drank a little more beer.

"But that was a lie," I said. "The ship's engineer told me he'd taken Mrs. Wells to the airport at Trellis Bay fairly late that night for the last flight out on the way to Miami."

I drained the rest of the bottle.

"You can bet your paycheck she didn't make that trip in the yacht's backup dinghy, the small gray one."

"I'm following you," said Millet. "Keep going."

"Wells didn't have any reason to kill Brownell," I said. "Wells had suspicions, but he didn't know that his wife was cheating with the crew until I confirmed it over a week later. So I don't think Wells killed Brownell. But you found Brownell's blood on the yacht tender, the same one that mysteriously reappeared the night he was killed."

Millet stood to watch the men on the launch pull Schuster's body aboard.

"That still doesn't prove Schuster killed him," he said.

"No, it doesn't. That's why I baited the hook and trolled it around behind me. He took the bait, followed me out here, and proved my theory. And I'll bet that the ballistics on the bullets you pulled out of Brownell are a direct match to the pistol Schuster brought with him today."

Millet thought for a moment.

"That was quite a dangerous stunt, Mr. Greene. I would have preferred it if you would have given me the facts you'd uncovered and let us in the RVIP handle police business."

"Like you've been handling Cattrel?" I asked. "You've been pussyfooting with that guy for years. Are you ever going to get around to arresting him?"

Millet's eyes narrowed, and his head cocked about ten degrees to the right.

"Why are you asking me about Jimmy Cattrel?" he asked.

"You already know why. Because he wants to kill me," I said. "And because he's tried to. And because he's going to keep on trying. That tends to draw a guy's interest."

A larger swell swept under the boat and Millet sat back down in the cockpit.

"Tell me where you've been since five o'clock this morning," he said.

"My mouth is a little dry."

"You have been shot in the arm and you are in shock," he said.

"I'm thirsty. Can you get me a drink?"

He went down the companionway and came back with a glass of water. I drank about half of it. It wasn't nearly as good as beer.

"So where have you been, Mr. Greene?" he asked.

"I was anchored at Biras Creek last night. All night," I said. "I called you from the boat this morning and motored over to the Bitter End for lunch. I've already told you what I said to Schuster when I saw him at the bar. And I've already told you how he followed me out here, how he pulled a gun on me, and how he lost the toss."

"You have witnesses to place you at the Bitter End this morning?" Millet asked.

"The dock boy I threw my lines to, I suppose. Maybe the guy tending bar will recognize me."

Millet was silent for a moment. He tossed the bagged .45 from one hand to the other and back again.

"You want to tell me what's going on?" I asked. "I've solved Brownell's murder for you. That's in the bag. What are you doing about Cattrel? Can't you give me that much?"

The police launch returned and pulled up to *Figaro*'s port side. There was a dripping body bag lying in its cockpit. Millet looked up from the bagged pistol.

"Mr. Cattrel was found murdered on the beach at Long Bay around ten o'clock this morning," he said. "We found his driver in the car's trunk."

58

"I don't know anything about that," I said.

"One of our officers was watching for Mr. Cattrel this morning in Trellis Bay. He saw Cattrel walk off the boat that came in from Guana Island around a quarter to nine. Cattrel's car arrived, he got in the back seat, and it drove off toward town. He did not get very far."

"Well, I didn't shoot him," I said.

Millet stood up, walked over to the police launch, handed the two bagged pistols to one of the officers, and turned back to me.

"He wasn't shot, Mr. Greene. Jimmy Cattrel's throat was slit from ear to ear with an extremely sharp knife by someone who knew exactly how to do it. His driver, Germaine Walker, was shot in the temple at close range."

I thought of Al, his nasty-looking combat knife, and the silenced .32 automatic.

"Later this morning, one of our officers found five of Cattrel's employees at his house on Virgin Gorda. All had been killed."

"How'd they die?"

"One had been shot twice in the chest, one had his neck broken, and three others had their throats slit just like Jimmy Cattrel's. Every one had been heavily armed but none of them had fired a shot."

"And you think I did that?"

Millet thought for a minute.

"Sounds like a hit from some crazy Venezuelan drug lord trying to send a message," I said. "I hear that they sometimes go a little over the top when disappointed with employee performance."

"Five men murdered yesterday and two more this morning," he said.

It sounded like they hadn't yet found the guy in the apartment. I decided not to tell them.

"Whoever it was," continued Millet, "left Mr. Cattrel's body on the beach at Long Bay, walked into the water, and disappeared."

Al was as comfortable in the water as a dolphin, and he'd been trained to disappear. He could have anchored a boat around the point west of Long Bay and swum the two miles there and back with no difficulty.

"Can you tell me where your friend, Mr. Higgins, is at the moment?" Millet asked.

"No," I said. "He and his girlfriend recently became engaged. I think they ran off to celebrate."

Millet weighed my answer in his head for a few minutes. I knew it was light as far as answers went.

"Venezuelan drug lord," I said. "Bet you a million bucks. His name's probably in the book Phillips gave you. The DEA's probably got the guy's phone number. You might give them a call when you get back to the office."

Millet thought quietly for a moment as though he had a lot of unanswered questions. Then he told the other officers to take Schuster's body back to Road Town. The police launch cast off and powered back toward Tortola with *Petty Cash* in tow.

"Aren't you going home, Constable?" I asked.

"You have been shot in the arm, Mr. Greene. You also appear to be in a mild state of shock, and you may even be slightly inebriated. You are definitely in no shape to sail this boat back to Road Town."

He took off his shoes and socks, shed his tie, and rolled up the sleeves of his uniform shirt.

"And it has been far too long since I have had the opportunity," he said.

A thin smile graced his lips.

I sat with my back against the cabin and watched him disengage Kyle, reset the genoa, and turn *Figaro* off the wind. The guy knew what he was doing. *Figaro* caught the strong easterly and sailed rail down through the channel on a broad reach. Constable Millet smiled. He couldn't help it. No sailor can.

"Are you still on duty, Constable?" I asked.

He looked at his watch and smiled back.

"No, Mr. Greene. I am on my own time now," he said.

"Then call me Sim," I said.

I went below and got two more cold ones. He smiled again when I returned, and he accepted the proffered bottle.

The wind held strong and *Figaro* lifted to race down each swell that came up from behind. We made nearly seven knots. I could have squeezed out another half knot if I'd had to, but we weren't racing. And Millet was enjoying himself.

We sailed quietly in the sweet sound of rushing water. An hour later, Millet broke the silence.

"Sim, we absolved your friend of Derek Brownell's murder three days ago," he said. "Your friend had an iron-clad alibi that, quite frankly, still surprises me. Yet you pursued the case, you put yourself in harm's way with a dangerous criminal, and you ferreted out the real perpetrator. You managed to get yourself shot up in the process."

"Uh-huh," I said.

"It could have turned out much worse for you."

"Could have," I said.

"But why?" Millet asked. "Why do all that? Your friend was already cleared of the charges. What was in it for you?"

"Honor is its own reward?" I said.

He cocked an eyebrow.

"Okay," I said. "Let's just say I'm Scottish stubborn."

59

"ARE you sure there's anything down there to find?" asked Al.

"Pretty sure," I said.

It was the day after Christmas. We had changed into our second set of tanks and were about to head back down from the surface for another try.

Henry had taken Al and Liv to Anegada after he picked them up off my boat that Saturday night. Henry had taken them to a place on the north shore he owned; a place where Al and Liv could hide out for a while. But as soon as they got there, Al remembered that he had to "run a little errand" and he borrowed Henry's boat. He brought it back the next day. I never asked Al about what happened that Sunday morning in Long Bay, but I'd already drawn my conclusions.

The newspaper spent the following few days bemoaning the murder of the respected former RVIP constable Jimmy Cattrel. When the news ultimately surfaced that he had been laundering money for a drug cartel, the paper changed its tune considerably.

Constable Millet went on record as stating that Mr. Cattrel and several of his employees had been murdered "by persons unknown but presumably associated with the trade of illicit drugs." A fine and understandable, if entirely inaccurate, version.

I was wrong about Levon being killed by Ronnie. The redhead had scared him so much that night at the bar at Gun Creek that he'd stolen a small power boat and ran it all the way to St. John during the night to hide out at a friend's house. He saw the newspaper report of Cattrel's death and decided it was safe to come back home.

Spencer, the special agent who'd offered me a pistol in San Juan, showed up at the docks the day before Christmas in chinos, loafers, and a flowered Hawaiian shirt; a fed on holiday. He wished me a Merry Christmas and "congratulated" me on dispatching Jimmy Cattrel "the old-fashioned way." I told him I had no idea what he was talking about. He smiled broadly, winked, and handed me another one of his mostly blank business cards. He ended our conversation with the recommendation that I should call him if I ever needed a favor. Given the context, I wasn't sure I wanted to know what he considered a "favor."

I called Jack Penn, thanked him for his help, and asked him if he'd ever heard of a federal agency whose operatives carried business cards with only a first name and a phone number. He sucked in a quick breath and hung up immediately.

Al and Liv returned to Tortola after a week's rest, and I told Al about my theory regarding sunken treasure. We promptly borrowed Lars's boat and dropped its anchor at 18°47.8275' North latitude, 64°46.0314' West longitude off the southern shore of Great Dog Island. A reel of line tied to the anchor chain allowed us to make sweeping concentric circles around the spot nearly thirty feet down to see if my theory was correct.

We hadn't seen anything of interest during the first dive and had exhausted one tank of air each. We each had two more full tanks left.

"Keep your eyes open," I said.

"For what?" asked Al.

"How should I know?"

I let the air out of my buoyancy vest and dove back down to the search reel. We took our positions four feet apart and started to trace the next concentric circle away from the anchor. We were slow and methodical. There was no hurry.

Al found them twenty minutes later. Two military ammunition cans lying between a large outcropping of brain coral and a couple of big rocks that somebody had moved to shield them from view. Another hefty rock was on top. The oversized ammo cans had been painted Desert Storm camouflage. Al was lucky to see them. We examined the area carefully but could find no more ammo cans.

I tied a marker buoy to the two cans, inflated it, and sent it to the surface. Al headed back to the anchor chain to untie the search reel and I met him at the boat. We pulled the boat's anchor and powered the short distance to the buoy.

"You think it's booby-trapped?" asked Al.

"No," I said. "But it never hurts to be careful."

I tugged on the buoy's line. There was some strong initial resistance, probably the weight of the rock on top, but no explosion. I reeled in the line, and the two cans surfaced near the boat. Al reached over and pulled them in over the side.

He tugged at the locking handle on the first one and opened it. The can was stuffed with plastic bags like the one that had held the passport for Derek Brownell's alter ego. Each bag was filled with U.S. currency.

"Oh, baby," I said.

"Well, I'll be dipped," said Al.

I opened the second can; more bags. But it wasn't the time or place for a thorough examination, so we closed them both, put them on the floor of the boat, and piled our diving gear on top. There was no point in sticking around. Al fired up the boat's ancient outboards, and we laid a straight, if sedate, wake to Road Town.

We didn't open up the cans again until we were back at Al's house. Each plastic bag was tightly packed with carefully wrapped bundles of hundred-dollar bills. It took us nearly an hour and a half to count it.

"You think that's enough to set us up with a decent dive boat?" I asked.

"That's enough to buy us each one," said Al. "And a spare."

"Easy, Al. Extraordinary expenditures can draw unwanted attention."

I walked into the kitchen, grabbed an ice-cold Carib from the refrigerator, and squeezed a slice of lime into it. I took it out onto the patio and sat in one of Al's comfortable wooden chairs.

The sun had set hours before, and I looked northwest of Guana Island into the darkness of a moonless Caribbean night. There were no ships to be seen, no airplanes overhead, no lightning-infused squalls on the horizon.

Several hundred miles beyond that dark barrier and just north of the Dominican Republic lay a string of remote and largely ignored islands. I thought of a large wooden schooner with maroon sails and a tall, beautiful woman standing at its helm.

I sat back in the chair and pulled at the bottle.

"Al?"

"Yeah?"

"Are there any direct flights to the Turks and Caicos?"

60

THERE weren't any direct flights to the Turks and Caicos. Not by a long shot. Three different planes, two long layovers, and almost a full day of travel for what amounted to a 400-mile trip. And the round-trip cost half as much as a new outboard. While money was no longer a problem, I've never been one to spend it needlessly.

Figaro covers an honest 150 miles a day without pushing hard, and it seemed like a three-day sailing trip would be a fine way to unwind and relax. I emailed Marie on Saturday morning and spent a few hours provisioning and getting ready for the trip. I cleaned and greased Kyle's gears, lashed my dinghy to the foredeck, and stowed the outboard. Marie hadn't replied to my email by the time I left Ft. Burt, but I left anyway. I wanted to clear Customs, get out of the channel, and sail into clear water before dark.

I turned to a course of west by northwest once we passed Jost Van Dyke. My fishing line sang out as the last limb of the sun dropped away behind St. Thomas, and I pulled in a fine dorado, sliced it up in the last fading rays of sunlight, and slipped the fillets into the icebox. I thought how nice it would be for a guy to live like this the rest of his life and then realized that I was that guy.

The lights on St. Thomas passed by eight miles to the south as we pushed on. The winds were steady, Kyle kept us pointed in the right direction on a broad reach, and there was nothing but clear water ahead. There were no large ships sneaking up on me, no bad weather on the horizon, no major concerns, so I took a short nap. When I woke up we were passing the lights of Culebra well off to port. A few hours later, we passed the warm glow of Fajardo, Puerto Rico, just below the southern horizon.

The next few days were quiet with steady trade winds off the starboard quarter. *Figaro*'s drifter pulled us along at seven knots, and the sun felt warm and comfortable on my bare skin. Grand Turk appeared shortly after sunrise on Tuesday, and I made ready for landfall. A couple hours later, I skirted the south end of the island, turned *Figaro* into the calm water of the island's lee, and anchored about a half mile north of a massive cruise ship. I had no idea how long I would be staying in the Turks and Caicos, so I paid for the full ninety-day cruising permit.

I checked my email at an internet café and opened the reply from Marie. She was staying with her dad and brother at David's client's estate on the island of Provo. She wanted to see me. I felt like making way immediately, but Provo was at least eighty miles away and I needed a cold drink, a long nap, and a shave. I replied and told her that I would spend the night at Salt Cay and head for Provo in the morning. She could look for me in the harbor the next night.

I had that drink, bought a few groceries, and walked back to my dinghy. It was a short beam reach to the tiny harbor at Salt Cay and the place was empty; not another boat or person in sight. I set the anchor into the sandy bottom, put up the bimini to shade the boat, and opened all the hatches to catch whatever breeze I could. The lack of sleep that comes with single-handing caught up to me, and I lay down on the starboard settee for an afternoon nap.

I woke to the sound of an approaching outboard motor and stuck my head out the companionway. The lower limb of the sun touched the horizon and began to sink into the Caribbean as a large center-console fishing boat turned into the harbor. Marie stood by the boat's pilot and waved when she saw me. She had a small carry-on in her left hand.

I helped her aboard *Figaro* as the other boat came to rest against the port rail. She thanked the boat's driver and turned to kiss me.

She smelled like vanilla and orchids and she tasted like ripe raspberries and champagne. She was the most beautiful woman in the world.

"I suppose it could be a whole day's sail from here to Provo," she said. "But it's only a couple of bumpy hours by outboard. And I couldn't wait until tomorrow."

We kissed again as the other boat left the harbor. We barely made it to *Figaro*'s cabin.

We spent the next week swimming with dolphins in turquoise-tinted water, catching lobsters and spearing fish for dinner, and baking ourselves brown on secluded white sand beaches. The wind would pick up in the afternoon, and we'd weigh anchor and sail *Figaro* to the next small cay or secluded sandspit. There were wonderful sunsets and midnight swims. We didn't get to Provo until well after New Year's.

David insisted on my sharing the details of Derek Brownell's murder and my investigation; the redheaded kid that swam to *Figaro* with a gun in his hand one night and then landed with mortal finality in her cockpit a few days later; how I deduced that Captain Schuster had killed his own first mate over smuggled drug money; and the violent death of Jimmy Cattrel. I blamed the last on a Venezuelan hit team.

I didn't mention Jack Penn, an unidentified federal agency, the vicious murder of a criminal's wife, or the deadly skills of a highly trained, if aged, former military operative. There are things best left unsaid.

We shared fine dinners with David and his client on a balcony overlooking the Caribbean, danced at the clubs in Provo, and listened to steel drum bands play their music until late at night. We swam in warm, clear water off white sand beaches and we shared a room on the second floor of the large home.

Moonlight illuminated that room late one night, and we watched the ceiling fan carve a lazy circle against the ceiling. We listened to the night birds make their gentle noises in the trees outside our bedroom as she rested her head on my chest.

"I think I may truly love you," she said. "More than any man I have ever known or ever hoped to know. And I've been thinking about the suggestion you made this morning."

Here it comes.

"It sounds idyllic," she said, "and I know I would love almost every minute of it, but I don't think I could ever give up my job and move in with you on your marvelous little boat. I enjoy teaching high school in Stamford and I am good at it. I don't think I could leave it, even for a life on a boat in a paradise like this with a wonderful man like you."

Thunder rolled in on the slight breeze like a huge wave crashing and roaring on a distant beach. I stroked her hair in silence.

"And I don't think I could live thousands of miles away from what's left of my family," she said. "Not yet, anyway."

I kissed her forehead.

"I also know that you wouldn't be happy back home with me," she said. "I don't think you could ever leave the sea."

There was a dim flash of distant lightning. I thought for a moment and waited, listening for the thunder.

"I want you in my life, Marie. Somewhere, anywhere. Even if it's only for a few short months in the Caribbean," I said. "Even if I have to wait years."

She moved up to kiss me again and we stopped talking of jobs and boats and hopes of permanence. More lightning crashed well out to sea and the thunder rolled across the water into our room. Much later, raindrops fell on the leaves outside our window as she fell asleep smiling.

<<<<>>>>

1

WE keep a picnic table at the back of the dive shop. A six-sided umbrella plastered with Coca-Cola logos sticks up out of the middle and shields it from the seasonally hot Caribbean sun. And the sun was definitely in season that day in mid-July. Ninety degrees, humid, and windless. The water wasn't much relief. Like cooling off in a lukewarm bathtub. The locals call it "hurricane weather."

Three thousand miles away, a low pressure tropical wave will march off the west coast of Africa into the warm Atlantic. Warm moist ocean air rises into that wave and the earth's rotation swirls it into a counterclockwise tempest. Somebody at NOAA will call it a tropical depression and give it a number. Days pass and the depression eases into the central Atlantic where it grows into a tropical storm. By the time it reaches the Caribbean, it's a full-fledged hurricane worthy of a name and a number—on a scale of 1 to 5—to tell you how tough it is.

The vast majority of the hurricanes during the six-month season pass either to the south of the British Virgin Islands into the Gulf of Mexico or to the north to attack the Bahamas, Florida, or, occasionally, the east coast of the United States. The BVI gets some strong winds and heavy rains. The power goes out for a half-day or so. A few boats will break free of their moorings and crash on some rocks somewhere but the islands themselves rarely get hit hard by a catastrophic hurricane.

Sometimes the weather is so hot and nasty during the summer that local folks will openly hope for a hurricane to pass close enough to bring the wind and the heavy rain and a break in the monotony of summer.

When there isn't a hurricane, the picnic table with the Coca-Cola umbrella behind the shop is a nice place to relax with a cool drink and to watch the sun set across the harbor. Our dive shop is little more than a warehouse in front of a small wharf between the fuel dock and that ratty forgotten section of the harbor where derelict commercial vessels rust and list and sink their keels into the harbor mud. The shop is where we store the equipment we use to take vacationers on underwater tours. We do salvage work, too, raising the chartered boats or lost outboards that those same tourists occasionally leave on the bottom. Regardless of the job, we always go to the customer in our new dive boat. We almost never have visitors.

We had a visitor that day, though. Constable Millet sat on the bench under the Coca-Cola umbrella and watched the three of us back *In Depth II* up to our little dock and tie her off. I hadn't seen him in nearly a month. He looked awful.

Al jumped off the boat with the passenger manifest and the day's receipts and jogged past him to the office to fill out deposit slips and enter figures into our accounting system. Running a diving tour business isn't all just air compressors and swim fins anymore and Al handled the books. Eryn and I carted the empty SCUBA tanks and other gear off the stern while Millet watched quietly. I asked Eryn to wash off the regulators, buoyancy vests, and other dive gear with fresh water and hang them to dry. She ran to the job with her characteristic enthusiasm and I walked over to talk with the good Constable.

I led him into my office, tossed my L.A. Dodger's bill cap onto the top of my filing cabinet, and sat down in my old steel and naugahyde desk chair. He sat in the chair across from me and crossed his excessively long legs. I don't run into many guys who are taller than me and I'd always wondered if, at six-five, he'd have made a decent point guard had he been raised in the States. His British upbringing probably steered him toward cricket. He was way too skinny for rugby.

"What can I do for you, Constable?" I asked.

He pierced me with an icy stare and I wondered what obscure island law we had unknowingly violated.

"I'd like to have a beer if I may," he said.

"You're off duty?"

He nodded and I reached into the small refrigerator under my desk, pulled out two Caribs, and plucked the caps off the bottles with the church key that hung from the wall. I handed him one and he drained half the bottle in one go. It wasn't like him to do that.

"Who's the young lady?" he asked.

"Eryn? She's from the States. She decided to take a year off and intern with us as a dive instructor before starting law school. Bright young woman."

"Very pretty," he said. "And a bit young for you, wouldn't you say?"

He forced a smile.

"She's too young for anyone," I said. "Sweet and innocent. Not exactly a woman of the world. Goes to church on Sundays over at the Bin-Cal building. Doesn't even drink."

I hoisted and drank some of my beer in celebration of that last comment about Eryn and wondered what this interview was all about. A Detective Constable of the Royal Virgin Islands Police Force doesn't usually show up at our dive shop—off duty or not—requesting cold beer and information about our employees. This was, in fact, a first.

"Do you consider me to be an okay bloke, Mr. Greene?" he asked.

"You're an honest cop," I said. "You work hard at your job and you're not sloppy in your procedure. You're okay in my book."

He nodded.

"And I've probably told you at least fifty times to call me Sim," I added.

He smiled slightly.

"Are we friends, then, Sim?"

"I'd like to think so," I said. "We crewed together on *The Tiger* during the Spring Regatta and you've had Al and me up to dinner at your house with your family. I've played with your kids. Your wife's a babe and I'd steal her from you if I had half a chance. Of course we're friends."

He forced another smile and emptied the bottle. I grabbed a replacement from the little fridge, opened it, and handed it to him.

"You did an excellent job last Christmas figuring out who killed that Brownell fellow," he said.

"Thanks."

It hadn't been an easy case and Constable Millet had not exactly encouraged my involvement at the time. He thought Al had murdered the guy and I had to turn over quite a few rocks to find the real killer and get my best friend out of jail. But it had worked out all right for most of those involved.

I sat there wondering exactly where this conversation was headed.

"What was the killer's name?" he asked.

"Does it matter?" I said.

"I was more than a little miffed that you'd shot him dead," he said.

"It was self-defense, you know."

He nodded and tipped the second bottle back.

"I didn't really have a whole lot of choice in the matter," I said.

He waved his hand as if my killing the fellow was merely the stuff of small talk among friends.

"You seem to have a gift," he said. "Weighing issues and probabilities. Drawing connections between seemingly unrelated facts. Finding things that cannot otherwise be found."

I took a drink from my beer and tried to draw a few connections between the unrelated subjects we'd covered in the current conversation. I didn't see any.

"You're dancing around something that's bugging the hell out of you, Constable, and I'm not seeing it," I said. "Why don't you cut to the chase and ask me straight out?"

He put his half-empty beer bottle on my desk and placed his hands on the arms of his chair. He looked straight into my eyes. There were new lines in his face that spoke of nights without sleep and days filled with worry.

"Our daughter has been missing for almost three weeks."

You can find out more about DEAD DOWNWIND, and other Sim Greene mysteries, at **www.robavery.com**.

- **Finding Figaro** (March 2018)

In this prequel to *Close-Hauled*, Sim Greene is tasked with providing additional security for a scheduled visit from the Secretary of the Navy to the US Navy's "mothball" fleet. Threats are received, a body is found, violent activists are dealt with, and.....Sim discovers a boat. This novella can be found downloadable and free of charge at https://robavery.com.

- **Close-Hauled** (December 2016)

"Remember Travis McGee, the hard-boiled liveaboard protagonist who prevailed through 21 John D. McDonald crime/mystery/detective books? Sadly he's frozen in time, but readers hungry for more now have a new protagonist: Sim Greene, a modern-day liveaboard sailor in Southern California. In this first installment of a series I'm eager to consume, Sim Greene finds a murder victim outside Ventura Harbor. Right away, the discovery shoves him down the twisting unknowable path that pits his intelligence and intuition against those determined to take not just his life, but also the lives of those close to him." — *Cruising World* (September 2017).

- **Broad Reach** (November 2017)

"Book two in this series doesn't disappoint. Sim is back on a perilous trail, this time on a tropical island, getting to the bottom of a mystery that tangles bad characters with good and pits loyalty against love." – Michael Robertson, Editor, *Good Old Boat*.

- **Dead Downwind** (August 2018)

Summer is hurricane season in the Caribbean. It's hot and humid and nice people can turn nasty. A young woman disappears under mysterious circumstances and a second is brutally murdered. The first is the daughter of a Detective Constable; the second was Sim Greene's employee. Sim and his friend, Al Higgins, investigate the crimes, track down the culprits, and take on an evil organization powerful enough to operate in broad daylight. Sim and Al will either destroy this sinister group or die trying.

ACKNOWLEDGEMENTS

There are too many people who have helped me during this project for me to adequately thank them all. But I'll list a few anyway (in no particular order): Jeff and Cheri Earl, Wes and Cari Clark, Gordon and Frances Smith, Dean and Deanna Sonnenberg, Brett Boulton, Jay Allen, John Arthur Taylor, my family (Emily, Cameron and Allison, Jay, Frances, and Henry), and my agent and friend, Jacques de Spoelberch. I could not have finished this book without their encouragement and advice.

ABOUT THE AUTHOR

Rob Avery was born and raised in Burbank, California, but spent as much time as he could at the beach or in the Pacific Ocean. He is a criminal defense lawyer by profession and has a passion for sailing. His writing combines the two. Rob also hates referring to himself in the third person but can do so when pressed.

www.ingramcontent.com/pod-product-compliance
Lightning Source LLC
Chambersburg PA
CBHW070821190726
48292CB00006B/2078